WHITE WEDDING FOR A SOUTHERN BELLE

BY
SUSAN CARLISLE

WEDDING DATE WITH THE ARMY DOC

BY
LYNNE MARSHALL

MILLS & BOON

Summer Brides

Two unexpected journeys to 'I do'—
two perfect summer weddings…

Stunning Ashley Marsh and beautiful doctor
Charlotte Johnson have vowed never to risk it
all for love—but the hotshot docs they work
with are an irresistible temptation!

ER doc Kiefer Bradford and army doc
Jackson Hilstead are hotter than the summer
sun, and before they know it these two
guarded heroines find their vows undone…

Now they must find the courage
to make the most important vows of all.
And what could be more romantic than
not one but *two* summer weddings?

Find out what happens in:

White Wedding for a Southern Belle
by Susan Carlisle

Wedding Date with the Army Doc
by Lynne Marshall

Summer Brides

Available now!

WHITE WEDDING FOR A SOUTHERN BELLE

BY
SUSAN CARLISLE

MILLS & BOON

Published in Great Britain 2016
By Mills & Boon, an imprint of HarperCollins*Publishers*
1 London Bridge Street, London, SE1 9GF

© 2016 Susan Carlisle

ISBN: 978-0-263-91498-6

Our policy is to use papers that are natural, renewable and recyclable
products and made from wood grown in sustainable forests.
The logging and manufacturing processes conform to the legal
environmental regulations of the country of origin.

Printed and bound in Spain
by CPI, Barcelona

Dear Reader,

I've had a love affair with Savannah, Georgia, for over thirty years. I should—I spent my honeymoon there! The setting of this book made it extra-fun to write. When my fabulous fellow Medical author Lynne Marshall suggested that we place our Summer Brides books in Savannah I didn't hesitate to agree.

I knew who my characters would be as well. Ashley, a feisty local politician who believes deeply in improving her community, and Kiefer, a doctor who starts a clinic in the neighbourhood. These two have so much in common, but both have such strong personalities they almost can't get past themselves to see the love they have for the other.

It was an exciting story to write, and I hope you enjoy reading it. I love to hear from my readers. You can find me at susancarlisle.com.

Susan

To Joan May, my mother-in-law.
Thanks for sharing your son with me.

Susan Carlisle's love affair with books began in the sixth grade, when she made a bad grade in maths. Not allowed to watch TV until she brought the grade up, Susan filled her time with books. She turned her love of reading into a passion for writing, and now has over ten Medical Romances published through Mills & Boon. She writes about hot, sexy docs and the strong women who captivate them. Visit susancarlisle.com.

Books by Susan Carlisle

Mills & Boon Medical Romance

Midwives On-Call
His Best Friend's Baby

Heart of Mississippi
The Maverick Who Ruled Her Heart
The Doctor Who Made Her Love Again

Snowbound with Dr Delectable
The Rebel Doc Who Stole Her Heart
The Doctor's Redemption
One Night Before Christmas
Married for the Boss's Baby

Visit the Author Profile page at
millsandboon.co.uk for more titles.

Praise for
Susan Carlisle

'Gripping, stirring, and emotionally touching…
A perfect medical read!'

—*Goodreads* on
His Best Friend's Baby

CHAPTER ONE

ASHLEY MARSH PUSHED through the crowded ballroom filled with St. Patrick's Day revelers dressed in costumes and lit by nothing but small green lights. As an alderman on the Savannah City Council, part of her job was to attend these types of events. Still, a fund-raiser hosted by Maggie Bradford wasn't an invitation she could ignore.

Savannah, Georgia, with its large Irish history and a disposition toward a good party did St. Paddy's Day right, even to the point of turning the river green. She'd always enjoyed the festivities but costume parties were a little over the top for her. Recognizing who she was speaking to tonight probably wasn't going to happen. It made her a little nervous knowing that when people were behind a mask they tended to do things they wouldn't otherwise. Experience told her that she wasn't always a good judge of character anyway.

The crowd around her wore anything from big green shamrock glasses to Irish kilts. She'd chosen a green tunic and tights, and a leprechaun hat. With a glittery gold mask over her eyes, she had some anonymity yet she didn't look as foolish as many of those in the room. She smiled to herself. More than once someone had told her to lighten up. Maybe tonight she would…a little. After all, few in the room could identify her.

"Ms. Marsh."

Maybe she was wrong.

She knew that voice. It was Alderman Henderson, a thorn in her side most of the time. He was dressed as if he were the mayor of an Irish village in a green suit with yellow plaid vest and buckled top hat.

"Ralph, how're you doing? Having a good time?" She already knew he wasn't.

He shrugged. "I guess so. The wife is really into these things. Anyway, I want to let you know that the hospital has agreed to partner with us on your clinic idea. I just spoke to the administrator a few minutes ago. I'm going to agree to support it for the trial period of six months. Be aware, if there's just one issue I'm going to withdraw that support." His tone was firm, indicating he wouldn't be changing his mind if all didn't go well with the clinic.

Excitement filled her. She'd been working for this opportunity since she'd been elected. "Thanks, Ralph. You're doing the right thing here."

"I'm not sure about that yet, so we'll see." He wandered off into the crowd and Ashley wasn't disappointed.

Suddenly feeling like celebrating, she looked around the room and spied a tall man with brown hair standing by himself. He was near a door to the outside as if he was preparing to run at any moment. He wore a dark suit with a green tie. Over his eyes was a mask of small yellow plaid. He was certainly understated for the occasion. Surely he would be safe enough for a dance or two?

Ashley made her way in his direction. Stopping in front of him, she said, "Happy St. Patrick's Day. How about giving a leprechaun a bit of luck by dancing with her?"

Dark green eyes looked at her for a long moment. He nodded then set the drink he held down on a nearby table. Following her, they moved out onto the dance floor. A fast song was playing and she turned to face him. The man was a good dancer. They shared two more songs.

When a slow number started she said, "Thank you for the dances."

He inclined his head. "You're welcome." The sexy timbre in his deep, rich voice was something she wouldn't soon forget.

Ashley walked away. She wasn't into being held by strange men, so she was both surprised and relieved that he hadn't insisted she dance the slower song. If she was less cautious she might have enjoyed being in this stranger's arms, but she knew too well what could happen when you weren't careful...

Dr. Kiefer Bradford watched the tiny leprechaun cross the room and speak to a few people as she left him on the dance floor. He might have pursued her but his mother wouldn't appreciate him picking up a one-night stand at her event and he'd no interest in anything longer. After what his ex-wife had done to him he had no intention of stepping into a serious relationship again. She'd seen to it that he didn't believe anything a woman said.

The only reason he was at his mother's costume ball was because he'd been in town for a job interview. When his former best friend, Josh—now his ex-wife's husband—had been made director of the ER at the Atlanta hospital where Kiefer worked, it had been time for him to get out of town.

He was tired of dodging Josh. The whispers of the staff. The pitying faces of his friends. And, worse, the anger he continued to feel. Savannah was his home. He still owned a place here. He'd come back and leave all the ugliness behind.

Kiefer saw the leprechaun a few more times around

the room but never on the dance floor. Twice they were almost close enough to speak but then she was gone. Anyway, he'd done his duty and he was ready to go. Enough green for him today. He'd watch and hear the rest of the fun from the balcony of his apartment.

As he was on his way out to the lobby, the leprechaun was coming out of a door to the right. Just as he was about to pass her Kiefer saw his ex-wife, Brittney, and Josh coming toward him among a group of people. Despite the festive dress, he recognized them.

Apprehension and anger rushed through him. Even here they still interrupted his life. They must have come to town for St. Patrick's Day. Brittney was from Savannah as well. Regardless of their history, his mother's party was the go-to event in town, so of course they wouldn't miss it.

Kiefer didn't want to speak with Brittney and Josh or want them to see him leaving alone. Without thinking, he grabbed the leprechaun as she passed.

Her small yelp of surprise made him pause for a second before his mouth found hers and he backed her against the wall. Her lips were soft and sweet beneath his. Her hands braced against his chest, pushed and then relaxed against him. Seconds later they slid to his waist. He shifted his mouth to gain a better advantage. One of his hands moved to cup her cheek.

Through the fog of desire welling up Kiefer heard the group pass. He forced himself to back away, letting his lips slowly leave the leprechaun's. The longing to find them again filled him but he'd already stepped over the line.

"Just what do you think you're doing?" she hissed, standing between him and the wall, his hand still cupping her face.

"Saying thank you for those dances."

The leprechaun huffed. "By accosting me?"

He shrugged and removed his hand. As he did so the button on the sleeve of his coat caught in the necklace around her neck.

"Stop. Be careful. Don't break it." Her voice rose.

Why was she overreacting about a simple necklace with a funny-looking stone on it?

He held his arm motionless while she worked to release the chain. The shamrock on top of her hat bobbed against his nose. She smelled like baking cookies.

"Got it." She looked up.

This leprechaun had the most beautiful doe-brown eyes he'd ever seen. Kiefer leaned in. She pushed against his chest. He stumbled backward and she hurried past him, disappearing into the crowded ballroom.

That leprechaun had certainly made this St. Patrick's Day memorable.

Three months later

Kiefer was back in Savannah and driving through Southriver. He wasn't having his first reservation or second but third about being in this part of town at this time of day. During his teen and college years Southriver had been the area where everyone had gone to find or buy a good time. Apparently that hadn't changed.

When the medical director of Savannah Medical Center had questioned him about working at the Southriver clinic during the interview, Kiefer had thought of it as more of a what-if sort of question instead of a sure thing. He liked the adrenaline rush a large ER offered but he needed to get out of Atlanta. Seeing Josh regularly after what he and Brittney had done to him wasn't working. The staff was too aware of the tension between them.

Being the clinic physician wasn't his first choice but at least it would prove his leadership and organizational skills for an opportunity down the road. Three to six months at the clinic and maybe he could transfer to the ER or apply for a departmental spot at the hospital.

As he continued down the street the number of people sitting on the steps of houses increased. It was already hot and steamy for the early days of summer and this evening was no different. These people were doing anything they could to catch a breeze. In front of a few homes children played. Maybe the revitalization of the area was starting to work.

The appearance of the neighborhood improved the farther he drove. The blocks behind him had empty buildings with grass growing in the cracks of the sidewalk and trash blown against the curb. All signs of inner-city apathy. In contrast, the closer he came to the address he was looking for, the better kept the houses and businesses looked. Many were newly painted, with fresh signs above storefronts and flowering plants hung from light posts. This went on for one block but the next started showing the neglected look of the earlier ones.

What the...?

Just ahead of him a group of males who wore their pants low on their hips and matching bandannas on their biceps stood aggressively facing a woman in front of a three-story brownstone. The woman was Ashley Marsh. Kiefer recognized her from a couple of TV interviews he'd seen since his return.

The best he could tell, she was a crusader of the highest order. As a child of someone who took on causes—sometimes to her own detriment—he was weary of what

Ashley's plans might be. In her interviews he'd found her articulate and intelligent, if not a little antagonistic for his taste.

Kiefer wasn't particularly impressed. He believed in helping people—after all, that was why he'd become a doctor—but he also expected people to help themselves. Not everyone could be saved. Sometimes people were just not worth it.

What he knew of Ashley Marsh reminded Kiefer too much of his mother. That "help everyone, all people are good" view of life made Kiefer a little leery of Ashley Marsh. Advocates often saw the picture through rose-colored glasses. Ms. Marsh struck him as being that type of person. If he were ever interested in a woman again it wouldn't be in someone who didn't show more restraint where people were concerned.

As he drew closer he could see that Ashley was talking to the group, gesturing with her hands.

One of the young men made an aggressive move forward. To her credit, she didn't back away.

Kiefer's hands tightened on the wheel. All the ugly memories of a day so long ago, when his mother had been attacked, came flooding back. The man off the street, his mother begging him not to kill her, his mother falling to the floor, the man going through her purse and Kiefer watching it all helplessly through the slats of the pantry door. He'd sworn then he would never again stand idly by while someone was being threatened.

His tires squealed as he quickly pulled into a parking lot next to the building. The group turned toward him. At least their attention was drawn away from Alderman Marsh. Kiefer hopped out and circled the truck, putting himself between her and the gang.

"Hey, man, who're you?" growled the man Kiefer had

pegged as the leader of the group. His dark hair was long and pulled back in a band. He wore a hoop in his ear.

"Dr. Kiefer Bradford. I'm the new clinic doctor."

"We don't need no more outsiders here."

Ashley sidestepped Kiefer. He put his arm out to stop her without taking his eyes off the men in front of him. He felt more than saw her move around him and he dropped his arm in frustration.

"I can handle this," she announced in a firm tone, confronting the guy in front of Kiefer. "Look, Marko, the clinic is to help the people around here, not to spy on you. What if your mother or sister needed medical care? Don't you want them to have a place to get it? This will be a no-questions-asked place."

It would be? That was the first Kiefer had heard of that.

"We don't need…" Marko lifted his chin toward Kiefer "…no outsiders coming into our neighborhood."

"This is my home as much as it is yours," Ashley stated. "I've known your family all your life. I used to change your diapers."

A couple of Marko's buddies snickered. He glanced at them. Their faces sobered. "All your do-gooding isn't going to work," Marko said to Ashley.

"I'm trying to make the community better. The clinic is the first step in doing that."

"Yeah, right, it's your way of trying to change everything." He spit on the ground then scowled. "I run this 'hood, and if I don't want you or your clinic, you'll be gone."

Kiefer took a step forward. "Don't threaten the lady."

Marko glowered at him. "Back off, mister, or you'll regret it."

A couple of Marko's thugs moved toward him.

Ashley pulled at Kiefer's arm, preventing him from going toward Marko. "He isn't worth it."

The horn of a police car had Marko's gang scrambling, each running in a different direction and disappearing into the dwindling light.

"Is there a problem here?" the patrolman asked out the car window.

Ashley left Kiefer's side and went to the car. "No, we're fine, Carl."

Carl looked at Kiefer and raised his chin. "Who's this guy?"

"This is Dr. Bradford, the new director of the clinic."

Kiefer nodded.

"Good to have you, Doc," Carl said. "Never a dull moment in Southriver."

"I'm finding that out."

"Carl, don't run him off before he even gets started," Ashley said with a half laugh.

"Sorry, Alderman, that wasn't my intention. Y'all have a good evening." Carl's partner drove the car on down the street.

After all the excitement Kiefer took a really good look at the woman beside him. Beneath the streetlight she wasn't at all like the person on TV, more like a college coed and less like a hard-nosed politician. Of average height, with midnight-black hair she wore pulled back in a ponytail. Her jeans had holes in them; not as a fashion statement but from actual use would be his guess.

His attention went to her tight T-shirt, which did nothing to hide the generous breasts but, in fact, drew attention to them with "not here you don't" written across them. What captured his attention was the necklace lying between her breasts. It was the same one that the woman he'd kissed on St. Patrick's Day had been wearing.

He looked into her dark eyes. Yes, those were the ones. He'd thought of that kiss and these very eyes many times since then.

"You!"

Ashley gave him a quizzical look. "Yes. Me."

She didn't recognize him. But why should she? He'd worn a mask.

Ashley put her hands on her hips and glared at the man before her. "What were you thinking?"

He blinked a couple of times as if he'd forgotten where he was. "What do you mean?"

Dr. Bradford looked truly perplexed. As if he couldn't imagine creating a situation that both she and he couldn't get out of. Marko wasn't someone to mess with. "Jumping in between Marko and me. I had things under control."

"Yeah, I could see that. Six against one is always a fair number. I was only trying to help."

What was it about his voice? Had she heard it before? That rich tone sounded so familiar. "You weren't. If anything, you were making matters worse."

Ashley clenched her jaw. She'd fought most of her life against being overprotected. To fight her own fights. After her childhood friend had been abducted it had seemed like her father hadn't wanted to let her out of his sight. For years she'd had to beg to walk the two blocks to school. Even when he'd let her she'd caught him or her brother following her. It had taken going off to college to break away. She loved her father dearly but she would never return to that way of life. Having this doctor ride to the rescue wasn't what she needed or wanted. She could take care of Marko and herself.

Dr. Bradford said sarcastically, "So, if I understand correctly, I should have just stood by while they scared you into doing whatever they wanted you to do, which, by the way, was what?"

"Marko doesn't want the clinic to open. He believes it's only here to keep tabs on him and his gang. You know, big brother watching and all that. What it amounts to is he's afraid that if the people in Southriver have something positive, they'll want more and stop letting him intimidate them. Push thugs like him out."

"That's what you want too, isn't it?"

"Yes. I want to make this a good place to live."

"Admirable. But if you're not careful you won't be around to see it happen."

That might be true, but she'd spent so many years feeling cloistered and controlled, as if she couldn't take care of herself, that as an adult she fought against it whenever it happened to her now. She wasn't that brave in her personal life, always questioning her ability to judge if she was seeing the real person. Fighting to truly trust. Her being fooled before had destroyed someone's life. She couldn't let that happen again to her or anyone she cared about.

"Look around you." She reached out an arm and directed it toward the buildings across the street. "Those were all businesses when I was growing up. Criminals like Marko slowly drove them away. I won't be driven out. This clinic is the first step in bringing people back."

"You have grand plans, Ms. Marsh."

"I believe in dreaming big."

"You have your work cut out for you."

"Maybe so, but when I ran for the city council I promised that I'd help make this area a better place to live and I intend to keep that promise."

"Even if it kills you?"

She shrugged. "It won't come to that. Let's go in and

I'll show you around. Then we'll get to work." She turned toward the building. "By the way, don't ever step between me and anyone again."

Kiefer blinked. He'd just been put in his place by a woman who had been wearing a leprechaun outfit when he'd first met her. She didn't recognize him. He was a bit disappointed. Then again, why would she? Their kiss had got to him but that didn't mean she had felt anything.

And what was this about working? He'd been told this was a meet and greet. He'd made plans for dinner tonight. Something about Ashley's demeanor warned him that wouldn't be a good enough excuse for leaving early.

She walked toward the redbrick structure with large window frames painted white. It had a heavy-looking natural wood door that had obviously been refinished with care. On either side of it were pots full of bright yellow flowers. She looked back as if she expected him to follow her. When he did she pushed the door wider. After he entered she closed and locked it. Despite what he believed was her earlier recklessness, at least she was showing some caution.

"The building used to be a hardware store," she informed him. "This large area will be used as the waiting room." All makes and models of wooden chairs were stationed around the room. "I have someone, Maria, coming in tomorrow morning to act as receptionist. She's a good girl. Let's go back here and I'll show you what I have planned."

Kiefer didn't say anything, just trailed after her down a long hallway that had obviously had new walls built to create smaller rooms on one side.

"These are the examination rooms. I couldn't make

too many permanent changes because I had this building declared a historical one so it wouldn't be torn down."

Was she a crusader about everything? Even buildings? He'd seen sound bites of her talking about revitalizing the area but he hadn't known that included defending old buildings. In his mind, constructing more modern ones would have been more effective and energy efficient.

"This is the supply room, where we'll need to concentrate our efforts tonight."

Kiefer stepped into the room. It was piled high with boxes. More than a night's worth of work faced them.

"What's all of this?"

"Donated supplies. You'll find they aren't hard to come by. Manpower is. People are more than happy to give as long as it doesn't require any real investment of time." She stepped forward and opened a box.

"Ms. Marsh, I'm sorry but I have another appointment at eight. I'll get started on this first thing in the morning." He had to stop looking at her mouth. Thinking of their kiss.

She made a disgusted sound. "I don't think you'll have time for that tomorrow and I have scheduled meetings so I'll be in and out."

"I doubt there'll be so many patients that I can't see to it over the next few days."

"You might be surprised. Were you told that this job would require long hours?"

"I understand those. I am an ER doctor. The issue is that I wasn't prepared to work tonight. I understood I was to come and see the clinic. Not set it up."

"Dr. Bradford, around here we all do what has to be done. Were you told you would have only one nurse?"

"No. I was just asked to start work here the day after tomorrow."

"You have the date wrong. Tomorrow is opening day."

He'd be there ready to go in the morning. She seemed to set high expectations for herself and others. Kiefer didn't need her reporting back that he'd not given his all to this project. He had to ensure this clinic ran smoothly.

Shrugging out of his lightweight jacket, he conceded, "I can stay for a couple of hours now. We won't get it all done tonight but maybe we can have at least one exam room operational. But first I have to make a quick phone call."

"Sounds like a plan, Dr. Bradford."

"Please call me Kiefer. After all, we have met before."

She tilted her head in question. "I don't remember that."

"Now my feelings are hurt. It was at a St. Patrick's Day party."

A look of concern came over her face. She studied him for a moment. "Really?"

"You invited me to dance."

Ashley sucked in a breath. Her eyes widened. "You grabbed me in the hall."

"I'm sorry about that. Heat of the moment and all that." Kiefer wasn't going into why he'd kissed her. He also wasn't going to let on how much he'd enjoyed doing so.

"I should have slapped your face."

He shrugged. "Probably."

Ashley's hands shook as she opened the first box. She glanced at Kiefer. He had been the one. The man whose kiss had turned her inside out. She'd pushed him away and had gone down the hall back to the party on wobbly knees. No kiss had ever lingered and stayed with her like his had. Even months later she could remember every detail. But could she trust him? Someone who just grabbed a stranger and kissed them?

Kiefer looked at her. She turned away. Was he thinking

of their kiss? Worse, laughing at her? She had to get past the moment and concentrate on the job at hand. What they had shared had been two adults being silly during a party.

He wasn't who she'd expected, on more than one front. She'd thought an older, more established doctor would be assigned to the clinic. The council had only agreed to support the clinic if she could work out an affiliation with the Savannah Medical Center. Only when she'd managed to make the connection had the plan come together. The six-month time limit meant the clinic had to look good from the first day and there could be no issues, like with Marko.

Her next concern was that if the clinic did make a go of things, would Kiefer stay and run it after the six months were up? Or would he be like so many others? All her life she'd seen people wanting to help come and go in her community. Civic groups, church groups, private companies, all wanting to make a difference. The problem was that they never stayed long enough to make a real change. Slowly the strides forward would slide back to the way they had been. They came in and did their projects for the allotted time then left, never really committing to Southriver. Ashley needed people who would stay and be a part of the community. Someone who would have the same conviction about the community as she did.

When she'd been elected from the Southriver district to serve as alderman, the establishment of close affordable medical care had been one of her main platform points.

If there had been a clinic close by, Lizzy might have lived.

The clinic was the first of many improvements Ashley planned to implement. The beginning of making restitution for not having been there for Lizzy. But she had to show success with this project before she requested funds for the next.

They spent the following few hours opening boxes. Kiefer would tell her where the supplies were needed and she would put them there. He was a clean-cut guy in an all-American way. Dressed in a knit collared shirt and jeans, which seemed worn enough that they might be his favorite, and loafers. He was a striking man. As much so as he had been on St. Patrick's Day. He oozed confidence, but she knew from experience that he would need to gain acceptance in this neighborhood. His eyes were his most arresting feature. They twinkled with merriment. She should have remembered them, but it had been his voice that had pulled at her. That timbre when he said certain words made it special.

Kiefer was a worker, she'd give him that. She had no idea what some of the items they were handling were or how they were used, but he seemed pleased to see each of them. On occasion she would catch him looking at her. It made her feel a little nervous. That kiss stood between them. Theirs was a business relationship and she was going to see that it stayed that way.

"I'll need to make a list of other things we need when we get this all finished," he said.

"Good luck with that. I had a hard enough time getting these donated."

"I know someone I could ask."

"Who's that?" Ashley pushed another empty box out of the way.

"My mother. She's always looking for a cause. I'll put her on it. It may take a while for us to get what we need, but we will."

"Your mother isn't Maggie Bradford, is she?" She should have known. Last name Bradford. She'd been at Maggie Bradford's party. Great. Another connection between them. Ashley knew his mother.

"That's her."

"She's a smart woman. Very persuasive."

"Yeah. That's Mom."

He didn't sound that pleased. "She has a big heart."

A shadowy look came over his face. "Sometimes to her own detriment. That's a characteristic the two of you share." He picked up another box and headed out the door.

What had he meant by that comment?

Sometime later he looked at the large, expensive watch on his wrist. "I'm sorry, but I've gotta go. I'll finish the rest of this tomorrow." Picking up his jacket from where he'd hung it, he pulled it on. "Walk to the door with me. I want to make sure you close up."

"You don't have to worry about me. I've lived in Southriver all my life and I'll still be here when you're gone. So please don't start trying to play hero."

"No hero here. Just put my concern down to having been there, done that, and humor me." He stood at the door, waiting on her.

What was that all about? She stopped what she was doing and followed him down the hall. Kiefer opened the front door. "Lock up."

"I will, but I'm going to wait here until you get into your truck. If any eyes are looking, they need to know you're with me."

He started toward his truck. On his way he called, "This lot needs a security light."

"I'll add it to the already long list." She watched him climb into his late-model truck. It was a nice one and she was afraid it might not fare well in this neighborhood.

Vandalism could be a problem. It also made him stand out as a visitor, and that could cause confidence issues with the locals.

He waited with his headlights shining on her until she turned and went inside. Oddly, she liked his concern.

CHAPTER TWO

KIEFER SPENT SOME of the late hours of his evening contemplating the curiosity of life. Who would have thought he would ever meet the leprechaun again and, even more amazing, be working with her. Life took funny twists. More than once as they'd stored supplies he'd thought about their kiss. Had that just been a onetime incredible kiss or would all hers be like that, causing that instant fire of desire? He'd like to find out but something about the all-business Ashley Marsh had said that wasn't going to happen. What a shame.

He arrived at the clinic the next morning a couple of hours before opening time. A group of young men stood across the street even at that early hour. A ripple of alarm went through him and his gut tightened.

Was Marko trying it again?

Stepping out of the truck, he used his key fob to lock it and walked toward the front of the building. The roar of a car going too fast filled the air. By the time he had reached the door the men had started across the pavement.

Surely these guys were just trying to intimidate him. Since the day he'd seen his mother beaten by the homeless man she'd brought home for a meal, he'd been on guard where people were concerned. He was a realist.

Some people were bad by nature. Defenseless he wasn't anymore and he'd sworn a long time ago that he would never again watch another person be hurt.

Trash had been dumped in front of the door. Kiefer stepped in it to knock on the clinic door, all the time aware of the approaching group. His entire body was on alert as he formulated a plan if they attacked him. He vowed to get his own key today.

"Hey, you looking for Ashley?" the guy who led the men asked.

Kiefer slowly turned. "Yes."

"You'll need to go around back. The door to her place is there."

Was the guy kidding him? Kiefer counted heads. Four to one. He wasn't going to put himself into a position of being jumped. Before he had to make a decision about how to handle the situation, the door opened.

"Good morning, Dr. Bradford," Ashley said with a smile. She was already dressed for the day in a pantsuit, giving her a professional and approachable air at the same time. He recognized this persona from TV. The one where she was determined to get what she wanted.

"Mornin'."

She looked around him. "Hi, guys. Everything's okay. Dr. Bradford is going to be the clinic doctor. It opens today."

One of the guys said, "Okay, we were just makin' sure you're okay. Marko is spreading the word that he's pissed about what you're doing around here. We'll get that trash cleaned up for you, Miss Ashley." The guy dipped his head respectfully.

"Thanks, Wayne. I appreciate that."

Kiefer shook his head as if confused. Then, indicating the garbage, he said, "Why do you put up with this?"

"Because this is my home. I'm not leaving it because someone doesn't like me."

She was a gutsy lady, Kiefer would give her that. Most of the women her age he knew were always looking out for themselves. How they could financially better their situation. Like Brittney. She'd certainly done a number on him. It had turned out she'd married him because he was a doctor and would be able to give her a good life. When she'd found out Josh's bank account was even larger she'd moved on to him. Now Kiefer had no use for women other than a casual night out and a few laughs. He couldn't trust one not to use him. As far as he could tell, they all wanted the same thing. What they could get for themselves.

"Come on in." Ashley opened the door wide. "We need to get ready. Patients should be here soon."

"Those guys said you live in the back." Kiefer followed her in.

"That isn't exactly right. The entrance to my place is there. I actually live upstairs."

"You don't mind living above the clinic?"

"It's my building and my idea. The people around here needed a place to come for medical care and I had the space."

Kiefer was impressed. She really was committed to seeing her ideas work, even to the point of financing them. Outside of his mother, few people he knew were that devoted to anyone other than themselves. How much Ashley reminded him of his mother made him feel uncomfortable. Did all her work to better the world leave Ashley with any room for anything more in her life? Did she have a boyfriend? Want children? Something to care about besides her political agenda?

That wasn't his concern. He believed in helping people. His mother had instilled that in him, but he was still aware that some people would take advantage of you. His impression was that Ashley Marsh hadn't learned that lesson yet.

She was saying, "I'm sorry I'm not going to be much help today. I have a speech to give this morning, a committee meeting with the local businesses and then a council meeting tonight."

"I didn't expect you to spend the day with me. I can handle the clinic. That's why I was given the job."

"I'd hoped to be here but these meetings were already on the calendar and couldn't be moved. I just thought I could help smooth things over with the community. My neighbors can be mistrusting until they get to know you."

"I'll be fine. I'll have a nurse to assist me, won't I?"

"Yes. Margaret will be here soon. She was also born and raised in Southriver. She'll be a great help. Well, I've got to get ready for my day."

Ashley left him and he started working on arranging the supplies they'd not got to the night before. Forty-five minutes later the buzzer sounded and he went to the main door. He checked out the window. After last night he wouldn't take any chances that Marko or his gang would catch him off guard. A dark-skinned, silver-haired, heavyset woman dressed in purple scrubs stood there. He unlocked the door and opened it.

"I'm guessing you're Dr. Bradford," she said before Kiefer had a chance to speak. "I'm Margaret Nettles. I'll be your nurse."

"Nice to meet you, Margaret. I'm sure I'll be glad of your help."

She looked around the waiting room. "Ms. Ashley has high hopes for this clinic and I agreed to help because she's such a fine person, but I don't know that it's going to work out. I'll do my part and help you do yours. Now, can you direct me to where I can put my purse? We need to get started. You already have a couple of patients waiting outside."

"I didn't see anyone."

"You wouldn't. They didn't come across the street until they saw me. They'll be along in a minute."

He glanced out the door. "But we don't open for another hour."

"That may be so but they'll be here nonetheless."

Margaret was correct. He closed the door and showed her to the office. She'd just locked her purse in the desk when the buzzer sounded.

"I'll see to that," Margaret announced.

"I only have the one exam room set up. I thought we'd have time to work on the other two between patients."

"I doubt that'll happen. Despite some in the neighborhood being against this clinic, the people around here need it. They'll come until they're scared away. I'll put your first patient in the exam room." With that she walked heavily down the hall.

What had he got himself into?

A boy of about three was his first patient. The mother didn't look much older than eighteen. Much too young to have a child. Her hair was pulled back, which added to her look of youth. The little boy was clean but his clothes were well-worn and a little small on his chubby body.

"Hello, I'm Dr. Bradford. What's the problem today?"

"Mikey has a bad cold."

Kiefer could see that clearly. The child had a horribly running nose and a wet cough. Kiefer went down on his heels. "Mikey, I need to listen to your chest for a minute. This won't hurt."

He placed the stethoscope on the boy's chest. His heartbeat was steady but his lungs made a raspy sound. After that Kiefer checked Mikey's mouth and ears. Both were red and irritated.

Kiefer looked at the mother. "Mikey's going to need antibiotics for ten days. Then I want you to come back."

The girl's face took on a troubled look.

Kiefer stood. "Mikey should be just fine."

"Is there something else you can do for him?"

"The medicine should fix him right up." Kiefer looped the stethoscope around his neck.

"I can't get the medicine," the mother said softly.

"Raeshell." Ashley spoke to the mother from the open door. "I'm on my way to the drugstore right now. Dr. Bradford can write that prescription and we'll have it filled."

How long had Ashley been standing there? Was she checking on him?

It dawned on Kiefer that the girl couldn't pay for the medicine. "I'll do that right away." He stepped out into the hall.

He would make some calls when he had a chance and see about getting a few drug companies to help out. A couple of drug reps owed him favors. He'd be calling them in.

Kiefer pulled the pad out of his pocket and wrote the prescription. He then removed his wallet and took out some bills. He handed them to Ashley. "This should cover it."

"You don't have to," she whispered.

"If I don't, you will. You can't pay for everyone that comes through here. We're going to have to get some help in this area."

"I hadn't given much thought to people's inability to pay." She shoved the money into her pocket.

"Well, it's time to do that."

"I'll be back in a few hours. Maybe you'll have a few minutes for us to discuss it then," Ashley said.

"I have some ideas of my own that I'll work on as well." Returning to the room, he told the mother, "Ms. Marsh is waiting outside to drive you to the store. Don't worry about the cost. It's taken care of. I'll see you and Mikey back here in ten days. You make sure he takes all of the medicine. It doesn't work if you don't."

"Thank you, Dr. Bradford," Raeshell said meekly.

"You're welcome. Bring Mikey back if he gets worse."

"I will." The girl gathered her child close and left.

By noon he almost regretted his words to Ashley earlier. He hadn't stopped once. There was a constant stream of patients, each with varying degrees of need but none that he couldn't handle. His worries about being bored were long gone.

Already Margaret was proving to be a treasure. She knew the people who came in and put them at ease. Maria, his receptionist, showed up around nine. By then Kiefer had already seen eight patients. Margaret handled telling Maria what to do, leaving him to see a waiting patient. If every day was anything like this one, working in the ER would look like spending a day at the beach.

Around two o'clock Ashley stopped in again. This time she was wearing a simple dress and sweater. She looked refreshing on a hot day. "How're things going?"

"Busy."

"I'm glad to hear it. I was afraid Marko might bully people into staying away."

Kiefer looked at the notes he'd made on his last patient. He was going to have to start a charting system. "I don't understand why he wouldn't want a clinic here. The police, yes, but the clinic, no."

"It's all about power and control. He's afraid I'm taking it away."

"Doesn't his family live in the area? Need medical service on occasion?"

Ashley brushed her hand over her skirt. "Sure they do, but he doesn't care. Look, I've got to go. I have that community meeting. I just wanted to see how you're doing."

"Afraid I'm going to up and leave, Alderman?" He gave her a pointed look.

"I can't say it hasn't crossed my mind."

"Rest assured, I'll be here when you come back." He wouldn't be got rid of that easily.

It was late that evening when Ashley opened another supply box and searched the contents. Having no idea what they were, she left the box for Kiefer to see to. Her afternoon meeting hadn't gone as well as she'd hoped. The businessmen were worried about retaliation if they participated in the block party she had planned to celebrate the opening of the clinic. They had complained about the cost as well. In her opinion, the neighborhood needed to come together, start acting as one, if they were ever going to make a real difference. She wanted it so badly and couldn't figure out why the community leaders didn't.

Her evening council meeting had gone better. At least she'd had the good news that the clinic was up and running. It had been dark by the time she'd returned home. She'd changed clothes once again and had come down to the clinic to start arranging supplies.

Kiefer was behind the nineteen-forties metal desk in the closet-sized office, dictating into his phone, when she went by. He hadn't even looked up. She'd been impressed with his treatment of Raeshell and Mikey, especially when he'd offered to pay for the medicine. Despite his impulsive behavior at the party, he seemed to be a stand-up guy since he had already put in a full day and was now doing extra hours. She'd been disappointed that he'd not stayed later the night before to finish up organizing the supplies, but he'd more than done his share today.

A few minutes later he joined her in the supply room. "Hey."

"Hi," she returned.

"It's been some day."

"It always is in Southriver." She opened another box.

"That would be a great slogan for your Welcome to Southriver signs," he said.

"I'll keep that in mind."

An hour later they passed each other in the hallway, she on the way to the reception area and he coming from the office. They bumped into each other and she fumbled to keep the box she carried from falling. Already aware he was a big guy, being this near him only emphasized the fact. His hands covered hers, helping her to balance the box again. He looked at her mouth. Was he going to take advantage of the situation and kiss her again? Her nerve ends danced. Something in her wanted him to, while her mind stated clearly that it was a bad idea. He was a stranger and she had no business letting him that close. She was glad for the space when he stepped back.

He said casually, "I don't know about you but I missed lunch and dinner today. Would you join me for a pizza? I'll have it delivered so we don't have to stop work except to eat."

Was he kidding? No one was going to deliver in Southriver after dark. She chuckled. "Good luck with that."

"What?"

"Getting something delivered around here after the sun goes down. Too many drivers have been robbed." She shifted the box so that she could see him clearly. Kiefer really was a good-looking man.

"You have to be kidding."

"Nope. Give it a try if you don't believe me." She was going to enjoy proving she was right. She walked down the hall.

When she returned he called from an exam room, "Pizza will be here in thirty."

She stepped back to the doorway. "How did you manage that?"

"I have a buddy who's a policeman and his family owns a pizza place. He happened to be helping out tonight."

"I'm impressed." And she was.

In a short while the front-door buzzer that she'd had installed the day before went off. To Ashley's amazement the pizza had arrived just as Kiefer had said it would. She hoped he always used his powers for good. Following him to the door, she said, "Check the peephole first. Never open the door after hours until you know who it is."

"You really should consider living elsewhere."

That wasn't going to happen. She'd made a promise years ago and she wasn't going to go back on it now. "That's not going to happen. It would defeat everything I stand for."

Kiefer looked at her for a second then out the peephole. "It's Bull." He opened the door.

A man as tall as Kiefer but much bulkier stood there with a large pizza box in his hands. "Well, Kie, you're sure slumming tonight."

Anger flared in Ashley. That was the way everyone thought of Southriver. If a person was in Southriver then it wasn't for a good reason, one of many perceptions she was working to change. She stepped around Kiefer.

Even in the dim light she could see Bull's eyes widen
and his instant embarrassment. "Ah, I'm sorry. No offense."

She said in a clipped tone, "None taken. That isn't the
first time my neighborhood has been insulted."

Kiefer chuckled softly as he gave Bull space to enter
and closed the door behind him. "Careful, Bull. She
might take you out, gun and all."

His warm sound of compassion took the edge off the
moment for Ashley.

"Truly my apologies, Ms. Marsh." Bull sounded sincere.

Ashley looked closely at Bull. "Don't I know you?
Aren't you the officer who caught the guy robbing the
café a couple of weeks ago?"

Bull squared his shoulders and gave her a look of
pride. "That was me."

"I appreciate that. The Gozmans are nice people.
They've lived here all my life. I'd have hated to see them
lose their business because they couldn't pay their bills."

Bull grinned. "Does that make up for my remark earlier?"

She smiled. "I'll let it go for now."

It bothered Kiefer for some reason that Bull was flirting
with Ashley. Worse, she seemed to like it. It appeared
innocent enough but he knew from past experience that
looks could be deceiving. Brittney and Josh had managed to conceal their affair for months. But Ashley was
nothing to him, so why should it matter if Bull was interested in her?

That wasn't true. Somehow his reaction to their kiss
had added an element he didn't understand.

"Okay, neighborhood hero, I'm hungry. How about that pizza?" Kiefer pulled out some cash.

Ashley wasn't his type anyway. He liked her high energy and understood her big heart to a certain degree, but her drive to change the world was over the top for him. Too much like his mother. If he was ever interested in woman again it would be less about commitment and more about enjoying life.

"Bull, why don't you join us?" Ashley asked.

"Yeah, do," Kiefer said, in a less-than-encouraging tone.

"Naw. I need to get going." Bull took the cash and turned back toward the door.

Kiefer opened it, letting Bull exit, and stepped out as well.

"Listen, man," Bull said, "you be careful coming and going around here at night. Also, you need to get a security light for that lot." He nodded toward Ashley's place.

"I didn't get much else done around here today but I did call the power company about that."

"Great. I've heard good things about what Alderman Marsh is trying to do but she has stirred up some trouble as well. I hope you don't get caught in the cross fire."

"I'll keep that in mind. Thanks for the pizza."

"No problem."

Ashley was waiting on him when he came back in. "I'm ravenous. Why don't we go up to my place to eat where there's a table?"

"Sounds good to me."

She led the way down the hall. At the end she opened a door he'd assumed was a closet. It turned out to hide a staircase. He climbed the stairs after her, getting a good view of her nicely round behind. When they reached the top they went through another door that opened into a small kitchen, which had obviously been remodeled. The brick walls and patchwork tablecloth gave the room a homey and functional feel.

Ashley placed the pizza box on the table. "What would you like to drink? I have soda, tea, beer, water."

"I'd love a beer, but I'd better settle for a soda." He took one of the matching chairs.

Ashley pulled two cans of soda out of the refrigerator.

"So how long have you lived here?" Kiefer watched as she filled glasses with ice and then poured the drinks over it.

"About a year. I bought the building two years ago and spent six months making it habitable. I still have work to do." She placed his glass in front of him.

"You did the work yourself?"

"All that I could. I had to cut corners where I could."

"I'm impressed. You've done a nice job, from what I've seen."

Ashley smiled. She had a nice smile. Sort of made him feel like the sun had come out. "It was a labor of love. And I do mean labor."

He flipped the box top up and took a slice of pizza. "If you don't mind, I'm about to starve."

"You need to pace yourself around here."

"Isn't that the pot calling the kettle black? You had meetings all day and still managed to check up on me." He took another bite of pizza.

"I wasn't checking up."

"Really? What would you call it?"

She shrugged. "Neighborly concern."

"We aren't neighbors."

"No, we're not. I'm pretty sure we grew up as different as daylight and darkness."

"You're making a big assumption. We might have

more in common than you think." Kiefer leaned back in his chair. "To start with, we both grew up in a neighborhood. Are your parents still married?"

She nodded.

"Mine are too. We both went to college. We both have jobs that help people."

Ashley raised a hand. "Okay, maybe you're right. But I grew up in a low-income, racially diverse area, while I'm sure yours was an upper middle class, private school community."

She had him there. "Yeah, but that doesn't mean we aren't both interested in the same things. I certainly have a mother who showed me the importance of helping people. You're making life better. And I make people feel better. We have more in common than you might think."

"Now we've moved into philosophy. I think that may be too deep a subject for me this late at night." Ashley took a bite of pizza. Kiefer watched her chew. Was he ever going to get that kiss out of his mind?

"You might be right. I've been at it so long today I'm starting to feel loopy."

They ate quietly for a few minutes before Kiefer stood and pushed the chair under the table. "I need to do a couple of things downstairs. Then I'm going to head home. Thanks for the nice place to have dinner."

"I'm the one who should be thanking you. You bought the pizza and against all odds got it delivered. By the way, the local TV station is coming to do a story on the clinic tomorrow. They've asked to interview you."

Kiefer wanted nothing to do with that. When his mother had been hurt and the case had gone to trial, he'd been on TV as they'd come out of the courthouse. It had been a horrible experience. He had been the child who had watched his mother being beaten nearly to death but had done nothing. The shame had been more than he could carry. Since then he'd shied away from that type of attention. He had no interest in getting involved with anyone who was always on a mission. He'd been raised by a person like that, knew the risks involved.

"I'll see if I have time." He headed down the stairs.

Ashley was waiting for the TV crew when they arrived. In the last year, since she'd been on the council, she'd learned to court the media but to always be wary of them as well. She needed good press to help move her ideas forward in the neighborhood revitalization. Shining a good light on what she was trying to accomplish in Southriver would hopefully not only get the city council behind the project but set a precedent for what could be done in other areas of the city and other cities in general.

It was just after lunch and she'd only seen Kiefer a couple of times that morning. No matter what they were doing their kiss seemed to pop into her mind. The more she tried to shove it away the stronger it became. She'd almost reached the point that she wanted to kiss him again so she could put it behind her and move on.

Ashley had come down early just to check in and see how things were going at the clinic. Kiefer was busy with a patient and Maria was overseeing a full waiting room. At least there shouldn't be an empty room when the news crew arrived. She'd gone downtown for a meeting and had returned in time to grab a bite to eat before she was due to meet the TV crew. Sitting at her table in the kitchen, having a sandwich, she looked at the chair Kiefer had filled the night before.

He was a big person but had seemed relaxed in her small kitchen. It had been too long since she'd shared even a simple meal with a man. Most of the men she had dated hadn't been happy with the prospect of living in Southriver, and she wasn't interested in moving elsewhere. Her world was here and she needed a partner who understood that, who supported that part of her life.

Her one truly serious relationship had ended when she'd decided to run for the city council. He'd wanted her support to further his business but hadn't been willing to do the same with her desire to become an alderman. She had been crushed by his attitude. This was a man who was supposed to love her. It hadn't taken long for them to part ways. Ashley wanted her relationship with a man to be a partnership. She refused to settle for anything less.

Since then she'd made her views and plans clear in the beginning and they had turned off any other men she'd dated. She was starting to miss male companionship. Someone to just have fun with.

Could she and Kiefer become friends? Based on their kiss there might be some benefit sexually as well. She'd enjoyed her conversation with him over pizza. One other good thing about him was that he wouldn't be staying in Southriver long. No outsider ever did. Kiefer wasn't her type anyway. They could part ways without hurt feelings, she was sure.

But what if her radar was off? What if she was misjudging him? It had happened before.

Thirty minutes later Kiefer walked up the hall in her direction as she made her way toward the waiting room.

"So, how's the alderman today?"

She smiled. "Busy."

"Are you ever not busy?"

Ashley thought about that for a moment. "Not really."

"That would have been my guess. You know if you

don't slow down occasionally you will burn out and not have enough energy to save the world."

"Save the world? I'm not trying to save the world."

"Sure you are. What you're trying to do in Southriver is to save a part of the world."

She'd never thought of it that way. "I'm just trying to help families in this neighborhood live better lives. That's all."

"If you say so."

Ashley stepped closer to him so that no one could accidentally overhear them. That was a mistake. She came to an abrupt stop. His aftershave smelled like citrus with a hint of spice. She forced herself not to inhale deeply. He didn't move away but instead he looked down at her. Her gaze flickered down and returned. They were uncomfortably close but she wasn't going to back away. "Dr. Bradford, your job isn't to evaluate me or concern yourself with what I do, but to run this clinic."

"Why, yes, ma'am, Alderman Marsh." He glanced behind him then leaned down as if he was going to kiss her and mumbled, "I believe your dog and pony show have arrived." He stepped around her and headed down the hall.

What was his problem?

She had one as well. He left her tingling all over.

Kiefer tried to stay out of the way of Ashley and the reporter followed by the TV cameraman. Maybe if he remained busy, which wasn't a problem because he was, he wouldn't have to be involved. He'd stopped by the office to make a quick note on a patient when Ashley stuck her head in the door.

"Hey, do you mind coming in to see Mrs. McGuire?

She's agreed to let us film her. We'd like to get you doing the examination." She turned to leave.

Kiefer wasn't interested in being part of her publicity. He was a doctor and a professional. There were patients to see. He didn't have time for her PR show. "I don't think so."

Her head popped back around the door. "What?"

"I'd rather not."

She studied him for a second. "It'll just be for a few minutes. No big deal."

Kiefer shook his head. "I don't think an examination of a patient is a place for a TV show."

Ashley stepped farther into the room. "Why're you being so difficult about this? I need this publicity for the clinic. To raise funds that are needed desperately."

"I understand that but I don't think putting a patient on TV is the way to go."

The reporter came to the doorway. Ashley glanced back then returned her attention to Kiefer. Her face held a beseeching expression. "Please. I won't ask you to do it again."

Something about her look had Kiefer reconsidering. What would be so bad about doing his job and trying not to pay any attention to the camera? He did understand the need to shine a light on what was going on in Southriver. He said tightly, "Okay, but you'll owe me."

"Thank you," she said, then turned to the man behind her. "Russell, we'll go to the exam room now and meet Mrs. McGuire."

Kiefer followed the party up the hallway to one of the two functioning exam rooms. The camera crew stopped outside the door and allowed him to enter first. Mrs. McGuire was a forty-something woman neatly dressed in a casual shirt and jeans. When he entered she looked up from where she sat in a chair in the corner.

"Hi, I'm Dr. Bradford. I understand you're Mrs. Mc-Guire."

Ashley, along with the reporter and cameraman, squeezed into the room.

Mrs. McGuire looked at the group with interest. "I am."

"Are you sure you're okay with this?" Kiefer nodded toward the people behind him. "I'll tell them to leave if you're not."

"Mrs. McGuire—" Ashley started.

"Is *my* patient."

Ashley said nothing more.

The patient nodded her assent. "Now, Mrs. McGuire, what seems to be the problem?" Kiefer asked.

"I've been having trouble with one of my toes." She lifted her right foot. It was covered by a sock and she was wearing a house shoe.

"Would you please remove your sock? I'd like to take a look." As she did so Kiefer pulled the other metal chair in the room closer.

A sweet smell of infection filled the room. He reached down and cupped her calf, lifting it so that her heel rested on his thigh. Mrs. McGuire's large toe was a deep purple color that was extending to the next one.

The cameraman took a step closer.

"How long has this toe looked like this?" Kiefer asked, trying not to let his concern show in his voice. He didn't want the reporter to get the idea that this might be more than an ordinary hurt toe.

"Oh, I don't know. Maybe a few months."

Kiefer nodded. She should have been seen long ago.

"Mrs. McGuire, have you ever been told you were a diabetic?"

"It's been so long since I've been to the doctor I don't remember."

Kiefer took a deep breath, trying to remain calm. Why had she let this go on for so long? Did she realize how bad it was? He turned to the reporter. "I need you to leave now. I would like to talk to my patient in private."

"But we really didn't get anything," the reporter complained.

"Dr. Bradford, could I speak to you outside?" Ashley followed the reporter and cameraman out.

"Mrs. McGuire, I'll be right back," Kiefer said.

Ashley waited in the hall. He closed the exam room door behind him. The reporter and cameraman were walking toward the waiting area.

"Why're you making this so difficult?" she demanded, before he could say anything.

"Because that woman in there needs to be in the hospital. She's going to lose that toe. If she waits much longer she could lose her entire foot. I don't think that's something that should be said in front of a camera."

Ashley's mouth formed an O of comprehension.

"That's right, oh. Now, if we're done here I'll see about making arrangements to have her admitted."

"I'm sorry. I didn't know. I'll see that she gets there. I know she lives alone and will need a ride. That's probably why she hasn't been seeing a doctor regularly."

Kiefer had to admit Ashley's focus turned quickly to compassion and willingness to help. Despite her appearance of having a one-track mind, only concerned about her agenda, she genuinely seemed to have the woman's best interests at heart.

She headed down the hall toward the reporter and Kiefer returned to Mrs. McGuire.

He took the chair again and explained the situation to his patient.

Mrs. McGuire surprised him with her reaction when she said, "I'm not going to the hospital. Nothing good happens there."

That wasn't generally true but in her case it might be. Kiefer wasn't sure if her prognosis might be worse than he'd anticipated. At a knock on the door he said, "Come in."

Ashley entered. "Mrs. McGuire, I'm going to drive you to the hospital."

"I'm not going."

Ashley's eyes widened as she gave Mrs. McGuire an incredulous look. "Why not?"

"Because I don't want a bunch of people I don't know poking at me."

"Please, Mrs. McGuire, you need to have your foot seen to. I'll be there with you. Didn't Dr. Bradford tell you how important this is to your health?"

"I did," Kiefer said.

"I understand the doctor is trying to help but I'll be all right." Mrs. McGuire started putting on her sock. "I'll just give it a good soak and it'll get better like it always has."

Kiefer leaned forward, capturing her gaze. "That might work for a little while but not forever, and when it stops you'll be in bigger trouble. Please reconsider."

Ashley placed her hand on his shoulder. He was far too conscious of it remaining there as she said, "Dr. Bradford, would you let me speak to Mrs. McGuire for a second?"

"Sure." He left. What did Ashley have to say that couldn't be said in front of him? As he went into the next exam room he saw the reporter and cameraman still standing in the waiting room.

A few minutes later Ashley stopped him in the hall. "If you'll make all the arrangements, I'll take Mrs. Mc-Guire to the hospital as soon as we go by her house and pack a bag."

Ashley could work miracles. "What did you say to get her to go?"

She grinned. "What's said between two women stays between two women."

"That's not been my experience."

She looked at him with her chin tilted to one side. "Why, Doctor, I do believe you're a bit jaded."

"No, I've lived long enough to know differently. But it doesn't matter. I'm just glad you convinced her."

CHAPTER THREE

ASHLEY DROVE HOME well after dark. She'd got Mrs. Mc-
Guire settled in the hospital, but not happily so. Her only
hope was that Mrs. McGuire would stay long enough to
get the care she needed. Now having the clinic in the
neighborhood, the older woman would have a place to go
to for care. The clinic was already making a difference.

If only it had been around that day for Lizzy.

As she drove by the front door of the clinic she saw
a couple of boys on either side of it. They were pushing
over the urns. Ashley honked her horn and their heads
jerked up. She recognized them as members of Marko's
gang. Rolling down the window, she hollered, "Hey, stop
that!"

That was all it took for them to take off running.

With a sigh, she parked and climbed out. She walked
over to see how big a mess had been made. It was late,
she was tired and didn't feel like cleaning it up. But if
she didn't do it now, what was left of the flowers would
be dead by morning. She reached the door just as it was
opened. She almost fell but Kiefer's strong hands gripped
her shoulders and steadied her. Her heart beat faster. She
wasn't sure if it was from surprise or from the jolt of having him touch her.

"Y-you scared me. I d-didn't expect you to still be here," she stammered.

He let her go. Disappointment washed over her. Not a feeling she should be having.

Kiefer stepped out. "I was finishing up some paperwork and getting ready to head home when I heard something going on out here. I came to check it out."

She waved her hand around. "A couple of kids have been busy."

"More like Marko trying to make a point."

He was right but she wasn't going to let him know that. "I'd like to just consider it a prank. I've got to get this cleaned up."

"Can't it wait?"

"The flowers could die overnight." Ashley started picking up the plants.

"Ah, a woman and her flowers."

"What does that mean?"

"Just that women have a thing for flowers." He handed her part of a plant.

"You sound pretty cynical. Someone used flowers against you?"

"Something like that. Why don't you get the broom and dustpan?" Kiefer began picking up pieces of the broken urns and putting them into a pile near the wall of the building. "I'll get started cleaning this up."

It was nice of him to offer to help. "You've had a long day. Go on home and I'll see to this."

"I'm not leaving you out here by yourself after this happened. So forget it. Get the broom and dustpan."

"Don't tell me what to do."

"I wouldn't have to if you weren't so hardheaded," he retorted as he continued to work.

Ashley put her hands on her hips and glared at him.

It gave her little satisfaction because he wasn't looking at her. "I am not hardheaded."

"You're sure acting that way. I've made a simple offer of help and you're still standing there."

"Are you always so bossy?" Ashley glared down at the top of his head.

He looked over his shoulder at her. "Are you?"

With a huff, she stomped through the door and down the hall. Kiefer's chuckle followed her. She hadn't enjoyed growing up with a father controlling her every move and she sure didn't like Kiefer telling her what to do. It was time to make that clear to him. She snatched the cleaning supplies out of the closet along with a bucket and returned to the front door. Kiefer had all the pieces picked up and the flowers laid off to the side.

"I tried to save your flowers but I'm not sure they're going to live."

He really was making an effort at being helpful. Maybe she could cut him some slack. "Thanks. I was afraid of that. Would you like to do the honors of sweeping or holding the pan?"

"I'll take the pan." His hand brushed hers as she handed it to him. A shiver went through her.

"I rather like the idea of you at my feet," Ashley said as she swept the dirt into a pile.

"Don't get carried away with the idea." Kiefer held the pan while she moved the dirt into it then dumped it into the bucket. "Maybe if we put the flowers in here they might make it."

"Sounds good to me." She went back to sweeping. It was nice not having to clean up all by herself.

A few minutes later Kiefer said, "I think that's got it."

"I'll carry the broom and pan in if you don't mind bringing in the flowers. You can just set them beside the door."

Her body skimmed his as he waited for her to enter ahead of him. Why did the most insignificant touch between them make her heart flutter?

After putting the bucket on the floor, he said, "I'm going to call it a night. Lock up. I'll see you in the morning."

"Hey, you didn't even ask about Mrs. McGuire."

"I'd just got off the phone with her doctor when I heard the crash out here. She's doing fine. I plan to visit her before I get here in the morning."

He really was a good doctor. "Thanks for what you did for her today."

"No big deal. All in a day's work."

"It's a big deal to Mrs. McGuire and the people around here." *And to me.*

Kiefer nodded. "I'm just glad I could help." He grinned. "And I didn't have to spend too much time at your feet."

The next morning just after sunrise Ashley woke to the sound of large vehicles pulling into the parking lot. Crawling out of bed, she went to the window and looked down to find a truck towing a power pole. It pulled to the end of the lot closest to the iron stairs leading to her front door. Behind it was another truck with an industrial posthole digger attached.

What was going on?

She'd been trying for months to get a streetlight put in near the lot. More than once she'd been informed that it wasn't going to happen. Now all of a sudden the power company was showing up. She watched as Kiefer's black truck turned into the lot and took a spot out of the way of the trucks. He climbed out and walked over to one of the men from the power company.

Ashley quickly pulled on a long housecoat and hurried down the hall to her apartment door. Stepping outside onto the small iron deck, she leaned down over the rail. "What's going on?"

Kiefer looked at her. "Harold and his crew are going to put a security light in for you."

"I knew nothing about this."

"I called in a favor."

Ashley pressed her lips together. The light was needed but she didn't want Kiefer taking it upon himself to see that she got it. She could take care of herself, get things done without his influence. After years of fighting against stifling concern, she wouldn't let it take over her life again. She could grow to trust and depend on him. What if she did and he disappointed her? "I wish you hadn't done that."

He climbed the stairs. "What do you mean? You know this light is needed."

"I do, but what I don't need is someone trying to take care of me."

Kiefer joined her on the landing. She suddenly felt small and underdressed with him standing next to her in his golf-style shirt, tan slacks and loafers. He made her think of things that could happen between them that were better left alone. Her nipples tightened in reaction to his nearness and she crossed her arms over her breasts.

"What brought that on? You said the other night that you'd been trying to get a light installed out here and I just asked the hospital administrator to give the power company a call."

"Okay. I appreciate your efforts." She turned to go inside.

"You still didn't answer my question. What's the chip on your shoulder about people being concerned about your welfare?"

She turned to glare at him. "I spent most of my life with overprotective parents, especially my father. It took me a long time to break away and I'm not going to let anyone control my life like that again."

Kiefer's shoulders and head went back. "Whoa, I didn't expect that blast."

"Then you shouldn't have asked." She opened the door, entered and closed it firmly between her and the man who saw too much and managed to send her emotions into a tailspin.

Kiefer hefted a cement urn out of the bed of his truck. He was glad he'd backed up to the front door, instead of trying to carry it across the parking lot. It weighed more than he'd anticipated. The man at the garden shop had loaded the two pots for him. He had asked for their sturdiest and apparently had got his request. Positioning the urn beside the door, he returned to the truck for a bag of potting soil.

After Ashley's reaction to him arranging for the security light, he probably shouldn't be replacing the flowers without discussing it with her, but he'd not seen her again. She'd left just after daylight, that much he knew, because her car was no longer parked near her stairs.

He poured half the bag of dirt into the pot. What he couldn't figure out was her over-the-top reaction to him trying to help. The security light just made good sense. Was she one of those women who didn't want anything done unless she was the one to do it? She probably wouldn't like him replacing the flowers but she would just have to get over it. He'd tell her it was for the clinic and not her. That he was confident she would accept.

Why he cared he had no idea. After what Brittney had done to him he'd promised himself not to care about a woman one way or another and here he was planting flowers for one who wouldn't be grateful. Brittney liked flowers. She'd kept fresh ones in a vase all the time. It had turned out some of those had been from Josh.

Stepping inside, he used more force than necessary and picked up the bucket with the dirt and flowers he and Ashley had rescued the night before. Kiefer took a deep breath then headed outside. He was doing this during the only lag in patients he'd had in the last two days. Instead of eating lunch, he was out here planting flowers, something that was well out of his wheelhouse. He really needed to get a move on so he was done before a patient showed up. He'd handle Ashley's reaction when the time came.

That was sooner than he'd expected. He was in the waiting room, speaking to Margaret about how he would like the charting handled, when the sound of heels on the old pine planks of the floor headed in his direction. Kiefer didn't have to guess who the *clip-clip* belonged to.

Ashley joined him and Margaret at the old office desk being used as Reception. "Hey, Margaret, how's it going?"

"Fine. We've been busy."

"Great. At least we can prove to the council that the clinic is needed." She turned to him. "Dr. Bradford, could I speak to you for a minute?"

Kiefer didn't like her tone. It reminded him of when he was in trouble and his mother used his full name. Ashley must have noticed the flowers, on which he believed he'd done an exceptional job.

He followed her down the hall. She wore a pencil skirt and dark hose that made her slim legs look sexy. He'd always been a legs man and hers were some of the finest he'd ever seen. The swish of her hips did something to his libido as well. He shouldn't get involved with a controlling, political do-gooder. She wasn't his type and even if she had been he'd sworn off women. He'd been kicked in the teeth and wasn't going to put himself in that position again. Still, he could look and appreciate, couldn't he?

Ashley stepped into his tiny office. He joined her and closed the door. She regarded at the door as if she feared she might have made a tactical error.

"What's going on that you thought we needed to talk alone?" He was taking the offensive before she could.

"I, uh, I noticed the flowers out front. I'm assuming you did them."

"I did."

"You know that isn't part of your job description…"

Kiefer took a step closer and she moved back until her bottom was against the desk. He pinned her with a look. "I do, but it needed to be done and I wanted the guys that did the destruction to know that the clinic was here to stay. I also had the security light erected for the patients as well as you. Soon it'll be getting darker earlier."

She gave him a perplexed look. Maybe he'd managed to stymie her. Something she'd not been for the entire time he'd known her.

"I thought—"

"That I'd done it for you?" He took a half a step closer. There was that fresh-baked cookie smell again. He wanted to breathe deeply, take it in. He raised a brow. "You made it perfectly clear the evening we met that you didn't need my help."

"I guess I did."

Apparently when she didn't have the upper hand she could be dealt with rather easily. "Well, if we have that cleared up then I'll get back to my patients."

"Before you go I have one other thing to discuss with you." Her voice had taken on the tone of authority again.

"Yes?" He looked down his nose at her.

"Next Saturday is the community block party. You will need to attend."

"Is that a request or a demand?"

Ashley's eyes widened. "Why, I'm asking."

"That's not what it sounded like."

"Are you trying to pick a fight, Doctor?"

He leaned toward her. "No, I'm just trying to remind you that I'm not one of your subjects."

"S-subjects?" she stuttered.

Ashley truly looked as if she had no idea she'd become so wrapped up in what she wanted that she'd forgotten that others might have different ideas or plans. "I'm not employed by you. I like to be asked to do something, not told. Especially when it has to do with my spare time."

She huffed. "Would you please come to the block party?"

He acted as if he was giving it a great deal of thought before he said, "I'll be there. Do I need to bring something?"

"No, all the food will be taken care of. I just need the neighborhood to see you as part of them."

"I understand. Now, if you're through with me, I have patients waiting." He stepped toward the door, stopped and returned to face her. His hands cupped her face. "You know, it's time I get this out of my system." His mouth found hers. It was as sweet and perfect as he remembered.

Ashley made a small sound of resistance before she returned his kiss. Her hands went to his forearms and squeezed.

Yes, that fire was still there. Flaming.

He let her go almost as abruptly as he had taken her. She rocked back on her heels.

Ashley raised her head, giving him a haughty look. "I have an appointment downtown."

Kiefer opened the door and spread an arm wide, indicating for her to leave first. Her shoulder brushed his chest as she moved past him. A buzz of awareness shot through him. To make it worse, her scent lingered behind her. He licked his lips.

He enjoyed pushing Ashley Marsh's buttons. She exasperated and intrigued him at the same time. As for kissing Ashley, it was far from being out of his system. All he could think about now was doing it again.

Three evenings later Ashley was in her kitchen, preparing a simple dinner after a long day of ensuring that the plans for the block party were properly handled. She wanted the event to go off without a glitch, providing another step toward community solidarity and pride.

She hadn't seen or spoken to Kiefer since their last discussion. Or kiss. Boy, the man could kiss. Where the first one they'd shared had been hot, this last one had been steamy and delicious, and far too short. She still didn't remember her drive downtown.

If she was honest with herself she might admit she'd been dodging Kiefer. Something about him unnerved her. Made her want to let go of something she'd fought hard to earn. Could she believe in him? Trust him to be who he seemed to be?

She'd thanked him for the new security light more than once. It had been reassuring that she didn't have to worry about coming home to no light other than the one over her door. It was also nice to have someone to help her out. She liked it that he'd seen to replanting the flowers. Somehow it made a statement that the clinic and he were here to stay, at least for a while. But how long would that be for? Should she let herself depend on Kiefer? Dared she? She'd trusted people before and been wrong. Could she be wrong again?

His truck was still in his parking space when she'd come home. She'd made a point not to go into the clinic. Kiefer was correct—it was his domain and not hers to oversee.

As she chopped the vegetables on the cutting board beside the sink, she sang along softly to the love song on the radio. She stopped and looked over her shoulder through the arched doorway to the hall.

Was someone there?

It wasn't so much what she heard but how she felt. Seeing nothing, she started to place vegetables into the skillet for a stir-fry. She gave the pan on the burner a shake. Between songs, the creak of a board she knew well had her turning around. Marko stood in the doorway. She dropped the skillet, spilling half-cooked vegetables across the floor.

"How did you get in here?"

He had a smirk on his face. "The same way I go anywhere I want."

"You broke in." She walked to the center of the room and pointed toward the door. "Get out, Marko."

"Who died and made you the boss of me?"

"Marko, you know I'm not afraid of you." He stepped toward her. Ashley remained where she was, refusing to be intimidated despite her heart beating against her ribs.

"You should be," he snarled. "I own Southriver. Don't force me to make you pay."

"Don't threaten me."

He moved into her personal space. Ashley couldn't stop the shudder that went through her. She smelled his beer-laden breath as it brushed her face. He snarled, "I'm not threatening you. I'm making you a promise."

Ashley backed away until she butted up against the counter. Marko matched her step for step. He leaned in and picked up the knife she'd put in the sink. She sucked in a breath when he brought it to her face.

"I'd hate for you to have an accident."

"Ashley." Kiefer's voice came from the stairwell seconds before he stepped through the door.

Marko was already disappearing around the opening in the direction of her outside door.

Kiefer looked from him to her. "What the...?"

Ashley slid down the cabinet to the floor. Her pulse raced. She put her arms around her legs and her head on her knees.

Kiefer wasn't sure what had been going on but it was too close to déjà vu for him. The situation reminded him of what had happened to his mother. In two strides he was across the width of the kitchen and looking down the hall. The outside door stood open. The screen was still slapping against the frame. He pushed the main door closed and locked it before returning to the kitchen.

Ashley still sat on the floor and he crouched down beside her. Gathering her into his arms, he held her. To his surprise she didn't fight him, instead buried her head in his chest. Soft sobs racked her body.

He brushed his hand over her hair. "Shh, I'm right here. You're safe."

They stayed that way for a few minutes until Ashley slowly pulled away. Kiefer let his hold ease but didn't completely release her. He brushed her hair from her face and looked into red eyes and a pale face. The strong woman he was so familiar with had disappeared. Compassion filled him. "Will you tell me what happened?"

She looked at him for a moment as if she didn't understand him. Finally she said, "Marko stopped by for a visit."

"There was more to it than that." He looked at the food surrounding them.

She gave him a sad smile and a little nod that reminded him of a young girl who had broken her doll. It was less about heartache and more about disappointment.

"He threatened me with the knife."

"He what? I'm calling the police." Kiefer reached in his pocket for the phone.

"Don't." She grabbed his wrist.

"You have to report this."

"I can't. I babysat him. Our families were friends. I wasn't crying over what he did just now but over the loss of that sweet kid, the one who wasn't so angry with life and injustice."

Kiefer leaned back and looked at her. She was an amazing person. Here she had been threatened with a knife in her own home and all she was worried about was the person who had threatened her. How like his mother. Where did they get that type of fortitude? What he wanted to do was kill Marko or at the very least see that he was put in jail. Kiefer had no compassion for anyone who treated a woman that way, particularly one he cared about. It had killed him to see his mother defenseless in front of him and here it was happening again.

"So you're just going to allow him to go around threatening people?"

Ashley stood. "He didn't hurt me."

Kiefer came to his feet too. "He might have if I hadn't shown up."

"I don't think so. He was trying to scare me."

"I'm not willing to take that chance." Kiefer glared down at her.

"I'm not yours to worry about."

He looked everywhere but at her, trying to contain his irritation. "I hope your big bleeding heart doesn't get you—or someone else—into real trouble someday." He needed to do something or he would really become angry. "Point me in the direction of the broom and dustpan and I'll clean this mess up."

To his astonishment she indicated a small closet door without argument. The recent events must have got to her more than she wanted to let on.

"I've got oil all over me. I think I'll get a shower." She didn't look back as she walked down the passageway.

Kiefer swept up and gave a quick soapy mop to the floor. She'd been preparing a meal, so she couldn't have had dinner yet. He looked in the refrigerator and found ingredients for an omelet and salad. He was impressed with her well-stocked kitchen. Most of the women he knew would rather eat out than cook. Apparently Ashley dined at home often.

Ten minutes later he had put a simple salad together and still no Ashley. He didn't want to cook the eggs until he knew she was ready to eat. He went down the hall in the direction of what he guessed was her bedroom. The hall led into a wide room that had to be her living area. An eclectic group of furnishings filled the space. He'd bet his paycheck the tables had been yard-sale finds Ashley had refurbished. Was there nothing the woman couldn't do?

Small canister lighting and lamps gave the room a warm feel, but the fireplace with the whitewashed mantel was the focal point. Two comfortable-looking chairs were pulled up close to it. This was a place where Ashley really lived. There was nothing pretentious about it. Down-to-earth and natural, just like Ashley. Two doors led off the area.

He went to the doorway of one. It looked like an unused bedroom. He tried the other.

This was her bedroom. It suited her. A white iron bed covered in a multicolored quilt faced the door, with windows on either side draped in some gauzy material. A large free-standing wardrobe stood to one side and an old-fashioned dresser on the other. His mother would say the room was charming.

"Ashley? I've put some supper together."

There was silence.

He stepped farther into the room. "Ashley?" A whimper came from a doorway he'd not noticed before. Steam hanging in the air told him it was her bathroom. "Are you okay?"

A weak "Yes…" reached his ears. Through the fog he could see her dressed in the robe she'd worn the other morning and the necklace he'd seen at the St. Patrick's Day party. Did she wear it all the time? She sat on the toilet lid with her hands clasped together. Her body shook.

Kiefer reached for her. Taking her forearms, he helped her stand. Her lack of resistance indicated she was at the end of her rope. As he led her to the bed he said, "Come on. Let's get you warm and something in your belly."

He jerked the covers back, helped her under the sheets and pulled the coverlet over her, tucking them under her chin. "How about dinner in bed?"

"You probably think I'm weak," she mumbled.

"No, I just think you've had a shock and need to process it. You'll be back to your old demanding self in the morning, I'm sure. Now, you stay put and I'll have something for you to eat in five minutes."

"I don't want—"

"I'm sure you don't but I'm going to wait on you until I know you're feeling better."

"How did you know what I was going to say?"

"Because I know you. Enough talk. I'll be right back."

Ashley wished she could crawl under the covers and never have to face Kiefer again. How could she lose it like that? It wasn't like her. After her best friend, Lizzy, had been kidnapped she'd promised herself she'd never be in that position, vulnerable. She'd been in her own home and Marko had invaded it. He had been right there before she'd known it. Was that the way it had been for Lizzy? Had she been as scared? She'd known Ron, just as Ashley knew Marko.

If word of what had happened got out, not only her parents but the neighborhood would be fearful. If the city council heard, it might be the end of the clinic. She couldn't let that happen. The clinic meant so much to her. It was a way for making up for the selfishness of her past. To compensate in some small way for her part in what had happened to Lizzy.

How could she have been so wrong about Marko? She would have sworn that Marko would never have done what he had. She'd believed that behind that bravado he'd just been putting on a show. In reality, she put on the same show. She didn't want anyone to know how scared she could be.

Trying to shake off the fears from long ago, Ashley pulled her covers close. She had to get control or Kiefer would think she was going nuts. Could he see how much Marko's visit had affected her? That was a joke. Kiefer had found her in the bathroom in the middle of an emotional breakdown. Of course he now knew she had been scared witless. That she'd been putting on a front of confidence. What if he told someone and it got back to her parents? They would start in again about her living elsewhere in the city, even though they wouldn't leave South-river themselves.

Kiefer was as good as his word. He returned with food on a tray. There were two bowls of salad and plates with omelets that looked perfectly cooked. The man had talents other than being a fine doctor. And he really was that. She'd been astonished at the number of people who had come to him for care. She'd imagined that the people of Southriver would have been much more standoffish but apparently word had circulated that Kiefer could be trusted. Did she believe what she saw enough to agree? What if he fooled her like Marko had? Like Ron?

"If you don't mind, I think I'll join you."

She nodded. "I guess so. You can have it all, as far as I'm concerned."

"Oh, no, you don't. You're going to eat too. I'll shame you into feeling guilty that I slaved over a hot stove if I have to."

Ashley couldn't help but grin at that. She scooted up in bed, adjusting the housecoat so that it didn't gape over her breasts. "Okay, you're being nice, so I'll at least make an effort."

"That sounds more like the Ashley I know." He set the tray on the bed. "I'll get our drinks. I didn't trust myself to walk all this way without spilling them if they were on the tray."

Kiefer was back in less than a minute with glasses of iced tea. He placed them on a table beside the bed where she could reach hers. Afterward he handed her a bowl. "Eat up. It'll make you feel better."

Ashley wasn't sure that was true but she took a bite anyway. Kiefer started in on his salad with gusto and was soon working on his omelet.

"So where did you learn your culinary skills?" She had

managed to finish her salad and was placing the empty bowl on the tray.

"I think 'culinary skills' is stretching it a bit. If you're asking where I learned to cook then that's when I was in med school. It was either learn or starve. I had to eat whenever I had a chance at all times of the day. I can do the basics. From what I could tell about what I swept up off the floor, you might take cooking more seriously."

She finished chewing the forkful of omelet that might have been the best she'd ever had. "I like to cook when I have time. I was raised standing beside my mother in the kitchen, watching her."

"So does your family still live in Southriver?"

"Oh, yeah. You couldn't blast them out."

"Kind of like you."

"I guess that's true." She and her parents did have that in common.

"Your family ever think of moving somewhere else?"

"Only once, a long time ago." Those had been dark days.

"What changed their minds?"

She concentrated on putting her plate on the tray. "Mother and Daddy didn't know where they would go. They had never lived anywhere but here."

"My family isn't much different. Even my first cousin, who now lives in California, still considers Savannah home. Once you have Chatham County sand between your toes, it's hard to get it out."

Their families might have that sand in common but outside of that they had to be as different as swampland was from a desert. "Thank you for the meal. You didn't have to do this."

He grinned. "Sure I did, if I wanted to eat."

"Thanks also for not making me feel more ashamed

of my breakdown. Please don't mention this to anyone. It would upset my parents if it got back to them."

"Nothing to be ashamed of. You had good reason. And what happens at the Southriver clinic stays in the Southriver clinic."

He needed to leave. Kiefer was far too charming. She was also far too aware of her state of undress and of him being in her bedroom, sitting on her bed. She'd not had a man in here in so long that if he was any nicer to her she might grab him and pull him under the covers. After their last kiss it truly was temping. "Well, I appreciate your help."

"And that sounds like my cue to leave." The bed gave when he stood. "I already know what the answer will be before I ask this question but I have to."

What was he talking about?

"Are you going to be all right here by yourself?" He studied her.

Ashley met his look and said in a firm voice, "Yes. I'm fine now. I just overreacted for a few minutes. I'm good now. Thank you."

"You've already said that. More than once."

"Well, I am grateful."

"The problem is that you sound too grateful for you. That's why I think you might still be a little rattled."

He saw too much, too easily. She leaned forward and glared at him. "What's that supposed to mean?"

"Now, that sounds more like the Ashley I know."

"Now it *is* time for you to go."

He chuckled as he picked up the tray and headed out the door. "I'll be locking up behind me. You do have your cell phone nearby?"

"Right here." She picked it up off the bedside table.

"If you even hear a noise, call 911."

"I'll be fine. Now, please leave so I can get some sleep."

"Call me if you need me. Even just to talk."

"I won't."

With his back to her as he went out the door he said, "I know. Good night, hardheaded Ashley Marsh."

Where was a shoe to throw when she needed one? She smiled. He'd managed to irritate her but he'd also got her mind off what had happened. Kiefer Bradford was a smooth operator. That she could admire.

Kiefer double-checked the locks on Ashley's front door and the one to the stairs going to the clinic. Even the main clinic door he rechecked. He walked round the building, making sure there were no broken or open windows.

How had he been sucked into a woman's life that was so much like his mother's? In the past he'd made a point to date women who were nothing like his crusading mother. Brittney was a case in point and look where that had got him.

In his truck he called his buddy Bull and told him what had happened. Ashley wouldn't be happy he had but that didn't matter—her safety came first. Bull said he would see that the clinic was patrolled more often that night.

Sleeping at Ashley's had crossed his mind but he had no doubt that she would have objected strongly. He wasn't going to pick that fight but he would do what he could to see she was safe. The woman was too self-confident for her own good. Tonight had proved it.

Around midnight Kiefer woke to the sound of rain on the windows. That was one thing about living on the coast—the weather could go from flaming hot to a strong thunderstorm overnight. He immediately reached for his phone and tapped in Bull's number. He answered on the second ring.

"So how are things?" Kiefer asked.

"A little overprotective, aren't you, Doctor? Have things become personal with the pretty alderman?"

"No, I'm just concerned. Nothing more. Nothing less. So answer my question."

"Everything is quiet. Last time we cruised by no one was around. There was one upstairs light on but that was it."

Was Ashley having a hard time sleeping? Scared and turning a light on? "Thanks, buddy. Please continue to check on the place."

"Will do."

Kiefer put his phone down then picked it up, placed it on the bedside table then picked it up again. What was the worst she could do? Get mad at him for waking her. Scream at him tomorrow morning for calling. He should check on her. Just to make sure she was okay. Or maybe to just satisfy his need to know.

He touched Ashley's number, which he'd programmed into his cell phone when he'd been given it as contact for the clinic. On the first ring she answered. There was a hesitant note in her voice as if she was unsure about who it might be.

"Hey, it's Kiefer. I wanted to see how you are."

"Do you have any idea what time it is?" Her voice was stronger.

That was good. "Yeah, about one a.m."

"Don't you know better than to call people in the middle of the night?"

"I heard a light was on at your place. I thought you might be up."

"How would you know that? Either you're standing

below my window or having me watched." She paused. "Bull. I asked you not to tell the police."

"I told a friend."

Ashley made a sound of disgust. "Same difference."

"I just wanted to make sure you were okay."

"You don't have to do that. I'm not your responsibility."

He pushed at his pillow, getting comfortable. "After what I walked in on I wouldn't be human if I wasn't concerned."

"Why do you keep pushing it?"

He didn't want to go into that full explanation. "Because I swore a long time ago that I wouldn't sit by again while someone hurt another person."

"What happened?"

It wasn't something he talked about much, certainly not to a virtual stranger, but for some reason he wanted Ashley to understand. "My mother was attacked when I was a child."

Ashley made a shocked noise. "I'm so sorry to hear that." For the first time since she'd been attacked she sounded like herself. "No wonder you overreact."

"I didn't realize I overreacted. I thought I was rather calm, considering. So are you sitting in front of the fireplace or are you lying in bed?"

"This conversation has suddenly taken a creepy turn," she said in a light tone.

"I was only asking to gauge whether or not you were really having trouble sleeping."

"So now you can make diagnoses over the phone. Impressive, Doctor."

He liked this quick-witted Ashley. It would be nice to see more of her. "I can. If you're sitting in your living room, that tells me you're still rattled, but if you're in your bed, there's a good chance you're recovering and will go back to sleep."

"Well, if you must know, I'm in bed."

"Good. You aren't still in that robe, are you?"

"Now you're really getting personal."

He guessed he was but it was for a good reason. At least her mind was off what had happened to her. "You need to have on something comfortable to sleep well."

"I changed into a gown soon after you left."

Kiefer hated that he'd missed that. Whoa, that wasn't what he needed to be thinking. He wasn't going to get involved with Ashley on that level. They were business associates only. He'd sworn off women. Those with an agenda didn't interest him and Brittney had cured him of taking a chance on being used. But those kisses between him and Ashley pulled at him. Said there might be something there.

"Good. Then why don't you turn off the light and try to sleep? I'm sure you have a full day ahead."

"You think you know me so well."

He was surprised just how much he did know about her in such a short time. The interesting thing was that he found he really liked her when she wasn't on her high horse about how she wanted something done. "Well, enough." The sound of her yawn came through the phone. "Am I boring you?"

"Maybe." She chuckled.

Warmth spread throughout his chest. "Then I'll say good night, Ashley."

The click of a lamp being turned off reached his ear then a soft "Good night, Kiefer."

What would it be like to hear that firsthand as he gathered her close in his arms? He was headed in the wrong direction. Backing off was what he needed to do. Ashley had been taking care of herself long before he'd come along and she would be doing it when he was gone. Tonight was an exception to the rule. Period.

CHAPTER FOUR

ASHLEY WOKE WITH a jerk. She'd overslept. She had been more shaken by Marko's threats than she'd wanted to admit. Sleep had been easier to find after Kiefer had called. There was something about his deep, smooth voice that made her feel safe, as though he was right there with her instead of miles away.

Now she was ready to face her day. There were arrangements to make for the block party and she had a meeting with the zoning commission to get help with some buildings that needed restoration on the next block.

As the day went on she settled down, no longer thinking twice about leaving the house or going about business as normal. Marko had made his move and as usual was all talk. She'd seen Kiefer a few times in passing but they hadn't had time for anything more than a casual hello, no real discussion. What that would have been about she had no idea. Still, she missed their talks—or sparring was more the word for it.

The next evening she was in the kitchen, cooking, when there was a knock on her door. Her heart picked up speed for a second. She put it down to still being a little jumpy, not over-excitement at seeing Kiefer, who had just stuck his head around the door.

"Hey, I was on my way out for the day and wanted to say bye."

His eyes studied her too closely. Too watchful for her comfort. "I'm fine, if that's what you want to know."

Kiefer stepped farther into the room. "Never doubted it for a minute."

She smirked. "I bet."

He put his nose in the air. "Mmm, something smells good."

Ashley turned back to the stove and stirred the pot of black-eyed peas. "That would be my supper."

"It sure smells wonderful. Well, I guess I'll leave you to it."

"Kiefer." She turned around just as he was starting through the door.

He looked back at her. "Yeah?"

"Would you like to join me?"

"I sure would."

She laughed. "It didn't take you but a second to answer."

"I only get a home-cooked meal when I visit my parents. But those meals come with an inquisition from my mother about when I'm going to get married. When will she be a grandmother? Why don't I settle down?"

"Why aren't you married?"

He gave her a pointed look.

"I'm sorry. That's one of those questions you don't want to answer."

"I don't mind answering it. I just don't want to talk about it at every meal. I've been married and have no plans to do it again."

"That bad, huh?"

"My wife left me for my best friend."

She didn't say anything. What could she say that would

make that any better? He'd had his own issues. "That's tough."

"Yeah, it was. Now, how can I help?"

"You can get the knives, forks and spoons and set the table." She pointed. "The drawer to the left."

"Okay. What about you?"

"What about me?" She looked at him.

"Ever been married?"

"No. Guys don't seem to like sharing their time with my desire to work for social change."

"Understandable."

She caught his look. "What do you mean by that?"

"Just that you're a force to be reckoned with."

"I'm not sure that's a compliment. But I'm going to take it as one." She pulled a pan out of a drawer under the stove. "Where are the glasses? I'll pour us some tea."

He hadn't agreed with her. Did he think she came on too strong? Why should she care what he thought? "They're in the cabinet next to the refrigerator."

Kiefer had to reach past her to get them and his chest brushed against her back. Suddenly the kitchen became closet sized. Her hand shook as she moved a pot off a burner.

"Careful with that. You might get burned." His breath fanned against her neck.

She shivered, very aware of him being near. "If you'd give me some room then you wouldn't have to worry."

He straightened. "I'm used to worrying about you."

"I wish you'd stop."

"It's part of the job of being the local doctor."

Ashley poured the beans into a bowl. "Did you always want to be a doctor?"

"No. I dreamed of being a beach bum. I still love

the beach. How about you? Did you always want to be an alderman?"

"I was going to be a great journalist."

"So that's why you're so good in front of a camera." Was she?

"I guess. I didn't know I was." She pulled the pot roast from the slow cooker and put it on a platter.

"You seem very natural. I hate it." He took the platter from her.

"I noticed that the other day. It just takes practice not to be intimidated."

Kiefer walked to the table. "I don't want to practice. My one real experience wasn't fun."

"What happened?"

"When my mother was attacked the TV cameras were everywhere. Always in my face."

She looked appalled. "You were just a kid."

"They didn't care. But enough of that talk. I'm hungry."

She grinned. "I've never known you not to be. Sit down and I'll get the potatoes ready."

He did as she requested. When all the food was in front of them she sat. Leaning over the table, he made a big show of smelling and studying the food. "Do you always cook like this?"

"Once a week I treat myself to an all-out meal that I prepare. I'm usually so busy I don't eat right, so this is my way of compensating." She picked up a bowl and handed it to him.

As he spooned out mashed potatoes he said, "Well, I'd like to get on your regular dinner guest list."

Warm pleasure filled Ashley. It was nice to have a man appreciate her, and Kiefer in particular. "I'll take that under advisement." She watched as he took a large hunk of roast beef from the platter in the middle of the table.

She filled her plate and glanced over at Kiefer. He was waiting on her to begin eating. His parents had taught him manners. Picking up her fork, she took a bite and he dug into his meal with gusto.

"This is the best thing I've tasted in months." He raised a forkful of meat.

Ashley couldn't help but glow under his praise. "Thank you. You know I'm not going to kick you out. You don't have to keep going on about how good the food is."

He glanced up. "I'm telling the truth."

"I'm glad you're enjoying it." It was nice to cook for someone who appreciated it. Kiefer was starting to endear himself to her. She liked him the more she was around him, slowly learning to trust him.

"So when you're not cooking or being an alderman, what do you do for fun?"

"Fun?"

"Yeah, you know when you smile and frolic. Fun."

She chuckled. "Frolic. You pulled that out of the vault."

"You've never frolicked?" He raised both brows.

"Sure I have. When I was about four."

He asked between bites, "So you do remember fun?"

"Never said I didn't."

"Okay, now we're talking in rounds. Let me try again. What do you like to do on your days off?"

"I don't have many of them but when I do I like to go to the movies."

"What kind of movies?"

"I like old romances. *Rebecca, Casablanca, An Affair to Remember.*"

He stopped chewing. "Now, that's a facet of your personality I didn't expect. I took you for more of a shoot-'em-up person."

Was he saying that she didn't have a soft side? Hadn't she heard that before from other men? The idea really hurt coming from Kiefer.

Her chair scraped the floor as she stood. Taking her plate to the dishwasher, she put it in. "Well, people can surprise you."

Ashley returned to the table for two bowls and carried them to the counter. A large hand slipped around her and placed the platter of leftover meat on the counter just as she turned. She bumped into Kiefer's chest. His hands came to rest on her shoulders.

"Hey," Kiefer said softly, compelling her to look at him. "I didn't mean to hurt your feelings."

"You didn't."

His gaze held hers. "I think I did. You don't have to be the tough guy all the time."

Her hands went to his chest. "I'm not."

Kiefer pulled her closer. His look dropped. He intended to kiss her. The thrill of anticipation made her heart rate increase.

"I know for a fact that parts of you are very soft." Slowly his mouth lowered to hers.

Ashley closed her eyes as his lips touched hers. They were firm and sure. Wonderful. She wrapped her arms around his neck and returned his kiss. How did he manage to make her brainless when his lips were on hers? She pushed up against him, finding solid warmth that she wanted to bury herself in.

His lips left hers. "Let's go somewhere more comfortable."

What was she doing? She didn't have time for a complication like Kiefer. If they became involved and then broke up, which they surely would because they were so incompatible, what would happen to the clinic? It would make their relationship extremely uncomfortable. Should she believe in him? No, she'd been misled before. Be sure. Very sure. Ashley pushed hard against his chest, breaking their contact.

Kiefer looked at her with questioning eyes. He leaned toward her again.

She backed away. "I think it's time for you to go."

"Ash—"

"It won't work."

"How do you know?"

"I just know. I don't have time to play games."

He continued to watch her. "What games?"

"You know, the one where we get together, we play house and then we break up. I don't have time for all that emotional upheaval." What if she was wrong about him?

"You got all of that from three simple kisses?"

Was she overreacting? Maybe so, but she'd been there before, and during this time in her life she didn't have time to be sidetracked by getting involved with someone who was just here temporarily. Who would let her down in the end. "That's the problem. Your kisses aren't simple. I'm sorry—I'm tired. I think it's time for you to go."

"I will, but I won't be going far." He went to the door to the stairwell. Before he stepped through it, he looked back at her. "Just know that if it was up to me I'd still be kissing you. All over."

Heat washed over her. Just the idea made her blood hum. If he tried again, would she stop him?

Thursday evening Ashley was on her way home from a monthly council meeting. She'd drawn flowers on her notepad as Alderman Henderson had expounded on how too many funds were being used in the Southriver district and needed to be redirected to the infrastructure of the downtown where tourists visited. Ashley had heard it all before over and over. All she wanted was to go home and have a hot shower.

She glanced at the Southriver Community sign that had only been erected two weeks earlier. The sign showed the outline of brownstones with a river in the background. She hoped the signs gave the community a sense of pride because with that came ownership, which made a neighborhood strong.

As she drove up to the clinic she noticed the light was still on. Kiefer must have been working late. He had become a real asset to the clinic. The people in the community liked him. She shouldn't be so amazed because she did too. Too much. His kisses, though brief, still lingered. She bit her bottom lip. It still tingled whenever she thought of Kiefer's touch.

Seconds later she saw him step out of the clinic door and reach in to turn off the outside light.

A *pop-pop* drew her attention away. Not even a second later there was a *tink-tink* of something hitting the right front panel of her car. Was someone throwing something at her?

She saw a blur of movement that made her think of Marko. Another *pop* and the windshield cracked loudly.

Was he shooting at her?

Pop.

Ashley stomped the brake pedal, shoved the car into gear and leaned down over the console. Her arm stung. She must have hit the steering wheel. She felt a dampness there as well.

Before she could react further Kiefer was beating on her window. "Are you all right? Unlock the door!"

He was already jerking on the door handle as she pushed the button to release it. He slung it open before she could sit up.

Kiefer's head was inside the car. "Ashley. Ashley. Are you hurt?"

"I don't think so. Was someone shooting at me?"

"You're damn straight they were!" His hand was around her, pulling her into a sitting position.

"Did they shoot at you?"

"No, he ran off. He was after you."

"After me?" She tried to look out the windshield. "Oh, look at my poor car. Insurance is never going to believe this."

"Forget the car. How about you? I need to check you out. Are you sure nothing hurts?" He helped her out of the car.

"My arm does a little bit."

Kiefer said a string of words that could blister faster than the sun on a hot day in August. "You've been hit." He put an arm around her waist, supporting her weight against him.

"What?" She held her arm to her chest. Blood started to drip off her elbow.

"Stay still and let me have a look."

She did as he requested. Looking at her arm, she could see that there was a ragged tear in the lightweight material of her shirt.

Kiefer ripped the cloth, enlarging the opening.

"Hey!"

"Hush, your shirt was already ruined. I need to look at this." His finger probed along her skin.

"Ow!"

"Sorry. Do you have any napkins or a cloth in here?" he asked, looking toward her car.

"There are a few napkins in the door pocket." Her arm was starting to really sting.

Kiefer reached into the side pocket and came out with a handful of restaurant napkins that she'd stored there in case of a spill. He placed them over her wound, applying pressure. It stopped the stream of blood running down her arm.

She pulled back. "You do know that hurts, don't you?"

Kiefer didn't ease up. "I'm sorry but it's necessary. I need to get you inside where I can see. Can you hold your hand over it?"

Her head was becoming fuzzy but she said, "Yes."

"Good girl. Let's go." Kiefer supported her as they walked across the parking lot.

The sound of a siren and the flash of blue lights came toward them.

She tried to pull away. "You called the police?"

"Yes, I did. Someone was trying to kill you."

"No, they weren't. I'm sure they were only trying to scare me."

He brought her back against him. "Well, as far as I'm concerned, they were. Enough talking."

The police car pulled in next to them.

Ashley, despite her best efforts, weaved on her feet. "I'm feeling light-headed."

Kiefer grumbled something and pulled her tighter against him. He called to the officer, "I'm Dr. Bradford. Someone shot at Ms. Marsh." He gestured to her car and where the shooter had been with his free hand.

Kiefer kept moving toward the clinic as the officer took off in the direction he'd pointed. At the door Kiefer continued to hold her close. She moaned. Her arm was throbbing.

"Hang in there, Ashley. I'll have you taken care of

in no time." He pushed the door open. As they entered Ashley stumbled. Kiefer scooped her into his arms and stalked to an exam room. There he placed her on the table. "Do not move."

Ashley had never heard him sound so forceful. Even if she'd felt like doing so, she wouldn't after that demand. "Don't worry, I'm going nowhere."

In almost no time Kiefer had returned with an armload of supplies. He dumped them on the table and then tore into a box, pulling out some gauze pads. Taking a bottle of saline, he opened the top and wet a square. She hissed as he dabbed around the wound.

"I hate that it hurts but it can't be helped. Can you lift your arm? I need to see if the bullet went through."

Ashley raised her arm and Kiefer tore her sleeve farther. His fingers were gentle and careful as he pushed against the skin around the wound. "I don't feel any bullet but I can't be sure until you have an X-ray. I'm going to clean you up and then get you to the hospital."

"I don't want to go to the hospital."

"Even if I didn't think you needed to go, you would still have to. It's the law that all gunshot wounds be seen in an ER." Kiefer added more saline to a clean pad. "Let's get the bleeding stopped and you wrapped up."

Over the next few minutes Kiefer cleaned the area around the wound and put a bandage around her arm.

"Do you think you can walk to the truck?"

She nodded but when she stood she was unsteady on her feet. "With some help."

Kiefer pulled her close and guided her out to the truck.

"What're you looking for?" Ashley asked, when he slowed to look around for the second time.

"I'm making sure that someone isn't out here, waiting to take shots at you again."

"The police are here. They wouldn't dare."

"I'm not taking any chances." He steered her to the truck and lifted her inside. On the way round to his side he called to the officer who was examining her car, "I'm taking her to the hospital. It'll be quicker than waiting for an ambulance. We'll give our statements there."

The officer nodded his assent and said they'd meet them at the hospital. Kiefer glanced at her and checked her pulse again before driving away. For once Ashley was grateful to have someone taking care of her.

Kiefer paced the waiting area of the ER. They had told him to get out of the exam room. Go have a cup of coffee. Like he wanted some. His real worry was that someone had shot Ashley. Marko had been bad enough, but this… He'd known the neighborhood wasn't the best but he'd never imagined this would happen.

He made another trip across the floor. Ashley could have been killed.

Not soon enough for him, Will, the ER doctor and an old friend from medical school, pushed through the door to the waiting room. Kiefer didn't give him time to speak before he stalked toward him and asked, "How is she?"

"She's going to be fine. Has a few stitches in her forearm. The bullet didn't hit the bone. It was just a graze."

"You checked her over completely?"

Will eyed him closely. "I did. You act as if you and Alderman Marsh have something going on."

Kiefer couldn't meet his eye. Maybe he was overreacting but the thought of Ashley being hurt sickened him. After Brittney he had no intention of ever having something "going on" with a woman. He liked Ashley and didn't want to see her injured—that was all. "We're just friends. She owns the building that the clinic is in."

Will nodded and gave him a look that implied he thought there was more to it than what Kiefer was admitting to.

"Can I see her now?"

"Sure. She's going to stay overnight just for observation."

"Thanks, Will." Kiefer stuck out his hand.

Will shook it. "Come on back. But you have to behave."

Kiefer didn't dignify that statement with a remark. He'd been alarmed for Ashley when they'd made it to the hospital. Her head had been on his thigh and her eyes had been closed. He'd brushed her hair back from her pale face and quietly reassured her. The realization that he knew almost nothing about her clawed at him. That had been the way he'd wanted it until now. The less he knew the less involved personally he would be. The thought of her dying changed things. He wasn't going to let her push him away again.

He slid the exam room glass door sideways just far enough for him to slip in. Ashley was as white as the sheet pulled over her. He took her fingers in his. More than once he'd seen loved ones touch family members the same way. When had this woman started mattering to him so much? Slipped past his defenses? His reaction meant nothing. He'd be this concerned about anyone he'd seen shot.

Ashley's eyes opened but were heavy as if she would go to asleep again in the next second. "Hey."

"Hi. How're you feeling?"

"Like I got shot. Did they hurt you?"

"No."

"Good." Her eyelids fluttered for a second.

"Can you tell me your parents' names so I can call them?"

Her eyes went wide. "Don't. I don't want them to know."

Kiefer squeezed her hand. "They need to know."

"It would just worry them. Please don't. They don't need to know."

Kiefer settled into a chair beside the bed. Minutes later a police officer entered. "I need to take a statement."

Over the next half hour he and Ashley told their stories as the young officer made notes. Against Ashley's objections Kiefer also mentioned the vandalism incident and Marko's visit. It was so reminiscent of what had happened to his mother. All those emotions had swelled in him. The blind rage of watching Ashley shot, the helplessness of not being able to do more, the fear that he might lose her. He wanted to hit something.

"We are aware of who Marko is. He isn't someone to mess with. Ma'am, you need to be careful."

"I will be."

"If there's any further trouble, call right away. We'll be making a thorough investigation of the incident."

"I wish you would keep this quiet."

"Ma'am, a shooting is serious business. You were lucky. You could have been killed."

Ashley settled back in the bed. "I know," she said quietly.

The sun was shining when Ashley's voice woke Kiefer. "What're you doing here?"

Sometime during the night they had moved her from the ER to a room on the sixth floor. "Sleeping," Kiefer grumbled.

"You look awful," she mumbled, as she started working her way into a sitting position.

Kiefer jumped up.

She gave him a quizzical look. "My arm hurts."

"Here, let me help you." He raised the bed and moved the pillows around behind her.

"Thanks. Have you been here all night?"

"Yes." He stood looking at her.

"Why?"

"You didn't need to be alone and you wouldn't let me call your parents."

They were interrupted by a doctor entering. She checked Ashley out and said that she could go home but that she couldn't drive for a week. Her stitches would need to stay in for ten days.

An hour later Kiefer picked her up at the discharge exit of the hospital. He'd been driving fifteen minutes through traffic when Ashley asked, "Where're we going? This isn't the way to my house."

"To my place."

Ashley squirmed in her seat. "I need to go home."

"No, you don't. Someone was waiting on you. You're not going back there until I know it's safe."

"You can't tell me what to do."

Kiefer glanced at her. "I can tell you. What I can't do is make you do it. But if you give me a hard time I'll let your parents know what happened. It's time you trusted me."

"That's blackmail."

He shrugged. "If that's what it takes to get you to take care of yourself, so be it."

Ashley couldn't believe she'd been shot. Who would shoot her? Worse, she had to stay at Kiefer's house. Her emotions were swinging one way and then another. She didn't know him well enough to be his houseguest.

She glanced at him as he drove. He looked almost worse than she felt. There was some blood on his slacks. He wore a green scrub top. "What happened to your shirt?"

"It had your blood all over it, so I borrowed something to wear."

Ashley was wearing scrubs as well. She wished she had her own clothes. Leaning her head against the car window, she closed her eyes. "I'm sorry I messed up your clothes."

"Not a problem. I'm just relieved you weren't more seriously injured."

She must have slept because the next thing she knew Kiefer was opening her door. "Here, let me help you."

"What did they give me? All I want to do is sleep."

"That's the pain meds. You need to sleep. That way you'll heal faster."

He kept an arm around her waist as they walked to an elevator. "But I have things to do. I need to call people about the block party. And—"

"What you're going to do for the next couple of days is take it easy," he said as they rode up three floors.

The elevator opened and they exited to face a metal door. Kiefer unlocked it and pushed it open. Ashley entered and he closed the door behind them.

"Why don't you sit down while I get your bed ready?"

"I don't need to be in bed." She sank into an overstuffed couch.

"Even if you don't, I do. A man my size shouldn't sleep in a chair. I want you in a safe place where I know you're comfortable so I can get some sleep."

"Who's covering at the clinic for you?"

"I have a buddy who fills in sometimes. He agreed to take a couple of days for me."

"Aren't you afraid for him?"

"Not really. They were after you. Whoever it was didn't even try to shoot me. And I've hired a couple of off-duty policemen to watch the place."

"I wish you hadn't done that. The people of Southriver are suspicious enough as it is. Another stranger only makes it worse."

"The clinic should have already had security. With the drugs and supplies in it there should be security. The two guys I hired are from Southriver, so that should help ease the residents' concerns."

"You've thought of everything."

"I tried."

He'd managed to make her feel childish and selfish at the same time. "Kiefer, I really appreciate you taking care of me. I'm sorry I'm such a difficult patient."

"It's understandable under the circumstances. You stay put and I'll be right back." He went through a doorway, leaving her alone.

It wasn't that Kiefer's place wasn't a nice place to stay. It looked like a comfortable enough apartment. It was in one of the old warehouses that had been converted to apartments. It had all the basics but outside of that it showed little of Kiefer's personality. It was as if it was a place for him to stay but not a home.

Her head dropped to the couch cushion and her eyelids closed.

CHAPTER FIVE

KIEFER RETURNED TO the living area to find Ashley asleep. He grinned. The pain medicine had really knocked her out. She had a real thing about showing weakness and accepting help, even when she needed it. What had happened to make her so independent? Picking Ashley up, he carried her to the spare bedroom. Kiefer had given a moment's thought to letting her have his room, but he was afraid she would pitch a fit and demand he take her home if she discovered she was sleeping in his bed.

He settled her and pulled the covers over her, taking care not to move her arm unnecessarily. When the pain medicine wore off Ashley would be unhappy. Leaving the door open, he plopped into his favorite spot on the sofa and propped his feet on the footstool.

What was going on with him? Insisting Ashley come and stay at his home? He hadn't invited any other woman to stay since his divorce. He'd gone to their places, yes, but never had them to his. Truthfully, bringing Ashley here had more to do with his concern for her safety than intimacy.

But those kisses were personal. Each had been far too short. Far too right. He drifted off to sleep remembering them.

* * *

Someone was watching him. Kiefer opened his eyes. Ashley stood over him. "What're you doing out of bed?"

"I'd like to go home. I need some clean clothes."

Scooting to a sitting position, he retorted, "I thought we'd settled that. I understand your need for independence, but right now you need help even if you don't realize it. By the way, are you in any pain?"

"A little but I'm more worried about having a bath. I feel all yucky."

"We'll work on getting you clean but you'll have to settle for a shower. I'll find you something to wear. Then I'm sure you'll need pain meds and some food."

She continued to glare down at him. "Since you won't take me home I might as well take advantage of your hospitality."

Kiefer wiggled his brows. "You haven't seen anything yet. I'm just getting warmed up."

"Hey, I didn't mean like that."

He chuckled and stood. "Nothing like having an appreciative guest. I'll get a plastic bag to cover your bandage so it won't get wet. I'll be right back." When he returned he said, "Come this way."

"Where're we going?" Ashley moved to follow him.

He wiggled his brows again. "My bedroom."

She jerked to a stop. "Why?"

"Because my bathroom is through there and I have a walk-in shower you can use." He stopped at the bathroom door and looked back. Ashley stood in the opening of his bedroom. "Problem?"

"I'm just not completely comfortable with using a man's shower."

"You'll be fine. I won't join you unless I'm invited."

She smirked and walked past him into the bath. "That won't happen."

"Let's get that bandage covered." Kiefer dug under the cabinet for a roll of surgical tape. Finding it, he placed it on the counter. "I'm going to tape the bag around your arm but you'll still need to be careful not to get it any wetter than necessary."

"I know, Doctor."

"Hold this…" he indicated the bag "…while I wrap it with tape."

She held out her arm. He pulled a length of tape and secured it. He did it once more a little farther down. "I think that should be good enough. I'll get you a clean towel and leave you to it. I'll be right outside if you need me."

He pulled a clean folded towel from a cabinet and tossed it on the sink counter.

"I'll be fine."

Kiefer listened for Ashley as he went about finding her some clothes to wear. Thoughts of her naked in his shower were better left locked way. That was an involvement he couldn't afford despite the pull Ashley had on him. He was already far more involved than he'd ever dreamed he would be.

Because she wouldn't be able to raise her arm to pull a shirt over her head, he decided on one of his old button-up shirts along with a pair of sweatpants. Both would be too large on her but they were the best he could do on short notice.

The water stopped running. "Hey, you okay in there?"

"Yeah."

"Open up."

"Why?" She sounded suspicious.

"I'm trying to give you something to wear."

The door opened a crack and a hand came out. He

dropped the clothes on her arm. The door closed again. A few minutes later a groan came from inside the bath.

Concern flashed through him. "Ashley? You okay?"

Another groan.

"I'm coming in."

"Don't."

The word had hardly left her mouth before he was standing beside her. Ashley had one arm in the shirt and the other wrapped across her. She already had the pants in place. They were too large but at least they covered her. "What's wrong?"

"I can't get my arm in the sleeve. Hurts."

"I was afraid of that. Let me help." He reached out to her.

Ashley put her back to him. The shirt fell away from her shoulder, giving him an enticing view of her bare back, the creamy smooth skin inviting him to touch it. He had to remind himself to treat her as a patient, to keep his mind focused on the task when what he wanted was to take her into his arms. "I'll hold the sleeve out and you slip your arm in. If we have to, I can cut it out."

"I don't want to ruin your shirt."

"I'd gladly sacrifice it for the cause of not hurting you."

Ashley inched her arm into the sleeve. "My, the next thing you know you'll be fighting off my foes. Oh, yeah. You've already done that once or twice."

"It's nice you recognize it."

"I might do that, but it doesn't mean I like it. Or want it to continue."

He straightened the shirt over her shoulder. "Need help buttoning it?"

Ashley gave him a pointed look over her shoulder. "No, I think I can manage that."

"All right. I'll go see about getting us something to eat."

Had she looked disappointed? As if she'd expected another suggestive remark? Good. Maybe he was getting to her as much as she was to him.

Unlike Ashley's, his wasn't a well-stocked kitchen. He was home so rarely and at such odd hours that he did little but sleep here. Having her here made him see how sparsely he lived now, since the divorce. As if he just existed. Compared to Ashley's kitchen, his was cold and functional.

He phoned in an order to his favorite seafood restaurant just a block away along River Street. When Ashley was settled again he would walk there and pick up their meals.

The *pat-pat* of Ashley's bare feet on his wooden floors reached Kiefer's ears before she joined him in the kitchen. "Do you have some water or something? I'm thirsty."

"Yeah, just a second." He reached into a cabinet and brought out a glass. "What can I get you? I have water, week-old milk, and I can make some iced tea."

"Wow, what a selection. I'll take water for now but iced tea sounds wonderful."

"How does the arm feel?" He went to the refrigerator and used the ice dispenser.

"I would be lying if I said it didn't hurt. I still can't believe someone shot at me." She took a seat at the table.

He handed the filled glass to her. "Well, believe it."

"I really need to go home. Tomorrow is the block party. I have a list of things to do. Need to be doing."

"Don't you have a committee that's overseeing the event?"

Ashley drank half the water. "Yes, but I need to make sure everything gets done."

"No, *you* need to be in control. Why is that?"

She straightened her shoulders. "I don't. I just want things to go off without a hitch."

Kiefer sighed in exasperation and leaned a hip against the counter, studying her. "Well, I would recommend you request a police presence."

"If I did it would defeat everything I'm trying to accomplish. Too many police make it look like we have problems."

"Too few gives the criminals a chance to cause trouble. Again, why're you pushing so hard? I know you grew up in Southriver, but what you're trying to do consumes you to the point of being unsafe. You take chances and can talk of nothing else but what you are trying to do in Southriver. Don't you ever take a minute just to rest or have fun? Are you using Southriver as a stepping-stone to a state position? What drives you?"

Her eyes widened and mouth went slack. It appeared she couldn't believe he'd asked those questions. Had no one ever pointed that out to her?

Ashley clasped her hands in her lap in an effort to contain her resentment. She was trying to better Southriver for everyone. Her jaw tightened. Kiefer's implication that the work she was doing was self-motivated irritated her. How dared he?

She met his look and reached for the necklace around her neck. "It's none of your business what motivates me, but I'm going to tell you anyway." Although she worked to control her emotions, the moment she opened her mouth they came flooding out with her words. "When I was younger Lizzy, my best friend in elementary school, was abducted by the boy who lived next door to me. We knew him. He even babysat me and my brother when our parents and his went out for dinner. We all trusted him. Adored him.

"Lizzy knew him too because of all the time she spent at our house. We both thought he hung the moon, but one day when she was walking home from school he dragged her into the woods. He raped and beat her. By the time she was found Lizzy was in such a bad condition that she died on the way to the hospital. They said that if she'd had access to closer medical care she might have made it."

She didn't look at him as she continued. "I felt so guilty. Because of me Lizzy was by herself that day. I was supposed to go home with her but I didn't for my own selfish reasons. She trusted Ron because of me. After that the entire community was terrified for their children. My father never let me outside to play without someone watching me. I couldn't walk home from the family store by myself. I was so overprotected I was smothered. I understood why but that didn't mean I liked it.

"When I had a chance to go to college I was so glad to leave. But I missed my home and came back hoping to make a difference. Make it a safer place. I ran on the platform of improving the neighborhood. Headway is starting to be made and I won't, *can't*, let it slip backward. It's not about me—it's about making this a better place to live for everyone. Especially the children. I can have fun later."

"I'm sorry about your friend. That must have been a horrible time for you. At least now I understand why the clinic is so important to you."

"You have no idea."

A stricken look filled his eyes. He'd mentioned his mother being attacked when he'd been a child, but was there more to the story than he'd told her?

"Our meal should be ready. I'm just going down to

Ship and Shore Seafood. Will you be okay here for a few minutes by yourself?"

For someone who was so insistent that she share so much about herself, he sure had dropped the conversation fast when it came to his turn. She nodded. "I'll be fine."

His eyes narrowed. "I can trust you to be here when I return?"

"I'll be here. I'll make iced tea while you're gone— how about that?"

"Great. I'll see you in a few." He headed out the door.

Ashley had the tea steeping when he returned twenty minutes later. She'd also taken the time while he was gone to call a couple of people about the block party. Thankfully it seemed as if everything was running smoothly.

Less than an hour later she took a deep swig of her tea and placed the glass on the coffee table. "Either that was the best meal I've ever eaten or I was super hungry."

Kiefer grinned. "My guess is that it's a little of both."

The sound of a tugboat horn drew Ashley's attention. She looked toward the window.

"Would you like to have our dessert out on the balcony?" Kiefer pushed his chair back.

"There's dessert?"

"Sure there is. What kind of host do you think I am?"

She gave him a questionable look. "I don't think you want me to comment on what some would consider kidnapping."

There was a tense moment as she registered what she had said. Surely he didn't think she was putting him on the same level as the guy who had taken Lizzy?

"You do know you can leave anytime you wish?"

She nodded. "I do. Perhaps I shouldn't have said that in light of what we had been talking about."

"I'll get our dessert."

Opening the narrow French doors, she stepped out on the iron balcony hanging over the cobblestone road below. She eased into one of the cushioned wicker chairs with matching footstools. Crossing her arms across her breasts, Ashley put her feet up and rested one ankle atop the other. A foghorn blew again as a barge slowly moved over the water of the Savannah River in front of her.

Kiefer joined her, taking the other chair. "Here you go."

She took the round plastic-covered disk he offered. "A praline."

"The best in the world are made here."

Ashley unwrapped it and took a bite of the sugary disk with a pecan in the center. "Mmm. Wonderful. Thank you."

"You're welcome."

Looking out at the river, she said, "You have a great view."

"It's the one thing I really like about living here. I spend what little time I'm home sitting out here."

"You don't like the rest of the place?"

"I got it in the divorce." Disgust and resignation sharpened his voice.

"Why don't you sell it? This is prime real estate."

"At one time I wouldn't do it because she wanted it. Now I need a place to live."

"So you live here out of spite." Ashley glanced at him from beneath lowered lids.

"The way you say it makes me sound rather small."

That wasn't her intent but he obviously wasn't moving on. "You said it, not me."

"Brittney left me for someone who could give her more prestige, fancier cars and a larger house." He couldn't keep the bitterness from his voice.

Ashley sat forward and looked him straight in the eyes. "No, she didn't. She left you because she is a self-centered, money-hungry, shallow person."

Kiefer sat back in the cushion of the chair as if she'd hit him with her outburst. "I've never really thought about it like that." Somehow hearing it said with such authority made him believe it.

"Well, you should."

"They were at the St. Patrick's Day party. I saw them coming down the hall just as I was passing you."

"So that's what brought on that kiss."

Kiefer looked at her. "I'm not proud of it but I used you. I won't say I'm sorry I did because that kiss made my day."

She watched him for a moment before she said, "I'm getting tired. I think I'll go lie down for a while."

Had he said too much and run her off? "You need a pain pill before you do."

Ashley struggled to stand. Kiefer hurried to place a hand under her uninjured arm to help her. She stepped away from him. "Thank you, Doc. I think I can take care of myself from here. I saw the medicine on my bedside table."

"Call me if you need me."

"I'm sure I won't." What would it be like if she let herself need and trust Kiefer? No, it might change her life forever. Relying on someone was more than she was willing to take a chance on.

It was late afternoon and Kiefer was again sitting outside on the balcony. He'd spent the last few hours looking over paperwork sent over from the clinic and making phone calls. The first of those had been to a couple of drug representatives whose companies had an indigent program for people who couldn't afford care. Both had agreed to look into what they could do to help with providing medicines for the clinic.

The next one had been to his mother. He'd listened patiently as she'd reminded him that he needed to visit more often now that he was closer. He'd promised he would soon. With her placated, he'd asked her about helping to raise money for supplies for the clinic. As always, his mother had been excited about having another project to focus her energy on.

"So how do you like Ashley Marsh, honey?"

"She's doing good things in Southriver."

"That sounds like you're evading the question."

"I'm not."

"You know Ashley attended my St. Patrick's Day fundraiser. Y'all didn't happen to meet there, did you?"

"We might have." That was an understatement. Thoughts of their kiss still slipped in right before he went to sleep each night.

"I would think that after seeing and speaking to her you would have more to say."

He did but they weren't words to share with his mother. "She can be difficult, demanding and exasperating, but she really wants to help Southriver. She's doing good things for the community. And, yes, she is attractive. And, no, Mother, I'm not thinking about getting married or having children." *Ever again.*

"She's a pistol. I'll give her that." His mother sounded impressed.

"Kind of reminds me of you." Ashley and his mother did have a great deal in common. Almost uncomfortably so.

"I'll be by to check out the clinic sometime next week and see what I can do to help. I'll call first."

"Thanks, Mom. I knew I could count on you." Despite what had happened to his mother, she had not ceased her efforts to help the less fortunate. Again, not unlike Ashley, who didn't seem deterred by what had taken place in her life. He seemed the one most shaken by both events. He still relived the horror of seeing his mother hurt anytime he saw or heard of a woman being threatened. Maybe that was why Ashley had got under his skin.

Kiefer went to the kitchen for another cup of coffee. On his way back outside he stopped in to check on Ashley. She was still curled under the covers. Her dark hair was a mass around her head. It was the first time he'd ever seen her truly at ease. Did she wear that same look of peace after making love? He'd like to give her that and more. But Ashley wasn't a good-time kind of girl. She would be all about permanence, something he wasn't willing to try again.

He backed out of the doorway. That was a place he had no business going. Based on the devotion Ashley showed her community and city, her relationships with men wouldn't be shallow and short lasting. She would give her entire heart to the man she was involved with and, worse, would expect the same depth of commitment in return. He couldn't give that. Wouldn't take the chance on rejection again. Yet the more he was around Ashley the more he wondered if it might be worth the risk.

Her statement about Brittney and Josh implied she had been angry on his behalf. Why would it matter to her how he had been treated? All he'd ever comprehended was that he had been betrayed under his nose by the two people he'd cared about most. Not why. He'd never thought that through. It wasn't about him but them. They were the ones with the issues. He'd just got caught up in their selfish wants and needs. Why hadn't he seen it that clearly before?

The sun had sunk to the point it was brushing the buildings with gold when Ashley joined him on the balcony. He'd been aware of her approaching even before he saw her. It was almost as if his body was in tune with hers. What was it about Ashley that touched him on levels he didn't understand? Didn't want to.

"Hey," she said timidly, which was completely out of character for her.

"Hi, there, sleepyhead. Feeling better?"

She slightly moved her arm, still in the sling. "It's pretty stiff."

"If you think so now, wait until tomorrow."

"Yeah, and I have the block party tomorrow."

"Join me." He nodded toward a chair.

Ashley slowly took the chair beside him. "I can't get over how wonderful this view is."

"Isn't there a place in Southriver where you have a view over the river or to the east?"

She thought for a second. "Yeah, there's one building but it's so run-down… I'd love to see it bought and redone into lofts like yours. It would encourage new people to move in."

"Your mind is always thinking about how to make Southriver better. Do you ever think about yourself? About a personal life?" She looked at him. Was she thinking about how poor his relationship track record was?

She propped her feet on the stool, getting comfortable. "I've had a personal life. My parents wanted me to live somewhere different. Raise their grandchildren where they wouldn't have to worry about them. I almost married right out of college. But it turned out he wasn't interested in my running for political office and he started running around on me. I decided then I was better off alone, doing my own thing."

"Not every man is disloyal."

She looked at him. "No, some just go around kissing strangers at parties."

"I explained that."

"You did." She looked into the distance. "Women like to be wanted for themselves, not as a way to hide from ex-wives."

"Okay, I deserve that, but in my defense the next ones were all about wanting to kiss you." He watched as pink found Ashley's cheeks.

She smiled and said quietly, "Thank you."

He'd put her on the spot enough. "Hungry?"

"I'm fine. You don't have to fuss over me. Is there any chance you'll take me home this evening?"

"Nope."

"You know you can't hold me hostage forever." Thankfully her tone was teasing rather than irritated. She didn't feel threatened if she was making a joke.

The last ray of daylight touched her face and the glow made her beautiful. He murmured, "You and I both know you could leave if you really wanted to."

Ashley shifted slightly in her chair but didn't look at him. "I need to be home in time to get ready for the block party. We both have to attend."

"Not a problem. I'll have you to your place first thing in the morning."

They settled into silence as the stars slowly began to come out. Kiefer couldn't remember the last time he'd been completely comfortable not saying a word when spending time with someone. There was something special about that.

* * *

Arms held Ashley. She pushed at them. "Stop, stop."

A large hand shook her shoulder. "Ashley, shush. You're safe. You're just dreaming."

The bed shifted and she was pulled against something firm and warm. All her fear faded away. Snuggling against the wall, she found sleep again, feeling secure and protected.

Suddenly awake again, she kicked at the covers, her foot making contact with a hard leg. At a loud *"Ow!"* her eyes flashed open. Kiefer rubbed his thigh.

"What're you doing here?" It was still dark. Ashley could barely make out his form stretched along her bed. Kiefer's arm was under her neck and her cheek rested on his shoulder. His other arm was across her waist.

He gently patted her hip. "You were having a bad dream. Now, hush and go back to sleep."

For a fleeting second Ashley started to order him to get out of her bed, but the temptation to snuggle back against his heat and continue to sleep was too great. She succumbed to that desire and closed her eyes once more.

The next time Ashley woke she blinked against the sunlight streaming through the windows. She lay on her side with her bad arm supported by the bare midsection of a muscular male body. She looked down to see athletic shorts at his waist.

He muttered, "Yes. You're draped across me."

How did Kiefer know what she was going to say? She moved enough that she could look at him. "What're you doing in my bed?"

"Still asking the same old question? Don't you remember me answering that last night? You had a bad dream. I came in to see if you were okay."

"And stayed." Her body tensed and her tone questioned his motives.

He shrugged, showing no shame. "Something like that."

Ashley jerked to a sitting position and groaned as pain exploded through her arm. She grabbed it and held it close. "What time is it?"

Kiefer twisted to look toward the clock on the bedside table. "Six forty-five."

"We've got to go. I've a lot to do." Ashley was already moving toward her side of the bed.

A gentle hand circled the wrist of her uninjured arm. "Hold up a minute. I need to have a look at that bandage."

"It can wait. I need to get a bath." She looked down at her clothing. "I need to change my clothes. I have to make my dish to take. I also have to be there to organize the tables and see that the media gets the story correct."

Kiefer put up a hand. "Whoa, whoa. You were shot the day before yesterday and you still need to take it easy. I'll help you with what you need to do but your health comes first. I'll cover the arm and you can get a shower. Then I'll put a new bandage on it. I had Margaret send over some clothes for you, but I'm sure they aren't what you want to wear to the block party, so after stopping by Home Cookin' Restaurant for a gallon of potato salad, we'll go to your place you can change."

Ashley gave him a blunt look. "Are you about finished organizing me?"

He dipped his chin and pushed himself up to lean back against the headboard, giving her an enticing view of male chest, enough that she almost lost her train of thought.

"Yes," Kiefer said.

"I'd rather just leave now for my house."

"I'm the one doing the driving, so I'm the one with the plan."

She could argue further but it would only take up valuable time. Based on Kiefer's body language and his tone of voice, things were going to happen the way he'd decided. "Okay, you win. Let's get this arm ready for the shower."

She watched Kiefer rise lithely from the bed. "I'll get a new bag and meet you in my bathroom."

That sounded sort of kinky. Why was she thinking that? Maybe because she'd awakened in his arms. She had to quit having such thoughts about Kiefer. She needed someone that would be with her for the long haul, a man she could trust to be there for her always. He didn't want a long-term relationship and she couldn't agree to anything less. He'd also made it clear he wasn't impressed by Southriver.

She must have made a face because he asked, "Problem?"

The man was far too perceptive. "No," she croaked.

His look implied he didn't believe her. "Okay, see you in a sec in the bath."

Ashley watched the half-clothed man go out the door as if he had no idea what he was doing to her. Ashley swallowed hard. There it was again. The suggestion, even in her mind, made her tingle all over. He probably wasn't aware of his physical effect on her. For all she knew, he had women over all the time.

She left the bed with a groan. Her arm was so stiff. Moving it gently, she worked some of the ache out. On bare feet she made her way to Kiefer's room. His bedcovers looked as if he had been asleep and had thrown them back in a hurry. She must have cried out and alarmed him.

"You'll need to take that shirt off." He entered the bathroom.

She turned her back to him.

"Come on. I'm a doctor. I've seen plenty of naked bodies."

Ashley removed her arm from the sleeve with a fair amount of pain. Pulling one side of the shirt over the other to cover her breasts, she presented her arm to him. "You're not my doctor and you haven't seen mine."

Kiefer met her gaze. "But I'd like to."

Heat washed over her and her knees went weak. That shouldn't be happening. Kiefer wasn't who she wanted. Certainly not who she needed. "Dr. Bradford, are you trying to take advantage of the situation?"

"Maybe, but it's the truth. Right now you're hurt but I'm giving fair warning that after you mend I'm going to take advantage of every situation that comes my way. For now, let's get this arm ready for a shower."

She looked at the top of his head and along his shoulders as he leaned over, positioning the bag and wrapping the tape. Blood still whipped through her veins at his words. He was mighty confident that she would be accepting his advances. Would she be able to fend them off? Did she want to?

"I'll leave you to your shower. Your clothes are on my bed. Call if you need anything. Meanwhile, I have a few phone calls to make."

She met his gaze. "Thanks. You really have gone the extra mile."

He shrugged. "Not a problem."

Maybe it wasn't a problem for him. Helping people seemed a part of who he was. She had to ponder that.

An hour later they were both dressed and ready to go. She'd had to ask him for help with her shirt and he'd been very professional, even averting his eyes a couple of times. They'd each had a quick bowl of cereal and Kiefer was now helping her settle into the passenger seat of his truck.

"I forgot one thing," he said as he stretched across her to belt her in.

Ashley looked at him in question.

"A good morning kiss."

His lips found hers. They were sure and tender. She couldn't resist pressing hers to his. Seconds later he pulled back, leaving her craving more of his touch. That had to stop. Anything extra might be detrimental to her heart. The life she planned.

Ashley's breaths were shorter than they should have been just from a simple kiss. What would it be like if he gave her a real one? Like their first one?

He circled the truck and climbed in.

Working to keep her tone light, she asked, "Is a morning kiss part of the ritual when a woman stays at your house?"

"Women don't come to my place." He started the truck.

Her heart flipped. She watched his profile as he backed out of the parking space. The man was starting to consume her life.

Kiefer twisted his coffee cup round and round on Ashley's table as he waited, not entirely patiently, for her to finish getting ready to go to the block party. When they had arrived at her place she'd gone full throttle. She'd started making calls, writing a list and hunting out clothes to wear. He worried that she was overdoing things but nothing he said was going to make her slow down. Ashley was in the zone. The best he could do was be there when pain overtook her or she wore out. At least he'd had the forethought to pick up food for them to take so she wouldn't be lifting pots and pans.

When he'd slid into bed beside her during the night he'd questioned the wisdom of doing so. The moment she'd snuggled up against him, all warm and sweet smelling, there had been no doubt he'd made a mistake. One that he would remember forever for both good and bad reasons. It had taken him too long to fall back to sleep with his body so painfully aware of hers. But he hadn't been able to act on that. She was hurt, needed comfort.

He'd watched her slowly wake up and had savored the moment she'd realized she'd been cuddled against him. There had been an appalled expression on her face before her gaze had fixed on his chest. Women had admired him before but never had one looked like she'd wanted to eat him up. His damaged ego had received such a boost of adrenaline he'd had to work at not grabbing Ashley and pulling her to him. If he had, she probably would have slapped him. She was the type of woman who needed to be finessed, romanced, unlike what he'd done when they'd first met.

When was the last time he'd romanced a woman? That had been his ex-wife and that hadn't turned out well. Romance wasn't what it was trumped up to be. Why did he feel compelled to do so now? Because of Ashley. For some reason she brought out the side of him he'd long ago squashed. He wanted to make her happy. Feel important.

Still, the honeyed way Ashley had returned his morning kiss had told him all he needed to know. She wasn't immune to his charms. She didn't need his romancing. All she needed was to make time for herself and her needs while she was trying to change the world.

A moan more of disgust than pain came from the

direction of her room. He walked that way. "Is there a problem?"

"Yeah."

Kiefer stopped at her bedroom door. Ashley wore a light blue flowing dress with small straps. The color contrasted beautifully with her dark eyes and skin. She almost took his breath away.

"I hate this thing." She struggled to get the sling into place over her shoulder.

Grinning, he walked toward her. "Let me help." She turned her back to him. For once she didn't complain about his offer of assistance. He started untwisting the back strap, his fingers brushing her skin as he worked. Positioning the widest area of the strap over her shoulder, he stepped around her and adjusted it in the ring clasps. This time his fingers were too close to her tempting breasts. He'd lost his perspective as a physician and was thinking only as a man attracted to an alluring woman. Capturing Ashley's gaze, he asked, "How does that feel?"

She blinked at him a couple of times. Was he affecting her? Ashley was sure getting to him.

Stepping back, she said, "We need to get going. Did you get the folding chairs?"

"They're in the back of the truck."

"Good. The potato salad?"

How like her to deny what was happening between them. Keeping his face stoic, he answered, "I'll get it now. Do not go outside until I'm with you."

"Kiefer—"

"I mean it, Ashley."

"I won't. I'll wait for you."

Her ready agreement made him suspicious. She might not understand the danger, but he did. He hurried to get the potato salad from the refrigerator. Ashley stood by the front door. Together they exited, and all the while Kiefer kept scanning the area for anyone out of place.

"Do you really think someone would come after me in the middle of the day?"

"I don't know but we're not going to take any chances. It doesn't hurt to be cautious." He led the way down the stairs.

"I'm sure I've not sounded like it but I am grateful for your help."

Kiefer glanced back, trying to gauge if she was being truthful. "Why the change of heart?"

"No change of heart. I was just thinking I might have been a little hard on you the last couple of days."

He steadied her when she faltered on the last step. "After all, what're friends for?"

She considered him a friend. That was unexpected and nice. Ashley would be a loyal friend, of that he had no doubt. Something that had been missing in his marriage.

CHAPTER SIX

WHEN THEY ARRIVED at a park area near the river, Kiefer could tell it had been cleaned and groomed recently. Even the shrubbery had been trimmed. The large beach oaks surrounding the area provided shade from the already warm sun.

A few men were busy setting up tables. As they finished, a couple of women came behind them, rolling out plastic tablecloths.

Kiefer carried a large salad bowl. Ashley had requested he transfer the potato salad into one of hers. He placed it on a table already laden with food. He leaned the folding chairs he'd carried over his shoulder against a tree before he and Ashley joined some others.

As they approached, a heavyset woman wearing a bright smile stopped what she was doing and hurried toward them. "Ashley, are you okay, dear?"

"I'm fine. It's really just a scratch. The doctors…" she glanced at him "…just want me to be careful for a little while."

"Honey, you need to be more careful not to fall."

Kiefer looked at Ashley, who gave him a pleading look before she said, "I will. Mrs. Nasboom, I'd like you to meet the new doctor at the clinic, Dr. Bradford."

Mrs. Nasboom smiled up at him. "Nice to meet you, young man. I've heard a number of good things about you."

He smiled down at Mrs. Nasboom. "That's always good to hear."

"What do I need to do to help?" Ashley asked Mrs. Nasboom.

"I think we just need to set up the drinks table. We decided to put it over there." Mrs. Nasboom pointed toward a spot under one of the trees. There were already a couple of tables leaning against a large oak.

"We'll see to that," Ashley said.

When Mrs. Nasboom was out of earshot Kiefer looked Ashley straight in the eyes. "Fall?"

"Hush," she hissed, "or I'll tell them you pushed me." She walked away looking regal, like a queen.

Ashley was something.

As noon approached a crowd started gathering. Almost everyone made a point to come up and speak to Ashley. More than one had been a patient of his in the last few weeks. They often had something to say to him as well. Being an ER doctor, he rarely saw a patient twice. As the Southriver clinic doctor, he not only saw them more than once but had an opportunity to get to know something about his patients. He hadn't realized how much he had missed that connection until now.

Taking the clinic job had been his way of escaping. He'd needed to get away from Atlanta, from his past, and start over. The plan had turned out to have other benefits as well.

By noon the park was crowded with people talking and laughing. The tables almost groaned from the weight on them. The block party was achieving what Ashley had hoped for, a community coming together.

"Oh, honey, what happened to you?"

Kiefer turned from a conversation he was having with one of the local business owners to see an older woman dressed in a simple shirt and slacks hugging Ashley. When she released her, Kiefer could see Ashley favored her.

"Hi, Mom." Ashley looked at the balding man who reminded Kiefer of a banker standing behind her mother and said, "Hey, Dad. I'm glad you both could come."

"What're you talking about? We wouldn't have missed it," Ashley's mother said.

Her father gave her a hug and kissed her on the cheek. "Hi, sweetheart. What happened to you?"

Ashley seemed to hesitate. She didn't want to lie to her parents.

Kiefer walked over to them and said, "She took a tumble over the last step at her house. She'll be right as rain soon."

Her father studied him.

"I'm Kiefer Bradford, the clinic physician." He offered his hand to her father and they shook.

"You're the one Ashley has told us so much about." Ashley's mother beamed at him as if she knew something he didn't.

His attention went to Ashley, who was blushing. It was nice to see her a little less in control. "I hope it was good."

Her mother looked from one to the other. "Very good. We've heard you're a wonderful doctor, not only from Ashley but from others too."

"Thank you for the compliment. I try to be."

"We were long overdue for medical help around here," Ashley's father said gruffly.

Kiefer met his look. "That's what I understand."

"Jean, Robert," someone called.

"We'll see you later, honey," her mother said to Ashley.

Mrs. Nasboom, still moving at the same speed as earlier, came up to them. "Ashley, we want you to say a few words before Pastor Marks says the blessing."

"Today isn't about me."

"No, but this was your idea. You need to say something," Mrs. Nasboom said as she turned to go.

"Okay, I'll be right there." Ashley adjusted her dress around her.

At least she hadn't been planning to use the event as a political stepping-stone, like so many politicians would have.

Ashley made her way through the crowd to a small group standing in front of them. Kiefer remained at the back. Ashley spoke to a man then turned to everyone and raised her hand. The crowd quieted. "Welcome, everyone. I'm so glad you came today."

Kiefer was impressed with the way she held the people spellbound. He'd always thought of himself as a people person but Ashley had real talent for commanding attention. She really was loved by the community. He could understand that. She was hard not to care about. But he wasn't going there.

"I hope this is the first of many community events that Southriver will host as we all work to make it a wonderful place to live. Before Pastor Marks blesses the food I'd like to introduce the new doctor at the clinic to anyone who hasn't already met him. Dr. Kiefer Bradford, wave your hand."

Kiefer did so and the people turned toward him and clapped enthusiastically. The man he assumed was Pastor

Marks stepped up next to Ashley and offered a prayer. After that everyone lined up on both sides of the table and started filling their plates. Ashley was at the front of the line and he at the back. He spoke to those around him as he waited for his turn. They seemed like nice, honest people who were proud of their neighborhood. With his food in hand, he looked for Ashley. Normally he was uncomfortably aware of where she was. Now he felt lost without her, something he couldn't remember feeling with Brittney even after they were divorced.

A group of girls in their twenties stopped him. Between giggles they explained they were friends of Raeshell's, and he smiled at remembering his first patient's mother. Kiefer asked their names, which they offered with large smiles. They then talked about Raeshell and Mikey for a minute before he excused himself to find a place to eat lunch.

Seeing Ashley at one of the small picnic tables spaced around the area, he headed in her direction. He hadn't gone far when his name was called. It was Mrs. McGuire.

"Come join us, Doctor." She indicated an empty chair beside her.

Kiefer glanced at Ashley then walked over and joined the group sitting with Mrs. McGuire. Over the next hour or so he enjoyed hearing the stories of the group's childhoods and how much the community had changed. They all admired Ashley and supported her because of who she was and her work in their neighborhood.

He didn't even have to get up to get dessert. A woman took his empty food plate and thrust a large plate of cherry cobbler into his hands.

"Marsha Hardy makes the best cherry cobbler in Georgia. It isn't to be missed," Mrs. McGuire said.

It smelled heavenly. Kiefer put a forkful of the warm red mixture into his mouth. "Mmm."

"I told you so."

Kiefer covertly glanced around for Ashley.

"Looking for Ashley?" Mrs. McGuire was wearing a curious smile. "She's a good girl but I sometimes worry that she's too busy seeing about us and not herself. She needs a good man in her life. Children." Mrs. McGuire gave him a pointed look.

"We're just good friends." And they were, something he hadn't had with his ex. Still, something in him nudged him to want more.

The older woman harrumphed. "Yeah, I can tell that by the way you don't let her out of your sight."

"I just don't want her to get hurt again. She still has a sling on."

"You know, you're really not a good liar," Mrs. McGuire said flatly.

Kiefer hadn't felt this uncomfortable since he'd picked up the girl he'd asked to the prom. "I think I'll go see if there's any cobbler left."

Mrs. McGuire's chuckles followed him across the park.

Instead of returning to Mrs. McGuire, he walked toward Ashley, who was in a serious discussion with a group of men not far from the drinks table. As he approached she broke away and came toward him.

"I can tell you're starting to like it here, Dr. Bradford." She looked pointedly at his plate piled high with cobbler.

He grinned. "The ladies of Southriver can cook."

"Especially Ms. Hardy. I've not had a chance to have any."

"Too busy politicking." Kiefer filled a fork and offered it to her. "It's the best I've ever tasted."

Ashley leaned in and took the forkful. "It's wonderful."

Kiefer watched the movement of her lips as they slid over the fork. Even that simple action made blood rush to his groin. Did she make that same sound when she made love? He desperately wanted to find out.

"I'd like to show you something. Come this way."

He'd liked to show her a few things as well but they weren't thinking about the same things. Still, he was stunned she'd asked. This wasn't like her. "Sure."

He put his plate on a nearby table and they headed out of the park toward a block-long brick building across the road. At one time it had been a small factory. Now it was just a neglected structure fenced in, with grass growing around it. Beyond it was the Savannah River and the salt marshes.

"This is the building I was talking about the other day."

"The one with the view?" Kiefer studied the structure.

"Yep. I've never been inside but I've always thought it was a great old building. After seeing your place, I think it has promise. I'd love to have the entire top floor. Even have a roof garden."

"So why don't you look into buying it?"

"I can't afford it. I would need an investor, and being on the city council, I can't appear to have any conflicts of interest."

They continued walking along the fence.

Kiefer looked out at the slow-moving river. "You're right—it would have a great view."

"Families would even have a place for their kids to play across the street." Ashley turned toward the park.

Suddenly people were rushing out from under the trees away from the park.

Ashley stopped one of them. "What's going on?"

"A couple of guys are threatening people."

Ashley's heart thumped in her chest. The day had been going so well. They didn't need any trouble. Holding her arm, she hurried into the park. Kiefer followed. As they joined the people still there, she could see the drinks table had been turned over. Marko, along with two other members of his crew, was standing in front of everyone.

A couple of other men she didn't recognize stood to either side of the trio but were taking no aggressive action. They just watched carefully.

Ashley slowed her pace and walked up to Marko. She felt Kiefer close behind. She put on a bright smile. "Hi, Marko. We're so glad you could join us."

To his credit, the look on Marko's face was almost comical. He obviously hadn't anticipated that welcome.

"Would you like a plate to go? I missed seeing your mother. I'm sorry to hear she has been sick."

"We're not here for food," Marko growled.

"Then what're you here for?" Kiefer and the others took a step closer. She waved them back.

"We're seeing what you're doing."

"It's a neighborhood party. Anyone is welcome. You're part of the community, so you're welcome as long as you behave yourself." Ashley held her position.

"No one tells me what to do."

"Whether or not you stay or go is your business, but you're not going to destroy things like you did over there." She pointed toward the drinks table.

Marko stepped closer to her. Feet shifted around them.

Marko jerked his chin at her injured arm and smirked. "That hurt?"

"It did," Ashley said.

"If you don't stop, you'll get more than that," he snarled.

Kiefer stepped up beside her. Through clenched teeth he asked, "Are you saying you shot Ashley?"

She put her hand on Kiefer's arm. "Please don't start anything here. Now."

"That's right, Doc. Stay out of my way." Marko knocked over a food table as he stalked off. One of his buddies lifted another table and did the same. Everyone watched in disbelief as they left.

When Marko was out of sight the area erupted in chatter. The men started righting the tables and the women picked their dishes up off the ground.

"Everyone," Ashley called. "We've had a wonderful time here today. Please don't let a couple of mean people ruin it for us. We're a community of good people. That's what we need to remember." The tension in the crowd eased. "I hope to see you at the next get-together."

She was so glad her parents had already left and wasn't looking forward to their call about Marko. People continued to work at cleaning up but at a less frenzied pace. As she did her part where she could, Ashley noticed Kiefer talking to the men she hadn't recognized earlier. They shook hands and left before he joined her.

"Who were they?"

He hesitated a moment then said, "Just some friends of Bull's."

She glared at him. "I told you no police."

"They live in Southriver. I thought everyone was invited."

Ashley gave him a pointed look. "Did you ask them to come?"

"I asked Bull to see if he could have help here just in case something like what occurred happened. They were to hang back unless needed. That's just what they did."

As much as she would have liked to argue, he'd done the right thing.

Kiefer looked at her with concern. "How're you feeling? You have to be tired. If nothing else, of people asking about your arm."

Ashley was starting to fade. It had been a long day. "I'm fine. Let's finish here and go home."

For the next half hour they worked at cleaning up the park. Kiefer was beside her, doing what he could and assisting where she couldn't. Marko's appearance and show of temper had put a dampener on the day, no matter how hard she worked to put a positive spin on it.

Mrs. Nasboom stopped beside her. "It was a good day. We'll plan to do this or something like it in the fall. The committee won't let those thugs destroy what we're trying to do here."

"Thank you for saying that." Smiling gratefully, Ashley hugged her with her good arm.

"I have to ask you," Mrs. Nasboom said. "What really happened to your arm? I heard the doctor say something about you being shot?"

Ashley told her the truth and hoped that it wouldn't get out, but realistically it was inevitable. Hopefully it would be another couple of days before her parents heard.

The short return ride to Ashley's place was a quiet one. She was wearier than she wanted to admit. The block party had been going so well until Marko had shown up. She hadn't expected him, but glumly realized she should have. Maybe Kiefer was right. It was time for her to recognize the problems wouldn't be easily solved. That she was going to have to ask for police help.

"Kiefer."

"Huh?"

"I just want you to know I appreciate your help today. Especially you being concerned enough to see that we had police support in case things got out of hand. I didn't think Marko would be so bold."

His voice rose in disbelief. "After he shot you?"

"We don't know for sure it was him."

He gave her a look of disbelief. "Come on, Ashley. Either he did it or he had someone do it. He's dangerous. He's not that kid you used to know."

"I'm realizing that." She still couldn't tell him that she thought she had seen Marko in the parking lot. Didn't want to believe it.

Kiefer took her hand and squeezed it. "It was a good block party. You did a great job."

"You sure looked like you were having a good time when you were talking to those girls."

He grinned. "Were you jealous?"

"I was not!" Ashley pulled her hand away. She had been a little bit.

He pulled into the parking lot of her building.

"I think I'll take a nap." Ashley released her seat belt.

"I'll carry this bowl up for you and then I'm going down to the clinic and see if I can help out." His friend was still filling in for him so he could go to the park with her.

Ashley wasn't sure how long she slept. Even though she was in her own bed, the rest hadn't been as sweet or deep as what she'd had in Kiefer's arms. She couldn't believe how quickly she'd come to depend on him for security. Her arm still ached but not like it had earlier. She moved it up and down, trying to judge her mobility.

Climbing out of bed, still wearing her sundress, she went to her kitchen for a glass of water. The door to the clinic stairs was open. Kiefer must have left it so in order to hear her. The man was very considerate. Muffled voices came from below. He was still seeing patients. Returning to her living room, she settled into her favorite chair and turned on the TV. Finding a romance movie, she tried to get involved in it but all she could think about was Kiefer. She missed him. He'd become an everyday and sometimes nighttime fixture in her life. How had he managed to weave himself into her life so completely?

Footfalls in her hallway made her back tense. Was it Marko again? She had to get beyond that. She'd felt fear enough as a child.

"Are you watching that channel that hates men?" It was nice to hear Kiefer's deep voice.

She smiled. "They don't hate men. It just looks like they do."

"I'm getting ready to head home. I just wanted to make sure you don't need help with anything and to make sure you lock up. A couple of security guys will be around here all night."

"Do you have to go right now?"

He blinked. "Not really."

"I'd like some company. How about watching a movie?"

Kiefer nodded. "Okay, but no chick flicks."

Ashley giggled. "Fair enough. All my movies are in that drawer." She pointed under the TV. "While you decide on one I'll fix some popcorn."

She made her way to the kitchen. What had got into her? What was she thinking, inviting the most attractive male she knew to spend the evening with her? Aggressive in almost every part of her life, asking a man to spend time with her was out of character. She was opening a box she might not be able to close again. Even if she wanted to.

Kiefer was sitting on the sofa with his shoes lying on the floor and his feet propped up on the coffee table when she returned. He looked relaxed, as if he belonged. She placed the bowl of popcorn on the table and took a seat beside him, but not too close.

"What did you decide on?"

"*Star Wars*. The original." He pushed a button on the remote and the movie started.

"Good choice."

She picked up the bowl and offered it to him.

He took a handful. "I ate so much today I don't know if I can eat any more."

"I know what mean." She placed the bowl on the table again and sat back against the sofa.

Kiefer put his free hand around her waist and gently pulled her over next to him. His arm came to rest on the sofa above her shoulders. "That's better."

It was. A lot better. She laid her head on his shoulder. That was even nicer. Kiefer's heart beat at a steady rhythm beneath her ear.

They were about half an hour into the movie when Kiefer whispered, "Ashley."

She looked at him. His mouth found hers. The smell and taste of salted popcorn filled her head. He pulled back slightly then brushed his lips across hers before settling firmly on them. Her toes curled and her fingers itched to cling to him. Warmth permeated her inside, melted her resistance. Desire flared. She couldn't remember the last time a man had been as sexually attentive as Kiefer. Or made her feel more.

Too quickly he pulled away. "I've wanted to do that all day and I just couldn't wait any longer."

Ashley put her good arm around his neck and tugged his mouth down to hers again. She wanted more, needed everything from him. During the last few days things had changed between them. She'd come to depend on him. He had to know she wanted him, craved him. Pressing closer, she ran her hand through his hair. His tongue teased the seam of her lips and she opened for him.

She found heaven. A warm paradise. A place of security. Her tongue joined his in a dance that made her center throb. She grazed the back of his neck with her nails as he lowered her to the sofa. With his lips never leaving hers, he shifted to cover her body.

When he touched her hurt arm she flinched. He paused. She shushed him and pulled him back to her. Her whole body quaked with desire. She wanted him. Now.

Kiefer's mouth skimmed her cheek. She moaned. He breathed, "I don't want to hurt you."

"I don't care." Ashley directed his mouth back to hers, pouring all her passion into the kiss. She flexed her hips against him.

He broke away. Kissed her temple. "If you keep that up, this might be the fastest lovemaking session ever."

"I want you."

He rose up enough that he could look down at her. "In this you aren't in charge. We're partners."

She met his gaze. "Whatever you say."

"That's more like it. First off, and I can't believe I'm asking this, is this what you want? I'll accept no regrets in the morning."

Ashley nodded agreement as she fumbled with a button on his shirt and slid a finger through the opening to touch his skin. "Very sure."

"Are you feeling up to this? I wouldn't hurt you for the world."

She lifted up so that she could kiss the side of his

mouth. "Why, Dr. Bradford, are you trying to talk me into or out of bed?"

"I've been thinking about this for days and don't want to mess it up."

How like him to be concerned for her. "Then why don't you shut up and kiss me?"

He cupped each side of her face, sliding his fingers into her hair, and brought his mouth to hers. The kiss was powerful, going straight to her soul. Kiefer had some type of power over her. This was more like it. She sighed. Her hand kneaded his shoulder while the fingers of the hand in the sling brushed along his ribs.

His mouth moved over her lips, begging and giving at the same time. He shifted and pressed against her arm. She squeaked with pain.

He was off her in a flash. Oaths were said low and sharp.

She stood and took his hand. "I'm fine. Let's find somewhere more comfortable."

Ashley tugged him toward her bedroom. She paused halfway there, turned to give him a kiss. To her pleasure he groaned. She flicked her tongue over his lips. Without warning, he took control, turning it hot and wet. A growl rolled from deep within his throat as he wrapped his arms around her. Her feet came off the floor. Kiefer carried her into the bedroom. At the bed, he let her slide down his body. "I'm going to do what I wanted to do the other night. Undress you."

He slowly removed the sling from her arm then brushed a kiss over her lips. His hands came to her shoulders and skimmed her flimsy dress straps down her arms. He placed a kiss on the ridge of her shoulder. Briefly he fingered her necklace.

Ashley shivered. Could she stand this much attention until he was done?

"Turn around." His hands went to her waist and gently guided her so her back was to him. His lips flicked over the skin just below her neck. She shook.

"Like that, did you?" He didn't wait for an answer as he stroked his fingers at the top of her dress where the zipper started. Slowly, almost painfully so, he opened the closure until her dress hung by the straps at her elbows. His large, warm hands traveled along her rib cage until his fingers cupped her breasts still secure in her strapless bra.

"Perfect," he murmured in her ear, before he placed a kiss below her earlobe.

His hands began to work magic, making her breasts tingle and her nipples harden. Stepping closer, Kiefer pressed his ridged manhood against the small of her back. As one of his hands continued to lift and test her breasts, the other skimmed along her body, pushing her dress over her hips until it fell to the floor. One of his palms settled over her belly and pulled her back against him. She moaned.

Kiefer's hand left her and seconds later her bra fell away. Ashley shivered as the cool air of the room touched her sensitive breasts. That same hand returned to twirl a nipple between two fingers, making her womb contract. She leaned her head back against his chest, her breathing turning to short gasps.

Teeth nibbled at the top of her shoulder before his lips journeyed up her neck. "Sweet. So sweet," he murmured, as he took her earlobe between his teeth. "I'm hungry for you."

His hand at her breasts captured her other one, his fingers circling that nipple. Kiefer's other hand moved farther along her skin until he found the top of her panties. His fingers traced the distance of the lace at the top then back again before they slipped beneath.

Ashley sucked in a breath. Held it. Waited. Wanted.

His fingers tormented her breast. Warm, wet kisses found the spot behind her ear. The tip of his tongue flicked out to taste her skin. Kiefer's hand moved lower, brushing curls. "Share with me."

She widened her stance. He sucked gently on the curve of her neck as his hand cupped her heat. A finger found her core. Slipped in. Exited, to return.

Her panting was the only sound in the room. Blood roared in her ears. Kiefer's hand left her center and his thumb hooked in her panties, pulling them down. They rolled along her thighs and he shoved them to her knees. From there they fell and she stepped out of them. His hand glided up her leg, across her thigh to cup her again.

Kiefer's finger entered and left her core as his other hand rhythmically massaged her breasts in turn while his mouth kissed and nipped over her skin. She was on fire, the throbbing becoming a drumming. Urgency tightened in her, twisting and swirling, squeezing until she squirmed against him. Ridged with tension, she was being driven to begging, gasping for release. Yet Kiefer continued his assault.

Another thrust of his finger and she closed her eyes, pushed against him and keened her pleasure before becoming weak in his arms. Her knees buckled. Kiefer's soft, satisfied chuckle brushed her ear as he held her close.

Turning her around, he pulled her tightly against him and gave her an openmouthed kiss that only made her desire more of his attention. She'd never imagined fore-play could be so powerful. Or perfect.

"This time I want to watch you." Kiefer breathed as he looked into Ashley's flushed face. She was so beautiful. He lifted her to the bed.

"Unfair. You have your clothes on," she teased.

"That's easily remedied." His eyes locked with hers as he jerked his shirt over his head. She watched him unbuckle his belt and release it. He pulled a packet from his wallet before pushing his pants and underwear over his hips. They fell to the floor. He stepped out of them. With perverse pride he watched as Ashley's eyes widened as she gazed at his manhood. When her lips curved into a small smile, his heart beat hard against his ribs. She liked what she saw. His chest swelled. With her he wasn't lacking, like he had been with Brittney. Ashley had a way of making him feel like a man among men. Kiefer was tempted to thump his chest.

"Come here," Ashley all but purred, as she pushed back on the bed.

Maybe where lovemaking was concerned, having a self-confident woman in bed could have its advantages. He opened the foil package and covered himself.

"I don't have to be asked twice." Kiefer came down between her legs and moved over her to place his hands on either side of her head. His mouth found hers. She was waiting, warm and wet, to welcome him. Ashley wrapped her good arm around his waist. He was careful not to apply any pressure to her other one. Shifting, his length nudged her opening.

His arms trembled with the effort not to slam into her. He wanted her so badly. But she deserved care, tender-ness. Ashley broke the kiss and looked at him. Pushing forward, he found her opening and stopped. Her gaze still held his. She lifted her hips in invitation. With a thrust he filled her. She smiled and pulled his lips down for a kiss.

Mouths locked, Kiefer pulled back and moved forward, setting a rhythm that Ashley joined. Had he found heaven? He thrust again and Ashley's eyes widened. Her mouth formed an O before she tensed and pushed her hips upward. He watched as a look of wonder filled her eyes, a brush of amazement eased her features and she came apart before him.

With one more shove of his hips Kiefer joined her in the joy of suspended satisfaction.

CHAPTER SEVEN

ASHLEY WOKE CURLED against Kiefer's side, with her injured arm resting on his chest. It felt right, safe, being there. Her lips found skin.

In a raspy, low voice he murmured, "Mmm."

She'd had the best night of her life. Too good. It made her want more. But was that possible?

Kiefer's hand followed the curve of her hip and returned to cup a breast. "Good mornin'."

He sounded so sexy. So much so that she wanted to hang on to him forever. But that wasn't the way things worked in Southriver. He was a transient person and would be gone when his time was done. But until he left she planned to enjoy the time she had. Make the most of having him around. Was it selfish? Yes. But for once she was going to do something for herself. She'd deal with the fallout when the time came.

She kissed his chest again.

"I'd stop that unless you plan to back it up with something more."

"Oh, I have every intention of backing it up. Can you handle it?"

"You just take your best shot."

Ashley rolled, came up on her knees and straddled him. His manhood was already standing at full attention. She leaned forward with the intention of claiming his mouth.

He stopped her with a hand to her shoulder. "How's your arm?"

"You let me worry about that. You need to be concerned about whether or not you can stand up to what's coming your way."

He gave a throaty chuckle. "Bring it on, Alderman."

She caressed him with her tongue as she lifted her hips and slowly slid down his shaft.

Sometime later Ashley noticed that the sun streaming through the bathroom window came from high in the sky. She was enjoying Kiefer running his fingers through her hair as he shampooed it. She'd found a number of ways she liked being taken care of. "I would like to try this in your shower sometime. It's a little roomier."

"You're welcome anytime. But I rather like the closeness of yours." He rubbed his wet body against hers as he reached for the conditioner.

When she turned, licked a rivulet of water from the skin over his heart, Kiefer pinned her against the side of the shower, his intention clear in his eyes and in his body.

Ashley laughed. She'd done that more with Kiefer than with anyone else in her life and she liked it. For those seconds she forgot about the pain there could be in life. "Hey, what about my arm?"

He backed away. "Now you're going to use that as an excuse?"

"It worked, didn't it?" she said as she stepped out of the tub and grabbed a towel.

"I think you're teasing me." Kiefer joined her on the bath mat.

She grinned up at him. "Every chance I can get."

He reached over and lifted the stone that hung on her necklace. "You wear this all the time. What is it about?"

She took it from him. "Lizzy gave it to me. The day she died."

"You've worn it every day since?"

She nodded.

"You want to make sure you remember."

Kiefer understood. "I don't want to forget. It's too easy to forget."

He kissed her forehead then took her towel from her and started drying her off. A few seconds later he said, "Hey, it's Sunday. Why don't we go over to Tybee and spend the day?"

When was the last time she'd just taken a day for herself? Not thought about the next council meeting? Had to meet with someone? She looked at Kiefer, tall and naked in front of her. "I'd like that."

"Great. You put on your tiniest bathing suit so I can admire your beautiful body, and pack a bag, and we'll go to my place on the way for my suit."

He was like a kid happy to play for the day and it was rubbing off on her.

An hour later they were driving over the short causeway to Tybee Island. The sun was shining brightly as Kiefer pulled his truck into the last open parking spot in the lot next to the Tybee Island lighthouse. Together they carried their bags and beach chairs toward the water.

He picked a space away from the crowd but near enough to the water for Ashley to enjoy the sound of waves lapping, then opened and set the chairs next to each other.

His low whistle of admiration when she removed her shirt and shorts made Ashley blush. She savored knowing that he liked her body. He'd certainly shown it last night. "I'm going to lie on a towel for a while. Maybe take a nap." Ashley adjusted her towel on the sand.

He grinned. "Didn't sleep much last night?"

"No, but I did enjoy myself."

Kiefer took the chair closest to her. "That was the plan. Turn your back to me and let me put some sunscreen on you. I don't want you to burn."

She did as he asked and relished the feel of his strong hands applying the lotion. He'd changed her in a significant way. This care she could get used to. Lying down, she was soon asleep.

"Hey, sleepyhead. Let's go swimming." Kiefer was using the point of an inflatable raft to tickle her back.

Ashley rolled over and offered him her hand. He took it and pulled her to a standing position beside him. "There's no rest for the weary around you," she grumbled.

"I'm not that bad, am I?" He sounded concerned, raft tucked under his arm.

She caught his hand and pulled him toward the water. "I'm just kidding."

As they entered the water Kiefer pulled back. "I brought this float so you could rest your arm on it. That way, maybe you won't get it too wet."

He really was thoughtful. How could his ex-wife have ever wanted more than what he could give? "You think of everything. The salt water will be good for it."

"Yes, but you still need to keep it as dry as possible."

Ashley splashed him. "Wasn't the beach your idea?"

"Yeah. It might not have been my best. I forgot about your arm."

"Why, Doctor, where was your mind?"

Kiefer wrapped an arm around her waist and pulled her to him. "I was thinking about you, just not your arm." His lips found hers. Abruptly releasing her, he dived under, coming up again farther out in deeper water.

She floated as she watched him make strong, sure strokes through the ocean. After a while his head went under, to reappear near her. He took the other end of the float.

She played in the water as she asked, "I've been meaning to ask you—where did you get the name Kiefer?"

"From my parents."

She splashed him. "You know what I mean. It's such an unusual name."

He grinned. "My mother and my aunt Georgina had this big crush on a movie star who had the name. They both said they were going to name their sons after him. My uncle said his child would be named after him. So I got the name."

"Your father didn't mind?"

"No, he was just happy to have a son. Mother could have named me anything she wanted."

"Do you have brothers and sisters?" Ashley enjoyed dabbling her hand in the sway of the waves.

"Yeah. A brother—he and his family live in Atlanta—and a sister. She lives in Jacksonville, Florida. How about you?"

"One brother. He's in the service. We don't see much of him, but the internet and cell phones are great things." Richey would like Kiefer.

"You miss him?"

"I do. He was sort of my buffer between me and my daddy."

"How's that?" Kiefer pushed his wet hair back off his forehead.

"As long as I was with him, my parents would let me go places. He became my ticket out into the world."

"I know what happened with your friend was tough but were your parents really that overprotective?"

She nodded. "They were. It destroyed our family's friendship with the family next door. My parents questioned why they hadn't seen the ugliness in Ron. They feared what he might have done to us. They started second-guessing every decision they made until it was easier just to have us stay home than it was to take a chance on something happening to us."

His face turned serious. "I know something about that second-guessing."

She watched him, waiting for him to say more. Finally he did but it came out harsh and painful.

"You know I mentioned my mother was attacked?" She nodded and he continued. "She brought a homeless man home for a meal. What he wanted was money for drugs, not food. I watched him beat my mother for her purse and did nothing. I should have done something. At least your parents tried to protect you."

Ashley studied him closely. Pain filled her for the kid who had seen such brutality. They had more in common than she'd first thought. "How old were you when that happened?"

"Seven."

"You were just a kid! What did you expect you could do?"

"Instead of hiding in the laundry closet, I could have hit him or something. Anything. Screamed." The disgust with himself filled his voice. Did he really carry this around all the time? Why wouldn't he? She always carried the pain of Lizzy.

"And been hurt yourself?"

"That doesn't ease the guilt."

Ashley was well aware of what selfishness did to a person. All these many years later she still felt responsible for refusing to walk home with Lizzy that day. It might have made the difference. She hadn't wanted to get her fancy new boots muddy, walking across an empty lot, so she'd said no, despite Lizzy's begging.

Rubbing her hand up and down Kiefer's arm, Ashley said, "I'm sure your mother doesn't blame you. Did they catch him?"

"Yes. I had to give a description of the guy because Mother was in the hospital. When the reporters and TV found out a kid had seen it all, they were everywhere."

"That's why you didn't care anything about being on camera when the TV crew was at the clinic."

"Yeah, I've had enough of that to last a lifetime." A wave bumped their bodies against each other. "Enough of that depressing talk. I'd rather be touching you."

He let go of the raft, leaving Ashley to hold it. Standing, with the salt water at chest level, Kiefer faced her and placed his hands under her arms. Slowly he followed the path of her curves down to her hips. Cupping her butt, he squeezed then brought her to him for a kiss.

A wave washed over them, ripping them apart. Laughing and spluttering when they came up, they saw the float being carried away.

"I think you need to go dry off your arm," Kiefer said. "I'll get the float and be in in a minute."

"You're not coming with me?"

"This is a family beach, and if I come out of the water right now, after that kiss, I'd be an X-rated view."

Ashley laughed. "Need a cold shower, do you, Doc?"

He started toward her. "Maybe the alderman wants

to be on the front page of the newspaper for swimming topless."

Ashley shrieked and hurried for the beach.

"That'll teach you to make fun of me!" Kiefer called, as she walked up the sand toward their chairs.

Kiefer saw the grin spread across Ashley's face when he joined her. This time she had taken a chair next to his.

"Feeling better?" she cooed.

He put the float down and dropped into his chair. "Yes, no thanks to you."

The view of her backside as she'd walked up the beach hadn't eased his pain. His feelings were too sharp and intense for his peace of mind. What he had worked so hard to prevent had happened. He cared about Ashley.

They had been drying off in the sun for a few minutes when she asked, "Can we walk over and see the lighthouse?"

"Sure, why not."

Ashley pulled on her T-shirt and shorts over her bathing suit. Kiefer didn't bother with a shirt. They both slipped their feet into flip-flops. Hand in hand they walked toward the tall brick tower painted black with a white band three-quarters of the way up.

"I've always loved lighthouses." She sighed. "There's something romantic about them."

Kiefer stopped and looked at her. "And the surprises keep coming. First romance movies. Now lighthouses. What could be next?"

"I'll give you a real shock. I read romance novels."

His mouth gapped in exaggerated shock. "Are you learning anything in those books I could benefit from?"

She swatted his arm. "Maybe."

"I look forward to finding out."

They walked along the road a distance across a grassy area to the white picket fence entrance then toward the red-roofed house that was attached to the light tower. Beside it was a large white event tent. White netting had been tied in bows on the chairs and netting draped to create an altar.

"Look." She smiled broadly. "They're getting ready for a wedding. This is a beautiful place for one."

"Every woman likes a wedding," he said, more to himself than her. His ex had. That apparently was the only thing she'd liked about being married to him. Except for the best man. Neither weddings nor marriage interested him but he had no doubt they did Ashley. It was a gulf he wasn't sure they could cross.

"And how like a man to be cynical about them."

"I have good reason."

They walked around the outside of the lighthouse. "I've always wondered what it would be like to live in a house like this, with the water surrounding you. Listening to the rush of the waves during a storm and knowing that the light above was the difference between a sailor's life or death."

"You really are a romantic. I've always wondered how the light-keeper walked all those steps every day."

Ashley laughed. "We do see things from two different perspectives."

He pulled her close for a quick hug. "Yeah, but we see eye to eye on a few things."

They spent an hour looking through the museum and talking about the life of a caretaker.

"Well, are you ready for it?" Kiefer asked.

"For what?"

"To climb to the top." He opened the door to the spiral staircase.

"If you can, I can." Ashley gave him a determined look. He admired how she approached everything with a can-do spirit.

"Okay, but don't overwork that arm just to try to outdo me."

"Eat my dust." Ashley took the lead and she started up the stairs.

They climbed and circled, stopping a couple of times to catch their breath before they stepped into the lamp room.

"Oh, my, you can see forever," Ashley said in wonder.

"You've never been up here?"

"No, our family didn't journey far. With the business to run, there wasn't much time to do anything else."

Kiefer contemplated how very different their family lives had been. "And you've not been out here since leaving home?"

She continued to stare out at the ocean. "You know how it is. We don't visit the places closest to us." With a sigh she turned away from the view. "They sure have done a great job of preserving this place. I wish someone with money would take a real interest in Southriver."

"Always a crusader."

"What's wrong with wanting to make things better?"

Kiefer opened the door to the catwalk and she preceded him. "Nothing, unless it consumes your life until you don't have time for anything else."

Ashley turned to look at him. "I'm taking time today."

"Yeah, but when was the last time you did?"

She stood thinking.

"Exactly."

"I'm doing something important," Ashley threw over her shoulder as they walked around the top of the tower.

"Agreed. But what're your plans once you get Southriver into shape?"

"I don't know. There's always another area of the city that can be improved. Who knows, I might run for senator and work on the state."

There was what he'd been expecting. It wasn't all about Southriver. She was thinking of her future as well. "So you never plan to get married or have children?"

She gave him a speculative look, brows raised. "Why? You asking?"

"That was a general question, not one in particular. I've gone down the marriage route and it didn't work out."

"So you're done with it?"

They started down the stairs. "Apparently I'm not any good at it."

"Maybe you didn't have the right partner," Ashley offered.

Ahead of her, Kiefer muttered, "Learning to trust again is a tough thing to do." Something he wasn't sure he could ever do again.

She nodded, understanding more than anyone. "Yes, it is."

Two afternoons later Ashley was at home when her cell phone rang. She was surprised to see on the ID that it was Kiefer, who she'd seen downstairs only a half an hour earlier. Why would he be calling? He could just come up.

"Hey, what's up?" she answered.

"I thought you might like to know that your mother is here."

"What's happened?" Panic filled her.

Kiefer said in a calm voice, "She had a small kitchen accident. She'll be fine."

"I'll be right down."

As Ashley came out of the stairwell she saw Margaret in the hall. She pointed to an exam room and Ashley headed that way. Giving the door a quick knock, she entered the room. Her mother was sitting on the exam table with Kiefer on a stool beside it, holding her hand.

Ashley rushed to them. "Mother, what have you done?"

Her mother's eyes held pain. "I was pouring boiling pasta water into the colander and spilled it on my hand. Stupid mistake. And painful."

Ashley studied the angry red skin over the top of her mother's hand that Kiefer held.

"I'm going to need to clean and bandage this. If you don't take care of it you'll be vulnerable to infection," Kiefer said as he pushed the stool back and stood. "I'll be right back."

"Mom, where is Dad?"

"At the store."

"You drove yourself here? You should have called me." Ashley pulled the chair out of the corner.

"Like you called us when you were shot?" Her mother's voice was accusing yet laced with concern.

"I was fine. I didn't want you to worry. I was in good hands. Kiefer was right there to take care of me."

"And he lied to us."

"Please don't blame him. I asked him not to say anything. Made him promise—and he's a doctor, so it's patient confidentiality. I know I should have told you but I couldn't believe it at first."

"Ashley, we're your parents. We're going to worry. And we deserved to know, not hear it from someone who came into the store."

Ashley hadn't thought about that happening. She'd been so caught up in her own inability to accept that someone would do such a thing.

"You should have told us."

"You're right. It won't happen again. You deserve to be treated better." Ashley pointed her finger at her mother. "But it works both ways."

Kiefer entered, carrying a handful of supplies and a plastic bottle under one arm. He set a metal pan and a couple of bandage boxes on the exam table beside her mother, then the bottle. Looking at Ashley, he said, "Margaret is seeing to another patient. Do you mind helping me a sec?"

Ashley had no nursing experience but she would do what she could. "Sure."

He handed her the pan. "I'm going to pour the saline solution over your mother's hand and I just need you to hold the pan below it."

"I can do that."

"Mrs. Marsh, this will sting a little but I assure you it's necessary."

"Can I believe you?"

"Uh?" Kiefer gave her mother a perplexed look.

"You've lied to me before." Her mother glared at Kiefer.

"Mother!" Ashley barked.

He glanced at Ashley then looked back at her mother. "I promise never to mislead you again."

Her mother nodded. "I expect to hold you to that. Now, let's get on with this."

Kiefer appeared relieved to no longer be under her mother's scrutiny. He opened the top to the bottle and handed the pan to Ashley. Kiefer carefully took her mother's hand and held it over the pan. Slowly he poured the saline over the tender area until the container was empty. Using a gauze square, he cautiously patted the area dry.

The man was amazingly gentle. That was a rare quality in any person. He'd proved to have a number of positive attributes.

"I'm done with the pan," he said, and Ashley placed it on a nearby stand. "Mrs. Marsh, I would like you to hold it up like this." Bending her arm at the elbow so that it was at a ninety-degree angle, Kiefer opened and applied a tube's worth of salve to the damaged area. With that done, he wrapped gauze over it and neatly applied a purple elastic bandage.

By the time he was done, her mother was biting her lower lip. Kiefer stood and patted her on the shoulder. "Take an over-the-counter pain reliever and keep it dry. Let me see you again in a week. Call me if there is a problem."

"Thank you. You really are as good as they say you are," Jean said.

Kiefer smiled. "I consider that a high compliment, coming from you. Thank you."

Ashley took her mother's uninjured arm and helped her from the table. "Come on, Mother. I'll take you home."

As they passed Kiefer, Ashley reached out and grabbed his hand for a second and caught his gaze. He was one of the good guys. Someone who truly cared about people. A man she could trust. She mouthed, "Thank you."

The next week went by, with Kiefer waking up to Ashley nestled against him or her arm wrapped around his waist and her body spooned against his back. There was contentment in this arrangement he didn't wish to examine. More often than not, they showered together in the morning, a ritual he was enjoying too much. They spent their time at both of their places depending on where Ashley's schedule took her. Despite doctor's orders, she insisted that she would have no problem driving. She would do what she pleased, no matter what he said.

Her strong personality, independence and genuine love of people were what he liked best about her, but they were also the traits that made him worry. She went headlong and heart open into everything she did. If she wasn't more cautious she would be in serious trouble one day, but for now he was there for her.

As far as he was concerned, life was good. There had been no more incidents around the clinic, and according to Bull, there was no evidence strong enough to arrest Marko for shooting at Ashley. Kiefer still kept a cautious eye out for anyone or anything unusual. A security man watched the clinic at night, which added some comfort.

Thursday afternoon, Kiefer was coming out of an examination room when he saw his mother sitting in the waiting room. "Mom, what're you doing here?"

"I have some supplies and I thought I'd just deliver them."

Kiefer kissed her. "I wish you had called first. I could have got them from you."

"I wanted to see the place."

"This isn't a part of town you need to be in by yourself."

She put her hand on his cheek. "Honey, I'll be fine."

That was exactly what she'd said the day she'd lain bloody and bruised on the floor of their kitchen. She sounded so much like Ashley.

"How about telling me where to unload the supplies and then show me around." His mother's suggestion dispelled the dark memories.

"I can do that." Ashley's voice came from behind him.

Kiefer gave her a huge smile, always glad to see her even if they'd only been apart a few minutes. "Hi."

"Hey."

He wanted to give Ashley a kiss but they had agreed not to make their relationship public because of her position on the city council. They didn't want to give the media a news story. Plus they just wanted their personal lives to remain private.

Kiefer turned back to his mother, who was grinning and watching them closely. They weren't covering very well. He cleared his throat. "Mom, I think you know Ashley Marsh."

"Yes. We have met a number of times. Hi, Ashley."

"Hello, Mrs. Bradford. It's nice to see you again."

"Please make it Maggie," his mother said.

"Maggie it is. Why don't you show me those supplies and we'll get them in?"

Both women ignored him as they walked down the hall toward the waiting room. Kiefer smiled. Two peas in a pod.

Sometime later he heard talking in his office, which doubled as a storeroom. Ashley and his mother, both wearing business dress and not letting it matter, worked side by side as they unloaded boxes. They were deep in a conversation that he wasn't going to interrupt and hoped wasn't about him. He wasn't sure how he felt about the two most important women in his life spending so much time together. Coming to an abrupt halt, he focused on his realization. That was what Ashley had become to him—important. He'd stepped over the line and wasn't sure if he could step back or even wanted to.

Some hours later Kiefer had seen his last patient and was locking up the clinic behind Margaret when he realized his mother hadn't said goodbye before leaving. That was unlike her. He must have been so busy that she hadn't wanted to bother him. Flipping off the hall lights, he climbed the back stairs to Ashley's place. He tensed at the sound of voices. Ashley should be by herself. Was Marko making a move again?

He slowly stepped back down the stairs and picked up the baseball bat he'd bought and placed inside the stairwell for just such an occasion. Picking it up, he crept up the stairs again. With the bat raised in his hand, he slowly pushed the door open.

His mother and Ashley looked up from what they were doing at the table, saw the bat and stared at him as if he had gone crazy.

He looked at his mother. "I thought you had left."

His mother looked puzzled. "No, not yet. Why're you carrying a bat?"

"I didn't know someone was with Ashley."

"You visit her with a bat in hand all the time?" His mother turned in her chair to face him, concerned.

"Only when I'm worried she might be attacked."

"Why would you be concerned about that?" his mother asked.

Ashley took the bat from him. She placed it on the first step of the stairs. "Because someone I know came in unexpectedly the other week."

"And she was shot at!" Kiefer couldn't help but say.

"What?" Maggie's alarmed gaze met his.

"I'm fine. Nothing to worry about." As usual, Ashley played down the problem.

That might be the way she saw it, but he didn't.

His mother stood. "It's time for me to go anyway. Ashley, thank you for an interesting afternoon. It was nice to get to know you better. I look forward to working with you on our fund-raiser."

So his mother and Ashley had been up here, hatching some plan.

"I am too. Thanks for all the supplies. I promise they'll be put to good use."

"I'm confident they will be. Kiefer, why don't you walk me out to my car?"

Ashley led the way to her front door. Kiefer followed his mother out. He checked the area as they walked toward her car. He nodded at the security guard standing near the front corner of the building.

"She's a smart girl, Kiefer." His mother patted his arm. "Try not to worry so."

"Ashley's like you. She takes chances that she shouldn't."

"You can only do what you can do. I know you feel guilty that you didn't do anything when I was beaten. But you aren't the one who should feel that way. I'm the one who should carry that burden. I had no business bringing home that man. I overstepped. I put you in danger."

"Mom—"

"No, you hear me out. No child should witness that. It created a vein of distrust in you. I watched you become wary of people. When you finally did let someone in, of all things, she made you distrust more. I'm sorry for that. But not all people are bad. You must remember that. Have a little faith in Ashley and ease up on yourself." His mother settled behind the wheel of her car. "You deserve to be happy. Give yourself a chance."

"We're just friends, Mom."

His mother smiled. "Friends don't look at each other the way you two did in the hall today."

"Just don't build it up into something it isn't."

She patted his hand, which was resting on the door window. "And you should recognize when you have someone worth fighting for."

Kiefer returned to Ashley's apartment to find her in the kitchen, cooking supper. "I'm sorry if I overreacted."

She turned to him. "I understand. Really, I do."

"I hear a 'but' in there."

"Yeah. You're going to have to learn to control your protective instinct." Ashley turned the stove off and came to him, wrapping her arms around his waist.

"I can make no promises." He pulled her into a hug.

"I'm not asking for any. Just asking you to try."

"That I can do."

She kissed his chin. "I think your mother knows there's something going on between us."

"I think she does too." He grinned. "You made it pretty obvious that you were glad to see me this afternoon."

"Me? You're the one who looked happy to see me."

Kiefer squeezed her butt. "I was. I am now." He kissed her deeply, walking her back against the wall. His mouth went to her neck. "Almost as sweet as Marsha Hardy's cherry cobbler."

"What about supper?" Ashley asked.

He started removing her clothes. "I'm interested in dessert."

CHAPTER EIGHT

A WEEK LATER Kiefer was dressing for the day when Ashley said, "I'll be late tonight. I've got a council subcommittee meeting until ten."

"I'll pick you up."

"Kiefer, I understand your concern for me. I truly do, but you can't watch over me 24-7. I don't want it and you have a job to do. I'll be fine."

"I'm sure you will be but I'd like to do it anyway."

"I've been taking care of myself for years. I'm not going back to the way it was when I was a kid. Lighten up."

Wasn't that what his mother had told him? "Okay. I'll see you at my place?"

"No, back here. I have an early meeting with local businesspeople tomorrow."

He would feel better about her coming to his place but didn't push it.

Kiefer saw nothing of Ashley during the day. He kept an eye out for her car but it was never in the parking lot. His day was busy and apparently hers was as well. After closing the clinic, he climbed the stairs to her place. He missed the noise and smell of Ashley cooking their dinner, and more than that her waiting with a smile. He had it bad. Worse than ever. To have been so determined to just have a good time and not get attached, he'd failed miserably. He'd fallen in love with the one woman who could drive him crazy emotionally and physically.

In love! After Brittney he'd sworn never to go there again. But he was completely absorbed with Ashley.

Time clicked slowly by as he waited for her to return. Having alerted the night security man that Ashley would be coming in late, he watched the evening shows, listening for a car. When the nightly news started and it was half an hour past time for Ashley to come home, he called her. Her phone went to voice mail.

Kiefer paced the floor, stopping long enough to look out the window, hoping to see car headlights. Taking a shower, he tried to convince himself that when he'd finished Ashley would be there. She wasn't. He'd left his cell phone on the bathroom counter in case she called. Before he dried off, he checked to see if she had. No luck.

Still searching for light crossing the windows signaling Ashley's return, fear became a tighter knot in his chest. His imagination had him seeing Marko and his gang driving Ashley off the road. After an hour and a half the sound of a car door closing told him Ashley was home. He waited on the landing of her front door when she started up the stairs.

"I expected you ages ago. Where have you been?" he demanded, hands balled tight at his sides.

Even in the dim light he saw her body language change, stiffen. Become defensive. "We were in a deep discussion and a couple of us went out for coffee after the meeting."

"Why didn't you call?" He was coming on too strong but didn't know how to stop the raging emotions boiling in him.

"I tried. My phone battery died," she said over her shoulder as she passed him on her way through the door.

"Something could have happened to you. I didn't know where you were."

She turned to face him. "Yes, it could have but it didn't. I came and went without any problem before I knew you. I can take care of myself now as well."

"Yes, but that's before Marko started making threats."

"Look." She lifted her hands, letting her purse and the papers she carried fall to the floor. "I'm home safe."

He'd pushed too far and now she was pushing back. Worry and anxiety had done a number on him. Didn't she understand his distress at not knowing where she was?

"Kiefer, I don't think this is going to work. I can't take you hovering over me. Being on call to you. You reprimanding me when I don't show up on your timetable. I need the space and you can't seem to give it."

Had someone punched him in the stomach? He couldn't breathe. "Why? Because you can't understand that after what has happened, you need to be careful?" he spit. He hadn't talked to his ex-wife with such harshness even when he'd caught her kissing his best friend. Didn't Ashley understand that all this anger came from being concerned about her?

"No, because all you can think about is being that kid who didn't protect his mother. So now you overreact when you think someone might be in danger."

"Might? Like someone being shot at? That's a real danger. At least everyone but you thinks so."

She paused for a moment. "I know, I shouldn't ignore what happened. That's why I haven't made more of a fuss about the security men being here at night. But what I can't live with is this hypervigilance from you about where I am and when I'm coming home. I had enough of that during my childhood."

"But you've gone overboard the other way. Your parents convinced you that someone was out to get you at every turn. Now you believe no one will harm you. You take chances. Like facing up to Marko. Coming home at a late hour by yourself as if no one would be waiting to do you harm. You've been lucky so far. All I'm asking for is a simple phone call to let me know you aren't in a ditch somewhere."

"Not being a little overdramatic, are you? You think everyone is out to get me because the man your mother trusted turned on her. Your wife and friend betrayed you. You have to trust in people and believe in the best in them. My parents couldn't do it and I hated that."

"Trust. Is that what you were doing when you lied to your friends about being shot? Refused to tell your parents? If you would do that to the people you're closest to, how do I know I can trust you to act safely?"

"I would never purposely hurt you by putting myself in danger. I need you to trust me to make my own choices. I know you have a hard time with that and you have a good reason."

"But you're not being safe."

She took a step toward him. "How can you say that?"

"Because you're so caught up in doing and fixing for everyone else that you can't see what you should be doing for yourself. It's like you think that if you keep busy, pushing for an improvement here and rebuilding there, you won't have to think about what could happen or did happen. You want things to be perfect so another little girl won't be hurt. The world has depraved people in it, Ashley. You can't save everyone. Even Marko you're trying to save by not wanting to get police help. Some people are just bad."

She stepped toward him. "Like the guy that beat your mother. Your ex-wife. You want to carry the burden of hurt and guilt where they are concerned. You need to face that they were just bad people also. It seems like you might have the same problem as I do."

That statement hit home. "This isn't about what happened to my mother or with my ex-wife and what she did to me." He pointed to her and then to his chest. "This is about you and me. Why can't I get through to you? I'm not just worried about what happened tonight but your attitude about being aware of what is happening. It's as if you can't accept that someone has tried to do you harm. You seem to have gone into a mental shell where you're pretending you're unshakable. You're denying reality. Is that what you did after Lizzy went missing? Did you zone out so that you could deal with it? Look at you— you still wear your guilt around your neck."

Ashley fingered her necklace.

He couldn't stop himself. "You didn't hurt Lizzy. That guy did. You want me to move on but you haven't. You're still trying to make amends. Guess what, Ashley? You can't. You just have to live with what happened. You also can't save everyone."

She glared at him. "Like you do?"

That deflated him, his anger vented. "Maybe you're right." He hated to admit it. "Our issues are too large for us to get past."

Ashley's heart was splitting in two. It was excruciatingly painful. She didn't want to lose Kiefer but she didn't know what to do to hold on to him either. Giving up the freedom she'd fought so hard for wasn't easy.

Somehow she managed to say in a calm voice, "It's been a good ride while it lasted, Kiefer. I'm not going to change. You can't either. I wish you the best."

He stepped back, his shoulders slumped. "Then I should resign from the clinic."

Panic filled her. "Are you trying to blackmail me?" She needed him to work at the clinic. Only with a doctor would the clinic be successful. The council would want to know why if he did leave.

"No. I just don't think we can maintain a daily professional relationship after this. You're more to me than an associate and I'll never get past that. We obviously disagree fundamentally. It would be harmful for the clinic and what you're trying to do here."

"You talk about trust," she spit. "I trusted you to see the bigger picture. The one beyond us. You're no different than all the other people who come here for a few days then leave feeling good about themselves without truly investing in the neighborhood. Southriver is just something to look good on your résumé. I thought you were starting to devote your heart and life to this place. I believed, of all people, you understood loyalty. You were getting to know the people. Becoming part of us. Now here at the first bump you're trying to figure out how to get out."

"What're you talking about? *You* are more than a bump to me. I came here and worked my butt off, giving my all to the job. Not everyone wants or needs to spend every waking hour trying to save Southriver. You know what I think? I think you *need* to have a crusade. Something that will fill the void where you should have a personal life. You're afraid to care about anyone because you might lose them."

His accusation froze her for a moment. Was she really doing that? Was she covering up being scared? Pushing him away? But what was he offering her? The same thing they had been doing? There was no real commitment there.

She started picking the stuff up off the floor. "I just want people to have a happy life."

"It's not your job to provide that for them. Yours is to represent them. You're thinking only of Southriver and leaving no room for yourself. Me."

Had she really become consumed by her ideals? "I know it isn't working between us but I still need you to stay at the clinic. I was given six months to prove this clinic should be funded. If you leave now they'll pull my funding. Close the clinic. It'll affect my reelection as well."

That stuck like a knife in Kiefer's gut. Just as he'd suspected. It was about political gain. Once again he'd been fooled on more than one front. "That's all you care about. Your clinic. I thought we had something real and all you can say when I tell you I'll be leaving is what's going to happen to your precious clinic. Tell me how you're so different from my ex-wife. All that talk of her being selfish. Even if the cause is a good one, it's still more important to you than us. I've played second seat for the last time to the last person I'm going to. I knew better than to get involved. But I let myself do it anyway. No more. Not again."

"I'm sorry you feel that way." Ashley put the papers and purse on the kitchen table. She sounded casual but all she wanted to do was drop to her knees and sob.

Kiefer walked toward her bedroom and returned with his shoes on and a bag in his hands. "I'll stay at the clinic until a replacement can be found."

"Thank you for that."

"Good-bye, Ashley."

"Bye." The word was weak and sad, just like how she felt.

The next few weeks were beyond painful for Ashley. Just knowing that Kiefer was only steps away made life almost unbearable. Still, she couldn't come up with a way to make the situation better. Surely a new doctor, an old and stodgy one, would replace Kiefer soon. She desperately wanted the clinic to succeed, but how she was going to survive when he was gone forever she had no idea.

She tried to force herself not to look out the window when it was time for Kiefer to leave for the day, but most of the time she couldn't resist just watching his back as he walked to his truck. The trick was to make sure she moved away from the window so he wouldn't see how pathetic she was if he happened to look up toward her apartment. The first week after their split she'd made a point of not returning home before she thought he would be done for the day. For the most part it had worked, but then she was driven to have just a glimpse of him whenever she could.

Did he ever do that? From what she could tell, he was honoring her request to avoid any contact outside of what was necessary for the clinic. Which had been little. He was an excellent administrator and the clinic was running smoothly. Ashley just hoped it wouldn't be damaged by Kiefer leaving. The community had started accepting him. It was ironic that her personal issue with Kiefer might ultimately damage what she had worked for years to accomplish in Southriver.

The time came when she had no choice but to go to the clinic. It had been open for weeks now and she needed to submit an updated report to the council about how it was doing. She hoped she could see Maria to get some statistics and be gone before she had to face Kiefer. Going in the front door instead of down her stairs seemed like the best way to accomplish that.

With purse in hand, she entered. The waiting room was full. She hated it that so many people felt ill, but it also demonstrated the need for the clinic. Kiefer was no-where in sight as she approached the desk.

"Hey, Maria. I need to get an idea of how many patients have been seen since the clinic opened. How many were serious enough to send to the hospital and what the needs are."

"Wouldn't you rather talk to Dr. Bradford about that?"

Ashley glanced down the hall. Could she be a bigger coward? "No, I don't want to bother him. You should have all the information I need in your computer files."

"Sure, I'll pull it up if all you want is numbers. Problems and needs you'll have to talk to him about."

Ashley waited impatiently, all too aware that Kiefer could walk in at any moment. She believed in facing life head-on, yet she was hiding from the very person she cared the most about. A fact that had become agonizingly obvious to her over the last few days. What to do about it she didn't have an answer to.

The clinic door opened behind her.

"Oh, no," Maria whispered.

Ashley turned. Marko stood there with a wild look in his eyes and a gun in his hand. He slammed the door and locked it behind him.

Ashley's heart beat faster and fear lodged in her throat.

"No one move. Keep your hands where I can see them," Marko snarled. "Everyone that has a cell phone, take them out and put them on the floor. You two get over here." He pointed to her and Maria, gesturing that they join the others in the waiting area. "Cell phones on the floor."

They did as they were told. It sounded and looked like a bad movie drama. But this was sickeningly real.

Marko pointed the gun at Ashley and commanded Maria, "Get the doctor."

"Marko, I'm sure Dr. Bradford will be glad to see you."

Ashley worked to keep her voice level. "Put the gun down and I'll get him for you."

An older man sitting in the waiting room stood. Marko rounded on him.

"Sit down. Now." The man hesitated a second. Marko raised the gun. "Sit down now." He turned back to Ashley. "Call the doctor." The last word was a shout.

Before Ashley had a chance to move, Kiefer came hurrying up the hall. "What's going on here?"

He stopped short when he saw Marko.

"You're coming with me," Marko stated. He pointed the gun toward Kiefer's chest. "Let's go."

Ashley's heart missed a beat and she held her breath. What if Marko shot Kiefer? It was her fault Kiefer was in danger. She should have told the police weeks ago about Marko's threats.

"Where?" Kiefer asked. There was a note of defiance in his voice.

"You don't need to know." Marko waved the gun toward the door.

"I'm not going anywhere until I know what this is about." Kiefer's voice was firm.

Marko pointed the gun at Ashley. "Let's go or I'll shoot her."

Kiefer's jaw tightened, his lips thinned. Pain filled his eyes. "I need to get my bag. If you'll tell me what this is about, I can get the correct supplies."

Marko took a second before he answered. "Knife wound. You stay here. She can get the supplies." He pointed the gun at Maria.

She was in tears. Quaking, she looked as if she might become hysterical at any moment. Her voice wobbled when she said, "I can't. I don't know what to get."

Marko looked at her for a moment then turned to Ashley. "You do it. Don't try anything. All of you, let's go." He directed the gun toward the waiting room.

The group stood and headed down the hall. Ashley followed with Kiefer close behind.

"Get in that room. All of you."

As Ashley started to crowd into the full exam room with everyone else, Marko said, "Not you. You're going with us."

"She doesn't need to go. You have me," Kiefer said.

"Shut up. She'll be my insurance. You do what you're told and don't try anything."

"You already have me. Leave her." Kiefer sounded as if he were about to beg.

"I said shut up. You don't make the rules here." To the people in the exam room he said, "First person who opens this door will be shot." He pulled the door to the exam room closed. He looked at Ashley. "You get what's needed."

"I don't know what that is. I'm not a nurse."

Marko looked at Kiefer. "You tell her what to get from here."

Ashley went into the supply room while Kiefer remained in the hall.

"My bag is on the floor by the desk. Open it and I'll tell you what to put in."

Ashley found his backpack behind the desk and faced Kiefer, who stood at the door. With her hands shaking, she bent to pick it up. Opening the pack, she placed it on the desk chair.

This wasn't the Marko she'd known. Why hadn't she listened to Kiefer? Had she been so caught up in what she'd wanted that she'd been unable to see anything else? She would die if anything happened to Kiefer. She couldn't live if she was the cause of him getting hurt.

His phone.

It was under a stack of papers on his desk. She glanced at Kiefer. His gaze met hers. He shifted, drawing Marko's attention.

Marko shouted, "Be still!"

With her heart in her throat and all the possibilities of what might go wrong swirling in her head, she acted as if she was surprised and knocked the papers off, making sure the phone fell into the pack. Now all she had to do was pray that the phone didn't ring.

"Hurry up," Marko growled.

Ashley gathered the supplies as Kiefer listed them, shoving them into the bag.

"Let's go," Marko announced.

Ashley zipped up the bag and joined Kiefer in the hall. He took it from her. Pulling it over one shoulder, he turned to go toward the front door.

"No, the other way. Up the back stairs."

Marko pushed Kiefer forward. "Doctor, you first."

"Marko," Ashley said, "you know this is kidnapping. A federal offense. If you stop now, Dr. Bradford and I won't press any charges."

"She's right, Marko."

This time Marko gave her a shove. "Both of you shut up and get moving."

Kiefer didn't look pleased but he didn't argue further. Ashley climbed the stairs behind Kiefer, all too aware of Marko's gun aimed at her back. She glanced at the bat still standing at the top of the stairs, hoping Kiefer wouldn't be a hero and pick it up. Thankfully he didn't.

In her kitchen Marko said, "Let's go. Down the back steps."

Again Kiefer led the way. At the bottom of the steps

Marko said, "Now through that hole in the fence. Doctor, you first."

Ashley stepped through after Kiefer. Her pants leg caught on the broken wire. Kiefer snatched her up before she fell, bringing her hard against him. Just the feel of him eased her fear.

"Get moving," Marko snarled.

Kiefer released her. She moved ahead of him and Marko made no complaint. They followed a path through the vacant lot behind her building. The knee-high grass pulled against her legs. Her pumps sank into the sandy ground. A couple of times Kiefer supported her with a hand to her arm, helping her to stay on her feet.

Halfway across the lot Kiefer asked Marko, "Why don't you release Ashley? I'll go with you with no complaints."

Ashley wanted to scream no. He could be killed. Maybe she could talk some sense into Marko. He would never listen to Kiefer.

"Shut up and keep moving," Marko growled.

At the next block Marko directed them to a waiting car. "Ashley, get in the front seat. Doctor, in the back. I'll shoot her if you give me any trouble," he said pointedly to Kiefer.

When the doors were shut behind them, the driver passed a dark T-shirt to her and one over the seat to Kiefer. Marko said, "Put it on your head. Make sure to cover your face."

Ashley did as she was told. The stench of body odor almost made her gag but she pulled the shirt in place. She hardly had it situated before the car lurched forward.

For what seemed like forever they wove in and out of streets, taking corners too fast. She held on to the door handle, trying to stay upright. Where were they going?

They had traveled so far that they could no longer be in Southriver.

A tugboat horn blew. They were near the river. They bumped over railroad tracks a couple of times so hard that Ashley's head almost hit the roof. They made a final turn and the car came to a screeching halt, slamming Ashley forward.

"Ashley, are you okay?" Kiefer's voice was muffled under his shirt.

"I'm fine."

"Shut up. Pull those shirts off your heads and get out," Marko ordered.

Doing so, she saw they were inside a warehouse. There were boxes stacked to the roof and empty wooden pallets on the floor. After the harrowing ride, she climbed out of the car on shaky legs. Kiefer joined her with his bag in hand.

"This way." Marko indicated some type of office-looking area in one corner of the huge building. Lit from within, it had one door, and windows made up half the walls.

The driver jerked her toward Kiefer when she didn't move. They walked side by side with Marko behind them.

"Tell me what's going on," Kiefer demanded.

"You'll see soon enough," Marko said.

The driver opened the door to the office and Ashley, then Kiefer with Marko behind him, entered. Inside was a man lying on a dirty mattress that had no cover on it on an old metal bed frame. Based on the amount of bloody rags on the floor, he'd lost a large amount of blood. His pallor was deathly white.

Kiefer hurried to the bedside in full doctor mode. Slipping the bag from his shoulder and setting it on the floor, he unzipped it, found plastic gloves and pulled them on.

He lifted the material that looked like a T-shirt from the wound in the man's midsection.

The man moaned.

"I'm Dr. Bradford. I'm here to help you. I'm going to have a look at you and then I'll give you something for pain. What's your name?"

"Jorge," he said in little more than a whisper.

"He needs to be in a hospital," Kiefer said to Marko.

"No," Marko barked.

Ashley watched Kiefer look into Jorge's eyes. His hand went to the young man's forehead. "He needs surgery. He's running a fever. Has lost too much blood."

"You take care of him here," Marko said.

"He's already on the road to an infection." Kiefer looked around the filthy area. "Sewing him up here will only make it worse."

Marko pointed the gun at her. "You'll do it."

Kiefer glanced away but his look returned to meet hers. There was pain, worry and resignation in his eyes. "I'll need your help, Ashley."

"I've never done anything like this." She couldn't keep the quiver of fear out of her voice.

He gave her a reassuring smile. "I'll tell you what to do every step of the way. I have complete faith you can handle it." Kiefer looked around. "Is there water?"

"In there." Marko nodded toward a door.

Kiefer looked back at her. "See if you can find something to put some water in. If not..." he pulled a bag of bandage pads out of the backpack and handed them to her "...wet these." He gave her another reassuring smile that didn't reach his eyes.

"I'm sorry," she mouthed to him.

He nodded and turned back to his patient.

Marko leaned against the wall where he could see

both of them. "Get busy." To his driver he said, "You go watch outside."

The guy left.

Ashley went to a door that she guessed led to a bathroom. It turned out to be a small kitchen area and there was a bath off that. The place was nasty. Apparently someone had been living there for a few days, if not longer. Open food packages were everywhere. How was she supposed to find anything in here sanitary enough to hold water? Searching under the sink, she located a mop bucket, and pulling it out, she put it under the sink faucet. The water ran brown.

"Yuck." She jerked the bucket out from under the tap, emptied it while leaving the water running, then waited for the water to turn clear.

Marko stuck his head in the door. "Get busy."

"I am. Everything in this place is nasty. Marko, let us take your friend to the hospital. He's going to die if you don't."

"No more talking. Get busy."

The water had started to run clearer and she shoved the bucket under the faucet again. Using her hand, Ashley washed the bucket the best she could. With it full, she carried it back to Kiefer and set it down next to him. He glanced at her as he continued to apply pressure to the patient's abdomen. "Good girl. I need you to go around to the other side of the bed."

It had been moved into the middle of the room.

"Take my bag. Pull that chair up close and put the supplies on it." He indicated the wooden straight-backed chair behind a metal desk.

This could be her chance. If she could just figure out some way to use the phone. Glancing at Marko, she then looked at Kiefer. His expression said clearly that he trusted her. That he knew she would do what was necessary. She wouldn't disappoint him. Wouldn't let him down this time. Ashley went to her knees beside the bed and started pulling supplies out.

"I'm going to need the scissors first and the bandages."

She removed items until she found what Kiefer had requested. Her fingers brushed the cell phone as she pulled a box from the pack. Could she push numbers without Marko noticing? No, the time wasn't right. She'd have one chance and she would need to make that count. She handed Kiefer the scissors and bandages.

"I'm going to need a suture kit and the bottle of saline."

As he cut away the man's shirt and started to clean around the wound, Ashley continued to unload the backpack. Thankfully she had Kiefer and the bed between her and Marko. If she could just slip the phone out far enough to touch 911... Her heart beat faster as she reached into the backpack again. Her fingers circled the phone. Her hand shook. She gave a quick glance at Marko. He was still glaring at them, watching too closely. Not yet. She laid the backpack flat on the floor, setting the phone close to the zipper opening.

"I'm ready to suture. I'm going to need your help. Put some gloves on," Kiefer said.

Ashley did so. Her fear must have shown on her face because he reached across and squeezed her hand. "We'll get through this."

"Stop all the talking and get going," Marko said, shifting impatiently.

Kiefer put a hand on their patient's shoulder. "Jorge, I don't have any way of making you more comfortable. I'm sorry. This is going to hurt." He said to Ashley in a resigned tone, "Please open one of the suture packages."

Over the next hour she watched as Kiefer meticulously closed the wound. Jorge groaned through the first few stitches then passed out. Kiefer said little other than to occasionally tell her to move a finger here or dab a bandage there as he worked. If she hadn't known he was a good doctor already, she had no doubt of his abilities now.

Kiefer looked back at Marko. "That's the best I can do under the circumstances. He needs antibiotics that I don't have. If he doesn't get them soon I can't promise what will happen. We'll just have to wait and see. If you really care about Jorge you would take him to the hospital."

Marko snorted, "And go to jail. That's not going to happen."

Ashley started cleaning up the area. There were a few supplies left to pack away. Pulling the backpack to her, she was careful not to knock the phone out of the bag. Bumping the chair, she caused what was left of the supplies to fall off. Leaning over, she acted as if she was gathering the supplies. She pulled the opening of the pack back and touched 911.

"What's the deal over there?" Marko commanded.

She reached under the bed. "Nothing. I'm just getting a box."

Ashley's breath caught in horror. She hadn't changed the volume. Opening the bag, hoping Marko thought she was storing the box, she found the phone again. Fumbling, she searched for the buttons on the side of the phone and pushed the bottom one.

"What're you doing? Give me that." Marko headed in her direction.

Ashley palmed the phone.

Kiefer took that moment to stand, bumping against Marko. It gave her time to push the phone under the mattress.

"Get out of the way. I should kill you." Marko pushed Kiefer.

Pain swamped her. She wouldn't survive if something happened to Kiefer.

"Give me that." Marko pointed the gun toward the backpack. "What do you have in there?"

"Nothing but the supplies the doctor told me to put in here," she said as evenly as she could.

Marko jerked it out of her hand and dumped the contents on the floor, kicking them around. "I said not to try anything."

"Look for yourself. There's nothing there." Kiefer came around the end of the bed and offered her a hand.

She slowly rose, her knees stiff from being on the concrete floor for so long.

"What're you doing?" Marko growled.

"Helping Ashley up. We both need to stand. We've been kneeling a long time." Kiefer gave Marko a defiant look. "So what's the plan now? The police will be looking for us. Jorge shouldn't be moved. You're stuck. You need to turn yourself in. Why don't you let Ashley go and get help?"

Kiefer was still trying to protect her. She appreciated it but she wouldn't leave him. This was all happening because of her. Why couldn't she have accepted Kiefer's warnings that Marko was a threat? She'd give anything to turn back time, make this go away. Have her and Kiefer returned to the intimacy they'd shared. If they got out of this she would do everything in her power to make it up to him.

"No more talking. Get over there and be quiet. I need to think." Marko pointed to a corner.

Kiefer held her hand as they moved to the farthest spot

from the door. They stood against the wall. Her knees were just starting to recover.

The driver of the car came in and Marko conferred with him too low for her to hear, glancing at them a couple of times.

Kiefer turned slightly, putting his back to them. His mouth came close to her ear. "Phone?"

Ashley nodded briefly as she watched Jorge. Kiefer's brows went up in question. She mouthed, "Under the mattress."

CHAPTER NINE

KIEFER SLID DOWN the wall to sit on the floor. He tugged on Ashley's hand, encouraging her to join him. She did, coming shoulder to shoulder with him. They were both tired physically and emotionally. Fear had fed an adrenaline rush. Now that it dropped, exhaustion took over. Neither extremes were healthy.

They needed to get to the phone somehow. Finding the right time was going to be the tough part. If Marko would only leave the room. Getting Ashley to safety was his top priority. There was no way of knowing if her 911 message had gone through. He wrapped his arm around her shoulders and pulled her close.

Ashley looked up at him with those big eyes full of misery. "I'm so sorry I got you into this." Emotion was thick in her voice. "I should've listened to you when Marko came into my house. I thought I saw him that night I was shot but I didn't say anything."

She was such an idealistic soul. That was part of the reason he loved her and yet shouldn't. It didn't matter now. He gave her shoulder a squeeze and kissed her temple. "We'll get out of this. We'll be fine. Hang in there."

"I hope so. I owe you big-time."

He gave her a wry smile. "And I plan to collect."

"Shut up, you two! I need to think." Marco pulled the

chair out from around the bed and put it in front of the closed door.

"It looks like we're going to be here awhile," Kiefer whispered. "We might as well get some sleep." He stretched out his legs.

"Thank you for all you have done. You were amazing."

"Shush. Sleep."

Ashley laid her head against his shoulder. It wasn't long until she was breathing evenly. He was glad to have her in his arms again but this wasn't the way he'd wanted it to happen.

Somebody kicked his foot, jiggling him awake. Kiefer didn't know how much time had gone by but he guessed it was in the early morning hours. He looked over at Ashley. Her eyes were open. Fear filled them.

"Tell me what kinds of antibiotics Jorge needs," Marko demanded from above them.

"Jorge needs to be in the hospital, getting intravenous ones," Kiefer said.

"That's not going to happen. What're the names?"

Kiefer named off a few common antibiotics. "They won't be strong enough to keep the infection under control. He needs to be in a hospital."

Marko's face became distorted and he pointed the gun at him. "Shut up about the hospital. He's not going. Do. Not. Say. It. Again. Stand up. Both of you."

Kiefer stood and then helped Ashley to her feet. Marco reached behind his back and pulled out plastic wire fasteners. "Turn around."

They did as he instructed. Marko fastened Kiefer's wrists together behind his back and did the same to Ashley's. He then used another band to attach them together at the hands, so that they were back to back.

"I'll be back." With that he kicked the chair out of the way and left. The door clicked shut behind him.

Kiefer whispered. "Let's wait until we're sure he's gone."

They stood not moving. Waiting. Listening.

"Let's check the door first then go after the phone," Kiefer said. "I'll walk forward if you can go backward."

There were a few missteps and a wobble back and forth until they found a rhythm. They made it to the door.

"Turn sideways and slide up next to the door and let's see if we can get our hands on it."

Ashley did just as he asked. Kiefer managed to reach the knob. It didn't open. "Okay, let's go after the phone. You forward this time and I'll follow."

Skirting the bed, Ashley led them to the spot where she'd left the phone.

"I don't know how we're going to do this," she said.

"Back up as close to me as you can. We're going to push against each other as we squat down. I want you to reach out and get the phone." This plan had to work. He needed to get Ashley out of there.

"What about Jorge?"

"He's passed out. Even if he wakes he's too weak to move. The best way to help him is for us to get out of here." Urgency filled him.

Kiefer waited until she'd pressed her back against his.

"On three let's go down. One, two, three." Slowly they moved toward the floor. Ashley pulled on his arms. His right shoulder strained to a painful point before she said, "I have my fingers on it."

Thump. The phone hitting the floor told him she had at least removed it from under the mattress.

"Okay, let's go up. Push hard against me and take

small steps backward." They worked themselves to a standing position.

"Now we have to get it off the floor." Ashley moaned. "Marko could already be on his way back."

"Let's not worry about that. Let's go down again and this time I'll reach for the phone. The more you lean on me the easier it'll be for you." He waited until she pushed against him. "Go." They worked their way toward the floor. Kiefer's thighs burned as he went into a squat. Ashley groaned behind him. "Just a little more. I almost have it."

Relief filled him when his fingers circled the phone. "Let's go up. Not too fast or we'll fall." It was a slow process but they made it to a standing position again. "Swing your arms to the left." Ashley did as he asked. Looking over his shoulder, he touched the screen of the phone. It still remained black. Disappointment washed over him.

"The battery is dead." The words were a cry of anguish from Ashley as she looked back.

"Well, we can't depend on that. We've got to get out of these handcuffs then out of this room." He swung the phone so that it landed on the bed at Jorge's feet. "Let's go see what we can find in the kitchen. Lady's choice—do you want to walk backward or forward?"

"I'll take forwards. You ready?"

"Lead on." At least he'd got a small chuckle out of her. They shuffled their way into the kitchen.

"Okay, let's start with the easy stuff and look through the drawers first," Kiefer said. They slid sideways to the counter. "Let's get it open."

It took some maneuvering but they soon had a drawer open. Nothing. They shuffled to the next one and then the next. It wasn't until his face and body were pressed against the wall and they had the last drawer open that there was a sliver of hope.

"I'm touching something." The excitement in Ashley's voice made his optimism soar. "I think it's an old dinner knife."

Kiefer held his position. "Get it out but don't drop it, whatever you do."

"I've got it. I've got it."

He felt the metal across the top of one hand. "Let me hold it."

"You don't trust me?"

There was the old Ashley he knew so well. He trusted her more than anyone else he knew. "Yes, but I want you to cut your strap off. How sharp is it?"

"Not very, but it does have some serrations."

"That's better than nothing. Get started." He held the knife while she worked her hands into position.

Moving her wrist back and forth, she pushed against the knife. "This is taking too long."

"Just keep at it. We don't have a choice."

After an agonizing amount of time, the plastic finally broke. Ashley's hands were free.

"Now I'll do you." She had already taken the knife from him.

"No, it takes too long. We need to look for a way out of here. Go see if you can open the door."

She hurried out of the room and he followed. Ashley pulled on the doorknob. It wasn't budging.

"Check the bathroom. See if it has a window to the outside."

Again Ashley rushed from the room. Kiefer stood looking at the structure of the door. The hinges didn't have pins. They were stuck.

"Kiefer, come here. There's a window."

He hurried to her.

"It's not a very big one but I think I could get through it." She was already standing on the commode, pushing at the window.

"You need to break it out. Pull off your jacket and wrap it around your hand. Pull your shirt over your face so that you don't get hit by any glass."

She did as he said and started striking the glass. It broke with a large crash.

"Now make sure all the edges are gone."

Ashley worked her material-covered hand around the window frame. She stuck her head out the window. "It's to the outside." Excitement filled her voice. "Now let's get your hands undone."

"No, you're going through the window. I couldn't get through it anyway. I need to stay with Jorge."

"No, Kiefer. No!"

His look met hers. "You're going after help. Now stop complaining and get moving. Climb up my back and wrap your arms around my neck. Then I want you to put your feet through the window, otherwise you would be going headfirst and I don't want you to hurt that pretty head."

She reached up and cupped his face, pulling his mouth to hers. Kiefer's heart jumped. He'd missed her kisses. Thirsted for them. He pulled back. "Quit taking advantage of a man with his hands tied behind his back and get going."

Ashley gave him a weak smile then stood on the commode to get into position. Kiefer backed up and straddled the commode. Ashley put her arms around his neck from behind and pulled herself up his back. Kiefer leaned forward as her body weight pushed against him. She lifted her feet, putting them through the opening.

She was halfway out the window when he turned around. "Run for the nearest lit area. I'll be right here waiting when you get back. Now, get." His gaze held hers until she dropped out of sight.

He wanted to say so much more but they were running out of time.

Ashley sprinted until her breaths were deep and her side hurt. Her blouse stuck to her in the warm, muggy night. Her feet throbbed from running in her pumps. She was in the warehouse district of the shipping area of Savannah. There was no life around, only the occasional dim security light. If Marko returned to find her gone he'd come looking for her. Surely kill Kiefer. A sick feeling filled her. That wasn't going to happen.

She ran again. Surely she would find someone soon. Wouldn't let herself think any differently. Headlights came toward her.

Joy made her heart jump. *Help!*

She stumbled and fell, pushed her way up again. Waving her hands back and forth above her head, she signaled for them to stop. A sick feeling hit her. For a second she dropped her arms. What if it was Marko? But what if it was help and they passed her by because they didn't see her? She had to take a chance.

Waving again, she watched as the car accelerated then pulled to a screeching halt beside her. With relief that almost had her on her knees again, Ashley saw it was a police car. A uniformed officer hopped out of the car. It was Bull. She fell into his arms.

"Help! Kiefer is locked in a warehouse. Marko kidnapped us. Call an ambulance. There's an injured man in there too."

"Get in. Show us where." He opened the back passenger door and Ashley climbed in. The policeman driving was already on the radio, letting other patrolmen know they needed help. When Bull was back in the car the driver stepped on the gas.

She sat forward, looking through the wire mesh and out the windshield. Could she recall enough to find the correct building? They all looked the same in the dark. She had to remember. Had to get the right one. Kiefer's life depended on it.

"It's down here. The third big building on the right. No, fourth. I came out between those buildings." She pointed off to the right despite the fact no one could see her do it. "The one with the trash cans beside it."

The patrolman stopped the car in front of the large roll-down door.

"You stay here," Bull said, as he leaped out and pulled his gun. The sound of sirens filled the air.

She watched as Bull and the other officer opened a smaller door beside the larger one and entered the warehouse. Watching with her nose pressed against the window, she waited. Time seemed to slow to a crawl. More police cars arrived and men flooded in. Still no Kiefer. Where was he? Was he all right? Panic became a living thing in her. She hung on to the edge of the car door and didn't take her eyes off the opening to the warehouse. Was this how Kiefer had felt when he'd been waiting for her that night? Tears filled her eyes.

Had Marko returned while she'd been gone? She couldn't think like that. Not now that she'd found help.

An ambulance pulled to a stop nearby. The EMTs unloaded a gurney and pushed it through the larger door, which was opening. Soon after Bull came out of the building and walked toward her. He opened the door.

"Kiefer?" She was almost afraid of the answer.

"Inside. He's fine. Asking to see you."

Ashley ran into the building and stopped. Kiefer walked toward her.

Happiness surged through her. She smiled as the band squeezing her heart popped open. She ran, tears streaming down her face, toward him. His arms opened wide. When she reached him he engulfed her, lifting her off her feet. Kiefer was solid, sure and safe. Best of all—alive. She never wanted to leave him again.

"I thought… Thought… I was so scared…"

He held her tight as if he never wanted to let her go. "Shh, sweetheart. I'm fine. You did good. I couldn't have asked for a better partner." Kiefer slowly placed her on her feet and looked at her. He studied her as if making sure she really was okay.

"Did Marko come back?"

"No, but Bull can tell you all about that. I have to go to the hospital with Jorge. I want you to go too and be checked out. Bull is going to see that you get to your parents'. No argument."

She would go gladly. If Kiefer wasn't going to be with her then she wanted people around her who made her feel safe. Her parents could provide that. Despite them hovering when she'd been a child, she had felt secure. Smiling up at him, she nodded. "No argument."

The emergency crew came past them with Jorge on a gurney.

"I've got to go." He gave her a quick kiss and followed Jorge into the back of the ambulance.

Bull joined her. "Come on. I'll get you to the hospital and call your parents."

Ashley slowly walked to the car with Bull. Kiefer had said nothing about seeing her again. Had anything really changed between them?

* * *

It had been three days and still Kiefer hadn't called. Ashley had begun to worry that he wouldn't.

Her parents had picked her up from the hospital. Her arm had been put in a sling again. Not because of her gunshot injury but because her shoulder had been hurt from being hyperextended when she and Kiefer had been tied together.

Bull had explained on the way to the hospital that 911 had received the call, but before they could pinpoint the location, the battery had gone dead. All they'd had was a vicinity. When they had been called to a break-in at a pharmacy, they'd suspected it was related but they'd still had a large area to cover. They'd started searching the area. That was when they'd found her. On the way to the hospital the call came through that Marko and his driver had been picked up.

By the time her mother and father had made it to the hospital they had been typical worried parents. This time Ashley had found it comforting. She'd appreciated the pampering, even though Kiefer hadn't been there to offer some as well.

The second day she was at her parents' she went for a walk along her old block. It was warm outside but not hot and steamy yet. It was summertime and children were playing in their yards.

She stopped and looked at the house next door. The one Ron had lived in years before. After what he'd done, his parents had moved away, no longer able to face their shame. The new neighbors had painted the place, but it still held the stigma of being where Ron had lived. How could anyone have known? Was there ever a way of knowing what people were capable of? Not really. Mostly she had to just believe in the goodness of mankind. That trust was something she'd had a hard time giving. Kiefer had more than earned it. Proved himself worthy.

Still, she had misjudged Marko. No, that wasn't true. She just hadn't wanted to see it. He had given her all the signs.

Ashley continued along the street, lifting her face so that the sun warmed it. It had been a while since she had really looked at the area. Little had changed yet somehow it seemed different. She went on another couple of blocks and turned right. There was her father's small grocery store. Entering, she saw her father behind the counter.

"Hey, sweetheart. It's nice to see you."

"Hi."

"How about a drink?" He walked toward an old soda machine.

"That would be great." She accepted the bottle from him.

"I'm not busy this morning, so come have a seat and stay a minute." He indicated a stool nearby.

Ashley took it and her father the other.

"How're you feeling?"

"Better. Much better. In fact, I think I'll be going home tomorrow." She took a sip of her soda.

"It's been nice having you but I know you have your own life."

Ashley nodded.

"I'm sorry about what happened to you. I never would've thought Marko would do such a thing." A dark look came over his face. "But then, I've made that mistake before. I know you had a hard time with how overprotective I was when you were a kid. It was only because I loved you."

Had her father felt the same way she had when Marko had pointed the gun at Kiefer? Or when she'd had to leave him behind, knowing Marko could return at any moment? Had that been the same alarm that had consumed Kiefer when she'd been shot?

She'd experienced that type of fear. "I understand that now, Dad."

"I hope so."

There had been no compromise with her father but Kiefer had offered one. Instead of accepting it, she'd all but slapped him in the face. She'd thrown away what could have been.

A customer entered. Her father kissed her on the forehead. "I love you, honey. It can make us act in strange ways."

"Yes, it can."

A few minutes later Ashley put the drink bottle down and left. She didn't return the way she had come but instead walked toward where Lizzy had lived. The house was still there but her family had moved away as well. Ashley stood looking at the house. In her mind she could see Lizzy running down the steps to meet her. Or jumping as she played hopscotch on the sidewalk where Ashley stood.

It was time to let go. Lizzy and what had happened to her had shaped her own past, but now it was time to find a future of her own making. Ignoring the pain in her arm, she reached up behind her neck and unlatched the necklace. It slipped into the other hand and she dropped it into her pocket. Kiefer was right. She needed to think about what she wanted and needed. And that was him. He was her future. If she could convince him to give her another chance.

Kiefer had wanted to go straight to Ashley's parents' house the second he left the hospital. He had called but she had been asleep. Her mother had assured him she was doing fine. Knowing she needed rest after their ordeal, he had decided to wait. He had things he had to get straight in his mind, in his life, before he went to Ashley and begged her to consider giving him another chance.

What he had learned was that life was unpredictable and could be cut short. Finding someone special was rare and worth fighting for. He hadn't been able to handle everything by himself during their situation with Marko, but with Ashley beside him they had made a great team. It was impossible to stop bad things from happening to her but he could be there to support her when they did. He'd not been able to protect his mother because he'd been a child. She didn't blame him and he shouldn't blame himself.

Ashley had told him more than once that he needed to face what had happened to his mother. He couldn't confront that man but he could face the man that had threatened Ashley.

The next day Kiefer sat on a metal jail chair in a cubicle, looking at Marko. After some fast talking on Kiefer's part, he had convinced Bull to arrange the meeting.

Kiefer picked up the phone on the wall. After a moment of hesitation Marko did the same.

Marko jerked his chin at Kiefer. "What do you want?"

"To tell you that your buddy Jorge is going to live. He'll spend some time in the hospital but he'll make it."

Marko shrugged from where he slumped in the chair. "Okay. So you could have sent a message. Why did you show up here?"

"Because I needed to face you. For you to see me on this side of the glass and know you are on that side. To tell you that you'll never again hold any power over me or Ashley. I'll be there to testify against you and when I'm done you'll be forgotten by me forever."

Marko bared his teeth. "You think I care."

"It doesn't matter to me. What does matter to me is Ashley. If you so much as say her name, I'll use everything in my power to see that you never see the light of day again." Kiefer pushed his chair back and stood. "Now, you have a good day."

Kiefer walked out into the sunlight. The day had just become brighter.

He rolled his shoulders and headed toward his car. As for Brittney and Josh, it was time to move beyond what they had done as well. They had been controlling his happiness and he wasn't going to give them that power anymore. They'd been allowed too much importance in his life for too long. He was tired of having others feel sorry for him and he was disgusted by how long he'd felt sorry for himself. He'd found something good in his life, and he was going to hang on for dear life.

Ashley would never betray him. She was loyal to a fault. To her community, her family and her friends. She would be the same to him as well. There wasn't a selfish bone in her body. She believed in commitment. Had proved that by her devotion to the people in her life. Ashley was the type of person he wanted beside him forever.

She had not only given him his self-esteem back but she'd given him a home. Not the sterile life that looked like his apartment but something comfortable like her place. He'd become part of Southriver in the short amount of time he'd worked at the clinic. People were no longer people who came and went. They were business owners, grandmothers, young families—friends. He'd had no idea he'd needed that until he'd had it and had been about to lose it. He needed Southriver as much as it needed him.

Now it was time to convince Ashley that they belonged together. That was going to require a grandiose gesture. He had just such a thing in mind.

CHAPTER TEN

ASHLEY GLANCED AT the crowd filling the city council meeting room. There were more people than usual attending. She spoke to another alderman, hoping to garner some support for the clinic. She was afraid she was going to have a fight on her hands.

Her and Kiefer's ordeal had made the news. She'd done numerous interviews. To her surprise she'd even seen one with Kiefer. She had fully anticipated him to dodge such a thing, but he'd given a good solid sound bite, glossing over what had happened to them and turning the focus on the efforts being made in the Southriver area and what he did at the clinic. He'd made an impressive spokesman.

Others on the council had also been interviewed. They had made it clear in one way or another that they weren't in support of the clinic or the methods being used to make improvements in Southriver.

Outside of seeing Kiefer on TV, she'd not seen him in ages. It hurt terribly. The clinic had been closed when she'd returned to her place. She had been told that Kiefer had been given some time off. He deserved that. She had also been informed that at this time there was no one to replace him. Ashley couldn't bring herself to ask any more questions. Whatever she had hoped for with the clinic and Kiefer was gone.

He'd not even called. Okay, that wasn't true. He had spoken to her mother, but that wasn't the same as him talking to her. All she could try to do now was accept what he wanted and that wasn't her.

All the media publicity had shone a light on Southriver, but it had been a negative one for the most part. That was a portion of what the council meeting was about tonight. The mayor and a couple of the aldermen wanted to rescind the funding. Their argument was that the city couldn't afford to take a chance that what had happened to Kiefer wouldn't happen to another doctor. The liability was too great.

As painful as it was for the clinic to close, losing Kiefer hurt far worse. It was a constant ache that didn't ease. More than once she'd been in her kitchen and had stopped what she'd been doing to look at the door to the stairs, thinking she'd heard his footsteps. It would take a long time for her to push memories of him out of her home and even longer for them to dim in her heart.

She couldn't think about that now. She had a council meeting to survive. A clinic and a neighborhood to protect.

"Okay, folks. Everybody find a seat. It's time for the meeting to begin," the city council chairman said, hitting the gavel on a block of wood.

A tingle went down her spine. She turned and looked out over the room. Kiefer had just entered. His gaze met hers and held. For Ashley all the activity in the room faded away. Her heart went into a wild pit-a-pat rhythm and her entire body hummed with awareness. Everything in her zeroed in on Kiefer.

"Alderman Marsh, if you'll take your seat we'll get started."

Ashley blinked. Warmth filled her face. Kiefer grinned. Her hand trembled as she pulled her chair out from under the table. When she looked up again Kiefer was no longer visible. Had he left? Searching, she found him sitting in a seat a couple of rows from the back.

What was he doing here?

The meeting was being called to order. Her focus was divided between what was being said and Kiefer. Normally she was a highly attentive woman where her work as alderman was concerned, but this evening all her focus was on the man who hadn't taken his eyes off her.

"Ms. Marsh, in light of what happened recently, we feel it's too risky to ask a doctor to work at the clinic," Alderman Richards, one of the council members, said.

That statement jerked her out of her Kiefer-induced trance. Alderman Henderson had been the most vocal about not supporting the clinic in the beginning. Now he was bringing others over to his side. She wasn't surprised he would be the one who would take advantage of the Marko incident to make his point.

"We can't let one problem close down the clinic. The people of Southriver should have the care they deserve," Ashley responded.

"Yes, but we can't expect the hospital to put their doctors in harm's way by working there," another alderman said.

She looked across the table at the woman. "You do know I live in Southriver? Was raised there."

"Where you live is your choice. The city council asking the hospital to send a doctor there is ours. We don't want to put ourselves out there for a civil suit if he or she is hurt doing so," Alderman Richards said, pushing his wire-rimmed glasses back up his nose.

Ashley had heard all the political rhetoric before. "The people of Southriver deserve to keep the clinic. They were supporting it, using it and, more importantly, benefiting from it. More than once Dr. Bradford..." she looked at Kiefer "...identified medical problems that would have been left undiagnosed if the person hadn't come to the clinic. The patients would have never gone to the hospital until it was too late. He's even taken care of my mother when she had a severe burn. The clinic is making a difference. Will make a difference if we continue to support it. Close it and it will be the first step toward telling the people of Southriver they aren't worth the trouble. They're part of this city just as the rest of the districts are and deserve to be treated that way."

"Thank you for that impassioned statement, but the problem still remains that the clinic was a scene of a kidnapping and the doctor was taken at gunpoint. We can't have that happen again or anything else criminal. The hospital isn't going to put their employees into that type of danger."

Kiefer stood. His gaze met hers before he looked at Alderman Richards. "I'm that doctor who was kidnapped. Dr. Kiefer Bradford. And I disagree with you. The hospital is going to continue to support the clinic. I am going to continue as director and hope to encourage an additional doctor to join me. I believe in Southriver and what Ms. Marsh is trying to do for the community. I ask that the council continue their support. But even if you don't, I'll still be practicing in Southriver. And the city council won't be able to take credit for the work being done there."

Ashley stared at Kiefer in amazement. She felt as though she had been picked up, whirled around and set down again. Kiefer was going to stay on at the clinic.

As elated as she was over him staying, she didn't know how she was going to survive seeing him every day and knowing there could never be more than friendship between them. Somehow she would have to come to terms with that.

The city council chairman said, "I don't see how we can disagree with that offer. If Dr. Bradford wants to continue to run the clinic after what happened to him, then I don't see how we can refuse to support it. The clinic is working to make Savannah a better place. A better place to live and visit. What's good for Southriver would be good for Savannah."

How like Alderman Henderson to posture to the positive. He was up for reelection at the end of the year. More than once he'd swung to whatever side had best suited him. Thankfully this time it was hers.

"I call for a vote," Ashley said.

It passed unanimously and Ashley only half listened to what was discussed during the rest of the meeting. All she could think about was speaking to Kiefer. Trying to understand what he was doing. As soon as the meeting was over she headed directly to him.

She wanted to jump into his arms and kiss him but she settled for smiling. "Thank you so much for what you're doing for the clinic."

"I'm not doing it just for the clinic. Can we go somewhere to talk?"

He could take her anywhere. "I'd like that. Let me get my purse. I'll be right back."

"I'm not going anywhere." He'd made the statement sound as if it had a deeper meaning.

As they walked out of the building Kiefer put his hand on the small of her back. A shiver went down her spine. She'd missed his touch. Any touch from him. They made their way to the parking deck.

"Did you mean what you said in there?" Ashley asked.

"Every word of it." There was no sound of wavering in his voice.

"Good. Southriver appreciates it."

Kiefer glanced at her. "I didn't do it for Southriver. Well, maybe some of it, but mostly it's for you."

"Me?"

Was that disappointment in his eyes that she might not believe him? "Yes, you."

Her pulse picked up speed. Did she dare hope? "Where have you been? I thought I'd never see you again."

"Around. I had a few things I needed to get straight in my head, then some things that I needed to do," he said almost too casually.

"I understand."

He chuckled. "I don't think you do. But I hope you will. Why don't you follow me?"

"Where?"

"Just trust me, why don't you?"

"Okay."

Sometime later Kiefer pulled through the gate of the old mill they had looked at during the block party and parked in front of the doors. What were they doing here? He waited for her to join him.

"Why're we at the old mill?"

"For that view."

"How did you get permission to go in?"

He directed her inside and then toward the industrial elevator. "Didn't have to. I own the place."

"How? Why?"

He grinned then pulled the door open to the elevator shaft and pushed up the wire door to the elevator car. "You're sure full of questions. But since you asked, I sold my apartment downtown. And bought this so I would have a place to live."

"You did what?"

He closed the doors, pushed a button and they started moving up. "It was time to give up my passion for living in the past and concentrate on the future. Since I was going to be working in Southriver, it made sense to live close by. It would be easier for being on call. I've kind of become attached to the community anyway."

"That does make sense."

"How like you to understand the practicality of decisions." The elevator stopped, he opened the doors and they stepped off. "Come this way."

They were in an enormous open space with windows along the entire wall facing the river. The orange and pink of the evening sun streamed through them. Lines were drawn out on the floor and work was already being done to build walls.

Kiefer took her hand and steered her toward a staircase at the far end of the space.

She pulled at her hand. "I want to look around."

"Later. We'll miss the sunset if we don't hurry."

Together they climbed the metal stairs. At the top they stood on a landing and Kiefer pushed a door open and let her go out ahead of him. They were on the roof.

"It's wonderful." From here Ashley could see where the river ran into the ocean. Birds swarmed then flew off above the marshland. The wind made the saw grass wave gently back and forth. It was amazing. Made more so by Kiefer being there with her.

Not far away were the chairs, footstools and table that had been sitting on Kiefer's balcony. A candle in a glass jar sat in the middle of the table.

"The only things I kept. Come sit." He took her elbow. They both settled into their chairs.

"This is wonderful. I know you'll enjoy living here,"

Ashley said, as she watched the colors of the setting sun change over the water. Over the next few minutes they sat in silence as night crept in on them. Unable to stand it any longer, Ashley had to ask. "Why did you decide to continue your work at the clinic? And live here?"

Kiefer said quietly, "Because this has become my home. When you have a gun pointed at you it doesn't take long for you to realize what is important. You said very clearly and pointedly that I needed to move on and make some changes. This is my first step toward doing that."

"I'm glad for you. You deserve happiness."

"How're you doing post-Marko?"

"It was hard for me to accept that he would do something like that. I've learned a few things about myself too. You were right—I need to be more careful. I fought so hard against my parents but I understand them better now. I do think I've been working to relieve my guilt where Lizzy was concerned. I don't think I can ever give up being a crusader, as you call it, for the children in this community or trying to improve it, but I do realize that I need some balance in my life. I'm working on it."

"I'm sure you will. I have complete confidence in you. And don't give up being a crusader. The world needs more of your kind."

"Thank you. That was nice of you to say."

"Seems like we both have learned and accepted a few things in the last few weeks."

Ashley smiled. "What's the saying? 'You're never too old to learn something new'? You know this really is a magnificent view."

"You could enjoy it every day. There's plenty of room here."

"Does the second floor have the same view as this?" She glanced at him. What was he asking?

"As far as I know. But I was thinking more of you having the upper floor."

Hope soared in her. "But that should be yours."

"It isn't like you to be so dense. I want you to live with me. Actually, that isn't correct." Kiefer put his hand into his pocket and pulled something out then slid out of the chair to bend on one knee. He held out a ring. "I want you to marry me."

Ashley held her breath. She couldn't believe this was happening. Hadn't dared to hope for the possibility.

"Ashley Marsh, I love you. Will you be my wife and share all the sunsets with me for the rest of our lives?"

She just looked at him, speechless. Was this a dream?

A flicker of doubt went through Kiefer's eyes. This big, confident, intelligent man was unsure.

"What did you say?"

He shifted. "I asked you to marry me."

"No, before that."

He looked confused. "That I love you?"

"Yes. Could you say it again?"

He captured her gaze. All the sincerity of his heart was in his eyes. "I love you."

"That's better than any sunset I've ever seen. I love you too." She leaned down and kissed him. When they finally broke apart she said, "You know, you don't have to marry me. I know how you feel about marriage. That doesn't change how we feel about each other."

"Yes, I do. Because I want everyone to know you are mine. I know you would never betray me. You are faithful to those you care about. A commitment with you will last forever."

"I'll not fail you."

"Nor I you. So you will marry me?"

"There's just one more thing."

Kiefer sighed. "Heavens, woman, it takes a lot to get you to say yes. What else?"

"About you being overprotective…"

"I'm going to try—"

She put her hand over his mouth. "We'll work at a compromise, something we can both live with. I understand where you're coming from, and as part of my love I'll try very hard to not make you worry unduly."

"As part of my love I'll resist calling in the army when you are a minute late."

She chuckled. "I would appreciate that. Now, if you'll ask me that question again, I have an answer."

"Ashley, you will make me the happiest man alive if you will marry me. Will you?"

"Just try to stop me." She threw her arms around his neck and kissed him.

Two months later, Ashley stood in the doorway of the Tybee Island lighthouse. Her father reached out a hand to help her descend the steps. She lifted the long skirt of the flowing white wedding dress she'd fallen in love with the minute she'd seen it. She felt like a princess going to meet her prince. Kiefer certainly was hers.

Taking her father's hand, she stepped down and placed her arm in the crook of his. Kiefer was waiting for her along with all their friends and family. Much of the community of Southriver had been invited to the wedding. Because of her position on the council, the media were also present. She didn't care. The only person who mattered was Kiefer.

They'd chosen to have a simple wedding. No attendants. Just them. She'd surprised Kiefer with deciding on the lighthouse as the venue and they had agreed on a dusk ceremony, knowing how much they both enjoyed sunsets.

As she walked across the grass and around the corner of the building, thoughts of how far they had come and what they had overcome went through her mind. She'd almost lost Kiefer. She would never take him for granted.

The large white tent came into sight. Kiefer would be waiting at the end of the white aisle runner. The man who would protect her, the man who would stand beside her and the man who would let her cry in his arms when she was hurt.

She and her father paused before entering the tent. Kiefer stood tall and handsome in his dark suit. A smile formed on his lips and his gaze held hers. If she hadn't felt like a princess before, she did now. The love in his look was crystal clear.

Half an hour later she was Mrs. Kiefer Bradford.

The reception was every bit the party they had hoped for. Kiefer swung her around on the dance floor and Ashley giggled as he brought her close for a kiss. He couldn't seem to stop touching her and she had no complaints about that.

"I love you. Do you know that?"

"I do. And I love you. Thank you for giving me this." Meaning the wedding. Her happiness. Him.

"Hey, there, mind if I meet the bride?" A man who favored Kiefer stood beside him.

Kiefer let her go for the first time and enveloped the man in a bear hug then stepped back. "Jackson, my man, it's so good to see you. I'm glad you could make it."

"Wouldn't have missed it."

"Ashley, this is my cousin, Jackson Hilstead the Third." Kiefer put emphasis on the last word. "You know—the one from California—Aunt Georgina's son."

Ashley smiled at Jackson. "It's so nice to meet you.

I'm glad you could be here. You're the one who missed out on the name Kiefer."

Jackson grinned. "Guilty as charged." He shifted and put a hand on a pretty woman's waist and brought her closer. "This is Charlotte Johnson."

"Hello, Charlotte, we're so glad to have you here," Ashley said, as Kiefer and Jackson went into a deep discussion.

"You're a beautiful bride," Charlotte offered. "Gorgeous dress."

"Thank you. I think anyone must look beautiful when they're in love."

Ashley noticed the other woman glance at Kiefer's cousin. "I guess they are."

"Is there another wedding planned in the near future?"

The men turned back to them before Charlotte could answer. She clearly had it bad for Jackson. Ashley recognized that look because she'd seen it in the mirror since she'd met Kiefer.

The men joined them again.

"Ashley, I want you to make Kiefer bring you out for a visit sometime soon," Jackson said.

"We'll put it on our calendar. It sounds like fun," Ashley assured him.

Jackson glanced back. "I see Mother signaling to us. Better go see who else she wants us to meet."

Kiefer and Jackson exchanged a hug again.

"That's a woman in love," Ashley said as Jackson and Charlotte moved away.

Kiefer kissed her. "You think everyone should be in love today."

"That could be true but what I do know is that I love you."

"And I love you."

Ashley took his hand. "Want to go to the beach and watch the sunset with me?"

"Every day. For the rest of my life."

* * * * *

If you missed the first story in the
SUMMER BRIDES *duet, look out for*

WEDDING DATE WITH THE ARMY DOC
by Lynne Marshall

And if you enjoyed this story,
check out these other great reads from
Susan Carlisle

MARRIED FOR THE BOSS'S BABY
ONE NIGHT BEFORE CHRISTMAS
HIS BEST FRIEND'S BABY
THE DOCTOR'S REDEMPTION

All available now!

WEDDING DATE
WITH THE ARMY DOC

BY
LYNNE MARSHALL

Published in Great Britain 2016
By Mills & Boon, an imprint of HarperCollins*Publishers*
1 London Bridge Street, London, SE1 9GF

© 2016 Janet Maarschalk

ISBN: 978-0-263-91498-6

Dear Reader,

A few years ago I thought up a story about a female pathologist and ran it by my editor. The story had many flaws and needed much work. At the time I opted to put it away in a drawer, but I didn't stop thinking about it. After letting the story rest for a while I went back to it and, with the extensive notes I'd received from my editor the first time around, I reworked everything. I'm so happy I did.

Charlotte, my courageous pathologist, made a life-changing decision based on a potential killer that many women have to face. Cancer. She opted to be pre-emptive, and her decision was radical, but in her mind it was saving her life. She had strong reasons for making this decision, based on watching her mother's battle with and eventual defeat by cancer.

Jackson had everything going for him in life until a second tour of Afghanistan on an army medical team changed everything. He came home wounded and lost, and the already weakened fabric of his marriage didn't hold up under the stress. But, having almost lost it all, he courageously fought his way back and changed direction. Unfortunately divorce was part of that change, but a new beginning three thousand miles across country in California turned out to be his saving grace.

Picture a small pathology office in the basement of a hospital, where these two wounded and healing people come together in a most unromantic way. Against all odds love still raises its head, as well as the consciousness of these two meant-to-be people. All it takes is their willingness to risk another chance at love.

Is it worth it? Come read Charlotte and Jackson's story, so you can make your own decision.

Lynne

'Friend' me on Facebook!

Many thanks to Flo Nicoll, with her uncanny gift of
pinpointing the missing link in my manuscripts
and for giving me the freedom to explore diverse and difficult stories.

Also, I'd like to dedicate this book to the 'Dr Gordon' I remember so
well from my first job, working in a pathology department. I learned so
much and was given many opportunities all those years ago! Knowing
'Dr Gordon' changed the direction of my life. May he rest in peace.

Lynne Marshall used to worry that she had a serious problem with
daydreaming—and then she discovered she was supposed to *write*
those stories! A Rgesitered Nurse for twenty-six years, she came to
fiction writing later than most. Now she writes romance which usually
includes medicine but always comes straight from her heart. She is
happily married, a Southern California native, a woman of faith, a
dog-lover, an avid reader, a curious traveller and a proud grandma.

Books by Lynne Marshall

Mills & Boon Medical Romance

The Hollywood Hills Clinic

His Pregnant Sleeping Beauty

Cowboys, Doctors…Daddies!

Hot-Shot Doc, Secret Dad
Father for Her Newborn Baby

Temporary Doctor, Surprise Father
The Boss and Nurse Albright
The Heart Doctor and the Baby
The Christmas Baby Bump
Dr Tall, Dark…and Dangerous?
NYC Angels: Making the Surgeon Smile
200 Harley Street: American Surgeon in London
A Mother for His Adopted Son

Visit the Author Profile page at millsandboon.co.uk for more titles.

Praise for
Lynne Marshall

'Heartfelt emotion that will bring you to the point of tears, for those
who love a second-chance romance written with exquisite detail.'
—*Contemporary Romance Reviews* on
NYC Angels: Making the Surgeon Smile

CHAPTER ONE

CHARLOTTE JOHNSON MADE the necessary faces to chew the amazing chocolate, nut and caramel candy she'd just shoved into her mouth between looking at pathology slides. Mid-nut-and-caramel-chew, she glanced up to see a hulking shadow cover her office door. Her secret surgeon crush, Jackson Ryland Hilstead the Third, blocked the fluorescent light from the hallway, causing her to narrow her eyes in order to make out his features. *Be still, my heart, and, oh, heavens, stop chewing. Now!*

Except she couldn't talk unless she finished chewing and swallowed, and she figured he'd come for a reason, as he always did Friday afternoons. Probably because of his heavy schedule of surgeries on Thursday and Friday mornings. He'd ask her questions about his patients' diagnoses and prognoses, and she'd dutifully answer. It had become their routine, and she looked forward to it. After all, as the staff surgical pathologist at St. Francis of the Valley Hospital, it was her job to be helpful to her fellow medical colleagues, even while, in his case, thinking how she'd love to brush that one brown, wavy lock of hair off his forehead. Yeah, she was hopelessly crushing on the man.

She lifted her finger, hoping her sign for "One moment" might compute with the astute doc, then covered her mouth with the other hand as she chewed furiously. Finally, she swallowed with a gulp, feeling heat rise from her neck upward. *Great impression.*

"Don't let me interfere," he said, an amused look on his face. "The last thing I want to do is come between a woman and her chocolate." Obviously he'd noticed the candy-bar wrapper on her desk.

She grabbed a bottle of water and took a quick swig. "You're sounding sexist. How unlike you," she teased, hoping she didn't have candy residue on her teeth. Of all the male doctors she dealt with on a daily basis, this surgeon was the one who made her feel self-conscious. It most certainly had a lot to do with his piercing blue eyes that the hospital scrubs seemed to highlight brighter than an OR lamp. She pulled her lab coat closed when his eyes surreptitiously and briefly scanned her from head to toe. Or as much as he could see of her with her sitting behind her double-headed microscope.

"Ah, Charlotte…" He sat down across from her. "How well you *don't* know me. If you weren't my favorite pathologist, I'd be offended." Finally responding to her half-hearted "sexist" slur.

The guy was a Southern gentleman from Georgia, and she wasn't above stereotyping him, because he was a walking billboard for good manners, charm and—perhaps not quite as appealing considering the odds in a competitive and overstocked female world, in California anyway—knowing how to relate to women. The word *smooth* came to mind. But it was balanced with sincerity, a rare combination. Plus there was no escaping that slow, rolling-syllable accent, like warm honey down her spine, setting off all sorts of nerve endings she'd otherwise forgotten. He spoke as though they had all the time in the world to talk. She could listen to him all day, and if she'd owned a fan she'd be flapping it now.

"Well, if you weren't *one* of my favorite surgeons," she lied, as he was her absolute favorite, "I would've eaten the rest of it."

One corner of his mouth hitched the tiniest bit. "I think you already have, but don't worry, your gooey-chocolate choice would be number ten on my list of top three favorite candy bars."

Busted, she batted her lashes, noticing his spearmint-and-sandalwood scent as he moved closer. She inhaled a little deeper, thinking he liked to change up his after-shave, and that intrigued her.

"And since you brought up the subject of sexism, I've got to say you look great today. Turquoise suits you."

He regularly paid her compliments, which she loved, but figured he was like that with all the women he encountered, so she never took them too seriously. Though she had to admit she longed for him to mean them. What did that say about her dating life? Something in the way his eyes watched her and waited for a response whenever he flattered her made her wonder if maybe she was a tiny bit more special than all the other ladies in the hospital. She liked the idea of that.

"Thank you," she said, sounding as self-effacing as ever.

"Thank *you*," he countered.

Their gazes held perhaps a second longer than she could take, so she pretended the slide on the microscope tray required her immediate and complete attention. "So what do you need?"

Intensely aware of his *do-you-really-want-to-know?* gaze—this was new and it was a challenge that shook her to the bone—she fought the urge to squirm. Yeah, sexist or sexy or whatever it was he just did with those eyes was way out of her comfort zone. So why did that look excite her, make her wish things could be the way they had been before her operation? Where was that invisible fan again? Shame. Shame. Shame. And she called herself a professional woman.

"Do you have the slides yet for Gary Underwood? A lung biopsy from yesterday afternoon. I've got an impatient wife demanding her husband's results."

"The weekend is coming, so I can understand her concern." Charlotte hadn't yet finished the slides from yesterday morning's cases, but she was always willing to fish out a few newer ones for interested doctors. Jackson was as concerned about his patients as they came. Another thing she really liked about the guy.

She turned on the desk lamp, sorted through the pile of cardboard slide cases, each carefully labeled by the histology technicians, and found the slides in question. They settled in to study them, their knees nearly touching as they sat on opposite sides of the small table that held her dual-headed teaching microscope. She put her hair behind her ears and moved in, but not before seeing him notice her dangly turquoise earrings that matched her top. She could tell from the spark in his eyes that he liked them, too, but this time kept the fact to himself.

Yes, he was a real gentleman, with broad shoulders and wavy brown hair that he chose to comb straight back from his forehead. And it was just long enough to curl under his ears. Call him a sexy gentleman. *Gulp.* Very, very sexy.

Being smack in the heart of the San Fernando Valley was nothing new for an original Valley girl like her, but she figured it had to be total culture shock for a man from Savannah. *Talk to me, baby. I love that Southern drawl.* Why did she have such confidence inside her head but could never dare to act on it? She didn't waste a single second answering that question. Because things were different now. She wasn't the woman she'd used to be. Enough said.

In his early forties with a sprinkling of gray at his temples, Jackson had only been in Southern California for a year. Word was, if she could believe everything she heard from Dr. Dupree, Jackson had needed a change after his divorce. Which made him a gentleman misfit in a casual-with-a-capital-C kind of town. She liked that about him, too—the khaki slacks and button-down collared shirts with ties that he'd obviously given some time to selecting. Today the shirt was pale yellow and the tie an expensive-looking subtly sage-green herringbone pattern. Nice.

She turned off the desk light so they could view the slide better. They sat in companionable silence as they studied it. Hearing him breathe ever so gently made the hair on the back of her neck stand on end. Good thing she'd worn it down today. Hmm, maybe that was what he liked? *Stop it, Charlotte. This will never go anywhere.* Maybe that was why she enjoyed the fantasy so much. It was her secret. And it was safe.

She fine-focused on the biopsied lung tissue, increasing the magnification over one particular spot of red-dyed swirls with minuscule black dots until the cells came into full view. They studied the areas in question together. "Notice the angulated nuclear margins and hyperchromasia in this area?" She spoke close to a whisper, a habit she'd got into out of respect for the solemn importance of each patient's diagnosis.

"Hmm," he emitted thoughtfully.

She moved the slide on the tray a tiny bit, then refocused. "And here, and here." She used the white teaching arrow in the high-grade microscope to point out the areas in question.

He inhaled, his eyes never leaving the eyepiece.

"Here are mitotic figures, and here intercellular bridges. Not a good sign." She pulled back from her microscope. "As you can see, there are variations in size of cells and nuclei, which adds up to squamous cell malignancy. I'll have to study the rest of the slides to check the margins and figure out the cancer staging, but, unfortunately, the anxiously awaiting wife will have more to be anxious about."

"Bad news for sure." Jackson pushed back from the microscope, but not before one of his knees knocked hers, and it hurt her kneecap, feeling almost like metal. Maybe he was Superman in disguise? "I'll get in touch with Oncology to get a jump on things."

The situation caused an old and familiar pang in her stomach. Charlotte knew how it felt to be a family member waiting for news from the doctor. She'd gone through the process at fifteen, the year her mother had been diagnosed with breast cancer. That was the day she'd first heard the term *metastatic* and had vowed to figure out what it meant. And after that she'd vowed to learn everything she could about her mother's condition.

"Is he young and otherwise healthy?"

"Yes," Jackson said. "Which will help the prognosis."

She nodded, though not enthusiastically. Her mother had been young and supposedly healthy, too. The loss of her mother soon after bilateral mastectomies had broken her family's heart. Her father had never recovered, and within a span of three years of his downhill slide, he'd also died. From alcoholism, his self-medication of choice to deal with the emotional pain. She'd already stepped in as the responsible one when her mother had first been diagnosed, and after she'd died Charlotte had kept the family functioning. Barely. At eighteen, along with applying to colleges, she'd signed on to be the guardian of her kid sister and brother, otherwise they'd have ended up in foster homes.

Her mother's cancer had changed the course of her life, steering her toward medicine, and later, with her never-ending quest to understand why things happened as they did, sending her into the darker side of the profession, pathology.

"Well, I've got to run," Jackson said, bringing her out of her thoughts. "I've got a dinner I can't miss tonight, and Mrs. Underwood to talk to first." He stood and took a couple of steps then turned at her office door and looked at her again thoughtfully. "Do you happen to know offhand the extension for social services? I think the Underwoods could use some added support this weekend."

Having put the desk light back on, she scanned her hospital phone list cheat sheet and read out the numbers, admittedly disappointed to know he had a dinner engagement.

"Thanks," he said, but not before giving her a thorough once-over again. "Really like those earrings, too." Then he left, leaving her grinning with warming cheeks.

Wanting desperately to read more into his light flattery than she should, she groaned quietly. The guy had a dinner date! Plus the man probably said things like that to all the women he encountered in his busy days. It had probably been drilled into him back in Georgia since grade school, maybe even before that. Treat all women like princesses.

Who was she kidding, hoping she might be more special than other women he knew? She was five feet nine, a full-figured gal, or had used to be anyway, a size ten, and not many men appreciated that in this thin-as-a-rail era. Besides, even if he did find her attractive, nothing could ever come of it. She'd pretty much taken care of that two years ago with her surgery.

Odds were most men wouldn't want to get involved with her. She pulled her lab coat tighter across her chest. Her ex-boyfriend had sure changed his mind, calling off their short engagement. They'd been all set to go the conventional route, and she'd loved the idea of having a career, marriage and kids. Her mouth had watered for it. Then…

She'd cut Derek some slack, though, since her decision had been extreme and radical even. They'd talked about it over and over, argued, and he'd never really signed on. He hadn't wanted to go there. He'd wanted her exactly as she had been.

The memory of her mother suffering had been the major influence on her final decision.

Her hand came to rest on her chest. The realistic-feeling silicone breast forms—otherwise known as falsies—she wore in her bra sometimes nearly made her forget she'd had a double mastectomy. Elective surgery.

She fiddled with Mr. Underwood's slides, lining them up to study them more thoroughly.

She'd accidentally found her own damn cancer marker right here in her office. Along with the excitement and anticipation of getting engaged and the plans for having a family, some deeper, sadder dialogue threaded through the recesses of her brain. One morning she'd woken in a near panic. What if? She'd shivered over the potential answer. Then, unable to move forward with a gigantic question mark in her future, she'd had the lab draw her blood and do the genetic marker panel. The results had literally made her gasp and grab her chest. Her worst nightmare was alive and living in her DNA.

Knowing her mother's history, the near torture she'd gone through, well, having preemptive surgery had been a decision she'd known she'd have to make. Why not take care of it before it ever had a chance to begin? She'd begged Derek to understand. He'd fought her decision, but he'd never seen what her mother had gone through.

Jackson appeared at her door again, making her lose her train of thought. He inclined his head. "You okay?"

"Oh, yes." She recovered quickly, and he obviously accepted her answer since the concern dissolved from his face.

"Hey, I forgot to ask just now. Are you going to that garden party Sunday afternoon?"

Her old concerns suddenly forgotten, the hair on her arms joined the hair on the back of her neck in prickling. Was it possible that the handsome Southern doctor was actually interested in her?

"Yes. I kind of thought it was mandatory." It was July, the newest residents would all be there and it was a chance to put names to faces.

"Good. I'll see you there, then." And off he went again, his long legs and unusual gait taking that Southern stroll to a new level.

For an instant she let her hopes take flight. What would it be like to date again, especially with a man's man like Jackson Hilstead the Third? But he'd made no offer to go to the garden party together, and after all the thoughts she'd had just now, she wasn't a bit closer to making her secret crush real. No way.

Feeling the fallout from rehashing her past, she exchanged the instantaneous hope for reality. There was no way anyone would want her. Not with the anything-but-sexy scars across her nearly flat chest.

She sat staring into her lap, letting the truth filter through her.

Dr. Antwan Dupree appeared at her door, a man so full of himself she wished she could post a "closed for business" sign and pretend no one was home.

"I brought you some Caribbean food from a little place nearby. Thought you might like to try a taste of your heritage."

"I'm not from the Caribbean."

"Yes, you are. You just don't know it. Look at your honey-colored skin and the loads of wavy, almost black hair. Darlin', you've got Caribbean brown eyes. There's no question."

"It's brown. My hair is dark brown. Both my parents were from the States. My grandparents were from the States. My great-grandparents were from the States. I'm typical Heinz Fifty-Seven American. The name Johnson is as American as it gets."

"I see the islands in you."

"And that makes it so? Must be nice to live in your world." She suppressed a sigh. She always had to try her best not to be rude to the young, overconfident surgeon, because she did have to work with him.

"I'm just trying to help you get in touch with your roots. Try this. It's rice and peas and jerk chicken. You'll love it."

"I don't do spicy." She opened the brown bag, pulled out the take-out container and peered inside. Black-eyed peas were something she'd never tried before, but the rice was brown, the chicken looked juicy and, since the doctor had gone to the trouble to bring the food, she figured she should at least taste it. "But I'll give this a try."

"When you eat that you'll be singing, 'I'm home, at

last!'" He had an okay voice, but she wasn't ready for a serenade right then.

"I doubt it, but thanks for the thought." Her number one thought, while staring at her unrequested lunch, was how to get rid of Antwan Dupree.

Just as Antwan opened his mouth to speak again Jackson appeared once more at the door, which pleased her to no end.

Would you look at me, the popular pathologist? The thought nearly made her spew a laugh, but that could get messy and spread germs and it definitely wouldn't be attractive and Jackson was standing right there. She kept her near guffaw to herself and secretly reveled in the moment, though inwardly she rolled her eyes at the absurdity of the notion. Popular pathologist. Right.

Antwan was a pest. Jackson Hilstead, well, was not!

"Give it a try, let me know what you think." Antwan turned for the door. "You have my number, right?" He made a point to look directly at Jackson when he said that.

"Thank you and good-bye." She'd never found swagger appealing. She'd also learned that with Antwan it was best to be blunt, otherwise the guy imagined all kinds of improbable things. The thing that really didn't make sense was that he was better than decent looking and had loads of women interested around the hospital. Why pester her?

He nodded. "We'll talk later," he promised confidently, and did his unique Antwan Dupree walk right past Jackson, who hadn't budged from his half of the entrance.

"Doctor." Jackson tipped his head.

"Doctor." Dupree paid the same respect on his way out. No sooner had he left than Charlotte could hear Antwan chatting up Latoya, the receptionist down the hall. What a guy.

"Sorry to interrupt," Jackson said.

"Not at all. In fact, thank you!"

Jackson smiled and her previously claustrophobic office, with Dr. Dupree inside plus him now being gone, seemed to expand toward the universe.

"Spicy beans and rice give me indigestion, but I guess I have to try this now. I was actually kind of looking forward to my peanut butter and jelly sandwich."

That got another smile from him, and she longed to think of a thousand ways to keep them coming. She also felt compelled to clarify a few things. "For the record," she said as she closed the food container and put it back in the bag, "there is nothing at all going on between me and Dupree. He, well…he's a player and I really don't care for men who are full of themselves, you know?"

"He does like the ladies." Jackson hadn't budged from his spot at the door, and she began to wonder why he'd made another visit. "But in this case he does exhibit excellent taste."

Really? He thought she was attractive? Before she let herself get all puffed up about his comment, it occurred to her that Jackson must have come back to her office for a reason. Maybe he wanted to ask her to go with him to the garden party? "Did you need something?"

"Yes."

She mentally crossed her fingers.

"I was just talking to Dr. Gordon. He said he'd like to speak to you when you have a chance."

The head of pathology, Dr. Gordon, was her personal mentor, and admittedly a kind of father figure, and when he called, she never hesitated. "Oh. Sure, thanks." She stood and walked around her desk, then noticed the subtle gaze again from Jackson covering her from head to toe. If only she hadn't chosen sensible shoes today! But she thanked the manufacturer of realistic-looking falsies for filling out her special mastectomy bra underneath her turquoise top.

Charlotte strolled side by side with the tall doctor down the hall. She pegged him to be around six-two, based on her five-nine and wearing low wedge shoes, plus the fact her eyes were in line with his classic long and straight nose, except for that small bump on the bridge that gave him such character. She forced her attention away from his face, again noticing his subtly unusual gait, like maybe one shoe didn't fit quite right. When they reached Dr. Gordon's office door, she faked casual and said good-bye.

When he smiled his good-bye, she secretly sighed— what was it about that guy?—and lingered, watching him leave the department.

"You coming in or are you going to stand out there gawking all afternoon?" As head of pathology, Dr. Gordon had taken her under his wing from her very first day as a resident at St. Francis, and she owed him more than she could ever repay. She also happened to adore the nearly seventy-year-old curmudgeon, with his shocking white hair and clear hazel eyes that had always seemed to see right through her. His double chin helped balance a hawk-like nose.

"Sorry. Hi." She stepped inside his office. "You wanted to talk to me?"

He grew serious. "Close the door."

His instruction sent a chill through her core. Something important was about to happen and the thought made her uncomfortable. He'd better not be retiring because she wasn't ready for him to leave! She did what she was told, closed the door, then sat across from him at the desk, hoping she wasn't about to get reprimanded for something.

He gave his fatherly smile, and immediately she knew

she had nothing to worry about. "I'm not going to mince words. My prostate cancer is back and Dr. Hilstead is going to do exploratory surgery on me Monday. I want you to read the frozen sections."

Stunned, she could hardly make herself speak. "Yes. Of course." She wanted to run to him and throw her arms around him, but they didn't have that kind of relationship. "Whatever you want." His wife, Elly, had passed away last year, and he'd seemed so forlorn ever since. The last thing the man needed was a cancer threat. Her heart ached for him, but she fought to hide her fears. "I'll go over those specimens with a fine-tooth comb."

"And I'll expect no less." Stoic as always. Pathology had a way of doing that to doctors.

"Is there anything I can do for you this weekend?"

"Thank you but no. My son is flying in from Arizona for a few days."

"I'm glad to hear that."

"Oh, wait, there is something you could do. I guess you could fill in for me on Sunday afternoon at that new resident garden party deal."

"Of course." Not her favorite idea, since she'd hoped she could find a way to comfort him, like make a big pot of healthy soup or something, but she'd planned to go to the Sunday event anyway.

The good doctor winked at her. "Whatever we find, we'll nip it in the bud, right?"

"You bet." With her heart aching, she wished she could guarantee that would be the case, but they passed a look between them that said it all. As pathologists, they knew when cancer reared its head the hunt was on. It was their job to be relentless in tracking it down, the surgeons' job to cut it out, and the oncologists' to find the magic healing potion to obliterate anything that was left.

Medical science was a tough business, and Charlotte Johnson had signed on in one of the most demanding fields. Pathology. She'd never get used to being the bearer of bad news. Usually the doctors had to take it from there once she handed over the medical verdict. She considered Jim Gordon to be a dear friend as well as colleague and any findings she came up with he'd know had come directly from her. The responsibility unsettled her stomach.

Now that she'd dealt with her own deepest fear—and Jim Gordon had condoned her radical decision two years ago at the age of thirty-two—she was damned if she'd give up being an optimist for him.

Come Monday morning she'd be ready for the toughest call of her career, and it would be for Dr. Gordon. Her mentor. The man she'd come to respect like a father. But first she'd have to make it through the garden party on Sunday afternoon, and the one bright spot in that obligation was the chance to see her secret surgeon crush again. Dr. Jackson Hilstead.

CHAPTER TWO

CHARLOTTE DIDN'T WANT to admit she'd picked the Capri blue patterned sundress only because Dr. Hilstead had liked her turquoise top on Friday, though the thought had entered her mind while searching her closet for something to wear on Sunday morning.

It had been a long time since she'd even considered wearing a dress cut like this, which made her feel uncomfortable, so she'd compromised with a white, lightweight, very loosely knit, three-quarter-sleeved summer sweater. To help cover the dipping neckline, she chose several strings of large and colorful beads. On a whim, she left her hair down, letting the thick waves touch the tops of her shoulders and making no excuses for the occasional ringlet around her face. And this shade of blue sure made her caramel-colored eyes stand out.

With confidence, later that afternoon, she stepped into the St. Francis of the Valley atrium, which connected to an outdoor patio where dozens of doctors had already begun to gather. At the moment she didn't recognize a single face, all of the residents looking so young and eager. But there was Antwan with a young and very attractive woman on his arm. Relieved he wasn't alone, she glanced around the cavernous room.

She recognized several large painted canvases and

they drew her attention to the bright white walls as she realized the ocularist down the hall from her office, Andrea Rimmer, had painted them. In fact, she'd bought several of her early paintings at an art auction because she'd loved her style so much, but these paintings were signed with a different name because Andrea had married a pediatrician, Sam Marcus, so her name had changed now. Anyway, the paintings of huge eyes peeking through various openings were amazing, each iris completely different from the next, and Charlotte was soon swept up in imagining their meaning.

Totally engrossed with admiring the newest paintings of her current favorite artist, she jumped when someone tapped her shoulder. That flutter of excitement flitted right on by when she realized it was Dr. Dupree.

"You're looking extra fine today," he said, making a show of looking her up and down.

"Thank you. Where's your date?"

"Getting some refreshments." His line of vision stayed on her chest. "All those necklaces remind me of the Caribbean."

"They're just some beads I threw on, that's all. Oh, look." She really wanted to divert his interest from her chest. "Your lady friend is searching for you."

"If I didn't assume you'd have a date today, I would have asked you myself."

"I'm here as the representative of the pathology department. This garden party is all business for me."

"Such a shame. If you ever want to actually have a good time, let me know. You don't know what you're missing until you've gone out with me."

Seriously? "If this is any example of how you treat your dates, count me out. Now go spend some time with the very attractive woman you've brought. Shoo." She used her hands to shoo him away, like the pest he was. Man, it ticked her off how he treated women as interchangeable objects.

Frustration and anger interfered with her enjoying the artwork, and though she already really wanted to leave, she had promised Dr. Gordon to be the face of Pathology today. So she forced herself to head toward the refreshment table, where several of the new doctors stood talking among themselves. She glanced up in time to see something to make her get excited. Jackson Hilstead was easy to spot, being a head taller than others in his group, as he moved into the atrium. Charlotte found her smile come to a halt when she noticed that to Jackson's right was the assistant head of the hospital laboratory, Yuri Ito. His hand rested on her shoulder, like he was guiding her. Obviously they'd come together.

Why had Jackson asked if she was coming to the party if he was bringing a date? Her previous excitement turned to disappointment, making the thought of eating sour on her tongue. What else was new? Why had she even let herself follow her fancy in the first place? Antwan may have been right about the surgeon. Maybe he was as much of a lady's man as Dupree. What was up with surgeons?

Halfheartedly, she moved on to the buffet and picked a few items to pretend she was busy, rather than try to make eye contact with Jackson. What was the point? She greeted a few of the new residents, introducing herself and inviting them to stop by anytime for a quick tour of the department. The two young women and one guy all seemed very receptive, maybe even a little too enthusiastic. The dip may have looked great but it tasted bland, matching her mood, since eyeing the tall surgeon with Yuri, but she forced herself to partake.

Another tap on the shoulder sent her heart skittering

once more, until she turned to face Antwan again. How did he keep ditching his date?

"Here," he said, handing her a glass of punch. "You'll like this—it's for grown-ups. And it reminds me—"

"Let me guess—of the Caribbean? Evidently everything does today." She took the drink and sipped, pleasantly surprised by the sweet taste with a kick, as it was definitely a grown-up beverage. "Thanks." She forced a smile and received a much-too-eager grin in return. The sight made her eyes immediately dance away in time to connect with Jackson's where he stood a few feet away.

"Hi," he said, over the crowd.

"Hello," she mouthed back.

Jackson couldn't miss Antwan standing right beside her, which was probably why he quickly looked away. But she'd been clear with him about having nothing going on with Dr. Dupree, and hoped he'd believed her. Which further proved that looks could be deceiving.

So much for getting all dolled up for a man. Except Antwan seemed to appreciate her efforts. Backfire! "Oh, look, there's your date. Isn't she one of the new surgical residents? I'm going to introduce myself."

Antwan's smile faded quickly, and that brought hers back to life as she made her way over to the pretty African-American doctor across the room. She particularly enjoyed watching the too-sure-of-himself doctor squirm.

As the afternoon wore on and she got to know a few of the new batch of residents, who'd just begun working at the hospital July first, she secretly kept tabs on Jackson, who never left Yuri's side, though it sure didn't seem like they had much to say to each other. As in her case with Antwan, could looks be deceiving there, too?

Don't get your hopes up. She felt the urge to adjust her specially made bra but fought it. *This further proves the uselessness of secret crushes. Oh, they're fine when you keep them secret, but start letting them out on a rope and disasters like this happened.* Reality was like looking into a magnifying mirror. *What I see up close is never pleasant.*

She glanced up to find Jackson watching her, and, as crazy as her thoughts had been seconds before, that mere eye contact from the man she'd let her guard down over got her hopes right back up again. She had it bad for the guy, which meant one thing—she needed to get over it!

When she'd felt she'd spent the obligatory amount of time mingling with the new doctors, inviting them to visit Pathology, and also with several of her staff colleagues, she decided to skip out, admittedly feeling disappointed. With no chance for witty conversation with her doctor of choice, that Southern charmer who appeared to be taken anyway, there was no point in sticking around another minute. Unfortunately, her path of exit brought her by Jackson and Yuri, who looked like they were edging their way out, too.

Yuri gazed at her, tension in her eyes. "Hi, Charlotte."

"Hi, Yuri." No hard feelings. Yuri was a nice woman. "See you Monday." She scurried on by but not before someone tapped her on the shoulder. A third time! That Antwan didn't know when to give up. She swung around, less-than-kind thoughts in her mind and probably flashing in her eyes, to see Jackson's laid-back smile.

"You going already?"

Switching gears fast, she skidded into sociable. "Oh, uh, yes. Got a big day tomorrow, with Dr. Gordon's surgery and all. Well, you obviously know that."

"Yeah, I'll be leaving shortly, too."

Hmm, he'd said "I'll," not "we'll." Stop it. Don't continue to be a fool. "Well, good-bye, then. I'll be ready with the cryostat bright and early. I promise to get those frozen sections cut, stained and read in record time."

"I'm sure you will. Well, listen, I just wanted to make sure you knew how stunning you look today. I could hardly take my eyes off you."

Was he saying this right in front of Yuri? What was with men these days? But Yuri smiled up at him approvingly.

"Well, thank you." Her head was officially spinning with confusion. "I guess." She glanced at Yuri again, who continued to smile. "Good-bye now."

Jackson grinned and nodded and let her leave with a wad of conflicting thoughts clumping up her brain. What was going on?

Once she hit the street and got some fresh air, she inhaled deeply to clear her head, then gave herself a stern talking-to. *That's what I get for letting a man get under my skin. I should know better!*

On Monday morning Charlotte came into work early, hoping to see Dr. Gordon in the hospital before he'd been given his pre-op meds. Unfortunately, he already had, but he wasn't yet so out of it that he couldn't squeeze her hand and give her a smile and a thumbs-up as they rolled him from his hospital room toward surgery. His slightly intoxicated grin nearly broke her heart.

The vision of him stripped down to a bland hospital gown, with a little blue "shower cap" covering over his abundant white hair, lying on the narrow gurney as the transportation clerk pushed him toward the elevator, made her eyes blur and her chest squeeze. It also brought back sad memories of seeing her mother in the same position years ago, and reinforced why she'd chosen the safety of the isolated pathology department to the hospital wards after medical school.

To distract herself, she stopped at the cafeteria and bought a large coffee, then headed to the basement to her department, where she'd double-check the cryostat before Dr. Gordon's first specimen arrived.

Jackson planned to send down from surgery a sentinel node for her initial study, and depending on her findings, they would proceed from there.

By eight-fifteen the OR runner appeared in her lab with the first node from Dr. Gordon. The specimen came with exact directions as to where it had been resected and she made a note of that with a grease pencil on the textured side of the first of several waiting glass slides. She carefully put the specimen in a gel-like medium and placed it in a mold for quick freezing in the cryostat. She helped the process along with special fast-freeze spray, then within less than half a minute mounted the fully frozen specimen on the chuck and set up the microtome to her exact specifications.

After dusting the initial cut away from the blade with a painter's brush, she made the next cut and got the full surface of the node on the microtome then pressed her labeled glass slide to pick it up. She used H&E stain for immediate results since the hematoxylin and eosin stains worked best for her purposes, then placed a coverslip.

Whisking the now stained slide to the lab microscope, she began her study, and soon her hope for a benign node was dashed. Within five minutes of receiving the first specimen, she had to report the bad news over the intercom that connected surgery to her little corner of the world. The protocol was not to get into histologic details with frozen sections, instead sticking to a "just the facts, ma'am" approach.

"Dr. Hilstead, this is Dr. Johnson reporting that the first lymph node is positive for metastatic cancer." The words tangled in her throat, and she had to force them out, refusing to let her voice waver in the process.

"I see," Jackson replied. "I'll proceed to the next lymph node. Stand by."

"I'll be here."

Jackson continued with abdominal lymph node dissection, and she dutifully and quickly made her cryosurgical cuts and examined each and every specimen under the microscope, tension mounting with each specimen. The head of histology poked her head in the door, wearing a sad expression. Word soon spread in the small laboratory section about Dr. Gordon. Charlotte worked on in silence. After three positive-for-cancer lymph nodes, her voice broke as she reported, "This one is also positive."

A lab tech standing silently behind her in the tiny cryostat room moaned and left, grabbing a tissue on the way out. Dr. Gordon was well liked by his staff because he treated everyone decently, and in Charlotte's case, taking her under his wing and mentoring her when she'd been a green-behind-the-ears pathologist. She owed so much to him, yet all she could do today was be the bearer of bad news on his behalf.

There was no hiding the fact her findings were tearing her up, and her favorite surgeon must have felt compelled to console her. "We're almost done here, Charlotte. Just a few more, I promise."

"Of course." She recovered her composure, knowing the entire surgical team could hear her over the intercom. "I'll be here, Doctor."

And so it went until they found a benign node after six specimens.

* * *

Early afternoon, stowed away in the comfort of her dark office, studying yesterday afternoon's surgical slides, Charlotte sipped chamomile tea. With her heart loaded down with emotions, feeling like a brick around her neck, it would be a long day that she'd just have to force herself through. She'd had plenty of experience willing herself through days at a time, beginning as a teenager and more recently two years ago after her surgery had been done and she'd had to deal with the reality of her decision. She'd stripped herself of part of her female identity and hadn't yet figured out how to move forward. Derek's reaction the first time they'd made love after surgery, his expression when he'd seen her, would forever be tattooed in her mind.

A light double tap on her closed door drew her out of the doldrums she'd been intent on wallowing in. "If it isn't important, I'd rather be left alone." She went the honest route, hoping the staff would understand, especially since they all seemed to already know about Dr. Gordon's diagnosis.

The door opened, and Jackson, ignoring her request to be left alone, stepped inside. He was still in OR scrubs, his wavy hair mostly covered with the OR cap as he closed the door behind him. "I thought you could use a friend right about now."

Not giving Charlotte a chance to respond, he walked to her desk, took one of her hands and, finding little resistance from her, pulled her to standing like a reluctant dance partner, then into his arms. He hugged her tightly and sincerely and the warmth washed over her like a comforting cloud, all soft and squishy, with every surface of her skin reacting to his embrace in goose bumps. Yes, she did need this, and Jackson had no idea how much it meant to her.

They stood together like that for several moments, her breathing in his scent and finding it surprisingly not sterile-smelling at all, even though he'd just come from surgery. She leaned into his solid body, enjoying it, knowing this was a man she could literally lean on. One of his hands wandered to her hair, as if unable to resist the opportunity to feel it. She liked that he was so obvious about it, and smiled against his shoulder.

Before standing in the dim light and holding each other became awkward, Jackson spoke. "Chemotherapy can work wonders these days. I've already got Marv Cohen working on Jim's case, and I feel that already shifts the prognosis into a more positive direction."

Who was he kidding, trying to cheer her up? He was talking to a pathologist. She was a doctor from the end-of-the-road department where patients wound up after all the great medical plans hadn't panned out. The thing that hurt was that she knew Dr. Gordon himself had taught her to think that way. "We have to be realistic, Charlotte," he'd say. How would he feel when he woke up and got the news?

With all her dreary thoughts, she appreciated Jackson's desire to make her feel better. But this fight wasn't about her, it was Jim Gordon's to fight, and she promised she'd do everything in her power to help him. "I'll read the slides first thing in the morning, and report directly to Marv, after you, of course, so he can come up with a magic potion and stop this mess." *No matter what,* her mother had insisted to the very end, *don't lose hope.* Becoming a pathologist had made her cynical.

"I'm sure you will." His hands slid to either side of her face, fingers gently cupping her ears. Then he studied her eyes. She'd never been this close to him before, and loved looking up into his angled features and, in her opinion, handsome face, into those often world-weary eyes. Distracted by the thickness of his eyelashes, she didn't see what was about to happen until his mouth lightly kissed hers. Surprising herself, she let him, relaxed and enjoyed the feel of his lips pressing on hers. This kind of comfort she could get used to really fast.

But wait. This couldn't happen! It meant things, like getting close to another human being again. A man. Which could lead to, well, sex. Which wouldn't happen because once Jackson found out about her surgery and the fact she'd stripped herself of many a man's favorite playground, the breasts, he'd be like Derek. Not able to accept her as she was—still a woman, but scarred and different.

The pain from Derek's walking away had sliced too deep.

She ended the kiss, not abruptly, just not allowing it to go any further. She prepared a quick cover, with a single thought planted in her head since yesterday. "Didn't I see you with Yuri yesterday?" By his confused expression, it seemed like she had the perfect antidote to stop this kiss cold.

"You did. I was doing her a favor."

Charlotte was very aware that even though they were no longer kissing, he hadn't let her out of his arms. "A favor?" Did he really expect her to believe that line?

"She's got a thing for Stan Arnold."

"The head of the medical lab?" Trying to picture petite Yuri with tall, gangly Stan made Charlotte smile.

"He would be the one. Apparently she's had a thing for him for years, and recently found out his wife had dumped him. So she cooked up this plan to make him jealous."

"I don't remember seeing Stan at the party yesterday."

"That's the joke. Yuri sets up this elaborate plan, me pretending to be her date, and the guy doesn't show up." He smiled and shook his head. "She's got it bad."

"I guess I shouldn't listen to everything Antwan tells me."

His eyes widened, as if amazed she'd listen to *any-thing* Antwan said, let alone everything. "Like what?"

"That you're a ladies' man, and you've dated a lot of women from St. Francis."

An odd look crossed his face. "Not at all true. I've had only a couple of dates since I've moved here, no one from the hospital, and once they got to know me, neither lady bothered to stick around." What was he telling her? Was there a Mr. Hyde to his charming Dr. Jekyll? Before she could delve into that loaded statement, Jackson spoke again. "And by the way, I noticed Dr. Dupree hanging around you a lot yesterday. If you hadn't already told me you don't have anything going on with him, I might have thought you were there together." He'd expertly changed the subject.

"Oh, no! I hope no one else thought that." She was well aware of still being in Jackson's arms, and was also dying to know if she'd made him feel jealous yesterday, even though she knew it was pointless, just a little ego bump.

"I don't really care what anyone else thinks, but *I'm* relieved." He kissed her again, this one far from a comfort kiss and sending shivers dripping down her spine. If she'd had any doubt about his interest before, he'd sure proved her wrong now. This kiss felt intimate, like they kissed like this every day, and she liked it. Kissing Jackson shut down her never-ending thoughts and questions, allowing her to stay in the moment and enjoy the soft yet persistent feel of his lips on hers. At first he kissed like a gentleman, but something she did—she'd got carried away and opened her mouth and pushed her tongue between his lips, to be exact—had fired him up. She reeled with the feel of him getting a little wild with the kisses because of something she'd set off. How long had it been since she'd done this to a man?

As his mouth worked down the side of her neck, finding many of her trigger points and setting loose chills, his hands began to wander over her shoulders and down her arms, soon skimming the sides of her chest down to her waist and back up. As much as she was enjoying everything, he'd moved into "the zone" and it shocked her back to reality.

This can't happen. Not here. Not now. Not ever?

She pulled herself together and stepped back, letting him know they'd crossed a line for which she wasn't ready. She searched for and found her voice, barely able to whisper the words. "Though this is really nice, it probably isn't the best way to work out my concerns for Dr. Gordon."

"Seems like a pretty damn good replacement, though." Jackson, like the perfect gentleman that he usually had been until about five minutes ago, took a second to pull it together. "I'm pretty sure Jim will be out of Recovery by now. Want to go visit him with me?" It had been spoken as if nothing monumental had just happened between them, like he kissed women in their offices all the time.

"I'd love to." She'd also love to continue kissing him, but only in her dreams could she have what she really wanted from Jackson. Just like the reality of Dr. Gordon with metastatic cancer, some things weren't easily worked out.

With more questions about Jackson than she'd ever had before, and a boatload of mixed-up feelings, both mental and physical, for him, she still managed a daring last kiss. She'd call it a gratitude kiss. Granted, it followed a quick hug of thanks and was only a buss of the cheek, but at least it was something.

After graciously accepting her parting gift, and searching her stare for an instant, he headed for the door and she followed him toward the elevators for the post-op ward.

Something significant had happened between them. Figuring out what it meant would be left for another time.

Before just now, never in her wildest imagination could she have seen that kiss coming.

Dr. Gordon's eyes were closed. The head of the hospital bed was elevated slightly, and the white over-starched sheets seemed to bleach what little color he had from his face. Oxygen through a nasal cannula helped his shallow breathing. The sight of her mentor looking so vulnerable made her stomach burn. She took his hand, the one with the IV, and his eyelids cracked open. He needed a few seconds to focus before he smiled.

"Hello, Jim. Glad to see you survived surgery," Jackson said, as if he'd had nothing to do with it.

"Yeah, some lunatic tried to kill me today." His gaze shifted to Charlotte rather than look at Dr. Hilstead any longer, and his tough facade softened as he did.

"How're you doing?" She could hardly hear herself.

"Besides feeling like I've been shot with BBs in my gut, okay, I guess."

"When was the last time you had pain medicine?"

"I lost track of time a while ago. I'm supposed to push this." He nodded toward the medicine dispenser attached to his IV pole, which allowed the patient to regulate pain control on the first day post-op. He pressed it. If enough time had passed since the last dose, he'd get more now, which of course would put him back to sleep.

"Can I give you some ice chips?"

"Sure." He let her feed the ice to him from a plastic spoon, and it struck her how over the past few years he'd spoon-fed her knowledge as her mentor. Helping now was the least she could do. She found a pillow on the bedside chair, fluffed it and exchanged it for the flattened one behind his head, just like she'd learned to do with her mother. He groaned with the movement but let her do it.

Their eyes met briefly. Appreciation, with flecks of hard-won wisdom, conveyed his thoughts. Jackson had probably already talked to him about the findings, and Dr. Gordon had assigned her to the frozen sections for the surgery. They all knew the outcome. There was no point in bringing it up.

She tried to keep sadness from coloring her gaze as they shared a sweetly poignant moment, almost like father and daughter. Emotion reached inside her and gripped until her throat tightened and she feared she'd start to cry. She inhaled as reinforcement. "You probably feel like sleeping."

He let her use the excuse, squeezed her hand one last time and let her go. "Thanks for coming by."

"I'll be back later, okay?"

He nodded, snuggled back on the pillow and shut his eyes again.

Jackson guided Charlotte at the small of her back from the bedside out the door to the nurses' station. "He knew before going in what the likelihood was of his having mets."

She hated this part of her job, verifying the worst outcome. Seeing her mentor's tired face just now, looking nothing like the strong head of the department she'd always looked up to, had knocked some of the air from her. She gulped and the swelling emotions she'd tried to ward off with little bedside tasks took hold. Her eyes burned, and her chest clutched at her lungs. Memories from nearly twenty years ago threw her to the curb, and she broke down.

Jackson swept her under his arm and walked her to

a quiet side of the ward, back near the linen cart. "Let's go get a cup of coffee, okay?"

Trying her best to get hold of her runaway feelings, she nodded and swiped at her eyes. He handed her some nearby tissues, and she used them. Then, with his arm around her waist, he led her back to the elevator, which they had all to themselves.

"I didn't realize how close you are to Jim."

"He's been like a father figure to me. I lost my mother to breast cancer when I was fifteen, and my dad a few years after that. Dad just couldn't go on without her, I guess. I still miss them." Jackson's grasp tightened around her arm. "Dr. Gordon pretends he's an old grump, but I knew the first time I met him that he was a teddy bear. I guess I let him step into that vacant parental role. I don't know what I'll do—"

"Don't go down that path. We've got a lot of options at this point."

She nodded, further composing herself in preparation for their exit from the elevator. "My mother's missed diagnosis and subsequent illness was the reason I went into medicine and pathology."

"I wondered why a beautiful woman like you had chosen that department."

His honest remark helped lighten her burdens for the moment, and she smiled. He thought she was beautiful? "Do you think I'm ghoulish?"

It was his turn to grin, which definitely reached his eyes, and he laughed a little, too. "I can safely say you and that word have never come to mind at the same time."

"Whew." She mock-wiped her brow. "Wouldn't want to make the wrong impression." *Because I really like you.*

They entered the cafeteria and, taking the lead, he grabbed a couple of mugs and filled them with coffee, after verifying with caffeine or not for her. Then he picked up a couple of cookies on a plate, and after he'd signed off on the charge, they went to the doctors' seating in a smaller and quieter room than the regular cafeteria. Leading the way, he chose a table and removed the items from the tray then waited for her to sit before he did. Yeah, a take-charge gentleman all the way.

"You feel like talking more about what tore you up back there?" He got right to the point.

She inhaled, poured some cream into her coffee and thought about whether or not she wanted to revisit those old sad feelings about her parents any more, and decided not to. "I'm good. Just worried about Dr. Gordon."

He reached across the table and squeezed her hand. "I understand."

She hoped her gratitude showed when their gazes met. From his reassuring nod she figured it did. She accepted a peanut-butter cookie and took a bite. "Mmm, this is really good."

He picked his up and dipped it in his black coffee before taking a man-sized bite. His brows lifted in agreement. "So," he said after he'd swallowed, "since we're going to change the subject, I have an observation. I'm thinking you might be dating someone?"

Her chin pulled in. "Why would you think that?" Hadn't they been making out in her office earlier?

"You put a quick stop to our…" He let her finish the sentence in her mind, rather than spell it out.

She lifted her gaze and nailed his, which was, not surprisingly, looking expectant. He was definitely interested in her, which caused thoughts to flood her mind. She'd gone through a long, tough day already, and it wasn't even two o'clock. She'd once again seen firsthand how things people took for granted, like their health, could change at any given moment. It made her think how much more out of life she longed for. Shouldn't she grab some of what it had to offer, especially when it, or rather, he, was sitting right across from her, dunking his cookie like it was the best thing on earth? Instead of day in and day out spending most of her time with the biggest relationship in her life, her microscope?

But would Jackson want her as she was? Admittedly, she'd always been proud of her figure, never flaunting herself too much but not afraid to show some cleavage if the occasion and the dress called for it. Now every day when she showered she saw her flat chest, the scars. There wasn't anything sexy about that. Yet she was a woman, lived, breathed and felt like a woman, but one who strapped on her chest the symbols of the fairer sex every day before she came to work. Pretending she was still who she'd used to be.

The decision had seemed so clear when she'd made it. Get rid of the tissue, the ticking time bomb on her chest. Never put herself in a position to hear the words that had devastated her mother's life. *You have breast cancer.*

Because of lab tests and markers, she'd thought like a scientist, but now she had to deal with the feelings of a woman who was no longer comfortable in her body.

Then there was tall, masculine and sexy-as-hell Jackson sitting directly across from her, smiling like he had a secret.

She bet his secret was nowhere as big as hers. "You took me by surprise earlier."

"I took myself by surprise."

She liked knowing that the kiss had been totally spontaneous. "So, since you asked, I'm not seeing anyone. Today's just been hard. That's why I—"

"I understand." His beeper went off. He checked it.

"Let me know when you're leaving later and after we pop in on Jim again I'll walk you to your car."

It wasn't a question. She liked that about him, too. "Okay."

Except later, when Jackson walked her to her car, after visiting the hospital and finding Dr. Gordon deeply asleep and looking like he floated on air, Jackson reverted to perfect-gentleman mode. No arm around her shoulder or hand-holding as they walked. Whatever magic they'd conjured earlier had worn off. He simply smiled and wished her good night, told her to get some rest, more fatherly than future boyfriend material, and disappointingly kept a buffer zone between them as she got into her car.

As she drove off, checking her rearview mirror and seeing him watch her leave, his suit jacket on a fingertip and hanging over his shoulder, looking really sexy, she wondered if he'd had time to come to his senses, too. Something—was it her?—held him back. Then, since she knew her secret backward and forward, and how it kept her from grabbing at the good stuff in life, she further wondered what his secret was.

CHAPTER THREE

JACKSON TOSSED HIS keys onto the entry table in his West-lake condo, thinking a beer would taste great about now, but knowing he'd given up using booze as an escape. It had cost what had been left of his marriage to get the point across.

A long and destructive battle with PTSD had led to him falling apart and quitting his position as lead surgeon at Savannah General Hospital just before they'd planned to fire him three years ago. The ongoing post-traumatic stress disorder had turned him into a stranger and strained his relationship with his teenage sons, frightening them away. It had also ensured his wife of twenty years had finally filed for divorce.

He'd lost his right lower leg in an IED accident in Afghanistan. It had been his second tour as an army re-servist. He'd volunteered for it, and for that his wife had been unable to forgive him. She'd deemed it his fault that the improvised explosive device had caused him to lose his leg. He'd returned home physically and emotionally wounded, and, piled onto their already strained marriage from years of him choosing his high-maintenance edu-cation and career over nurturing their life together, she couldn't take it.

His fault.

Their marriage had been unraveling little by little for years anyway. High-school sweethearts, she'd then followed him on to college. His grandfather used to tease him that she was majoring in marriage. Then they'd accidentally got pregnant the summer before he'd entered medical school. With their respective families being good friends, there was no way he could have let her go through the pregnancy alone. So he'd done the honorable thing and they'd got married right before he'd entered medical school.

It hadn't been long before they'd realized they may have made a mistake, but his studies had kept him too busy to address it, and the new baby, Andrew, had taken all of her time, and, well, they'd learned how to coexist as a small family of three. In his third year of medical school she'd got pregnant again. This time he'd got angry with her for letting it happen when he'd found out she'd stopped taking birth control pills. Evaline had said she wanted kids because he was never around. And so it had gone on.

Then at the age of twenty-seven and in the second year of his surgical residency, he'd signed up for the army reserves. One weekend a month he'd trained in an army field medical unit, setting up mobile triage, learning to care for mass casualties. When he'd finished his surgical residency and had been asked to stay on at Savannah General, his wife had thought maybe things would get better. But he'd started signing on with his reserve unit for two-week humanitarian missions for victims of natural disasters at home in the States. Soon he'd branched out to other countries, and when he'd been deployed to Iraq, Evaline had threatened to leave him.

He'd made it home six weeks later in one piece, his eyes opened to the need of fellow US soldiers deployed in the Middle East, and also finally accepting the trouble his marriage was in. They seeked out marriage counseling and he'd focused on working his way up the career ladder at Savannah General, and things had seemed to get better between them. He'd stayed on in the army reserves doing his one weekend a month, catching hell from Evaline if it fell on either of his sons' sports team events, but he hadn't been able to pick and choose his times of service. They'd limped on, keeping a united front for their boys and their families, while the fabric of their love had worn thinner and thinner.

Then, after a brutal series of attacks on US military personnel, they'd needed army reserve doctors and he'd volunteered to be deployed to Afghanistan. He had been one week short of going home when the IED had changed everything.

His fault?

He'd come home, had hit rock bottom after that, then eventually had got help from the veterans hospital, and had spent the next year accepting he'd never be the man he'd once been and cleaning up his act. He'd been honorably discharged from the army, too. But the damage to Evaline and his sons and his reputation as a surgeon had already been done. She'd filed for divorce.

As time had passed his PTSD had settled down and he'd felt confident enough to go back to work. That was when he'd figured there wasn't anything for him back home in Georgia anymore. His wife had divorced him. His oldest son had wanted nothing to do with him. So since his youngest son would be attending Pepperdine University in Malibu, California, he'd sought employment in the area, hoping to at least mend that relationship. St. Francis of the Valley Hospital had been willing to give him a chance as a staff surgeon. With less responsibility, not being the head of a department but just a staff guy for a change, not having to deal with his ex-wife and her ongoing complaints anymore and enjoying the eternal spring weather of Southern California, his stress level had reached a new low.

Until today, when he'd had to tell his friend Jim Gordon some pretty rotten news—that he had metastatic cancer—and they both knew there'd be one hell of a battle ahead. Then, in a moment of weakness, seeing the distress Charlotte Johnson had been in, he'd let his gut take over and he'd moved in to comfort her. But it hadn't worked out that way, because he'd played with fire. He knew he'd thought about her far, far differently than any other colleague. That he'd been drawn into her dark and alluring beauty while sitting across from her, looking at patient slides, for the last year. Come to think of it, could he have been any slower? How long had he had a thing for her anyway? At least three-quarters of the last year, that was how long.

Could he blame himself for kissing her when she'd fit into his arms so perfectly, and she'd shown no signs of resisting him? Still, it had been completely improper and couldn't happen again because he wasn't ready to have one more woman reject him because his lower leg had been replaced with a high-tech prosthetic. Maybe it wasn't sexy, but it sure worked great, and he'd been running five miles a day to prove it for the last two years. In fact, he'd never been in better condition.

Ah, but Charlotte, she stirred forgotten feelings, that special lure of a woman that made him want to feel alive again. Something about her mix of confidence on the job and total insecurity in a social setting made him hope what they had in common might be enough to base a new relationship on. When he'd kissed her, because of her response, he'd got his hopes up that maybe she felt the same way. But she'd stopped the kiss and an invisible barrier had seemed to surround her after that. He'd pretended everything had been fine when he'd walked her to her car—he hadn't noticed her need to be left alone—but the message had got through to him. Loud and clear.

He wandered into his galley kitchen and searched the refrigerator, hoping there might be something halfway interesting in the way of leftovers. He grabbed a bottle of sparkling water and guzzled some of it, enjoying the fizzy burn in his throat. Today he'd kissed the woman who held his interest more than any other since his high-school sweetheart. That was the good news. The bad news was he knew he couldn't do anything further about it. Her invisible force field wouldn't let him through, and if that wasn't enough, his boatload of baggage held him back.

Out of curiosity, though, he did have one little—okay, monumental—test for Charlotte, one that would really determine her mettle before he totally gave up.

Saturday was the annual charity fund-raiser five- and ten-kilometer run for St. Francis of the Valley trauma unit. Charlotte had signed·up a while back and had forgotten to train for it, but she showed up anyway in support of the event. What they'd neglected to tell her was that this year they'd added zombies. Someone had got the bright idea to raise more money by getting employees to pay professional makeup artists, who'd donated their time for the event, to be made up as the undead. The sole purpose, besides getting their pictures taken, was to chase down the runners and tag them with washable paint, and hopefully improve some personal best times for some participants in the process.

Being a good sport, Charlotte ran with the five-kilometer crowd, squealing and screaming whenever zombies crawled out of bushes or from behind nearby trees, heading straight for her. She checked her sports watch. Out of fright she had cut her running time—well, the last time she'd run, which had been a month ago—by a couple of minutes at the half-way point. Impressive. Go zombies!

Running always made her think, and today was no different. Since Monday, with Dr. Gordon's surgery and the amazing kiss from Jackson, the man had been missing in action. He hadn't even shown up for their usual Friday afternoon slide show. Had the fact that she'd stopped him from kissing her the way he'd wanted been the reason? Or was her hunch right about him having his own reasons for keeping distance between them? She didn't have a clue, but one thing was certain—she missed him even though she felt safer when he wasn't around. Talk about being mixed up.

Oh, man, here came another small cluster of zombies, heading right for her and the group of three runners in front of her. The rules said that if a zombie left a red mark on you, you had to subtract thirty seconds from your final time. Even though she knew they weren't real, they still freaked her out. She shot into sprint mode and caught those runners up ahead, nestling herself in the middle of them as protection. She had no pride when it came to fear. They all screamed and swerved together as the slow-moving zombies up ahead got closer. They fanned out to avoid their zombie touch, especially if they carried red spray paint. She darted around another zombie, leaving the group of nurses behind and winding up running solo again, checking every bush and tree ahead for any surprises.

Soon things calmed down, so she slowed her pace and

relaxed, enjoying the early morning sunshine and mild temperature. If she kept up like this she'd actually have a shot at finishing the run.

Already having finished his ten-kilometer race and finishing in the top twenty, Jackson had doubled back, deciding to run the five-kilometer route, too. He wasn't kidding himself. He knew that doing the shorter run as well had everything to do with searching for Charlotte, because he'd heard through Dr. Gordon she'd signed up to run.

Up in the distance he saw a woman with long legs and rounded hips, wearing tight running gear, with a high ponytail swishing back and forth with each stride. Her lovely light olive-colored legs and arms helped make the call that, yes, it was undeniably Charlotte. She wasn't what he'd call a sporty type, but was fit for sure, though with full-figure curves, and in his mind she looked fantastic. Man, he'd missed her this week and really liked spying on her now.

He picked up his pace, realizing there was no hiding his big secret since he was wearing jogging shorts. He'd noticed the looks all morning from hospital employees as he'd sprinted by with his carbon graphite transtibial prosthetic, including a flex foot that looked suspiciously like the tip of a snow ski. Their interest in his running blade didn't bother him, he'd had to get used to it over the past couple of years, but that little yet monumental test he was about to give Charlotte—finally finding out what she'd think of his prosthetic and below-the-knee amputation—made his stomach tighten.

He hoped she wouldn't be like the only two women he'd dated since moving out West, neither of whom had been able to get past his missing leg. He'd once played the pity-me game and had lost his marriage and family, and since then had promised himself to never let it affect him again. So why was he so nervous now, jogging up behind Charlotte?

Well, here goes nothing. He lunged forward and reached out then grabbed her shoulder.

A hand grabbed Charlotte's shoulder. She screamed and nearly jumped out of her highly padded sports bra. Being so close to the finish line, would she be disqualified by a fake zombie bite?

With her heart nearly exploding in her chest, she turned to see how ugly the zombie who'd taken her out was. Instead she found a face that managed to take what was left of her breath away. It was Jackson's, and she wanted to throttle him!

"You nearly gave me a heart attack," she squeaked, soon forgiving him when she noticed those broad shoulders and the fit physique beneath the tight T-shirt, and how handsome he looked in the early morning sunshine, his hair damp and curling around his face from his workout. She smiled.

"Sorry, couldn't resist it." He slowed down his pace to stay with her.

"Well, I'm amazed I've made it this far without being attacked."

"I'll protect you."

Oh, how those amazingly masculine words put new spring in her step. She couldn't resist and took a quick glance at his shorts and those strong athletic legs. And, holy cow, the man had a prosthetic limb! And he ran like an Olympic athlete, with smooth, even strides and barely any effort at all, not out of breath in the least. He looked like a wounded warrior running on that shiny high-tech blade.

Her mind worked at laser speed. He usually came to her office wearing scrubs or street clothes. Once or twice she'd noticed his masculine arms, muscles that'd come from weights at the gym, but she'd never had the opportunity to see his amazing abdomen and those runner's muscled legs. Had she mentioned, holy cow, that he had a below-the-knee amputation on the right?

That explained his slightly unusual gait.

So her crush for the better part of a year had been on a man who had more in common with her than she could have ever dreamed! They were both missing something. The next question was, why had he grabbed her just now, obviously slowing down his pace to run with her?

It had to be because he liked her, too. Hadn't he proved it Monday afternoon when they'd hugged and kissed? The fact that he'd stayed far away from her and her department ever since, so very unlike him, had made her think differently and had proved he had reservations about starting a relationship. Welcome to the club, buddy. At least now she understood why and it didn't hurt so much that he'd been avoiding her. But it scared her, and not in a zombie-chasing way but much deeper. Because it was as plain as the sun right there in the sky making her squint. This. Was. A. Test.

She took another glance at his leg, more blatant this time, keeping her expression blasé, and making sure he noticed. Then she acted like there was absolutely nothing unusual about him.

He gave her a relaxed smile. She noted relief in his gaze, letting on how much he appreciated her casual acceptance of his amputation. Yeah, her mind was spinning out of control in record time with thoughts and deductions, but she couldn't help it. This was such a surprise. And it leveled the playing field, which sent a shiver across her skin, warm and damp from running almost five kilometers.

"So now you know," he said matter-of-factly, sounding like it was a challenge.

Think fast for the perfect answer, because if there was ever a time for the right words, it was now. She tried not to remember how cutting Derek's words had been to her the first time he'd seen her chest. *That's pretty extreme, Charl, and to think it wasn't even necessary.* Who was she kidding? It wasn't just what he'd said but the shocked, nearly horrified and unaccepting expression that had accompanied it. Pain radiated through her chest as all these thoughts and memories flashed past in less than a second. Think fast! *He's waiting for a response to his comment.* "That you're not perfect? I think I already knew that, Doctor, the day you said you didn't like my all-time-favorite chocolate bars."

He laughed, and she felt good about dismantling the bomb he'd expected to leave her with.

Then, like the fact he was missing part of a leg meant nothing, they forgot about it and ran on, Jackson prodding her along and scooping her away from another zombie attack as they closed in on the last half-kilometer mark. For someone who hadn't trained, she'd make sure to finish this race if it killed her, rather than let her new running partner down.

"I take it you run a lot," she said, having to gasp the words since she was so out of breath.

"It's the best stress reliever I know."

"Hey, Dr. Hilstead, isn't this your second time around?" one of the OR techs called from the crowd on the sidelines as they approached the finish line.

"I'm helping my friend be safe from the zombies," he shouted back.

"Wait, so you've already finished this race?"

"I ran the ten kilometers." He looked straight ahead, rather than rub it in with a self-satisfied look.

Yeah, I run five in my sleep. She mocked how she figured what his smug thoughts were about now, though using the last of her quickly disappearing breath. Now she'd have to finish this race even if she had to crawl over the line, just to save face.

He laughed again, and she was happy a guy who'd taken a big chance and shown the entire hospital his secret was in such a good mood. She hoped she'd had something to do with it, too, because she wanted to think the biggest risk he'd taken had been with her reaction. That would make her special, and she'd passed with flying colors. She hoped so anyway. Was she special?

"Got any steam left?" he asked. "Let's finish strong."

She understood the "let's" meant "her" and he wanted her to kick it up for the next several meters. Typical guy. Show him a finish line and he'd have to make a run for it.

She nodded, lying, and pushed into a sprint, well, her version of a sprint anyway—no hint of form, arms nearly flailing and her feet kicking up in a girlie run way behind her. But in her world she finished strong, simply because she finished!

He grinned and grabbed her shoulder again, this time not scaring the life out of her but guiding her to the SAG station for water and a banana. Her knees were wobbly, she gulped for air, and her pulse tore through her chest, but other than that she felt great.

"Good job, Dr. Johnson!" several of the hospital volunteers said in unison.

She wasn't able to speak just yet, so she smiled and

sipped some water to prove she was still alive. Jackson stood there grinning at her, his chest hardly moving, only a sheen of exertion on his skin. She, on the other hand, was sweating big fat drops, her sports bra with the "natural-looking" silicone padding nearly sliding out of place. He nabbed a towel from the volunteers' table and put it around her neck.

"Thanks." She could finally talk.

"You did great."

"You made me."

"Then I'm glad I found you."

Oh, the things she could imagine with that statement. *I'm glad I found you.* Wait, he'd been looking for her? Further proof he might be interested, and now that she'd passed the test, why not go for it? She'd finished the run, was now high on endorphins, or was it light-headedness from low blood oxygen? Who cared? She felt good right now, and she could talk again, so she decided to go for it. "Hey, you want to have dinner with me later?"

After all they'd been through together for the last few minutes—his surprise test, her passing it, his forcing her to excel at a sport she could honestly live without, her probably setting a new "slowest five-kilometer" world record, him acting proud of her anyway, and probably for many reasons—he hesitated.

Every part of his facial expression put on the brakes, and it took her aback. So she thought fast and covered. "I've got an autopsy to do later this afternoon, and I thought if you weren't doing anything around five, you might join me in the cafeteria for a quick and easy dinner? Nothing special or anything. No big deal." Had that sounded professional enough? It was nothing like a *date* date, just dinner with a running buddy who'd shown her his BKA for the first time today.

Jackson's mind wandered in a half-dozen different directions. Why was a great and attractive girl like Charlotte spending Saturday afternoons doing autopsies and offering last-minute dinner invitations? Hell, yeah, he wanted to spend time with her, but tonight was a rescheduling of his usual Friday night dinner and a movie with his son. He couldn't back out from that, they still had too much to work through, and things continued to be strained. But they were making progress. His son attending Pepperdine had been his main motive for moving to California in the first place. What was left of his family had to come first.

Reality clicked in. Tonight wasn't the night. His fascination with the lovely pathologist, who now knew about his leg, would have to wait.

"Can I take a rain check on that invitation?"

James, the near-to-retirement morgue attendant, was ready and waiting after Charlotte had showered and changed into scrubs. By the time she'd donned the gown, shoe covers, face mask and clear plastic face shield, plus two pairs of gloves, he'd already weighed the body and placed it on the stainless-steel gurney-style table, complete with irrigation sink and drainage trough. A large surgical table was nearby with the tools of her trade—bone saw, rib cutter, hammer with hook, scalpel, toothed forceps, scissors, Stryker saw and more.

A family had requested an autopsy on their loved one, a twenty-five-year-old man, who'd arrived in the hospital three days earlier with signs of a bacterial infection. The hospital had agreed to the postmortem examination to identify any previously undiagnosed condition that may have contributed to his death, and to pin down what bacterium had suddenly run rampant throughout his system.

As a clinical pathologist, not to be confused with forensics like people saw on TV dramas just about every night of the week, her job was to see for herself what may or may not have caused his death. Knowing that up to a quarter of performed autopsies revealed a major surprise other than the notated cause of death, over the next two to four hours she'd systematically examine the outside and inside of this young man's body to get to the best and most logical diagnosis.

James, her diener, stood by ready to assist with each aspect of the autopsy. Turning on her Dictaphone, Charlotte described what she saw externally. Then she used a scalpel to make a Y-shaped incision. Before her afternoon was done she'd weigh and measure every major organ, take systematic biopsies and place them in preservation solution. She'd also collect blood and fluid for laboratory specimens, snap pictures and preserve the brain in fixative for future dissection. She wondered what the zombies would think of her now.

James labeled as they went along and would, after the autopsy, submit all specimens to the histology lab for Monday, when they resumed their work week. Once the autopsy was complete, James would wash the body and make it ready for the funeral home.

Though the family might want and expect immediate results, like they'd come to expect on those infamous TV dramas, it might be an entire month before she'd have the final report completed. Autopsies needed and deserved the extra time to make the right diagnoses.

Her beeper went off. Ah, damn, it was Dr. Dupree. Since he'd called on her official hospital beeper, she answered.

"I need a favor," he said, before she could even say hello.

She'd grown to expect the worst whenever Antwan said he needed anything. "Yes?"

"They told me you're on call, and I just got an okay from a family for an autopsy. Can you do it for me tonight?"

"Tonight? Why the rush?"

"The family gave me twenty-four hours until they send their daughter to the mortuary. I need this favor, please."

She wasn't used to hearing sincerity in his voice. "When did the patient die?"

"Just now. I operated on her two weeks ago. Removed her appendix. Everything went great. Two days ago she was readmitted for loss of consciousness at home. Medicine was doing a work-up on her. She seemed to be fine. Then a nurse found her unresponsive in the hospital bed. She was already dead."

"Okay. Send her to the morgue. I'll tell James about the add-on."

"Thank you. I owe you a special dinner out."

"No, you don't. This is my job." Why was it that every time she spoke to Dr. Dupree her hackles rose? Because he was such a player, hitting on every woman in a skirt or hospital scrubs. But just now he'd shown a new side, genuine caring for a young patient who'd died of mysterious causes that may or may not have had something to do with the recent surgery. He was either being extra thorough or covering his backside... CYA, as the saying went.

For the sake of the family and the concerned doctor, Charlotte would do her usual thorough examination, and if she got lucky tonight, she might solve an unfortunate mystery.

Four hours later, having completed the long and complicated second autopsy, with strong suspicions that the young female patient had most likely died from an undetected brain aneurysm, she opted to shower in the doctors' lounge. It was nearly ten by the time she was dressed and ready to go home, but she decided to make a quick stop at her office first to call Security.

The elevator dinged as she unlocked the door to the pathology department, which was a few doors down from the morgue. She glanced over her shoulder in case it was Security, in which case it would save her a call, but out came Jackson. Though tired from a long day, her mood immediately lifted.

"Hi," he said, looking as surprised as she was. "I took a chance and got lucky."

"Hi, yourself. What are you doing here?" She unlocked the door and opened it. He followed her inside.

"I realized I didn't have your personal cell-phone number, and thought I'd see if you were still around so I could get it."

He'd come back to the hospital at…she glanced at her watch…ten-fifteen p.m., hoping to run into her? Sure, she was happy the man was pursuing her, but it also made her wonder about his dinner date. She gave him her number and watched as he entered it into his cell phone. Then he insisted she take his. A good sign.

"How'd the autopsy go?"

"I wound up doing two."

"No kidding. You must be beat."

"Yeah, it's been a long day, starting with getting chased by zombies and ending with, well, you know." Out of respect for the dead she always recalled the Latin phrase— *Hic locus est ubi mors gaudet succurrere vitae. This is the place where death rejoices to help those who live.* It was her way of reframing the tough job she did as a pathologist, especially when both of the autopsies she'd per formed tonight had been on young people, which always seemed wrong.

His hand came to her shoulder and lightly massaged. "Yeah, I know. It must be hard."

"No harder than what you do in surgery." She turned and looked up at him. Though he stood behind her, she got the distinct impression he might like to kiss her again, and admittedly, with that warm hand caressing her tight shoulder muscle, the thought appealed.

But he didn't. "You've got a point. Why don't I stick around while you do whatever you've got to do? Then I'll walk you to your car."

The rule at St. Francis Hospital was for every female employee—or any employee who preferred to be escorted, for that matter—to call Security after dark for the walk to the parking lot. Charlotte had used the service many times. In fact, it was the sole reason she'd come back to her office, to make the call and wait until a security guard arrived. Now she wouldn't have to.

"Thanks for saving me a call to Security. It usually takes twenty minutes for anyone to show up, so I was going to look at a few slides while I waited."

"I'll stick around if you still want to check those slides."

"To be honest, I'd really like to get home."

"Let's go, then."

As they walked, Charlotte couldn't let her question remain silent. "So how'd your evening go?"

"It was good. I had dinner with my youngest son, Evan—or Ev, as he prefers to be called these days."

Relieved that his mysterious dinner date had been with his son, she smiled. "You get together often?"

"Yeah, usually on Friday nights, but he had other plans last night."

So that was who he rushed off to every Friday afternoon. Her spirits kept lifting with each tidbit of information Jackson dropped. "That's great." And she really meant it.

He grimaced. "Well, we've got a lot to work out. The divorce was hard on both my sons but particularly on Evan. I've got to rebuild his trust, and we're getting there little by little."

She admired how much Jackson's family meant to him. It put him in a good light—a man who loved his family. The more she learned about him the more she liked, and the fact he had a BKA had zero impact on his appeal. If only she could trust that her situation would be as easily dealt with by him as his was for her. Unfortunately, her experience with Derek had set her up to expect the worst.

Sooner than she expected, because they always found conversation easy, he delivered her to the car.

"So thanks, and good night, then," she said, and as she unlocked the door and prepared to slide behind the wheel, he pecked her on the cheek. It surprised her, but in a good way, though she'd kind of wished for more and sooner than now.

"So I'll call you later, okay?"

"Sure." She grinned, enjoying being pursued by a man she was definitely attracted to. Maybe that was why the second part of her thought slipped out. "I'd really like that."

From the look on his face, he really liked that, too. Good!

Once inside her car, as she placed the seat belt over her shoulder and across her chest, her elation ebbed a bit. What was she thinking, acting like she was just a regular woman living a regular life, hoping to have a regular relationship with a new guy? That was ancient history for her—love, marriage, a career and family—a dream she could never achieve now.

Mindlessly, her hand brushed over her silicone pads. She was anything but regular.

But forty-five minutes later, when Charlotte was home and in her pajamas, Jackson didn't waste any time before using his newly acquired phone number. He said he'd called just to make sure she'd got home okay and to bid her good night again. She went to bed wearing a smile and thinking of his handsome face. Maybe taking a risk on a man like Jackson made perfect sense. Who could possibly be better than a guy with a BKA to understand her sense of feeling incomplete?

CHAPTER FOUR

MONDAY MORNING, CHARLOTTE visited Dr. Gordon, who was still in the hospital. He was undergoing aggressive chemotherapy and the oncological team decided it would be best for him to be monitored round the clock for the first couple of doses.

She put on her optimistic face, hoping her mentor didn't see right through her, since she secretly worried the therapy might be too little too late. Surprisingly, Dr. Gordon seemed in good spirits, and though the chemo had to be tough on him, he didn't complain.

Already Charlotte could see his hair and white caterpillar fuzzy brows thinning, the shine in his always inquisitive hazel eyes dulled. Memories of her mother losing her beautiful light brown hair nearly broke her heart, and how toward the end a raging fever had changed her mother's eyes to a glassy stare. At moments like these, the harsh reminders, she was glad she'd had the radical surgery to ensure she'd never have to go through what her mother had. Deep down she also knew there was no guarantee against cancer.

Charlotte fluffed Dr. Gordon's pillow, assuring him his department hadn't yet gone to hell in a handbasket, to use one of his favorite phrases, thanks to a few other pathologists pitching in along with her to cover for him. She gently replaced the pillow behind his head.

"I would expect no less, Charlotte," he said gratefully. "I only mentor the best and brightest."

His confidence in her skills had always amazed her, and right now a warm sense of fondness expanded to the limits of her chest as she made sure his call light was within reach and the pitcher of ice water was nearby. "Thank you," she said, fighting back the tears that always threatened whenever she was around him these days.

"No." He inhaled, as if continuing to talk would soon be a burden. "Thank you." He gave a frail squeeze of her hand and she leaned forward and kissed his forehead.

"Don't tell anyone I did that."

He winked. "It'll be our secret."

She smiled and quickly left because her vision was blurring and she didn't want Dr. Gordon to see her cry. No sooner had she stepped outside his room than her cell phone vibrated. It was Jackson. She headed for the elevator and answered.

"Have dinner with me," he said the instant after she answered. "We'll call it our rain check. I've found a great place in Westlake and it's no fun to eat out by myself."

Well, it wasn't exactly the most romantic offer for a date, but she liked it that he'd thought of her. "Tonight?"

"Got plans?"

"I've got extra work to clear out, what with Dr. Gordon being off, and—"

"Tomorrow night, then. We'll take a rain check on our rain check."

It only took a second to make her decision. "That should work. Sure, I'd love to."

"Great! I'll need your address."

The guy clearly wasn't big on chitchat. Did she want

him coming to her town house in Thousand Oaks to pick her up? If he was any other first date, or someone like Antwan, she'd insist on meeting somewhere. On second thought, she'd never consent to meeting Dr. Dupree anywhere! But this was Jackson Hilstead the Third, her secret crush, the one guy in the hospital who might possibly understand her fragile body image, because he'd fought the same demons. "What time?" she asked, after giving him her street address.

"Seven."

"That'll work."

She hung up, grinning, her mind whirring. She had a little over twenty-four hours to clear her desk, clean up her house and find something sexy but not too revealing to wear. She hadn't been this excited about going out with a man in a long time.

Now, if she could just ignore that insecure whisper, *He won't accept you as you are*, starting up in her mind and concentrate on enjoying herself on their first date. Her first date in...she couldn't remember when.

Jackson finished his Tuesday afternoon surgery early and made hospital rounds on his patients, updating the doctor's orders on some and discharging a few others. Feeling a long-forgotten ball of excitement winding up inside over the thought of dinner with Charlotte, he grinned all the way to his car. He'd take a long run as soon as he got home to work off the edge. He hadn't looked forward to getting to know a woman like this in a long time.

He'd dated a couple of different women over the last year in California when he'd been feeling lonely and had needed a woman's company. His self-image had taken a serious hit when he'd lost part of his leg. But then, he hadn't expected to get a divorce at the time either. And when it had become obvious that his two dates hadn't been ready for an imperfect guy, he'd stopped looking around, because the rejections only a few months apart and the subsequent effect on his ego had turned out to be major. He'd been in the prime of his life and the thought of being alone from here on out had sometimes been too depressing to consider. So he'd pushed his feelings down and had gone about his days working hard and trying to put things right with his sons.

And he'd hated to admit it wasn't enough. Enter Charlotte.

He'd always taken solace in the safe haven of Dr. Charlotte Johnson's office. Reading slides with her had turned into his one indulgence with the opposite sex in the last year. He liked sitting close enough to notice whatever new perfume she chose to wear, and to catch the fire in her rich caramel-brown eyes whenever she found something interesting on one of his patients' slides to share with him. He liked it that she didn't lead with her sex, like so many other women around the hospital. They had it and they flaunted it, and it often made his basic urges get all fired up, which sometimes made it hard to concentrate.

Did a man ever grow out of that? He was forty-two, so apparently not.

But Charlotte was different. She had a fuller figure than many of the women at St. Francis Hospital, which he preferred to a woman being too thin, and though she dressed in a very feminine way, she was careful not to show too much skin. That made her interesting, and alluring in a far less blatant way than the others. Call it intriguing. But what appealed to him most of all was her no-nonsense personality. She clearly had her head on straight, and after the long, slow decline and eventual implosion of his marriage, when his wife had seemed to become his worst nightmare—granted, he'd turned into a nightmare of his former self, too—that was a welcome change. With a woman like Charlotte, maybe he could learn to trust again.

Was that asking too much?

Even the thought sent a shiver down his spine. Could he survive another rejection? Sure, she'd seen his leg and had acted as though she couldn't care less, and she'd accepted his dinner invitation, another good sign. But she was a nice woman who happened to be a pathologist and who'd probably seen it all in her job. Of course she wouldn't have let on if she'd felt disgust. He knew that much about her.

A memory of his wife finally telling him how much he repulsed her, even when he'd already known it, made his stomach burn.

He needed to make sure this date wasn't taken out of context. Yes, he wanted to get to know Charlotte more, see where it might lead, but there wasn't anything he could offer beyond that. He wasn't ready for anything else. Small steps. His policy was always honesty, so tonight he planned to put his cards on the table and see what she thought.

Keep things safe. Keep her at a distance. Protect himself.

He had to, otherwise he couldn't go through with the date.

Jackson picked up Charlotte at seven on the dot, fighting a swarm of jitters in his gut. Hell, he hadn't felt this nervous about a date since his high-school prom—and he'd taken his ex-wife as his date to that! *Man up, Hilstead. It's just dinner out. With a lady you can't seem to get out of your thoughts.*

He forced his best smile, even though he'd only made it to the security call box.

Once she let him through, he strode the rest of the way

to her town house, wondering if he'd made a mistake in asking her out. Maybe it was still too soon to get back in the game. Damn the nerves—how was he supposed to eat with his stomach all tied up?

Then Charlotte opened the door and blew him away. She'd worn her hair down, which always messed with his head. It waved and tumbled to her shoulders, framing her face and highlighting her warm and inviting eyes. Plus she'd dressed to kill in a cream crocheted lace dress with a modest neckline and cap sleeves. Her light olive-toned skin blended well with the choice. The only color in her outfit was from her rainbow-dyed strapped wedge sandals and bright red and orange dangly earrings. As it was early summer, she'd fit right in for the restaurant he'd chosen.

She smiled and let him in and he pretended he wasn't the least bit anxious about this date. He just hoped she didn't catch on.

Her earth-toned, stucco-covered townhome was built into the side of a hill along with dozens of others. The place had a nice view of the Conejo Valley sprawl, and he was impressed with her taste in decor. No overstuffed and patterned couches or chairs, her taste was modern, clean and almost masculine. Several canvases covered in bright colors highlighted a few walls, and he recognized the style as similar to many he'd seen in the hospital foyer after it had been newly remodeled. He vaguely remembered hearing that one of the employees had painted them, and these looked very similar in style. Seeing the paintings on Charlotte's walls, adding vibrancy to her otherwise beige palate, he wholeheartedly agreed with her choices.

But what he noticed most of all, and constantly since

stepping into her house, was her, and how fantastic she looked.

She'd grabbed her purse and was ready to leave, so he quit staring at the view from her living room—because the alternative was to keep staring at her, which he really wanted to do, but he didn't want to creep her out—then followed her out the door. He'd better think up some conversation or he'd be a total dud tonight. What was his plan? Oh, yeah, lay his cards on the table. Take control of the situation from the get-go. He could do it.

"Ever hear of a place called Boccaccio's?" he asked as they walked to his car in the building's lot.

"In Westlake? Yes. Wow, it's supposed to be really nice. Are you trying to impress me?"

"I should be asking the same question, seeing how great you look." She blushed and he not only liked how she looked, but the power her true response gave him. He could do this, have a date. "But don't get too impressed. Yes, the restaurant is right on a small lake and, yes, the view is great, but it's just a man-made lake in an otherwise landlocked city."

"Still sounds wonderful to me. I'll just pretend it's real. Can we sit outside?"

"I was planning on it."

She was tall and fit well next to his six feet two inches as they walked to his white sedan. So many things about her appealed to him, but he had to stand firm, let her know what he was and wasn't open to. Keep that arm's length between them, though after seeing her all decked out tonight, the thought was becoming less appealing. After they'd uncorked a bottle of wine and shared a meal together, maybe she'd understand why he needed to do things his way. He hoped so anyway.

Once they'd arrived at the restaurant, having talked

about work and Dr. Gordon the entire drive over, his unease had settled down somewhat. As it was a Tuesday night they didn't have long to wait to be seated outside. It was twilight, a gorgeous summer evening, and the small lake was tinted with a peach hue as the sun said goodbye for the day. There really was something special about Californian sunsets. Charlotte was impressed, he could tell by the bright expression on her face, and how she craned her neck to take in the view from every angle, and he thought it was cute. The choice of word struck him as odd for a woman who was so much more than cute, but something in the way she crinkled her nose with delight over her surroundings put it in his head.

"I've heard good things about this place. Now I understand why."

"The food is supposed to be as good as this view." So far his conversation had been stiff as hell. He ordered a bottle of a good sauvignon blanc with her approval, and they set about making their dinner choices. They ordered calamari, light and crispy, for starters to share. Next he ordered a salad and she lobster bisque. For the main, she chose baby salmon piccata, and he went for the Chilean sea bass. Then the waiter left and the sommelier poured their wine.

He sat back and relaxed in the comfortable woven wicker and wrought-iron chair, thought about stretching out his legs but realized he'd bump her with his prosthesis if he did, so he stayed sitting straight up. He glanced across the table at his date, who continued to enjoy the view of the small lake and the early evening lights around the shore.

Charlotte was his date. Wow, that was a new concept. She was pretty and so damn appealing, enough to shake him up all over again. She sipped her wine and he joined her. The sweet smile she offered him afterward warmed his insides far more than the wine. She could be dangerous. He took another drink.

"I should let you know that I haven't wanted to impress a woman this much in a long time." His honesty surprised even him.

She canted her head and gave a self-deprecating simper.

"But I've got to be honest, okay?" Build that wall.

Her intelligent eyes went serious.

"I've already told you I'm divorced, but you should also know it was a really bad one. So the thing is I'm looking for companionship, but I can't promise anything beyond that." *Oh, right, buddy, lay it on* her—*don't dare admit* you're *a coward.*

She didn't seem surprised by his opening statement, though he'd half expected her to be, and honestly, it did seem more like the opening remarks in a court of law rather than dinner with a great woman. "This is just our first date, so I'm on the same page."

Who was he kidding, trying to pull this off? What had happened to honesty? "I'm probably coming off like an ass, but I respect you too much to not be open." He leaned on the table, looked her in the eyes. "I'm not sure I ever want to get into a serious relationship again, not after what I've been through. I don't see myself ever marrying again, and I definitely don't want to be a father again."

She took another drink of her wine. "Hold on a second. Let's not get ahead of ourselves."

He had to laugh. He was jumping way ahead of a first date. "Yeah, I get that, but I think it's better to put it out there right up front." Wouldn't someone like her want the whole package, a career and a family?

"So now there are pre-dating rules, sort of like pre-nups? I guess I've been out of the loop awhile."

He laughed again, this time at how absurd he must have sounded. What a jerk he was being. Would she want to spend another second with him? He should have left well enough alone and never asked her out. But their kiss and the feelings she'd brought back to life for him had made him pursue her. Yeah, he still wanted that. He had to be honest with himself first.

Luckily the waiter delivered their starter and they spent the next minute or two distracted, sorting out sharing the appetizer. He took a bite and grinned over the taste of calamari done just right, surprised he could eat with the hard knot of nerves in his stomach. At least the food service was going well.

After she'd finished her part of the appetizer, she wiped her mouth and took another sip of wine. "I hear what you're saying, and that you're going out of your way to make sure I understand it. I get it. I know you've been there, done that, and you probably think I think my biological clock is telling me it's time to have babies." She swirled the half glass of wine round and round. "I'm thirty-four after all. So you figure you need to take the stars out of my eyes, not let me get any ideas. But I've also got reasons for not wanting kids. So don't worry about me getting any ideas about a long-term relationship. I'll be honest and say I like your company and I'd like to spend more time with you, but I don't plan to have children or, for that matter, get married either. Deal?"

Surprised she'd just released him from any future involvement, besides feeling relieved by her blunt answer, he wondered why a young and vibrant woman such as her would have ruled out marriage or having kids. Not with him necessarily, but with anyone. His laying his cards on the table had backfired, planting more questions in his mind than answers. "I wasn't suggesting we'd rush into anything."

"And I definitely don't want to rush into anything before I'm ready either."

If he had any question about what she'd been referring to before, he understood now. She'd like to date but not be intimate. At least, that was what he assumed her message had been. "I can understand that." Had he subconsciously been thinking about being intimate with her? Of course he had, but he'd already figured out he wasn't nearly ready for that. She'd probably read his mind and cut him a break. But, honestly, who in their right mind would want to get involved with him after all he'd just said?

Glancing at her in the evening light, with tiny decorative string lights in the background outlining her head like a sparkly crown, making her look even more beautiful, he wished he was ready to be with a woman again. Her.

"And just in case you're wondering, it has nothing to do with your leg." She interrupted his quickly shifting thoughts, and he was glad of it. She'd brought up his leg, or rather his missing leg, the elephant in the room. Good. "My hesitation comes from my side of things. For personal reasons. Though I do want to hear how you lost your leg, and anything else you ever feel like talking about." She reached across the table and touched his hand. "I really want us to be friends."

"Friends?"

"Let's see where that leads, okay? No pressure on either side."

He could live with that, if it meant he got to spend more time with Charlotte. "Fair enough."

Salad and soup arrived and Jackson poured another glass of wine for both of them. Since he figured they'd already ironed things out, he relaxed and enjoyed the company of a woman who turned out to be as witty and warm as she was great looking. But he'd already known that, and that was what scared the daylights out of him.

The words from an Adele song popped into Charlotte's head. She'd once played it over and over after Derek had broken her heart. *This man would never let her or any woman close enough to hurt him again.* Jackson was proving to be a true wounded warrior, right to the core. Keep her at a distance. Keep things safe. Take control right from the start. Very military or surgeon-like. And she thought she had a stick up *her* back. Whew. Jackson was hurting hard. She finished the last of her wine—he was driving after all.

But she still liked him, and could totally relate to what he'd suggested. Admittedly, at first when he'd started his spiel she'd thought, *Step away from the walking wounded. This guy is not for you.* But after savoring dinner and getting past the rule book, she'd enjoyed the evening out. He'd even opened up and told her how an IED had blown off his leg while killing two of his medical team and injuring a dozen others in the midst of performing surgery in Afghanistan. Maybe they could be good for each other. Why not give this a try? If he wanted safety and distance, in her current insecure state she was more than down with that.

When they arrived back home and he walked her to the security gate, he surprised her by stealing a kiss. She liked his surprises, and slipped right into the mood. He was a good kisser, and she liked putting her arms around his neck, leaning into him. Really kissing him. Close like this, could he tell her chest was different than real breasts?

Damn. She'd ruined the moment.

She dropped away from their kiss, seeing a hunger in his eyes that, to be honest, frightened her. What happened to safety and distance? His rules.

"Thanks for a great dinner and a lovely evening."

His waning smile was tinted with chagrin. "Thanks for putting up with me."

"I like you, Jackson. You get that, right?"

"I do, and despite the mess I made of things earlier, I'm really glad you do." He dropped his forehead to hers, the intimacy of the act seeming out of the boundaries of his dating playbook. "I like you, too." She didn't pull away, just kept her arms resting on his solid shoulders, gazing at his eyes up close. "You want to catch dinner together at the hospital tomorrow before you go home?"

An odd offer, but...

"Or we could go out for a quick meal."

Had he read her mind?

"I've got surgeries up the wazoo on Thursday, need to buckle down and mentally go over the procedures, get loads of rest, you know the drill."

"That you're a doctor with a busy and demanding life? Yeah, I think I do."

They smiled wide at each other again, standing there forehead to forehead, his hands warm and resting on her hips. "So dinner tomorrow?"

"Yes. I'd like that."

He kissed her once again, a quick parting kiss, but it was enough to send a flutter through her stomach. "Great. See you tomorrow."

As he walked away and she let herself into the building compound, she dealt with the warm and fuzzy feeling in her veins. Somehow, him laying down the rules had freed her. It might be okay to tiptoe into something with him. Who knew what could happen?

Because it turned out that she really liked that wounded warrior, Jackson Ryland Hilstead the Third.

For the next couple of weeks they kept their word and enjoyed each other's company at work and after hours several times, even spending the entirety of the last two Sunday afternoons kicking around together. Who knew running errands could be such fun? But because of what Jackson had proposed with their dating, and what she'd said about not being ready, they didn't sleep together. Never even came close. The amazing thing was, Jackson still wanted to hang out with her.

People at work began to catch on, giving knowing glances or making little comments to Charlotte. "I see you and Jackson are getting along." And "Was that you I saw having lunch with Dr. Hilstead for the third time this week?"

"You want to tell me what's going on?" The last remark came from Antwan Dupree. "Because I'm warning you, Dr. Hilstead is only trying you out for fun. If I were you I'd be careful not to get hurt."

"It's none of your business what I do." Was he for real? He'd come in here searching for a pathology report and had decided to lecture her on watching out for big bad wolves? He was the only wolf she knew. "Now, which specimen are you looking for a report on?"

He touched her arm, which in her book was a no-no, and she recoiled. "What I'm saying," he went on, unaware of how he'd turned her off already, "is that I'm for real." His cell phone went off and he took the call, having the nerve to carry out a brief conversation with "Baby," probably his current main squeeze, some OR nurse who didn't know any better. "I'll call you later, baby." He hung up, looked all earnestly at Charlotte and smiled.

The amazement on her face had nothing to do with his self-described—in her mind imaginary—charm. Check that. The appalled expression on her face. Did he have a clue about himself? She rolled her eyes in as big and overdone an arc as she could possibly manage to get her point across, in case Dr. Dense hadn't figured it out yet. "Mind your own business."

"I'm looking out for you, Charlotte. I'm just saying the guy's playing you. He'll drop you when he's done. Watch out."

"Your MO doesn't apply to every man, Antwan. Do me a favor and butt out of my personal life. It has nothing to do with you."

She gave him a quick report on the patient he was asking about and sent him on his way. But damn if her private insecurities about her body image hadn't flared up, letting the seed of doubt Antwan had planted about Jackson catch her off guard.

Yes, she did have continuing issues about believing any man would still want her once he discovered the truth. But Jackson seemed as reluctant as she was to take the next step. The truth was that over the last two weeks their make-out sessions had heated up and she wasn't sure how much longer it would be before she ripped off his clothes.

The attraction was definitely there for Jackson, too, if she judged rightly about certain body parts of his that had started becoming obvious in the last couple of kissing marathons. Wow. She longed to touch him, to feel the strength, the heat, but that would be playing with fire.

The man turned her on, often sending her home heated up and unfulfilled. How long could they keep this up?

She thought about him at night in bed, too, often imagining his sturdy body covering hers. Sometimes she'd touch her chest, running her palm across her scars, wondering what he'd think. Sometimes she'd fuel the fire of her imagination and let herself think about how it would be to feel him inside, bucking under him, or on top of him, taking him all in. How would he want to take her?

She was still a woman. Her breasts didn't define her. Her soul made her a woman. Would Jackson be able to get past her missing breasts and feel her soul if they ever made love?

She feared the answer, yet she imagined him panting on top of her; she dreamed about taking his weight and wrapping her legs around his hips so he could plant himself deeper inside.

Oh, yeah, she definitely wanted to rip off the man's clothes.

But the thought of the other half of that "ripping his clothes off" scenario—him seeing her completely naked—always sent her mind into a tailspin.

CHAPTER FIVE

JACKSON GRABBED THE pile of mail from his locked box at the condo building entrance and carried it into his apartment. It had been another long week, but spending a few evenings with Charlotte, plus looking forward to hanging out with her on Sunday afternoon, had made the grueling week completely tolerable. What more could he ask? He had a woman with a pretty face and an intelligent mind to look forward to being with soon. Actually, there was something more he'd like…

He shuffled through the mail, discovering an obvious—by the embossed gold foil envelope—wedding invitation from his cousin Kiefer. Aunt Maggie, his mother's sister, must be out-of-her-head happy. Then he thought of his own mother, who may have lost faith in him, and his mood shifted. He should call her more often.

The wedding was six weeks away in Savannah at Tybee Lighthouse. Hell, how many summers had he spent at the family beach house on Tybee? Too many to recall. Everyone had pretended not to mind the hot, sticky humidity while taking relief in the Atlantic Ocean. Mosquito-infested barbecues. Frantic capture-the-flag games after dark, which had inevitably turned into hide-and-seek scare fests. A smile crossed his lips again, remembering his younger cousin looking up to him like he was a god at fourteen. In fact, he sometimes wondered if Kiefer may have gone into medicine because of him. He sighed. Yeah, he had fallen far from that "god" title over the last couple of decades.

For one brief moment, a whimsical "what the hell" thought about going to the wedding and inviting Charlotte to be his guest nearly had him filling out the RSVP. Then reality forced him to think of the repercussions. His ex-wife, being a lifelong friend with his extended family, would most likely be invited. Having to face Evaline after a year, her still angry and feeling self-righteous. Facing his parents, Georgina and Jackson, the man he was named after. What about his still alert and oriented grandfather Jackson Ryland Hilstead the First? He'd be there, and so would the rest of his family.

How would it be to see them all again after leaving on such bad terms a year ago? It would be tough, for sure. To be honest, he didn't know if he was ready to handle it yet. Plus he didn't want his personal family drama to take away from Kiefer and…he glanced at the invitation to check the other name…Ashley's wedding.

His older son, Andrew, had sided with his mother. How much poison had she filled Andrew's head with concerning him? He understood—he hadn't been around as much as he should have when Andrew had been young. He'd failed him in that regard. But Andrew had zero empathy about his father falling apart from PTSD after his last army medical mission to Afghanistan, instead going along with his mother's opinion, insisting the loss of his leg had been his own fault for volunteering to go. Voluntary amputation, were they serious? The thought still hurt and angered him.

Jackson understood he'd scared people when he'd lost his grip on what was good and true and solid in life for those several months, but to blame him for losing a limb? He shook his head. At least he was making progress with Evan. Following him to Southern California had been the right move all around.

He set the invitation aside, not willing to say yes or no right away. Maybe he and Evan could make the trip together, and his son might act as Jackson's olive branch. He didn't want to write off all his relatives, but feared they may have already done the same to him.

Not wanting to slip into a funk over a simple wedding invitation, he thought about the gift of Charlotte. He'd practically blown any chance of getting to know her better on their first date, but she'd refused to be scared off by him. Hell, she'd even laid down a few rules of her own. He smiled at the memory. Spending time with a woman he liked and respected on so many levels had done wonders for his mental blues. She knew about his leg and it didn't seem to bother her in the least. Who'd have thought a pathologist would turn out to be warm and caring, not to mention easy on the eye? Now he grinned. She'd call him out in a heartbeat about painting all pathologists with such a broad brush. And that was what he liked about her, too. She didn't take his baloney.

Their make-out sessions had taken kissing to a new degree. Charlotte was responsive in every way, yet he sensed he couldn't cross an unspoken line, and so far he hadn't. As for him, he was definitely hot, bothered and ready for the next step. Sex! But Charlotte had been straight about taking their time the night he'd so brazenly laid out his terms for dating. *Don't dare think about marriage or kids.* As though he thought she'd been chomping at the bit to do just that. Maybe surgeons did have extra-big egos. So far she hadn't given any clear signals of change on the up close and personal level. He sensed something very private held her back, and he, of all people, needed to be understanding about that. But they'd been dating several weeks now and his dreams were growing more erotic by the night. Did taking things slow mean never?

There really was nothing worse than being forty-two, a father of two grown sons, an established surgeon, having a career that for the most part he could be proud of, still being well respected by his peers overall, and horny. Horny as hell.

He headed to the kitchen to grab a soda and digest the current state of his life. Wedding invitation. Possible trip back home. New woman. No sex. Yet. Maybe, if he remained patient, something about that last part might change.

Or was it time for him to take the lead?

Charlotte rushed to the skilled nursing facility where Dr. Gordon had been staying during his continued oncology care. She'd heard he'd be transferred off-site to another, smaller, extended care facility, which meant she wouldn't be able to pop in so easily anymore. They'd kept him far longer than usual in the hospital because the chemo barrage had wiped out his T-cell count, making him a sitting duck for infection and nearly killing him. He was stable now, staff member status granted, and they couldn't justify treating him as an inpatient any longer. She wanted to be there for him during this trying time, since his wife, Elly, had passed away and his son lived out of state.

When she arrived at his bedside, she found him smiling, which surprised her. Word was his treatment hadn't got the results the doctors had hoped for. Surely an intuitive and bright man like James Gordon knew the downward course of his prognosis?

"Hi." She tried her best to sound casual.

His milky eyes brightened at seeing her. "Hi, dear." Dr. Gordon had started calling her "dear" and the honor nearly tore her heart every time she heard it.

"So they're moving you to some swanky 'let's pretend this isn't a hospital' kind of place, I hear."

He chuckled. "Yeah, kind of like that place all the old actors go to die."

She flinched. "Please don't say that."

"Don't get your knickers in a twist, kiddo. I'm just being funny. You know my motto—life isn't about what might happen, it's about what's happening right here and now. Today I move. Personally, I fought with them, told them I can take care of myself. I don't see why I can't go home."

He was getting frailer by the day, and she'd heard he'd had a fall once and had almost fallen a second time but a staff member had caught him. If he were left on his own, he could wind up breaking something and making his situation worse.

"The bastards—pardon my French, but the medical insurance department ticks me off—say twenty-four-hour in-home care costs too much. I know they're lying. Hell, I'd even pay for it. I get I'm a risk to myself." He shrugged his bony shoulders. "So, I go, and I bid thee adieu." He touched his forehead as if lifting a cap.

She shook her head. "No. You can't say good-bye to me. I'm coming to see you at least twice a week."

"My dear Charlotte. The thing for you to know is I'm feeling good, no more fevers, and I continue to have high hopes of beating this blasted cancer. As crazy as it sounds, coming from a pathologist, I've decided to remain optimistic, to let my natural human spirit overtake the practical scientist inside. If they want to extend the treatment and move me to a smaller, cheaper medical facility, fine, I'll go. The only thing I resent is not having any say in the matter."

She wished she could take her mentor home with her—that she could request a leave of absence to care for him—but her job was to keep his department running and that, at least, could give him peace of mind. She held his hand and they sat quietly for a few moments until someone appeared at the door.

It was Jackson, and even now, after all the time they'd spent together, the sight of him made her pulse do a loop-de-loop.

"I wanted to come and say good-bye before they rushed you out of here. Damn hospital budget and all," he said.

"Yes," Dr. Gordon said. "You being a lowly staff surgeon wouldn't have an iota of clout, would you?"

They laughed together, Jackson being better at getting when a man was trying to be funny than she was. She could see past the thin facade of tough-guy banter, how Jackson cared for James, and the respect was mutual. The knowledge landed like a splat of thick, gooey warmth on her chest.

For the next several minutes they all sat around and chatted about anything and everything other than James's condition or his move. Which meant good old hospital gossip, the kind doctors enjoyed just as much as any other employees. Though Jackson did suggest there might be a good-looking nurse to ogle where he was going. That got a laugh, too. "I'm old but I'm not dead," he insisted. If there was such a nurse, he'd notice. He also wanted to know all about the pathology department, and had some suggestions for issues Charlotte had brought up before. She could tell he needed to feel useful, and she'd make sure he still knew how much he was needed as her mentor.

Two patient transfer attendants, a young man and woman, arrived in his room, and Charlotte and Jackson stepped aside as they packed up what little of James's personal effects were there, then got him on their gurney and carted him off to the waiting ambulance.

Charlotte and Jackson followed closely along until they were outside. She didn't care if it was inappropriate or not—she kissed James on the forehead and gave him a hearty hug before they could slide him inside. "I'll be in touch soon."

"I'll hold you to that." He patted her arm and she could tell he bit back a lot of emotion, so she stepped away to make it a little easier for him. And her. Soon the ambulance doors were closed and all she could see of her mentor was his chemo-ridden head with just a few remaining wisps of white hair through the small back windows. Her heart clutched and her eyes stung.

Once the ambulance had driven away, she let go of her tears. Jackson's warm grip on her shoulders gave her something to lean on. He turned her toward him and circled his arms around her. "You're a good friend to Jim."

"I think I've told you before he's my mentor, but in so many ways he's been a father to me these last few years."

"He's a good man."

"Yes. Just now he reminded me about something he says from time to time, and why I'd forgotten, I don't know. He said, 'Life shouldn't be about what might happen, it should be about what's happening right now.'"

The deep personal meaning of that statement, spoken the day she'd finally made her decision to have the radical surgery, plus the fact that James Gordon was the first and only doctor other than her personal surgeon to know, had made a deep impression on her. He'd told her that he didn't think she should spend her life worrying about getting the cancer that had killed her mother, and if the surgery could offer her peace of mind, then she should do it. Then he'd assured her she wasn't crazy for taking the matter into her own hands. Just now he'd admitted he wished he had more say in his own treatment, then just as quickly had told her he'd decided to remain optimistic about beating his cancer. His choice, and a good one.

"Sounds like a solid motto for a good life."

She nodded. "He blew me away, sounding so upbeat about his condition." She pulled back from his shoulder and looked up at him. "He said he's decided to be optimistic instead of thinking like a scientist. He intends to beat it from that angle."

Jackson squeezed her a tiny bit tighter. "Then let's do the same, be optimistic for him."

"Yes. That's good advice. My mother was hopeful until the very end. She was amazing." Oh, if she kept on with this line of thinking she'd be blue in no time.

"I've got an idea. What do you say we take a walk on the beach at Malibu? Then I'll take you to a funky but great little place Evan and I discovered a couple of weeks ago." Jackson must have read her mind about needing some serious distraction, and his suggestion sounded perfect.

"I'd love that, but isn't Friday your night with Evan?"

"He'll understand."

Before she could protest, Jackson had his cell phone in hand and speed-dialed his son. Because she needed and wanted his company, she didn't try to stop him.

"Oh," he said, returning the cell phone to his pocket and pulling something else from the other one, "I almost forgot this." He handed her a candy bar. Her favorite, a

Nutty-Buddy. "This should keep your blood sugar up until we eat dinner."

"How sweet of you!" This simple gesture proved his thoughtfulness and touched her more than she cared to admit. "Thanks. And the best part is I know I don't have to share it with you."

First dropping her car off back home in Thousand Oaks, they took the Las Tunas Canyon route through Agoura to the Pacific Coast Highway, and made it to the beach with plenty of daylight left. They parked and kicked off their shoes and walked a long stretch of sand, holding hands and listening to the waves crashing against the shore, while they inhaled the thick salty ocean air. They held each other as the huge-looking golden sun slipped bit by bit over the horizon, and Charlotte couldn't remember a sunset she'd ever enjoyed more. Because she was watching it with Jackson.

Then, as promised, he took her to a trendy though decidedly funky little hole-in-the-wall for a vegetarian meal complemented by organic pinot gris. Whatever they had done to the "green" wine, it tasted so good Charlotte decided to have a second glass. Why not? Jackson was driving.

Jackson wasn't being forward, but after dinner Charlotte seemed to have just begun to relax, so instead of taking her home, where she'd immediately start fussing about his needs, he decided to take her to his condo. Who was he kidding, calling it a condo? It was more like a glorified apartment, but it served his purpose, and since it was in Westlake, it cost a pretty penny for the privilege of living there. Why not show her how a new bachelor lived?

"So here's my place," he said, switching on the lights

in the living room. The curtains remained drawn along the sliding glass doors, and the air felt heavy, especially after being at the beach. He strode to the wall and pulled back the drapes then opened the sliders for fresh air, suddenly aware how nervous he felt, having her here. It was another warm and inviting early summer evening, without a trace of humidity, which always amazed him, and the light breeze quickly chased out the stuffy air. He inhaled, forcing himself to relax.

"Make yourself comfortable," he said, heading to the kitchen to open a bottle of wine. He hadn't ordered any with dinner, though Charlotte had raved about the organic "green" wine. His thoughts had been that tonight she needed to let go a little, and if enjoying a glass or two of wine was the way, he'd make sure she got home safely. He picked up two wineglasses by the stems and carried everything to the other room.

Charlotte had made herself comfortable on the small but functional gray linen upholstered couch overrun with brightly patterned pillows, which she'd pushed aside. The pillows were only there because that was how it had been displayed in the catalog. What did he know about decorating? That had always been Evaline's job. When he showed up back at the sofa, her amused expression changed to a wide smile. Combined with the light blush of someone who'd been enjoying her wine with dinner, the look was more than appealing. "You've been reading my mind a lot tonight," she said.

"I try." He opened the bottle of chilled chardonnay and poured them each half a glass. She sipped, and he joined her. "This is where I hang out when I'm not at the hospital." He wished he could read her mind a little more right now, but on the other hand, maybe he didn't want to know what had put that previously engaging gaze on her face. She was probably suppressing a laugh at his decorating skills, or lack thereof.

"Rented furniture?"

Okay. Maybe he had read her mind again. He dutifully nodded. Was it that obvious?

"Not bad, but it tells me you don't plan to stick around."

"I think I've told you that I came here to be near my son, and that was the extent of my plan. Oh, and then I found the job at St. Francis." He took another drink.

"And then you started showing up in my office." She quaffed more wine, looking self-assured. He liked it.

His eyes crinkled with another smile. The topic was starting to get good. Plus her attitude had taken a turn toward sassy. "That I did. There was a surprise beauty in that office."

He gave another half smile. She stared lightly at him. It made him think there was a lot going on inside her head right then.

"Did you have any idea how long I had a crush on you?"

So he'd been right about a lot going on behind that getting-more-relaxed-by-the-minute stare. "I thought *I* had a crush on *you*."

She sat sideways on the couch, one leg bent on the cushions, the other crossed over it. He faced her. With the tip of her now shoeless toe, she made contact with his knees. "I liked you from the first time I saw you, and I couldn't believe how interested you were in the slides."

"That's because I was interested in the person showing me the slides." He touched her, soon caressing her toes. She drank more wine, letting him have his way with her foot.

"I liked being in the dark with you, getting to test out whatever aftershave you threw on. You don't have a favorite, do you?"

He shook his head. Shrugged. He liked how she was opening up and he didn't want to stop her, so he kept quiet.

"I can remember the first time our knees touched. You inhaled and I thought it was so sexy. You realize how sexy you are, right?"

His brows shot up. This was really getting good. "Uh, I hadn't thought about that in a long time." Three years, to be exact. Since losing his leg.

"May I ask what happened to your marriage?"

Ah, damn, she'd pulled a quick one on him and changed the topic to something much less appealing, but Charlotte deserved to know the whole story. His version anyway. And, more importantly, he'd reached a point where he knew he could trust her with it. "Evaline was my high-school sweetheart, and she followed me to college. We got married sooner than I had planned. Actually, I wasn't even sure I was planning on it, but she, or rather we, got pregnant and, well, I did the right thing. We were parents at twenty-one, right when I started med school." He took a drink of wine, uncomfortable about reliving his past.

"Obviously, I wasn't around much, which didn't help things, but we muddled through. Two years later, she got pregnant again. I have to admit I was not happy. She'd stopped taking her birth control pills and didn't bother to tell me." He took another drink. "I'll be honest and say I kind of felt like she'd trapped me. Not very heroic of me, but I'm being honest with you."

"I can understand that. No judgment here."

"Thanks. She was the first woman I loved and I held on to that, and we just kind of kept moving forward. But when I signed on for the army reserve medical unit and was away from home a lot, I'd come home and feel distant. That's when I realized our marriage was in trouble. The thing was, she liked being a doctor's wife, and I liked being a surgeon, so at least we had that in common."

He tried to make light of it and even forced a laugh, but he glanced at Charlotte and saw understanding and empathy on her face, not sympathy. At least that was how he needed to interpret it. She reached across the couch and squeezed his forearm. *Keep going*, she seemed to say. "Fast-forward to my coming home from a second tour to the Middle East, this one voluntary, missing part of my leg and a total mental mess, and, well, I fell apart, and she fell apart, and so did our marriage."

An old lump of pain started radiating smack in the middle of his chest. He took a deep breath, feeling grateful to be here right now with Charlotte. He wondered about her, too. "And speaking of marriage, why isn't a fantastic woman like you married?"

Her brows lifted. She sipped from her glass, looking thoughtful. "I was engaged. I planned to have the American dream of a career, a husband, kids. We were all set for it, too. Then…" she slowly inhaled "…things changed." She stopped and looked at him. "Would you mind if we went back to talking about how much we like each other?"

So she didn't want to open up right now. Maybe it still hurt too much, and if anyone in the world could understand that, he could. "I'll start. Knowing I'll see you at work at some point every day makes me happy to wake up. I haven't felt anything like that in, well, a long, long time."

A sly smile crossed her full and kissable lips. "My turn?" He nodded, eager to hear what she'd have to say. "Your blue eyes are killers, and there's something about your almost curly hair that drives me wild."

He hoped she planned to come on to him because the compliments were making him hot. He took a draw from his wine then put down his glass on the nearby coffee table. Something told him if she kept on with this line of conversation, he might soon want the use of both hands.

"And you've been the highlight of my day more times than I can count. Even when I first started at St. Francis. There you were, sitting in the dark." He moved closer, took a lock of her thick brown hair and played with it. "You always seemed calm, maybe a little reserved, but it was a welcome change from all the type A personalities in my department. I always looked forward to seeing you. Always." He leaned forward, and having moved her hair away from her ear, he lightly kissed the shell. "I thought you were sexy but you didn't seem to know it, which made you all the more appealing." He nipped her earlobe then watched the flesh on her neck prickle. "Now that I know you better, you're driving me crazy."

She took a quick last sip of her wine and set the glass down. He couldn't help but get his hopes up that tonight might be the night. Soon after their gazes met and melded, planting a solid yes in his mind. He kissed her, pulling her closer. She settled into his arms and kissed more hungrily than usual. They were getting pretty damn good at this part. Making out. He deepened his kiss and a tiny moan caught in her throat. His me-man-you-woman switch clicked on and his needy hands roamed her shoulders and arms and soon slid over her waist and up to her breast.

She stiffened so noticeably he stopped kissing in order to look at her. This wasn't the first time it had happened. "Am I doing something wrong?" He spoke quietly, his version of tender. "If there's anything I need to change, tell me so I can fix it."

She shook her head, switching from the relaxed sensual compliment-giver of a few moments before to a cautious woman with glistening brown eyes. She glanced over his shoulder rather than look straight at him. A sense of dread seemed to hover around her. "You've heard me talk about my mother."

He nodded, and he knew the stats about breast cancer, too. Was that what held her back in life? The fear of getting cancer?

"On top of having the strong family history, I have the Ki-67 blood marker *and* the BRCA1 and 2 gene mutations, plus SNPs—single nucleotide polymorphisms."

So that was the rest of the story, and a tough one to accept for sure.

"Not good. Right?"

Still considering the stark reality of what she'd just said, he didn't answer right away, but he had to agree. The odds were against her. "Is that what stops you from getting closer?" Would she never let him, or anyone, into her life because of that?

She took a deep jittery breath, shifted her gaze to his hand, touching his fingers, playing with them. Every time she touched him he responded, and soon their fingers were laced together, his thumb rubbing along the outline of her palm. She worried her mouth. "So two years ago I had preemptive surgery, bilateral radical mastectomies without reconstruction." She may as well have blurted out there was a monster in the house—the sudden news felt as jolting.

He gripped her hand tighter as the realization of what she was telling him registered. This beautiful young woman had had her breasts removed to avoid being diagnosed with cancer in the future. As a surgeon, he knew exactly what she meant. He knew what unreconstructed mastectomy scars looked like. Hell, he'd given those scars to hundreds of women over the years. But most opted to have implants along with the surgery. From several of his own patients who'd taken Charlotte's route, he knew the sorrow the women went through afterward. Dealing with body image was always the toughest issue. Yet her surgery had been voluntary, and she'd made the choice not to have reconstruction.

It also became clear why her engagement had ended. The guy hadn't been able to take it.

So the natural curves on display in her clothes were thanks to that special bra he recommended to his own patients. It sure had fooled him. Now he understood why she always tensed up when he started exploring that part of her body.

He needed to make it clear that he wasn't that guy, the guy who couldn't take it.

He pulled her hand to his mouth and kissed it, kissed each finger and the inside of her wrist. He just wanted to love her, to ease her fears, to let her know that, though, yes, he was shocked, it didn't matter to him. His other hand caressed her neck. "If you're worried what I might think, I'm going to quote back to you what you told me Dr. Gordon said. 'Life's got to be about what's happening right now, not about what might happen.' And right now I want more than anything to make love to you."

She leaned into his hand, and his thumb traced her jaw and earlobe. He pulled her to his mouth and kissed her again, a long warm and sensual message he hoped would get through to her. But he knew she needed to hear it from him, to make sure without a doubt he understood.

"You have no idea how much it meant to me when you didn't react over my leg. I didn't see the look of horror in your eyes that I've seen before. And, believe me, there's no hiding it if it's there. I've seen people try." He took both her hands in his and squeezed them. "Look at me." She complied and he gazed gently at her. "So, of all the people in the world, I know how it feels to be insecure about an imperfect body." He kissed her once more to prove his point, to hold her near, feel close to her again, hoping he was getting through. She seemed to welcome his kisses, as she always did. His hand slid to her shoulder and upper arm again, where he held her firmly.

"Charlotte, I've been fortunate enough to have lots of time to get to know you and you should know that I think you're a beautiful person both inside and out." A light ironic laugh puffed from his mouth. "Hell, I'm the perfect *imperfect* person to be with you tonight. But only if you want it." He could only hope his expression and invitation looked and sounded as sincere as he truly was.

Her hesitant, dark and worried eyes relaxed the slightest bit. Her hands moved to cup his cheeks as a look of deep gratitude crossed her face. Her fingers felt cold, nervous. But there was something more in that gaze, some kind of promise, or was it blatant desire, like he felt firing up again inside. She leaned forward and kissed him, lightly at first, then released all the passion she must have let build during his confession. Because that kiss soon morphed into a ravenous need to be close, to feel, to excite and take.

To make love with him.

CHAPTER SIX

JACKSON HOPPED OFF the couch and began searching through cabinets and drawers, leaving Charlotte confused. Had she turned him off? She'd thought she'd been giving him all she had, sending the strongest message possible—*I trust you. Take me, I'm yours!* She followed him into his small kitchen. He looked over his shoulder, apparently clutching some stuff in his arms.

"My mom sent out a bunch of things that I never thought I'd use in a hundred years, but guess what." He turned, showing her his armload of candles in various sizes and containers. "Tonight is the night."

She laughed with him, then reached out and relieved his overloaded arms of a few of the candles to help before he dropped something.

"What do you say we put these babies all around the bedroom and…" now that he had a free hand he pulled her close for a quick kiss "…light them up."

The fact he wanted to create some atmosphere for their first time being together made a powerful impact on her wavering mood. The gesture of using faint candlelight as a buffer hit her like the thud of a palm to the center of her chest. They were going to have sex tonight. He would see her naked. Rather than make a big deal out of it, and possibly make him self-conscious about his eagerness, she sniffed one of the candles, vanilla, then another, rose. "Things should smell pretty good, too." She gave her best shot at sounding anything but the way she really felt— nervous! "One more thing. I don't take birth control pills. I use a diaphragm, and I didn't bring it tonight."

He watched her for a second or two, understanding and tenderness like she'd never seen centered in his bright blue gaze. "I've got that covered." His sweet gesture calmed her jitters. "Follow me."

There was nothing quite like a man on a mission.

Once the candles were strategically placed around his surprisingly spacious bedroom, she took a quick trip to the bathroom while he circled the room, lighting each one. Just before she exited she looked into the mirror. "Are you ready for this?" she whispered, her pulse quick- ening from her jangling nerves, her fingers slightly trem- bling. Then she noticed a subtle reminder, the crutches leaning in the corner. Jackson would need them without his prosthetic to get in and out of the shower. His pros- thetic. She'd made full disclosure just now in his living room. A man who wore a prosthetic partial leg would understand.

She refused to let Derek's memory ruin the chance for something new. Something better. Tonight she'd trust her gut—which seemed to have turned into a butterfly farm—trust Jackson, and maybe finally turn the corner to wholeness. She took a deep, shaky breath and opened the door.

Jackson stood in the center of his room, several feet from the foot of his bed, surrounded by soft candle glow, looking more handsome than she'd ever dreamed. While she'd been in the bathroom and he'd been lighting can- dles, she noticed he'd also found a condom or two, which were now sitting on the bedside table next to a tall, wide white candle. A man of his word.

He smiled at her, candlelight dappling the deep creases on either side of his mouth, looking sexy as hell, and she walked toward him. He took her into his arms and held her still for a few beats of her heart. She let go, melted into him, loving his welcoming warmth. He kissed her temple and ear and she inhaled the trace of his spicy aftershave along with the swirling candle scents, a mixture of vanilla and rose. And magnolia? Lifting her chin, she met his lips and soon didn't have to think, since their kisses always took on a life of their own.

Out of breath from his greedy kisses, her hands landed on his chest and slowly unbuttoned his shirt, mostly because she was nervous and her fingers weren't cooperating with her desire to get that thing off him! Pulling open the shirt, she reaped the benefit of her effort, being treated to the smooth skin of his muscled shoulders and his impressive chest dusted with brown hair. Her fingers traced over the tickly feel of him before she kissed him there and there and finally at the notch at the base of his throat.

He let her undress him, unselfconsciously needing to sit down when she'd pulled his jeans to the hard prosthesis with its silicone suspension sleeve. The layered muscles of his runner's thighs and his washboard tight abdominals distracting her from that detail. The thought of removing the prosthetic had never entered her mind.

"This one is different," she said, refusing to avoid the obvious, besides the fact they wanted each other.

"It's my everyday leg, complete with shoe." He smiled with understanding over her question. "The one you saw was my sports version."

"The blade?"

Now he grinned. "Yeah, I'm a blade runner."

She returned his smile, but wanted him to understand she was only being curious. "So how do I take this off for you?"

After a moment's hesitation, probably considering that he'd never been asked that question by a woman he was about to have sex with before, he showed her the button to click down toward the prosthetic ankle joint. She followed his instructions, and he guided her on how to slide down the bulkier and harder version of leg. As she studied it, he quickly removed the liner with the pin that clicked into the joint down by the ankle. And that was that.

She glanced at what remained of his leg beneath his knee, the flesh and bone part, then quickly back to the rest of him. Choosing to focus on everything about him, and not just the one area he might be self-conscious about, she ran her hands along the length of his thighs and looked into his darkening eyes. She perfectly understood how he'd feel if she stared at the part that was missing.

He pulled her to him, kissing her again, bringing things back on track—they wanted each other—with his hands roaming all over her. His fingers found the hem of her cotton pullover, his intense gaze seeking hers for the okay. Would she make this revealing moment one to dread or, just like him, a matter of fact? She pecked his lips in answer, so he gingerly lifted her top, giving her time to adjust to what he planned to do next. But when he reached for one of her bra straps, her hand flew to his.

"That look of horror you described earlier?" she whispered. "I know what it is."

His gaze narrowed with concern.

"I was engaged when I had the surgery. We were going to get married and go for the whole package—careers, kids, the works. He didn't want me to have the surgery, but I insisted it was what I needed to do. And afterward he couldn't accept me. He just couldn't. He tried, but I saw it. He was horrified. I disgusted him. He pitied me. I—"

Jackson stopped her from saying another word by lifting her chin with a finger and delivering a tender kiss. As their lips pressed together and their tongues found each other, he undid her special mastectomy bra and removed it, never breaking from her mouth, instead deepening their kiss. He lay back on the bed and pulled her with him on top until her nearly flat chest was flush with his. Being this close to him, skin to skin, excited her. His warm, large hands explored her back and moved downward to her jeans, pushing them lower once she'd unzipped them, then cupping her bottom. With his palms firmly attached to her backside, she remembered how much she'd missed being explored by a man, and how good it felt now, loving this moment.

He concentrated on every part of her, rather than putting her missing breasts at the center. Finally, when she was completely naked with him, the fingers of one of his hands crossed her chest as lightly as a butterfly. The surprise of how sensual it felt to have someone else besides herself touch her there sent a blast of chills across her skin. Soon, while he continued to devour her mouth, his palm rubbed where her breasts used to be, and though many nerves had been severed during the surgery, his touch warmed and excited her as if her breasts were still there.

"You're beautiful," he whispered over her ear, and for that instant she believed him.

As their bodies tangled and tightened together, clearly turned on—her aroused and longing for more, him noticeably hard between them—she forgot about what was missing from him, and he obviously hadn't been turned off by her surgery. Maybe, she hoped, he'd meant what he'd said about finding her beautiful inside and out. Hadn't he just told her so?

He rolled her onto her back, pushing her hands above her head and kissing her chest in several spots. She could swear, in her mind, the nipples that were physically no longer there responded. His kisses traveled onward to her stomach, igniting more thrills, and worked their way over her hips and down across her thighs until his mouth settled where her heat mounted, tightened and balled into raw need. As his tongue found her tender folds and circled the tip of her sex, setting off amazing sensations bordering on lightning and fireworks, every worry and insecurity about her body image left her mind, to be replaced by one thought. At her core she was a woman and nothing could take that away.

A few minutes later, when he sheathed and entered her, working her into another frenzy under the spell of his strength and persistence, and surrounded by flickering candlelight, she dared to look into his eyes. They were already locked on her face. Watching each other under the grip of bliss was more intimate than anything she could imagine. And like that she let go and shattered the boundaries she'd put on herself because of her wounds, and from his frantic reaction was fairly sure he'd done the same. She needed him and wanted to please him, bucking beneath him, and his near growling moan proved she was on the right track.

He cupped her hips, she tightened her legs around his waist, he steadily upped the tempo, and they soon ascended to that beautiful intensity she'd almost forgotten, where he suspended her with near agonizing magic. Faster and stronger, he took her there. Until she was so tightly wound and overloaded with sensations she lost it and came deep, long and forcefully. He soon followed her and they tumbled through that paradise together, and she felt more complete as a woman than she ever had in her life.

On Saturday morning her muscles ached from their making great use of the condoms and candlelight, until all had burned out. By then so had she, and falling into Jackson's arms, immediately going to sleep, seemed surreal. His rented bed was surprisingly comfortable, or maybe it was the man in bed with her? When she woke, she glanced up at him. He was already awake and watching her, lightly playing with her hair.

"Hi," she said.

"Good morning." His hand grazed her shoulder and arm. "You like eggs? I'm starving."

"I love eggs. You cooking?"

He sat up. "You bet I am. I intend to impress the hell out of you, too."

"I think you've already done that."

His slow smile and darkening blue eyes relit the lingering warmth right where they'd left off last night. He kissed her to help it along, and soon the thought of sleeping in on a Saturday morning seemed far more appealing than any old home-cooked breakfast.

Later, when they'd managed to make it out of bed, he loaned her a T-shirt to wear with her underwear while he planned to dazzle her with his culinary skills. Before putting it on, out of habit she reached for her fully formed bra, but he stopped her.

"You don't need that around me." He ran his hand across her chest, up her neck and across her jaw, then kissed her. "I like you exactly the way you are."

CHAPTER SEVEN

AFTER CHARLOTTE AND Jackson's first night together, some wild, wanton woman had been released, a part of her she'd never before explored. Complicating things, she never knew when Jackson would pop in her office, his mere presence reminding her how much she wanted him. Usually his visits were after a particularly stressful surgery. He would drop in, close the door, and dance her into the corner to kiss her hard and thoroughly then make no excuses for how much he craved her. And she loved it! Then, with her feeling all hot and flustered, they'd promise to spend the night together, and that would be that.

This time, late on a Friday afternoon, it was the night he routinely had dinner and a movie with his son. With that one earlier exception, they never planned to see each other on Friday nights, so they'd have to put their lust on hold. She'd worn a loose and flowing gypsy-style skirt to work, hoping he'd see it and compliment her. She loved his compliments.

When her lover came into her office and closed the door, he had a hungry look in his gaze. He took her hand and pulled her to him, kissing her, fingers digging into her hair, walking her backward to the wall, pressing her there. "Nice skirt," he said, playing with the fabric and just happening to find her hip and soon her bottom in the process.

In no time she had one thought on her mind and was totally grateful for her choice in skirts. Her leg lifted and attached to his hip, bringing his body flush with hers. Thanks to the thin fabric of his OR scrubs and her skirt, she felt nearly all of him as he stroked along her center. Wrapped up in the thrill of the moment, him igniting her and wreaking havoc with her good sense, she whispered, "Let's do it."

"You have no idea how much I want to." He kissed her roughly, slipped his hand between them and cupped her, moving up and down, fanning her fire nearly to the point of no return. He took a ragged inhalation to stop himself from going further. "But we could get fired, and I need this job," he reasoned. His hot breath tickled over her ear as she ignored his logical warning. "As much as I need you…"

"The department is practically empty," she interrupted. "Lock the door," she hissed, completely lost to him and the moment, and she meant it.

He gave her a questioning look and she nodded her undeniable consent. She saw the flash of heat in his eyes. He nipped her earlobe, then her lower lip. "I can't think straight around you."

With the oddest sensation, she'd have sworn she had nipples and they were tight and peaked with her longing to feel him inside her. "You do some pretty crazy things to me, too. Please," she begged, pushing her pelvis closer to him. "Lock the door."

It had never computed before how isolated her office was. Or the advantage of the other doctors routinely leaving early on Friday afternoons. She was at the end of a long row of offices in the basement of the pathology department. No-man's-land.

From having been with Jackson a dozen times before, she recognized the shift in his expression, his heavy-lidded stare. All resistance was gone. Her insides quivered, knowing what would happen next. "Just this once," he swore.

Lightning swift he locked the door and riffled through his wallet for a condom. They were back where they'd left off, his hand finding her secret places and working wonders, and when her powerful moment came she let him cover her mouth with his palm to stifle her response. The last thing they wanted to do was draw attention to what was going on in case anyone was within earshot. He loved watching her when she lost it. And just then, thanks to his skillful touch, she totally had.

Someone knocked on the door. "Charlotte, are you in there?" It was Antwan.

With Jackson's hand still over her mouth and tightening, her gaze shot toward the ceiling. *Really?* Of all the bad timing in the world.

Jackson removed his hand from her mouth and put one finger over his. *"Shh..."* She felt the sudden urge to laugh. This was ridiculous, and nothing she'd ever do! But her pulse hammered in her chest, more from what Jackson had just done to her than from Antwan's unwanted appearance. Though the risk of being caught having sex, well, partial sex, at work kept her heartbeat racing along.

"Has Dr. Johnson left for the day?" Dr. Dupree called down the hall.

"I don't think so," Latoya's distant voice answered from the reception area. "Dr. Hilstead came by. Maybe they went for coffee."

Antwan tried the door handle. The nerve!

They stared at each other, neither hardly breathing. She clutched Jackson's arms and squeezed tight, her mind flying in a thousand directions. What should they do? What would they say if they got caught? What would her mother think?

"Well, she's obviously gone." Finally, they heard footsteps going down the hall and Antwan's distant voice chatting up the young receptionist. "It sure feels dead around here."

Latoya gave the requisite laugh at his sorry attempt at a joke with the pathology reference.

"What are you still doing at work?" Antwan's attention had shifted. Good. They talked more, but Charlotte had quit listening.

Jackson gave her a stern look. "This can't ever happen again."

Feeling out of control and pumped up by the excitement, she grabbed his scrub top and pulled him near, then delivered a ragged kiss. "You're right—this has got to stop. But first it's your turn."

"We're crazy to risk it," he whispered over her ear, his hot breath melting her and dissolving into a cascade of chills down and over her breasts.

She got busy giving all of her attention to him, admiring how firm he'd stayed through the close call. He gave his rendition of a ragged kiss, far more intense than hers, taking her breath away. His weight pushed against her, her leg lifted again, and when he'd secured her to the wall, she lifted the other, clutching his hips.

"We really shouldn't," he murmured.

Farther down the hall, in the histology lab, the late shift technician stopped and listened, wondering where those muffled rhythmic thuds on the wall were coming from.

* * *

On a Monday, Charlotte had a phone message that Dr. Gordon was moving again. It was from his son Ely. He said he'd taken leave from work to be with his father and that Dr. Gordon wanted him to notify her.

She'd just got back from a quick but fun lunch with Jackson. No sex involved. Who knew how great hospital cafeteria food could taste when you were totally into someone? Now her lunch turned to a lump in her gut at the news.

Dr. Gordon had regained a lot of strength, and three days ago when she'd last visited he had been as feisty as ever. Maybe he'd figured out a way to beat the system. She wondered if Ely had volunteered to come or if Dr. Gordon had manipulated the visit. She wouldn't dare consider that his health circumstances had directed the move home. Had Ely implied he was there for hospice care?

Before she could form another thought her cell rang. It was Jackson.

"I just heard Jim Gordon left the extended care facility for home. Maybe we should go visit him this evening."

"I'm not sure if his family would want that, but I want to."

"I'll give a call, let you know."

"Thank you." She had a stack of slides fresh from histology to study from Saturday's surgeries, and though her heart and thoughts were with her mentor, out of respect for him she knew his department needed to carry on.

After work, Ely had given the okay for a visit, so Jackson drove as Charlotte let several scenarios play out in her thoughts, though she never expected the scene they found when they arrived.

Dr. Gordon was sitting in an obviously favorite chair, judging by the wear and tear on it, and how perfectly the man fit into it, too. He gave an ethereal smile, his skin ghostly white. "Hello, dear."

She bent to kiss him on the cheek, which felt warmer than he looked. "Did you have to pull some strings to move home?"

No longer a curmudgeon, his gaze more impish now, he smiled. "Ely and Sharon are staying with me for a while." He officially introduced Charlotte to his son and daughter-in-law. "The hospital decided I was in as good hands here as there. At much less cost to them!"

"That's wonderful."

Ely was a younger version of his dad with thinner eyebrows, though a bit taller with a friendlier face, and personality-wise, probably thanks to his mother's input, less off-putting. He hovered around his father, and Sharon seemed to sense her father-in-law's every need. Beyond giving him all the care and attention he'd require over the next few weeks, they radiated something that couldn't be faked—love for him.

Knowing her mentor would be surrounded by family and seeing how at peace he seemed, being back home, helped ease her worry about the significance of the move. No one mentioned the term "hospice care," and there wasn't a sign of medical equipment in the living room. Charlotte hoped for the best.

"I've asked Jerry Roth to take over as department head," he said. "There'll be a memo going out tomorrow."

So much for hope. Her heart ached at the news and what it might imply.

"He'll do a great job," she said, trying to sound upbeat. Jerry was the logical replacement—though she hated thinking that word—being the second most senior in Pathology at St. Francis of the Valley. Even with her foolish hope lagging, she wanted to reassure Dr. Gordon about his choice. "He's been steady as a rock while you've been in the hospital." Sitting nearby, Jackson subtly took her hand and squeezed his support.

"When I come back, it'll only be part-time."

The emotional teeter-totter had her sitting straighter. "You're coming back?" She couldn't suppress her surprise and happy relief, and for a man who didn't do impish, she could have sworn he savored playing her.

"I've been officially deemed in remission." As much as it went against his nature, her mentor beamed. "Don't know how long it will hold, but I'm feeling stronger every day, and hopefully, with Sharon's healthy cooking and the company of my son and friends like you, I'll be back in shape in no time at all."

"That's fantastic news, Jim." Jackson spoke up, a sincere smile on his face.

"Thanks. I'm just being realistic about not taking on too much when I come back."

"Wise of you," Jackson said.

Elated, and grinning to prove it, except probably sending a mixed message with the tears that had simultaneously cropped up, Charlotte clapped her hands. "I can't wait."

"To be honest, I can't either. I need a purpose besides being a pincushion and lab rat."

After a long drawn-out hug, and Charlotte realizing that the move and their visit may have taxed Dr. Gordon, she decided it was time to leave. But first, remembering all the things she'd wished she'd said to her mother during her ordeal, before it was too late, in case she never got the chance, she sat on the ottoman where Dr. Gordon's feet rested. Having him captive, she looked into his eyes.

"It's been hard, not having my mentor around these last few weeks. I want you to know how much you've taught me and how special you are to me. How much I still need you." She took his bony hand. "I've kind of put you on a pedestal, sometimes wishing you'd been my dad." She glanced up at Ely, noticing his approving smile. "I'm a better doctor because of you, and since I can't exactly go around saying this at work, I want you to know I love you."

He tightened his frail grip in hers. "Thank you. You're very special to me, too. Now quit worrying about me. You know my motto: life shouldn't be about what might happen, it's—"

Ely and Sharon joined in on the last part of the phrase, clueing Charlotte in that it really was a saying he lived by. "It's about what's happening right here and now."

She studied the man in his comfy chair, back in the home he'd made with his wife of fifty years before she'd died, his son and daughter-in-law like bookends on either side of him. Him being there "right here and now" looked pretty darned sweet, so she said good night and they left.

Moved by the warm and squishy moment that had just occurred inside Dr. Gordon's house, Jackson stopped Charlotte before they reached the car. "I've got a wedding to attend back home in Georgia next month, late August. Would you do me the honor of being my guest?"

Surprise registered in her eyes, and she didn't answer right away.

"I figure if Jim comes back on the job part-time, you should be able to take a few days off." He opened the car door and let her slip inside, then walked around and got in, still waiting for her answer but not quite ready to hear it. "Before you make your decision, let me just say it's because we've got really close and I was hoping you'd come with me. The truth is, I'd feel better confronting the mess I left behind with you at my side."

"I'd love to go."

It was his turn to be surprised, especially because of the poor excuse he'd given for wanting her there with him. As backup? What had he been thinking? "You would? I didn't mean to imply you'd be a crutch or anything."

"I understand."

"Really?" Over the last few weeks he'd grown to know Charlotte's body as well as his own, and he marveled over that gift. Since they'd started dating, he knew her intelligence was both a source of challenge and comfort. They understood each other. Hell, he'd torn a page right out of Jim Gordon's rule book to help convince her to give him a chance: *Right here, right now. To hell with the future.* Her warm and loving attitude seemed a gift from heaven, yet she'd just dazzled him again by being so willing to step into his past without knowing how bad it could be.

"Yes. I'd love to go."

How much more proof did he need about how special she was? "Well, in that case, I think it's about time you met my son."

Charlotte snuggled into Jackson's arms in her bed after making love later that night. Being tall, it took a lot to make her feel petite, but his broad shoulders and long frame did just that. Now that her personal shock of having a double mastectomy had barely made waves for him, often, when they were just staying in and hanging out, she'd walk around in a T-shirt or sweater without strapping on her bra, her chest as flat as his. And it didn't faze him. He'd been the one to suggest it after the first time they'd been together. She considered that freedom a special gift from him. He really had proved to be the perfect *imperfect* man for her.

Just before she drifted off to sleep, one last thought crossed her mind: how life was looking up. Her mentor was in remission, the new guy in her life had just asked her to a wedding in his hometown, which proved he trusted her with a fragile part of his life. And now he wanted her to meet his son. She couldn't help but feel special. Yet he'd never come close to saying those three little words.

The big question was, was it safe to get her hopes up? Maybe he was just a guy like the rented furniture in his condo, temporary, useful for now, nothing to take for granted. He'd been very clear about never wanting to marry again or to have any more kids. Now that she knew the full story, she understood, too. He'd moved to California to be near his son, who would eventually graduate from college and move on. Why would Jackson stick around after that?

But right from the start, having laid down a few personal safety rules of her own for Jackson, like taking it slow before jumping into a physical relationship, she knew how easily a rule could be broken. Tonight that fact fed her hope.

Jackson was on his way out of the lunchtime surgical conference when he saw Dr. Dupree across the room. He'd had something on his mind and made a point to confront him.

"Dr. Hilstead. You need something?" Antwan was in the middle of sharing a recent conquest with a young resident.

"Yes, if you have a minute?"

The long-haired resident took the cue—in fact, looked relieved—and headed out of the auditorium with everyone else.

"I just wanted to let you know that Charlotte and I are a thing now, so you can step back."

"A thing?"

"Yeah, we're a thing."

"She knows this?"

"Most definitely. Anyway, you can step back now."

"Step back?"

"Yes, step back." Jackson emphasized the words for the guy who seemed to be playing dense.

"Sometimes ladies don't know what they're missing until they've tried it." His overconfident smile grated on Jackson's nerves. Was it a challenge? He also knew the jerk was referring to himself, Antwan, not Jackson, so he decided to spell it out for him.

"Trust me, she's tried it and liked it. I'm asking you nicely to leave her alone." Was he on the verge of flapping his arms and making monkey noises? *My territory. Leave!*

"If that's what she wants, fine."

Jackson stared at the dense doctor long and hard. But he didn't dare say the words that had just been planted front and center in his head. *She's mine.* That would make him feel a bit like he'd traveled back in time to a more dramatic stage, high school or college, when guys got all wrapped up in their women and proudly staked their claim. He was a mature adult now, in midlife, sophisticated and above getting into the fray. Yet feeling the intense need to make his point perfectly clear with a womanizing bozo like Dupree couldn't be denied, and it shocked him.

Where had that come from? What had happened to the civilized forty-two-year-old surgeon? He bit back the long list of things he'd like to say, deciding to go for terse. "It's what she wants. We want." Like he had the right to speak for Charlotte, as Antwan had already insinuated. But it was. It was what *he* wanted. And he was pretty sure she wanted it, too.

He turned to leave, deciding to let Antwan figure out for himself what that meant, thinking the Southern gentleman-turned-caveman was a welcome change. He'd just publicly admitted he and Charlotte were "a thing," whatever the hell that meant.

The revelation of admitting he had intense feelings again on *any* level, and in this case for someone else—for his lovely *Charlotte*—made him grin. He left the meeting feeling taller than when he'd arrived, though admittedly he glanced over his shoulder for any evidence of a feminist posse hot on his trail for daring to be the tiniest bit chauvinistic. That didn't stop him from grinning, though.

That Friday night, Evan turned out to be tall, like his father, with piercing blue eyes, but much fairer and with lighter, straighter hair. From this Charlotte deduced that Jackson's ex was a blonde. She let her insecure imagination go wild and envisioned a stereotypical image of a pretty petite Southern belle, a Georgia peach, as she'd heard it called. The thought made her cringe and hurt all over. But she'd thought about all she and Jackson had shared over the last several weeks, and how close they'd got. Then on the spot she decided it was better to be the extreme opposite from an ex—tall, olive-toned skin, dark hair and eyes, big-boned—than a dead ringer. Wasn't it?

Occasionally during dinner the strained dynamics between Evan and Jackson were evident, but only on certain topics, like the wedding and whether or not Evan planned to go. They agreed that Evan should fly out a few days early to spend time with his mother and brother, and as an observer the decision lifted a weight from Charlotte's heart.

Didn't they know that they had the same laugh? A few times she had to double-check who had said what because they sounded so much alike, too. The kid was his son, there was no doubt, and they shared a lifetime together, well, Evan's lifetime, anyway. And she suspected the same would be true with the older son, the one who'd yet to offer Jackson a touch of grace. They shared genetic traits and familial similarities, and no matter how hard Andrew might try to ignore it, there was no way to forget it. Again, her heart ached for Jackson and his troubles.

As the evening moved on over tapas and beer at yet another trendy Westlake restaurant, Charlotte realized something important. When they talked about Evan's Bachelor of Arts major at Pepperdine, excitement radiated from the nineteen-year-old, and fatherly pride was obvious in Jackson's eyes, which were decidedly sexier and bluer than his son's. Then again, she was biased. She quickly figured how to keep the conversation focused on university and life dreams, and soon Evan seemed to see her as an ally instead of an adversary—the woman threatening to take his father away from him.

She made it clear how important she felt a well-rounded liberal arts degree was to send a person out into the world. Evan couldn't have agreed more. Jackson's endorsement may have come in delayed, but he finally chimed in.

After a couple of glasses of beer Charlotte let her truest thoughts slip out. "Thanks to science and extended longevity, what makes parents think their kids can know where their journey will lead at the ripe old age of nineteen?" Charlotte mused.

"Exactly!" Evan agreed. The look of appreciation she received from the young man nearly melted her heart. One day he'd have the world at his calling, but he needed to first figure out where he belonged. Pressuring him to make up his mind too soon would never help.

Then she glanced at Jackson, who didn't appear nearly as impressed with her statement as his son.

Evidently she'd hit a chord of contention between father and son, so she continued. "I mean, I know how I wanted to become a doctor at sixteen, and you, Jackson, probably had a similar experience, but not everyone knows for sure where they belong at such an early age. My sister tried going to college and discovered it wasn't for her. Now she's happy as a clam with three kids and running a family business."

She didn't want to imply that Evan should drop out, so she quickly added, "Getting a solid, well-rounded education seems like the best step forward for most. Right, Evan?"

Evan nodded.

"I want the best for my sons. If Evan is happy with his major, then I'm happy."

Charlotte believed Jackson, because of all the men she'd met in her life, he had proved to be honest and dependable, someone to trust, and these were three characteristics at the top of her "perfect man" list.

Before dinner was over Evan seemed to understand a little better where his father stood on his undergraduate degree choices, and Jackson had made extra points, proving he supported his son. Charlotte couldn't help but think maybe she'd had something to do with it.

Then, over dessert, the previously unspoken subject of Dad dating a new woman came up.

"So I guess you two are dating, right?" Evan said. "And you want my approval?"

Charlotte worked extra hard to not show her true reaction. *Yes, we're dating, but beyond that I don't know what's in store. Do we need your approval for that?*

Jackson glanced at Charlotte, she glanced back, and

then he reached for her hand under the table. "Now that Mom and I are divorced, I hope you're okay with that."

"Hey, it's your life." Evan seemed to toss the answer a bit too quickly, maybe in an attempt to leave out the emotion behind it. Pain. "I mean, I know a lot's gone on with your war injury and PTSD and all, and things didn't work out between you and Mom, but, Dad, you're entitled to pick up your life and date again."

Jackson reached across the table and clutched his son's forearm. "You saying that means the world to me, Evan."

When they all said good night, Jackson gave Evan a bear hug, and Evan fully participated. The sight of the two of them hugging moved Charlotte nearly to tears, but she managed to keep her response in line, not wanting in any way to draw attention away from the big event of the night. Until, in true Southern charm fashion, Evan extended his hospitality to her and hugged her good night. As she hugged the bonier version of Jackson, managing to feel his sincerity, she couldn't help the moisture that sneaked over her lids.

"It was so great to meet you." She said it over-enthusiastically, completely different from the response she'd intended to give. Cool. In control. Sophisticated. *Really fun to meet you.*

Evan smiled and nodded, as though he was also surprised about how well the night had gone.

On the drive home, overall Charlotte thought the meeting had gone well and that Evan seemed okay with his dad moving on. At least she hoped Evan was being honest. Though the question still remained—where exactly was Jackson moving on to?

"What did you think?" Jackson asked.

"I think you've got a great son on your hands."

While driving, he flashed her a grateful and reassured

look. "I think you're right." Then, with his eyes back on the road, he added, "I'm really looking forward to the day Evan turns twenty-one and my job as parent will officially be over."

"Is that job ever 'officially' over?"

"The part about being completely responsible for them, yes. The being-a-parent part?" He grimaced. "Nope."

Now that the hurdle of meeting his son had come and gone, Charlotte focused on the next big event. Truth was, she'd interpreted the invitation to the wedding in Savannah as a turning point in their relationship. Though Jackson hadn't committed to the trip meaning anything beyond a few days together on his home turf. *With her as his backup.* Her thoughts, not his. She felt otherwise. He *needed* her there.

But if that was all he wanted, backup, she'd oblige. Because she knew exactly how she felt about him—this could be the start of something big! Old song or not, it was how she felt, yet she chose to hold her thoughts close to her heart rather than test the waters on Jackson. It was still too soon.

Two weeks before the big event she went shopping for a special dress. She whistled while she combed through the circular racks in the showroom, happily looking forward to visiting a state she'd never been to before. She loved it already since it was the place that had shaped Jackson into the wonderful, charming and sexy man she'd come to know and…and what? Was she there yet? Or was she stuck in the "start of something big" stage? Maybe she was waiting for him to catch up.

All the new and optimistic feelings ebbed when a wave of insecurity and anxiety took over and her stomach threatened to knot up and push out her lunch. She swallowed hard and forced herself to pull it together. Shocked by the emotional reaction the act of buying a special dress had caused—or was it thinking about feeling something more for Jackson than she'd ever expected?—she took pause.

Sure, Jackson had seen her and accepted her for who she was, but how would she measure up to the people back home? Wondering and fearing how she'd manage in a sea of people she didn't know, her only lifeline being Jackson, who would no doubt be dealing with a boatload of his own issues, she fretted. Suddenly depressed about her tall and sometimes clunky-feeling appearance—the hair that would probably frizz up in the summer Georgia humidity, not being able to buy a perfect dress right off the rack, not to mention a subtle competitive feeling toward his ex-wife, which annoyed her to no end—she passed off feeling out of sorts and generally unsettled on nerves about the upcoming event. Not the other way around—feeling profoundly sick to her stomach on a perfectly fine Saturday morning, and getting nervous about what it might mean.

Then she went back to hunting for that perfect dress that would make her feel like a knockout. A dress that would cause Jackson to see her in a different light.

As a woman he couldn't live without.

CHAPTER EIGHT

ONE WEEK LATER Charlotte sat in the laboratory with one of the histologists assisting while she examined, described and cut sections from yesterday afternoon's surgeries and clinic procedures. This morning there were no less than twenty-five bottles of varying sizes, each prefilled with fixative. An appendix, a gallbladder with gallstones, a cervical conization, a large, dark and oddly shaped mole, a wedge resection of lung—removed by Dr. Jackson Hilstead, she noticed on the requisition, which meant he'd probably pop by tomorrow to look at the slide with her. That put a secret smile on her face. She'd been doing that a lot lately, smiling for no reason.

In walked Dr. Dupree, looking like he had something on his mind, and he immediately wiped her smile away.

"Haven't seen you in a while," she said, opening the first bottle. Not that she'd wanted to see him or anything. Oh, man, she hoped he didn't read anything into her off-the-cuff, trying-to-play-nice greeting. The man was incorrigible.

"I've been told to step back."

Well, it was about time someone did. Who, though—hospital administration, the sexual harassment team? She kept her smirk to herself. "Step back?"

Not wanting to let him slow her down on the job at

hand, she examined, then interrupted Dupree to describe and measure the dimensions of a piece of tissue, then used a scalpel to find the best possible section to represent the entire specimen for slides and put it into a cassette.

He waited impatiently for her to finish. "Jackson said you two were a thing and I should step back. It was a couple of weeks ago, so I'm just checking if that's still true."

Her line of vision on the specimen flipped upward, catching her assistant's gaze, whose eyebrows nearly met his hairline.

Jackson had staked a claim on her? Glad she was wearing a mask, she hoped her smile didn't reach her eyes, though the thought of irking Dupree even more was tempting. "Maybe in your world 'things' only last a week or two, but I'm sorry to burst your bubble. The official word is, yes, we are still 'a thing.'"

Did you hear that, world? Why did that put an entirely new spin on the right here and right now and make her feel amazing?

The histology technician pretended not to be listening to every word as he labeled the cassette then placed it in a large buffered formalin-filled container in preparation for the overnight process. The next day, after cutting ultra-thin sections of the paraffin-encased specimens, the histologists would deliver a set of pink, blue and purple stained slides neatly laid out in cardboard containers for the pathologists to read.

This was tedious but necessary work, which took at least twenty-four hours to complete from the time of receiving the specimen to stained slides. Charlotte took her duty seriously and focused her attention on the specimens. Not Dr. Dupree. Even though what he'd said, not his visit, was responsible for her mood being lifted to one of elation. "If you'll excuse me, as you can see, I've got a lot of work to do."

Undaunted, Antwan waited for her to look at him. "I'll check back in a couple more weeks." And off he went.

The nerve of that guy. She huffed and the assistant shook his head. Yeah, they were on the same page about Antwan Dupree's reputation around the hospital. But beyond agreeing the guy was an idiot, no one could possibly understand where she was, in the condition she might be in, at this exact moment. She was on her own with that.

The room had special ventilation to suck out the caustic fumes, and she wore a duck-billed mask as well as a clear face guard to protect from any formalin splash into the eyes. It was the same thing she did on any given day at work without any side effects. Yet today, during the cutting process, she felt decidedly nauseous.

Who was she kidding? It wasn't just today.

Dreading what a week of all-day queasiness might mean, she promised to take a test once she finished the morning's lab work. She couldn't push it out of her mind another second.

At noon Charlotte stole away to the hospital laboratory and had a trusted and super-skilled lab tech draw her blood, barely feeling the prick of the needle. Then all she could do was wait for the result with fingers tightly crossed it would be negative. She couldn't let her mind venture into the realm of what she'd do if the pregnancy test was positive.

Absurd. She couldn't possibly be…could she?

As a resident pathologist, she'd seen and examined far more than her share of young women who'd wound up in the morgue, only to discover at the autopsy they'd died from blood clots related to their birth control pills. The clots may have lodged in their lungs or brain but, wherever they were, they'd wound up being the cause of death on the autopsy report. She'd stopped taking BC pills and, even knowing the odds of forming clots were extremely small, had chosen never to use them again.

So she'd been using a diaphragm with Jackson…except on that first night when he'd caught her by surprise and he'd used a condom. And that time in her office.

Later, with zero appetite, she forced herself to eat some lunch in her office when halfway through the intercom buzzer went off.

"Dr. Johnson? This is Sara from the lab. Um, your test is positive."

"Positive?" Had she heard right? Her heart tapped a quick erratic pace at those four little words. Her blood test was positive. She forgot to breathe.

"Dr. Johnson?"

"Yes, Sara, okay. Thanks." She'd done the worst job in the world of pretending she wasn't stunned. It seemed her little "thing" with Jackson, to use Dr. Dupree's term, had just turned into something much bigger. She was pregnant. No. No. *No*.

She hung up, reached for her trash can, bent over and lost the contents of her stomach into it. She was pregnant.

When she recovered, and was positive her voice wouldn't quiver, she picked up the phone and dialed Jerry Roth. "I'm not feeling well, just threw up. I'll need to take the afternoon off."

Since she was notoriously healthy and hardly ever called in sick, he didn't hesitate to let her go. "Go. Take care. Feel better." If it were only that easy.

Once at her town house, having been suspended in a bubble of disbelief so she could drive home safely but now feeling numb, she got out of her clothes and into her pajamas. Why she decided it was the right thing to do she didn't know. But it was. Even though it was early afternoon and summer, she wanted—no, needed—to snuggle into her soft bathrobe, to hide out and hope to find comfort there. Then she made a cup of herbal tea, noticing a fine tremor in her hand as she dipped the bag into the steaming water.

One little blood test had, once again, turned her life upside down.

What was she going to do? She didn't dare tell Jackson until she'd made her decision. The man had been adamant about never wanting another child. He'd warned her on their first date, hadn't he, almost coming off as fanatical about it. *No more children.* If she hadn't already made up her mind about liking him by then, he would have chased her away with his proclamations. Even though the "no kids" rule had matched her own.

The night they'd first made love he'd opened up and admitted feeling trapped into marriage by his ex-wife. Not that she wanted to get married to him because she was pregnant. But right from the start he'd made it known he was off the market in the marriage department. She wouldn't do that to him. But the baby. What about the baby?

Out of nowhere a long-forgotten dream from before she'd learned about her genetic markers whooshed through her. Her once-upon-a-time hopes of having it all—marriage, a career, *children*. She'd loved her rotation through pediatrics in medical school. Yes, she'd wanted children. Little knockoffs of her and whoever her husband turned out to be. Warm and lively little bodies that hugged better than anyone else on earth. The only munchkins in the world who would call her Mommy.

She plopped onto her couch and hunkered down for an af-

ternoon of soul-searching with a potential life-changing outcome. Who was she kidding? Her life had already changed
that first morning in the dress shop with that odd sensation
of illness that she'd brushed off as anxiety. She just hadn't
known it yet.

Was there a scientific way to handle the situation? She'd
already done the math and come to the conclusion the risk
for her getting cancer was too high, so she'd had the operation. She also knew without a doubt she never wanted
to pass it on. Now, though, she couldn't remember what
the exact percentage was for a potential "daughter" to in-
herit her markers and gene mutations. A lot had to do with
the father, didn't it?

She dropped her head into her hands, her thoughts fog-
ging up, and stared at the teacup on the table in front of
the couch. Besides being addled by nausea, her mind was
fuzzy around the edges with waxing and waning emotions
of fear and joy. She couldn't ignore the joy part, keeping
her thoroughly confused. What in the world was she supposed to do?

She'd sworn since she'd discovered she had not only
the breast cancer blood marker but also the gene muta-
tion, hell, she'd been adamant about it, *never* to have a
baby. No baby. No how. Any baby. Ever.

She remembered the day she'd begged her sister, Cynthia, to get tested and how she'd refused. Cynthia had
already had a child by then—a boy—so at least that was
one less concern for Charlotte. But when her sister had
informed her that she and her husband were planning to
try for another, Charlotte had stepped up her campaign.
Finally Cynthia had relented and had tested negative.
Charlotte had had to bite back her envy in shame. Of
course she was happy for her sister, who'd gone on to
have twins, one of whom was a girl, and she still worried

about little Annie's future. Cynthia had the same parents yet didn't carry the markers. Where did that leave Charlotte, the bearer of the unlucky genes? Where would it leave her baby if it was a girl?

Though what she carried would only potentially affect a girl baby, for personal ethical reasons she could never take a chance, get pregnant and wait to find out the sex before making a decision. No way would she be a designer parent, picking and choosing the child's gender, so she'd accepted it would be better to never have children. At all.

So here she was.

She needed another cup of tea. Maybe a gallon of it.

Somewhere during the course of cup after cup of calming chamomile, her anxiety rose, and several visits to the bathroom later, cautious excitement tiptoed into the mix of out-of-control feelings.

What? How could she be excited about something she'd sworn she didn't want? A baby.

Well, because she'd never *actually* been pregnant before. And now that she was, it seemed like a quiet miracle. A gift she'd never expected but somewhere deep inside had still always wanted. A bubble of joy insisted on making itself known. For a few seconds Charlotte let herself feel it, float on it, dream with that joy. A baby. *I'm going to be a mother!* Say it out loud. Make it real. She whispered it. "I'm going to be a mother."

Oh, God, she needed to hug that toilet again.

A little later, groaning and lying flat on her back on the cold tile of the bathroom floor, she stared at the white ceiling and remembered Dr. Gordon's words—*Life shouldn't be about what* might *happen, but about what's happening* right now.

She'd been born with a genetic marker she'd had no

clue about, had been a happy kid as far as she remembered, and a typical teenager, until her mother had got sick. Long afterward, she'd discovered her potential for cancer, something that could be measured and planned for, unlike most people who never knew or suspected anything until they got their diagnosis. She'd dealt with it in her own way, and now she had to search her soul to decide whether or not to allow that same chance for her baby because *life shouldn't be about what might happen*. The key word jumping out at her this time—life.

Right here and now a baby was taking form in her womb, and cells were dividing and multiplying at the speed of light. Amazing. A million things could change during the process of a pregnancy. The possibilities of "what might happen" were exponential. Extraordinary. But right this second it was a fact—she was pregnant. And it seemed amazing! But the scientific part of her brain sneaked back in. Yes, she was going to be a mother. Unless a long list of potentialities stopped the process. Most importantly, would she be able to live with the guilt if her baby turned out to be a girl and also carried the same genetic markers? Or the guilt of not letting her baby have a life at all?

Her head started spinning with overwhelming thoughts. Could a person overdose on chamomile?

She rolled onto her knees, stood and staggered to her room and her bed.

At this exact moment in time she, without a doubt, knew one thing and one thing alone—that she needed a nap.

The flaw with allowing herself to succumb to a long escapist nap—in this case several hours—in the late afternoon was having to lie awake with a gazillion thoughts winging through her head now, late at night. She couldn't get Jackson out of her mind. Of course. Every rule he'd laid down from the start. In spite of that, how wonderful and compassionate he'd turned out to be. What a great lover he was, how the thought of being with him always made her quiver inside. How he'd recently admitted to people other than her that they were "a thing," both at work with Dupree and his personal life with Evan. Hell, the whole hospital knew!

How he never wanted to get married again or have children.

Yeah, that part. Plus the fact his ex-wife had got pregnant and rushed him into marriage. There was that fear again—would he suspect her of trying to do the same thing?

She had to make sure he understood that wasn't her plan. Hell, she still had to wrap her brain around the pregnancy part. She was nowhere near ready to think about the concept of marriage.

Besides, he'd yet to tell her he loved her. A fact. Did she love him? If she ever married it would have to be for love, not because she'd felt forced into it. Nothing else would do.

What was she supposed to do about their relationship now that she was pregnant? Should she wait until after the wedding to tell him? Could she bear to be around him keeping such a life-altering secret, forcing a pretend face that communicated all was well, and, oh, hey, I'm having such fun, when in reality, since the wedding in Georgia was only a week away, she'd probably still be fighting morning sickness?

Would it be fair? To either of them?

She glanced at the clock. It was nearly midnight. Maybe he'd tried to call her this afternoon while she'd been passed out in a pregnant-lady stupor. She walked to the living room and found her purse. Sure enough, he'd called, not once but twice, and had left a message after each one.

"What's up? Where are you? I heard you left work sick. Can I bring you anything?"

And an hour later.

"So you must be feeling really crappy and you're sleeping, because I checked the hospital and you hadn't been admitted. Kidding, but not really. I'm kinda worried. Call me if you need me. Okay? I'm home."

The man deserved to know. Right here. Right now. She understood the bomb she was about to drop on him would probably— Who was she kidding about *probably*? It *undeniably* would jeopardize their relationship. Though the thought already broke her heart. She grabbed an already used tissue from the coffee table. He may only see what they had as a "thing," but for her he was the "start of something big" romance, the first man she'd trusted since Derek. For Charlotte trust was the step just before…

That didn't matter since it was probably all over now, and she owed him the truth. The man who couldn't wait for his youngest son to turn twenty-one so he'd be relieved of full-time parenting wouldn't want to start over again.

Making the call wouldn't be so scary if, in all the times they'd made love, he'd just once whispered that he loved her. She'd been foolish enough to hope he would, even while knowing it was too early for a declaration like that. Now, since the probability of him breaking things off was huge, and she'd never get the chance to hear those words from him, she had to prepare for the worst. She used that tissue again, wiping her eyes and nose. Would she ever hear "I love you" again? From anyone? *Stop thinking about what may or may not happen, get on with right here and now.*

One thing she knew without a doubt: telling a man something as monumental as this needed to be done face-to-face. Too much could be hidden over the phone. With the news she was about to lay on him she needed to see his eyes, to see his sincere reaction. And he needed to see how important this change in life plan was for her.

Her insides quivered, and it had nothing to do with feeling nauseous.

With trepidation she speed-dialed his number, making a snap decision to do something completely out of character, to lead with her feelings. Tell him how she really felt about him. Could she admit she loved him, or would it feel forced right now? Then, definitely, she'd have to get around to the other part of the issue. Or maybe she should feel him out first, to see how he felt about *her*. Oh, hell, nope. It was her call. Her "situation," and she should be the one to be boldly honest. She might not be able to say "I love you" yet, but she sure as heck had other feelings about Jackson.

An unexpected sense of hope took hold as his phone rang. *I know what I'm going to say. But the instant I hang up I need to jump into the shower and clean up because... man, oh, man... I'm a mess and he cannot see me like this when I break the news.*

Jackson stirred from a restless sleep and looked at the time. It was midnight. And Charlotte was calling. He hoped she wasn't horribly sick. He'd left those messages, asking her to let him know if there was anything he could do. He'd even considered stopping by on his way home from work. But knowing how independent she was, he'd opted to wait to be invited. On alert, he sat up and answered the phone.

"Are you okay?"

"I'm crazy about you."

"What?"

"I've been meaning to tell you how crazy I am about you for some time now."

Was she dialing drunk? She was the most practical lady he'd ever met. Why would she call and blurt out such a thing unless…? Maybe she had a fever and was delirious.

"Will you come over?"

She'd just told him she was crazy about him, was probably a little tipsy, and now she'd asked him to come over. With all the possibilities that proposition held, how could he refuse?

"I'll be right there."

As he cleaned up and got dressed, an odd thought about the midnight invitation to his lady's house made him smile. Plus she'd said she was crazy about him, which was totally out of character but made him feel like a prince. Who'd have ever guessed when he'd first noticed her all those months ago that the prim-looking and earnest-as-hell pathologist would have turned out to be a sexy drama queen? The funny thing was, he liked it. He *really* liked it.

Several other thoughts forced their way out of the recesses of his mind as he drove to her house. How Charlotte was healing him and how grateful he was for that. He'd been shedding layer after layer of protective defenses since he'd met her. Something about her had made him like her right off, but now that they'd got close—in fact, closer than he'd been to anyone other than his wife—it seemed he was becoming a new man. Because she'd made it okay. She accepted him. He felt things again. Life was something to look forward to, not simply to manage to get through day by day. And because of his changing, he thought about a future. Maybe right here in California.

Sometimes the way he and Charlotte got along made

him wonder if he had ever really been close to his wife like that. Their hasty marriage hadn't felt like his idea. He hadn't felt nearly ready for it, or for becoming a father twice before he'd turned twenty-four. To everyone else, his family, hers, he'd been a young doctor with a bright future. They had been the perfect couple. So he'd learned to work that to his advantage. A wife and kids completed his package as a safe bet to hire into a respected surgical practice, to groom for bigger and better things, like taking on the role of department head of surgery at Savannah General. His stay-at-home wife had made it easy for him to shine, too. He was grateful for it. While he'd spent hours and hours working his way up, she'd raised the kids. Mostly alone. Especially after he'd signed on for the medical unit in the army reserves and had started volunteering for disaster missions. Had they ever been close?

Andrew and Evan had been the highlights of his life, though—he couldn't dispute that, even when working sixty-hour weeks and going away one weekend a month. He smiled as he sat at a red light, remembering the heat he'd taken from his grandfather for not strapping Andrew with the name of Jackson Ryland Hilstead the Fourth. Evaline had stood by him on that decision. He sure hoped Drew appreciated it. So his ex-wife had given him his family and had stuck with him until he'd fallen apart. What more could a man have asked?

For better or worse? For both legs? For a wife who wasn't repulsed by him? Someone to stand by him through the toughest trials in his life, not just the successes?

His smile dissolved. Those wishes required a lot in return. He'd let their relationship grow empty. Truth was, he hadn't been there for her beyond providing a home and a lifestyle loaded with the perks of being the wife of a wealthy doctor. And that hadn't been enough. Because he hadn't been around. For most of their marriage that situation had been satisfactory for her. Until he'd changed for the worse after taking that second tour in the Middle East in the army reserves and had come home from Afghanistan.

Coming home a hot mess—to use his mother's favorite saying—broken and disfigured. Coupled with his PTSD and withdrawal, it hadn't been nearly enough for her anymore. He'd stopped being able to run a department. To do surgery! The one thing he'd come to think was the reason he'd been put on the planet.

Truth was, he hadn't been willing to fight for Evaline like he supposed he should have. He'd hit bottom so fast and hard his heart had splattered. He hadn't had anything left. It made him wonder if he'd ever really loved her. Or vice versa.

So now he was forty-two, driving after midnight to a new woman's town house because she'd dialed drunk, told him she was crazy about him and invited him over. Crazy, right? But he was excited about it. In fact, he hadn't felt excited about much in life since the war injury...until Charlotte. The woman who was helping him heal step by step. He was a better man because of her.

And if her calling meant she wanted to take him to bed, hell, yeah, he was all for it. Even if her virus or whatever it was that had made her leave work got him sick, it would still be worth it. Because there was something close and tender they shared beyond the crazy-hot sex. It was called total acceptance, and that special part, her accepting him as he was, and him doing the same with her, was bringing him back to life. He could only hope she felt the same.

Charlotte's heart fluttered when the security light came on from the entrance gate. She hit the entry button to allow Jackson to pass and park, her lungs forgetting to breathe on their own. With damp palms she finger-combed her hair and took a quick glance in the hallway mirror. Did it really matter how she looked? Something far greater than her appearance was at stake.

He knocked, and she nearly lost her nerve. Could she run to the bedroom and hide under her pillows?

Willing strength she wasn't sure she had, she bit her lower lip and opened the door. There stood Jackson in all his post-midnight glory. Hair dashingly disheveled, eyes bright and blue, huge questions in them. Late-night stubble. "You don't look sick to me. You look great." His expression was lusty and hopeful.

Her eyes closed as she inhaled before she could answer, picking up his fresh application of spiced aftershave and fighting a wave of nausea. "I'm not sick in the classic sense, though God knows I've been nauseous all day. Well, all week, actually."

He scrunched up his face, trying to follow her meandering explanation. With his high intelligence he was probably already putting the equation together. Or choosing to ignore it, in which case she'd have to hit him over the head with it.

"May I come in?"

Oh, God, she hadn't even let him inside. "Of course." She stepped back, but he reached for her arm and squeezed as he kissed her hello. She flinched, but for one instant the gesture, his warm lips pressing against hers, calmed her. What would he think? Then her roiling nerves took over again. "Have a seat."

His glance seemed to ask, *Why so formal? What if I want to stick around and keep kissing you?* Yet he dutifully went to her beige couch and sat. "I get the impression you have something important to say."

Her eyes lifted to the ceiling. "That's an understatement." She halted any further comment from him by using her hands to tap the air. "Let me figure out how to best say this. Okay?"

"How to say what?"

She paced and glanced at him, could read confusion or irritation in his expression, or maybe it was concern. She was being too obtuse, and needed to get to the point of why she'd called him out in the middle of the night. He might really think it was just to have sex. She stopped walking and faced him, then took a deep breath, deciding to go full speed ahead.

"Okay, let me start from the beginning." She had his total attention and the responsibility seemed more than she could bear, but she forced herself to pull it together. She had no choice, so she blurted, "It seems I'm pregnant."

The words had the expected effect of hitting him like a brick. He didn't smile or jump up to hug her with joy. No, that was the fantasy version of how this conversation would go. Instead, his eyes flashed wide and his head jerked back. Far too authentic for her to handle right now. Apparently she'd left him speechless. So, with her feet planted, she opted to continue her story. "I never expected to be pregnant. I'm not trying to trick you into marriage or anything." She assumed he'd gone right to the conclusion that history was repeating itself all these years later. "I swear. But since you're the father, I owe it to you to be honest and up front." She stopped to swallow and take a breath. "I'm choosing to keep my baby."

And there it was, the horrified look, the you-blew-every-great-thing-we-had expression. The tension around his brows reminded her how he'd laid out the rules right from the start. He didn't want to get married. He never wanted to be a father again. Her insides clutched.

"I know. You don't want to be a father ever again. You made it very clear. And yet here I am telling you I want this baby. After swearing I never wanted to pass my cancer genes on to a child of mine." Her chin quivered, but she refused to let the emotions gathering speed inside take over, so she bit down hard on her lip and counted to three. "I am afraid and filled with guilt about my decision, guilt for you and for the baby, but I can't say I'm sorry. I just can't."

Finally, she had the nerve to look into his face and eyes again. True, at first he'd looked horrified, or that was how she'd read it, but now his mien seemed perplexed, as though he was trying to solve a mathematical problem. A very big and complicated mathematical problem.

She remembered the words he'd repeated to her before the first time they'd been together, and the more that she was getting used to being pregnant and dealing with it, she bent those words from Dr. Gordon and decided to toss them back at him.

"You were the one who quoted the good doctor that 'life shouldn't be about what might happen,' otherwise we never would have made love in the first place, right?"

She suddenly had his undivided attention, the dumbfounded look nearly causing his mouth to drop open. She wanted to sit beside him and plead for him to understand, but she stayed right there, on the other side of the coffee table from him. "So that brings us back to what is happening right now. Yes, I'm pregnant."

"You're pregnant." Evidently he was still feeling stunned.

"Yes, and you made me that way." Her finger shot up.

"No, that isn't exactly right. We got that way together. *We're* pregnant."

Still Jackson remained painfully silent. It cut like a blade through her center.

She'd just laid her fear, pride and guilt on the table and he wasn't rushing to save any of it. Her decision to stay pregnant seemed to be hanging in the balance of his grace. She couldn't allow him to have that control over her body and her baby. Could she stand to hear him tell her thanks but, no, thanks? Oh, God, no, it would hurt too much. Fear took over about what he might say, and as was her pattern of dealing with fear, she rushed into a response before he'd had time to digest her news and form the words for a reply. She simply couldn't take this agonizing pause. If he wasn't going to say anything right this instant, she needed to step in, take control, preempt the outcome. "Please, leave. Now."

"Charlotte." She heard pleading and frustration in the single word of her name.

She shook her head. "I promise not to upset your carefully planned-out life. I get it. You told me from the start. You've done the fatherhood thing and never want to do it again. You're counting down the days until Evan turns twenty-one." Her fear seemed to change to anger from one breath to the next and she couldn't bite her tongue to stop the next thought from coming out. "I know you never want to get married again. Hell, you can be an old lonely man for all I care. I'm having this baby." Damn the break in her voice, the surge of hurt childishness, the threatening tears welling in her eyes. Damn them all. And damn him, too.

She scanned the table for more used tissues.

"Wait a second," he said. "You're reading all kinds of things into this, and I don't deserve your insults. Can you understand that I might need to digest everything you've just told me? You owe me a little time to think, don't you?" He stood, imploringly, it seemed, taking a couple of steps toward her.

She moved back. "Sure." She sounded terse.

Had she hoped for and maybe even expected too much from her Southern gentleman? He didn't rush to her or make a single promise. He'd simply stood there looking all befuddled. *You're what?* What he asked for was time. And a reasonable person would grant him that. But she was anything but reasonable in her pregnant and scared sightless state.

The saying that actions spoke louder than words hit her like a full frontal head butt, knocking her fear aside and fueling her anger. He obviously didn't want any responsibility for this baby growing second by second inside her. If he didn't want to jump on board with the pregnancy, that said all she needed to know, and so she didn't have time for him. If she were a princess, she would have him banished, but she was a modern woman dealing with a life-changing event, and it hurt to have to go through it alone, to not get from him the support that she'd secretly prayed for. Her secret dream. But so be it.

"Go," she said, trying to cover up her true feelings. "Think all you want. Nothing is changing on this end. Go. Go!" Had she actually yelled at him?

Because he didn't budge, she grabbed his hand, pulled and led him to her front door, and only because he was still stunned and didn't seem to have the ability to resist her did he allow her to push him out. Or maybe he wanted her to, to let him off the hook. *She kicked me out!* he could claim later—which only made her angrier. She closed the door with a bang, nearly in his face.

She wanted to cry and scream and drop to her knees

with disappointment, but the only thing she could do right that moment was respond to his muffled protests on the other side. "Charlotte. Charlotte. Come on. Don't be like this."

She searched for her voice and mustered all the nerve she had left. "Just to make it clear, I said nothing is changing on this end. Except whether or not I'll ever let you back."

CHAPTER NINE

JACKSON WASN'T EVEN sure how he'd made the drive home. His head swam with thoughts yet nothing seemed clear enough to grasp. Charlotte was pregnant, the one thing they'd both agreed from the start would never happen.

And she planned to keep the baby.

Where did that leave him? With an intense sense of déjà vu.

Think straight!

First, he needed to admit he loved her for helping him get his life back, and though he'd been on the verge of telling her—his midnight visit had seemed like the perfect time—the news that she was pregnant had knocked him completely off track. It had rocked the thoughts in his brain until they were so jumbled up he couldn't think.

The monumental revelation, that he loved something Charlotte had done for him, helping him heal and grow, deserved its own moment in time. He'd planned to indulge in the new thought for days to come, that he might be able to love again, to hold the concept in his hands and pass it back and forth, to get a feel for it, savoring the secret, and then and only then to find the nerve to say it out loud. To see how it sounded: *Charlotte, you've revived me, and I'm finally open to a complete relationship with you. Are you ready to see where this goes?*

It might sound awkward and clinical, but it was his true feeling, and she deserved to know.

But she'd just told him she was pregnant!

Now he'd have to jump ahead dozens of steps in the relationship to admit the big secret. The one he'd planned to carry around with him for days, taking his own sweet time to tease her with dumb grins, special touches, secret glances at work, all building to the big revelation. *I'm in love with you, can't you tell?* Now everything had changed. Because the pregnancy forced it. And long before he was ready he had to admit it. The truth shocked him, made his mouth go dry. This was never supposed to happen again.

She wasn't merely "a thing." She hadn't ever been.

He loved her. Damn it, he loved her. But there wasn't time or the luxury of basking in that knowledge because she was already making him a father. Again.

Part of him wanted to kick himself for getting into this position in the first place. Wasn't a man supposed to learn from his history? Why had he let himself think he could be normal, pick up his life, enjoy getting close with a woman again? He'd been playing with fire since he'd first asked her out. If only Charlotte hadn't made it so enticing and easy.

Sure, blame her. You wanted her long before she came around to the idea. His fingers flew to his brows and rubbed up and down, as if that might help clear his head.

He'd sat there just now at her house like a big dolt when she'd told him. His jaw had dropped open, mind numbed by the news, unable to respond. *This is all out of order. I need more time to get used to the first part! You're not just a thing to me. I think I love you.*

He'd seen her inconsolable reaction, as clear as her beautiful brown eyes. He'd hurt her to the marrow, ripped open her heart, left her bleeding, and she'd turned that hurt into anger and kicked him out. Could he blame her?

He paced his condo, unable to rest, wanting to call her but still not knowing what to say. *I love you but I'm not ready for more.*

A baby? He was forty-two, done with those things. They'd made a pact on their first date, hadn't they? She clearly hadn't keep her side of the bargain. But was that all they were to each other, a bargain? He stopped to breathe and felt the wall building itself around him, separating him from the living, keeping him safe from ever feeling again.

Was he done with Charlotte? Could he throw away that new love so easily? What kind of man walked away from a woman he'd finally and only just recently admitted he loved, because she was pregnant and he didn't want to be a father again?

An empty and damaged-for-life bastard, that was who. Write it down, put it in his packet—damaged goods. But was that who he really was? Now was the time to decide if he was still that other man. Or not.

He slid onto his couch, mind roiling, hands fisted, sweat beading on his upper lip. He wanted a stiff drink, the crutch he'd come to rely on years before. But he'd spent enough time on the dark side after the accident. He knew the path to hell backward and forward and never wanted to go there again. He'd traded in that prison cell for a new beginning in California. Which had opened him up...for Charlotte.

He called her. She didn't answer. He didn't leave a message.

He glanced at his watch—it was almost three a.m. His first surgery was scheduled for seven. He put on a pot of coffee, set the brew button for five a.m. then went to his bedroom, threw on his jogging shorts and exchanged his prosthetic for the running blade, then drove to Malibu for a long soul-searching run on the beach just before dawn. Maybe it would help clear his head.

Having a full surgical schedule would force him to compartmentalize. Charlotte deserved his undivided attention and so did his patients. He could only deal with one trauma at a time, and one hundred percent couldn't be divided during surgery. As much as it tore him up, since she hadn't answered earlier, he'd have to wait until that night to talk to Charlotte. Maybe he'd be more coherent by then.

In the meantime he worried what kind of a hard-hearted SOB she'd think he was. Because he cared. And because he was leaving her in limbo for a day, he deserved all of her negative thoughts about him. He could practically feel them with each step of his run. His pace was off, his muscles tight and tender, his breathing out of sync. Yeah, he deserved it for putting her through hell.

The problem with taking the "patients come first" approach in medicine was that when at the end of an unbelievably grueling day, when he hadn't had an hour's sleep the night before and had zero left to give, he wound up giving himself a pass on calling Charlotte. *I need to be well rested, to have my thoughts straight, to know exactly what I think and feel about the situation*, he rationalized. He hadn't had a moment to think about any of it that day, and with tomorrow's schedule he feared it would be no different then.

She'd probably be done with him by then. And he would deserve it. So he dialed her number again. She didn't pick up. Again.

He fell into bed, planning to call her once more in an hour, and amazingly slept through the night instead. But at five a.m. he was wide-awake, his head spinning with thoughts. It was too early to call her, so he dressed for another run. He needed to consider the consequences of his affair with the beautiful pathologist. The woman he loved. He was starting to get used to the phrase, the woman he loved. That was progress, wasn't it? Maybe by the time he had finished jogging, she'd be up. He'd call her. This time she might answer.

But what would he say? Could he make things right with her after this torturing delay?

It wasn't a good run—in fact, it was worse than the day before. Every step felt as sluggish as his brain. Anxious thoughts came to mind. How much he missed Charlotte. How he needed to talk to her, which left him edgy and stepping up his pace. One he could hardly keep up with. After the unheroic way he'd handled her news, why would she even want anything to do with him? She'd pushed him out of her house. Her life? Hell, maybe it was better to let things end as they had.

He wanted to kick himself for letting the negative and completely unacceptable thought slip in.

It was an old and sorry excuse, as familiar as a predictable movie. And totally unacceptable. Wasn't he a new man—a healing man, thanks to Charlotte—or had her news ripped off the new skin and left him back where he'd started three years ago with all of his old flaws alive and festering, dragging him down?

Was that really what he was made of? He hated to think of the answer. He was only forty-two, it had been over three years since everything had changed, and surely he was a better man now.

He stopped and called her. As predicted, it went directly to message. "Charlotte, we need to talk. When can I see you?"

He ran on, soon hearing a text message shoot through. Don't bother to call again.

Blast it all to hell. He really had blown it by letting the extra day go by!

Damn, he already missed her more than he had ever thought possible. His chest ached, fearing he'd lost her forever. She was pregnant with his baby. Their baby. He understood what an epic decision it had to be for her to have the baby. Her fears, her guilt of passing on imperfect genes. He wanted to be by her side every step of the way. Now all he had to do was convince her he wasn't the heel she must think he was.

Not an easy task.

He ran back to his car, remembering how important the role of being a father was, and how his wife had always complained he had never been there enough for the boys. If he was a new man, couldn't he be the kind of father for this baby that he hadn't been for his sons? Charlotte was giving him a chance to shine in life again. Together. Why would he want to crawl back to his "you call this living" cocoon?

Things could be completely different this time if she'd only give him a chance. Shouldn't she give him a break? Sure, he'd failed his first chance, when she'd told him the news. He could tell how hard her decision must have been—she'd looked like she'd been through the wringer. The fine skin beneath those beautiful eyes had looked bruised and tense. Her full, normally soft mouth bitten and tight. She'd left work early and had probably thought about her condition every second until she'd called him. She'd cautiously tiptoed her feelings out, testing him, and had blown him away with her words. "I'm crazy about you."

She'd put herself on the line and he could have been a

robot for the lack of response he'd given her. Of course she'd be furious with him. In his defense, he'd been completely stunned. But he'd had time to recover, and all he'd chosen to do had been to let her down in the name of needing time to think things through and his demanding job. No wonder she never wanted to hear from him again.

He got into his car, wondering what good was a man who didn't risk it all for the woman he loved? Yeah, he'd had enough time to admit it and now he knew without a doubt that he *loved* her. Maybe he'd been forced to come to the conclusion, but the feeling had already been there, well hidden, of course, because even a breath of admitting he could love again had scared the hell out of him, let alone the thought of becoming a dad again. He knew he wouldn't feel the love so strongly now if it hadn't already been there, starting as a seed and growing every time they'd seen each other. Why else had everything felt so right whenever they'd been together?

He drove to her town house and pushed the security button.

"Go away." Her voice came through the speaker a few seconds later.

"I need to talk to you."

She clicked off and didn't open the gate for him. After a few minutes he revised his plan. Because now that he'd had an epiphany, he knew what needed to be done. If life was all about what was happening right then, not the past or what might be in the future, he wanted and needed with everything he had to be there for Charlotte *now*. And when the time came, he'd be a proper father for their kid, too. That was the beauty of new beginnings—he could start afresh, get it right this time.

He glanced at his watch. It was almost six on Thursday morning and he had another big surgery in less than two hours. Tomorrow, Friday, was the day they were supposed to leave for Georgia and his cousin's wedding. He'd bought the plane tickets and made reservations at the grand old hotel on the banks of the Savannah River. But forget about the wedding. He wouldn't go unless Charlotte was by his side. There was no way he'd go without her.

He'd been told all his life he was smart, but what this situation called for wasn't brains. It called for heart…plus a bit of resourcefulness. For a methodical surgeon, every once in a while he surprised himself with his creativity. A great idea popped into his mind. Sure, it was a risk, a huge risk, which made it all the more necessary. Charlotte had done the same with him the night before last, had laid it all out there. Now it was his turn. She deserved no less. The only question was, how would Charlotte respond to his over-the-top plan?

It was seven a.m. Jackson had performed the five-minute hand and arm scrub, and donned the first pair of his sterile double gloves. His surgical nurse had just helped him into his gown, his cap and mask were in place, and he used his elbow to push the plate on the automatic door opener on the wall. The important surgery required a frozen section. He'd seen Dr. Gordon's name on the list for the morning, so he'd called and, calling in a favor, had insisted that Dr. Johnson had to do it. It would be up to Jim Gordon, now that he was back part-time at work, to come up with a believable reason for Charlotte to step in. Knowing what a team player Jim was, Jackson trusted it would be a good one, too.

An hour later, after they'd cracked open the patient's chest and he'd biopsied the mass on the right lung, he put the fresh tissue into the waiting petri dish, which was sealed and labeled and quickly handed over to the OR runner. Pathology knew the specimen was coming. "Don't give it to anyone but Dr. Johnson."

"Yes, sir." The young summer volunteer, garbed in full OR regalia, took the specimen and fled like his life depended on the mission. Did he even know who Dr. Johnson was?

The entire surgical team waited for the report as the surgery was held in limbo and the patient constantly monitored.

While he waited, leaving the assistant surgeon in charge, he knew beyond a doubt what he had to do once he heard Charlotte's voice. He wanted to be a man Charlotte could trust and depend on and look to for support, for everything, and he didn't intend to waste another minute before he told her.

Within five minutes he heard Charlotte's voice on the OR intercom. There was a noticeably cool clip to it. "The lung biopsy is benign for cancer."

Great news for the patient, though it was imperative for pathology to figure out exactly what the mass was with further studies. He cleared his throat before Charlotte could disconnect. He couldn't let it matter that he'd be in front of the entire surgical team and anyone who was within earshot in the pathology department. This was too important, and now was the time for desperate measures.

"Charlotte?"

A second, then two passed. "Yes?"

"This is Jackson, just to make it clear."

Another pause. "Yes."

He took a deep breath. "I never thought I'd have a shotgun wedding at forty-two, and I can't exactly get on bended knee here in surgery." The staff laughed and looked surprised, but when they realized he wasn't kidding around, everyone stopped to listen to what in the world he would say next. "But, Charlotte, will you marry me?"

"P-pardon me?" she stammered. "We're on the speaker-phone, Jackson."

"I know. And I don't care. You won't take my calls and I figured if I came down there you wouldn't see me. So, with the OR staff as my witnesses, I'm asking, will you marry me?" Then, taking the biggest risk of his life, well, after proposing in front of almost a dozen people, he said, "I'll give you some time to think." Then he nodded for his surgical nurse to click off the intercom.

The instant she did, the operating-room team broke into applause.

He tried to ignore them, having a patient lying on the OR table and all, though he felt fantastic, like he'd just climbed Mount Everest, and smiled beneath his mask. He'd done it. Excellent. A wave of insecurity knocked him back a bit. His stunt didn't guarantee a "yes" from Charlotte, but at least he'd made his case loud and clear. With witnesses! He loved her. He wanted to marry her.

Now forcing his personal life to the back of his brain, he focused on the patient, who deserved to be front and center. When he'd finished resecting the rest of the mass and tying off all involved vessels, he asked the assistant surgeon to close for him. He knew and trusted the young woman's skill. Plus the team was completely on board with him needing to leave.

He disposed of his dirty gowns and gloves, washed his hands again, then strode to the doctors' lockers. He grabbed his work kit and headed to the bathroom to clean up and shave, to make himself as presentable as he could possibly be, before facing the woman he loved. Once he passed the mirror test, he gave himself a reassuring nod. "You've got this."

First off, he stopped to speak to the family of his lung surgery patient, sharing his good report, watching the tension vanish from their eyes and foreheads. Then, on his way to the elevator, while passing through the surgical ward, he noticed a patient getting discharged and there was a beautiful bouquet remaining at the bedside on the movable table. The staff rolled the table out of the room and into the hall in order to get the patient into the wheelchair in the tiny private room.

"You taking this?" he asked.

"No. I don't want to be reminded of this place," the young man said. "Flowers aren't my thing anyway."

"Mind if I borrow them?"

"Take 'em, they're yours."

Jackson removed the bright white daisies and yellow sunflowers from the glass vase and shook off the excess water. He grabbed some paper towels from the nearby dispenser to wrap around the stems. Pleased it was a proper enough bouquet, one fit for following up on a marriage proposal, he headed down to the basement and the pathology department. Since he didn't have a ring to offer her, these bright summer flowers would have to do.

Charlotte stood bewildered, staring at the OR intercom in the tiny room with the cryostat machine. Jackson had just asked her to marry him. The thought set off full body chills. The good kind. This after she'd spent the last two days trying to force him out of her life and heart. And had failed miserably. Was he serious? He wouldn't dare play a cruel joke on her, would he?

Of course not!

She'd laid a huge surprise on him the other night, then

had gone ballistic when he'd been as stunned as she was right now. He'd needed time to think through the sudden life change rather than jump up and down with joy. Hell, *she* hadn't felt joyful when she'd got the news, yet she'd expected him to be. How unfair and unrealistic she'd been. But being frightened about her decision to become a mother, a decision as momentous as her double mastectomy surgery, she'd needed his instant support. Unreasonably so. And he'd been unable to give it to her right off. So she'd got mad.

It'd hurt, and sent her back to feeling like a needy teenager when her father had offered little support over the death of her mother. She'd freaked out and pushed Jackson out the door. Out of her life? She didn't know for sure because she couldn't think clearly at the time. All she knew was he hadn't met her unrealistic and unreasonable needs, so he'd become a villain.

Two miserable days later, deep down she knew without a doubt he was anything but.

He'd pleaded with her to understand, to give him time to think, to let him back in. Yet she'd said something hurtful and angry through the door about whether or not she'd ever let him back. How immature.

It hadn't been fair to him, not by a long shot. Most guys would have just walked away and given up. *Her loss*, they could have rationalized. Yet Jackson had just pulled the craziest stunt she could ever imagine. He'd proposed over an OR intercom, with his entire surgical staff listening in. That proved he loved her, didn't it?

She smiled, tears welled in her eyes and she pushed them away. Except he had yet to say the words.

Now it was perfectly clear why Dr. Gordon had made that shabby excuse for not being able to do his scheduled assignment for the morning. She'd checked the surgery lineup and had seen Jackson's name and nearly lost her breakfast. They'd conspired against her.

Someone cleared their throat. She turned to see her mentor, who'd stepped around from being just on the other side of the laboratory wall. Though thinner than he used to be, the flash was back in his old eyes. "That was quite a scene," he said, unable to hide his pleasure.

"Did you know he was going to do that?"

"To propose? No. But he begged me to make you do the frozen section. What was a man to do?"

She shook her head, letting herself float on air just a little. What a stunt, asking a woman to marry him with an audience. Yet *not* hearing the most important part first, *I love you*, kept her tethered to the ground. He was going the traditional, honorable route. Girl gets pregnant, the guy marries her. It was probably a golden rule of the South. Was she supposed to clap her hands in joy? Was this what she truly wanted?

Dr. Gordon stepped closer and patted her back. Her mixed-up tears kept coming. It was great to have him at work again, even if only part-time, and for how long, no one could possibly guess. She was especially glad he'd been in on the most amazing proposal she could ever have dreamed of—minus a single phrase.

"I hope you have the good sense to tell him yes."

She went quiet, in all honesty not knowing for sure what her answer would be. "I'll let you know when I figure it out."

With that, they walked back to their respective offices, where piles of patient slides awaited their diagnoses.

She took her seat in front of the microscope, adjusting the head, resting her nose between the eyepieces, and, still feeling as light as a feather with hope and love, she focused on the slide in the tray holder. From time to time, though, she considered how she'd forced Jackson into the corner, and being the wonderful man he was, he couldn't stand to let her down. She worried she'd never know for sure if he loved her or was only doing his Southern gentleman duty. The honorable thing.

Would that be good enough?

Charlotte spent the next hour and a half in her darkened office with the shine of his big moment and proposal fading, reading slides, trying to put the man she loved out of her mind. A nearly impossible task. What would she tell him?

Her door flew open, the light was turned on, and in barged Jackson. She jumped. "I believe we left off at the part where I asked you to marry me." He pushed the flowers at her.

Enough time had passed for her to come off her cloud—in fact, with her growing doubt those clouds had turned a pale shade of gray. She didn't want to force him into doing something he didn't truly want. With a guarded heart she spoke. "You don't have to do me any favors, Jackson." She took the flowers anyway, laid them on her desk.

He looked puzzled, as if he couldn't believe that she still didn't get it.

Jackson had been so swept away with carrying out his risky task, he'd forgotten some very important words. He'd managed to mangle the proposal. What a mess. The whole thing had started with Charlotte feeling insecure about being pregnant and having to break the news to him, a guy who'd never wanted to get married or have kids again. He needed her to know something.

"Forgive me. I forgot to tell you something first—the most important part." Jackson approached Charlotte's chair and took her hands, bringing her to standing so he could look into those warm brown, though suddenly skeptical, eyes. He noticed her hands were shaking, and for a guy who'd just performed flawless surgery, his hands were, too. Why wouldn't they be? They were both about to embark on the biggest journey of their lives. This time together. If he could get Charlotte to cooperate, that was.

"I want to be there for our baby, Charlotte."

"And?"

"And? Oh, of course, and you! I want to be there for you."

"Because?" Now she looked downright impatient.

Because? Oh, for crying out loud, he really was sleep deprived and not thinking straight. "I love you. Didn't I say it?" In all honesty, the proposal in the OR, fueled by anxiety and adrenaline, was a blur.

"No."

Damn. He'd blown it big-time, but couldn't she read between the lines? "But I asked you to marry me. Surely that implies that? You know—"

She canted her head as if he'd been singing a beautiful aria and had just hit a sour note. He could fix that.

"I love you." He hoped the sincerity he felt down to his bones was reflected in his eyes, because he needed her to understand how important this was to him. "I want to marry you, to be our baby's father, if you'll have me." She gazed at him, not as much as a whisper crossing her lips. He needed to step up his pitch. Maybe appeal to her practical side? "You'll need my help raising our kid because you have no clue what you're getting yourself into. Trust me, you need me. Our kid needs me." He would have missed her twitch of a smile if he'd blinked, because he was sweating through what had turned out to be a totally messed-up proposal. He hoped she needed him half as much as he needed her, now that he'd finally admitted it. He let go of her hands and framed her face then kissed her with everything he had, trying to communicate what he couldn't somehow manage to find the perfect words for. She kissed him back. A good sign. It occurred that she might need to hear him say it again. "I need you, because I love you. Marry me. Please."

She fell against him, and he held her tight.

"We've had a rocky patch," she said to his chest before she looked up at him. "It took a couple of days for you to come to your decision."

"You mean my senses."

"Yes." She smiled, but not joyfully, more of a sad or resigned kind of smile. Could his delay in figuring things out have taken that much life out of her? "Like you, I'd like to take some time to think over your proposal."

Had his hesitation and two days' lag time been enough to make her question what they had? He had no right to demand an answer right now, not after what he'd done, but it hurt to the center of his heart, realizing how he'd left her alone when she'd needed him most. Now he could say he truly knew how she'd felt. All he could do was hope she'd come to her senses the way he had and say yes. Yes to their future. "I don't want to wait that long, but I have to understand after what I've put you through."

"It isn't payback, Jackson. I've got to think things over."

Suddenly feeling like a man walking a tightrope, he went still. "That's understandable." What would he do if she told him no? He didn't want to let her out of his sight but he had to finish his afternoon clinic and tie things up for the next few days away. "What about the wedding this weekend? Will you still go to Savannah with me?"

She kissed him lightly, then looked into his eyes. "Yes. I promised I'd go with you and I'll go."

That gave him time and the chance to make things

right again. If he couldn't convince her that he loved her right now, maybe the beauty of his hometown would help her fall in love.

CHAPTER TEN

LATE ON FRIDAY night Charlotte stood at the window of her tenth-story hotel room in Savannah, watching a foreign container ship slowly pass by. The tall rusted ship loaded several stories high with colorful cargo crates almost reached her eye level. Definitely a working ship. With tons and tons of cargo, how could it possibly stay afloat?

"That thing's huge," she said loudly to Jackson, who was arranging clothes in the closet.

"Get used to it—this is one of the most traveled rivers for international shipping in the US."

"It's really fascinating. I kind of feel like the captain could be watching me with his binoculars."

"I wouldn't be surprised. Probably hoping to get a peep show."

That made her laugh. "Boy, would he be disappointed."

Out of nowhere Jackson was at her back, passing his arms around her waist and pulling her close and nuzzling her neck. "He wouldn't get the chance because I'd deck him if he tried spying on you."

She turned her head so they could kiss. "Thanks." She looked back at the ship, almost directly across from them. "Did you see that, Captain?" she called out.

Jackson chuckled along with her and hugged her closer.

It was the first time they'd gone away overnight and checked into a hotel room together, and the first time they'd cuddled today. He'd chosen a gorgeous and grand hotel and spa with a harbor view. Every detail about the place spoke of old wealth. For a San Fernando Valley girl who'd grown up in a lower middle class area, the obvious opulence, though beautiful and inviting, also made her a little uncomfortable. Even now, she'd never think to stay in such a place, but apparently the man with three names and a number was in his element.

Their spacious bedroom had plenty of room to sit on the love seat and enjoy the view. Like a grand lady wearing a shiny pearl necklace, the Savannah River looked extra pretty with the city lights from across the river.

"What's all that?" She pointed across the river to a long street still busy with activity at the late hour. Rather than deal with what was written on her heart, for now she'd stick to superficial talk. Which was pretty much what they'd done for the entire flight to Georgia.

"That's River Street. All those buildings used to be cotton warehouses. Now they've been converted into anything your heart desires."

"Wow."

She looked downward at the huge hotel pool accented with lights, then to the right where a white gazebo adorned in tiny café lights looked like a miniature toy in the center of a picture-perfect lawn. All the while, as she checked out the area, she enjoyed the warmth of Jackson's body against hers, his hands resting on her stomach. It made her think of their baby and how protected it was right this moment. "Looks like they have weddings here, too."

"They have weddings everywhere in Savannah. It's a very romantic city. I can't wait to show you the historic district tomorrow morning."

"In that case, I hate to be a party pooper, but since we've got a big day tomorrow I'd better get some sleep. I'm worn out from the flight and getting up so early." *And being pregnant and totally confused about your marriage proposal.* She glanced at her watch and realized that back home it was only eight o'clock. Was that what pregnancy did to a woman?

"I wanted to introduce you to an old college buddy of mine—we were roommates—but I can understand your needing more rest these days." Jackson had been completely accommodating the entire day, and now was no different. "You've got to take care of our baby, right?"

That was part of the problem. Since Jackson had come around and said he wanted to marry her and he loved her, she couldn't quite shake the feeling it was all about the baby. "I had no idea how exhausting being pregnant was."

He squeezed her a little tighter. "And I don't want to make you feel worse by pushing too hard. The point is for you to enjoy the wedding tomorrow evening. To enjoy Savannah." He kissed her cheek. "Would you mind if I met up with Jarod for drinks downstairs in the bar?"

"Of course not. Go right ahead."

"Okay, I won't be late. Just a drink and a little catching up on things."

Within ten minutes of Jackson leaving, Charlotte had done her nighttime routine and snuggled into the amazingly comfortable bed, choosing to leave the curtains open so she could continue to look outside before going to sleep. She may not have the energy to be out there, but she could still enjoy the hustle and bustle of River Street across the river. She was also rewarded with the grand entrance of another enormous cargo ship passing slowly through the waters. The sight put a smile on her face, making her feel oddly connected with the wide world while snug in her bed.

Unfortunately, she couldn't shut down her mind or stop her worries about Jackson. Honor was a large part of who he was, and she worried he was merely doing the right thing by asking her to marry him because she'd got pregnant. Just like he'd done with his ex-wife. Before the weekend was over she'd have to confront him about it. With her body dictating her needs, plus the fact she'd hardly slept last night from thinking nonstop about Jackson's true motives for proposing, within a few minutes she'd drifted off to sleep.

She heard voices and forced her eyes open. Glancing next to her in the bed, there was evidence that Jackson had slept there, and she remembered cuddling next to him at one point in the night, but he wasn't there now. Plus the sheets felt cold. How long had he been up? And who was he talking to? Should she hide under the blankets and play possum?

"Thank you," Jackson said, then closed the hotel-room door, before shortly appearing at her bedside with a full breakfast tray.

She sat up, mouth open. "Wow."

"Good morning, sunshine! Breakfast is served."

She had to hand it to him, he was really trying hard—the least she could do was be gracious.

She glanced at the digital clock on the bedside table. It was only seven-thirty in the morning. That would be four-thirty back home. "I feel like a princess. Thank you." She hoped the current wave of morning queasiness would pass so she could really enjoy the spread, rather than move things around her plate and hope he didn't notice. Especially after his obvious desire to treat her like royalty. She sipped some water. "Did you sleep much last night?" She threw back the covers, and in her sexy nightgown, which hung a little loosely around her chest, she stood.

Jackson came to her and hugged her good morning. They lingered in their embrace and she savored his solid warmth and the way he smelled fresh from the shower complete with yet a new aftershave, this one with a hint of sandalwood. Dared she dream about being his wife, secure in knowing it was her he wanted to marry, and not merely because of a ready-made family?

"Yeah, I was in before one. Had a good talk with my buddy. Got all caught up on a few things." It made her wonder if he'd talked about his current situation, having a pregnant girlfriend and having to get married *again*, but she didn't ask. It was too early for drama. "Let's eat. We've got a big day ahead of us."

"I'll do my best," she said, smiling up at him, hoping she'd make it through the day with such a heavy heart.

"There are twenty-two squares to share with you."

She popped her eyes wide open. "Twenty-two?"

"I drive fast, but we'll only have time for a few today, my favorites like Lafayette Square, Chippewa Square, Monterey Square and I'll tell you all about the Mercer house then. Oh, then we'll stop by Ellis Square so we can hit City Market. I've got a favorite restaurant there where we can have lunch. Then tomorrow we can spend a little more time checking out more squares. How's that sound?"

It sounded wonderful, but it surprised her that he hadn't marked out time for his family or for introducing her. Could he feel ashamed of the fact that, if she said yes, he'd be having another "shotgun wedding," as he'd called it in the OR? But she didn't want to spoil his enthusiasm first thing in the morning, so she kept her uncomfortable thoughts to herself.

"Great!" She glanced at the tray of breakfast food and thought about the wedding that evening. "But that sounds like a lot of eating."

He laughed. "Can you tell I'm really excited to have you here?" He sat and slathered a piece of toast with Georgia peach jam.

Maybe she should try to believe him. He wanted to share his world with her, and that knowledge set off a warm feeling tumbling through her body. Her queasiness vanished and she was suddenly more than ready to dive into the scrambled eggs and O'Brien potatoes. And, mmm, the fresh fruit and pancakes looked good, too!

Charlotte had never seen such a picturesque area as the historic district in Savannah. While they drove, she felt like she'd gone back in time with the beautifully preserved buildings and famous blocked-off squares, each with its own charm and individual appeal. Spanish moss draped every tree, and there were hundreds of oak trees throughout the area, as well as palmettos and magnolias.

"Lucky for you you're here in summer to see the crepe myrtles bloom."

The heat made her feel sticky, and she wasn't convinced she should feel lucky to be here in the heart of summer, but she completely agreed that the crepe myrtles were gorgeous. She was also glad he'd put on the air conditioner for the drive. "They certainly are beautiful. But with all the trees everywhere, everything looks beautiful here."

Jackson lucked out and found a parking spot. "We've actually got a nickname as the forest city because of that." He helped her out of the car and a wave of hot humidity hit her like a wet sauna towel. "But with heat like this, our ancestors had to plant trees just for the shade to survive. It was a practical idea that's brought all kinds of benefits."

She fanned herself as she felt a fine sheen of perspiration cover her face, wondering how crazy it would make her hair. Yeah, lucky her for being in Georgia in August. As a San Fernando Valley girl, she certainly knew about heat, but the humidity here brought "hot" to a new level. As they walked, she wondered how the bride would survive wearing a wedding dress in weather like this. She knew the wedding was out toward the beach at a lighthouse, which would probably help.

Holding hands and strolling to the heart of Ellis Square, they watched the children and a few adults playing in the big fountain, which was obviously meant for water play. The sight of little kids squealing with joy as the dancing water shot up made her think of her baby. She looked at the man she'd been positive she loved a few short days ago.

He pointed to the busy market and shop area. "Ever had shrimp and grits?"

"Had shrimp. Never grits."

"I'm going to take you for the gourmet supreme version of that dish. Follow me."

During lunch, she ventured to bring up one major portion of her worries. "Jackson, what if this baby is a girl?"

"Is that what's been on your mind?"

She nodded. "In part. Yes."

"You've got to quit thinking of yourself as poison for a girl baby."

"But if I pass on my genes..."

"You can't let yourself obsess about that. We could have a boy. Or a girl who'll be perfectly fine. If you want to have her tested, I'll stand behind you, but worrying and feeling guilty isn't going to help anything. Who knows where breast cancer research will be in twenty years? Please, stop doubting yourself. Think about the wonder of having a baby. Period. Not a single child born is guaranteed to come problem free."

Moved by his sentiment, she reached across the table and touched his arm. This was part of what she loved about him. "Are you really okay with me being pregnant?"

"Once I got used to the idea, I have to say I'm excited. It'll give me a chance to be the kind of father I should have been with my sons. I promise to be there for you, to help you raise our kid."

She believed him and burst into tears to prove it, but what he'd just vowed had sounded more like a dutiful co-parent than a loving husband. If she could only believe he felt as strongly for her.

After a huge lunch, and visiting a couple more beautifully impressive town squares, Jackson was considerate about Charlotte needing to rest before they got ready for the wedding. So he delivered her back to the hotel room so she could take a power nap and he headed out to the gym and then the pool. She definitely wanted to look her best for the wedding that night, for meeting his family, too, but most especially for him. She needed to see the love in his eyes before she made up her mind about his marriage proposal.

"Wow!" was all that came out of Jackson's mouth. Charlotte stood before him in a pale peach-colored dress that flowed in tiers to her ankles with a snug and wide fitted waist and a halter-style top embellished with a beaded and jeweled collar.

"The color is called blush." She looked anxiously down at her dress toward her toes. "I chose it because it works with my complexion. Plus I thought it would be comple-mentary no matter what the bride's colors are."

As far as he was concerned, she didn't need to ex-plain anything. Indeed, her light olive skin and dark hair glowed in contrast to the pastel shade. "You were meant for that dress, or I should probably say that dress was meant for you."

She smiled shyly and turned a slow circle, causing the skirt to flare out the slightest bit. The cut of the back of the dress was high, she hadn't gone for sexy other than a slit opening beneath the halter collar, yet she still looked like the sexiest woman on the earth to him.

"Thank you. Too bad I'll only get to wear it once."

The ironic statement made him grin. Not if his plans played out as expected. "After the bride, you'll be the most beautiful woman there." Because heaven help any woman who tried to show up the bride!

She shook her head, like she couldn't believe him. Anyone seeing her would never have a clue she'd had bilateral mastectomies. He hoped that didn't still make her feel self-conscious. How many times had he proved she was all he ever wanted or needed? He saw her as the woman he loved, a completely beautiful person, sexy and appealing, and though she had scars, they were part of her. Part of who he loved and wanted to spend the rest of his life with. Like the missing part of his leg was part of who he was now. The guy he'd finally accepted, with the help of Charlotte.

"Those sandals are a knockout, too." She wore strappy beaded silver sandals and had had a flashy pedicure. Though he'd memorized her body with all the times they'd made love, he'd never realized how sexy her feet were. Wow. "I may have to get a special permit to take you out in public. You might cause accidents and general chaos."

She smiled demurely and blushed, and he took a mental picture of that perfect moment in time to cherish and keep in his heart forever. Until she said yes to his marriage proposal, he couldn't let down his guard. He really wanted this. A life with her. Without a doubt. Now he had to convince her.

It wasn't until they got into his rented car that a tight coil started knotting in his stomach. He was ready to see his parents, had talked extensively to them about his plans for this trip back home. That wasn't the problem. He and Evan had worked things out, but Andrew was still avoiding him, and that hurt. Otherwise, if Andrew had been open to it, he would have spent time with him earlier today. The one break he'd caught had been Evaline deciding not to attend the wedding. That had taken a huge weight off his mind.

From what he'd heard, talking to his parents, well, mostly from his mother, Kiefer's future wife, Ashley, was a councilwoman from the tough town of Southriver and the wedding would be attended by the locals and act as a big thanks to her for helping revitalize her home front. She and his cousin Kiefer had met when he'd become the director of the new neighborhood clinic. People would be attending from all walks of life from blue collar up to high society. It should be an interesting mix. Knowing his community activist aunt Maggie, she was probably thrilled by Kiefer's choice of a wife. Since he and Kiefer had always kept in touch, especially as they were both doctors, Jackson knew he'd be welcomed.

Due to summer traffic it took Jackson almost twice as long as it normally should to reach Tybee Island Lighthouse Station. But what perfect timing for Mother Nature, at just about sunset. Once they'd parked, they headed toward a huge white tent set up on rich green grass next to the famous lighthouse, black with one wide white stripe in the center. It sat in the middle of five historic support buildings, a perfect little community. It had been made into a museum compound in 1961 and people lined up to have their weddings here. In the backdrop the sun quickly made plans to set in the west. To the east, the Atlantic Ocean made itself known with a light breeze scented with salty sea air. It lifted Charlotte's hair, which looked fuller and wavier since they'd got out of the car.

What could he say but she was the most beautiful woman in the world. His peaceful, loving observation quickly got jostled by his mother's strident voice.

"Jackson, yoo-hoo!"

He turned. "Hi, Mom." Her hair may be going silver and white, but there was no mistaking his mother's sharp blue eyes hadn't lost a hint of their passion for life.

She grabbed him and hugged him as if he were still a kid. "Look at you—you look so handsome!" He fought a grimace. "And this must be Charlotte. Aren't you lovely. Hi, I'm Georgina, Jackie's mom."

She greeted Charlotte in the same exuberant way, making her almost lose her balance. "It's great to meet you."

"You'll have to sit at our table later so we can get to know each other, okay?"

"That'd be great."

Did they have a choice? But Charlotte was being a wonderful sport, and he loved her even more for it. Off in the distance he noticed Evan, who waved to him, then shortly brought Andrew over. The fact that Drew smiled, and it seemed sincere, when they said hello meant the world to Jackson. Maybe all was not lost between him and his elder son, and maybe mending his relationship with Evan had helped. He'd make a point to talk to Andrew tonight, and to invite him out for a visit to California. Fingers crossed Drew would be open to that.

Music started to play as the sunset was imminent, and the open seating quickly filled up. Jackson guided Charlotte to the closest available seats. By the look of the large crowd, Ashley and Kiefer had a lot of friends in their community.

Handsome as always, tall, with brown hair and having Aunt Maggie's green eyes, Kiefer stood with the lighthouse as a backdrop in a dark suit, waiting for his bride. Ashley soon appeared in a classic white dress but with a light green sash, dark shoulder-length hair and eyes that reminded him of Charlotte's. She looked pretty and proud. She held her head high and smiled with all her heart at her friends and family as she walked down the aisle, but most of all she smiled for his cousin.

Jackson felt it in his gut—these two were meant for each other. Then he glanced at Charlotte, eyes bright with excitement over the wedding, the setting, the couple, and that same gut reaction helped him know he'd made the right decision in asking her to marry him. Now, if she'd only realize they were meant for each other and say yes.

The reception was a bit chaotic, thanks to the standing-room-only crowd and the low-key wedding plans, but everyone still managed to get fed. A local group played typical wedding reception songs, and Jackson even convinced Charlotte to dance with him a few times. He'd never get tired of the feel of her in his arms.

He didn't want to push the point, but she hadn't given him an answer yet. He was kind of hoping she'd get all swept away with the wedding tonight and tell him yes. The music was romantic, they were dancing, and it was time to prod things along. "You know I love you, right?"

Hope showed in her gaze. She rested her forehead on his cheek. "I know I love *you*."

He squeezed her tighter. "So let's get married." The song ended. No answer. He didn't want to let go of her, so he stood holding her close until the makeshift dance floor had cleared. She took a breath. He waited for her to say something.

"When are you going to come visit me?" the familiar voice of his grandfather called out from the edge of the dance floor.

Jackson led Charlotte to where he sat. "Gramps, this is Charlotte Johnson."

"Miss Johnson, it's my pleasure to meet you." His wiry, silver-eyed and white-haired granddaddy looked enchanted, and had obviously partaken of the champagne punch. She sat beside him and let him continue to hold her hand. They chatted briefly about the weather, where she'd grown up and a few other superficial topics. Then Gramps jumped right to the heart of things. "I've been around over eighty years, and I think I can judge when a man is smitten with a woman. It seems Jackson the Third here is sportin' the look of a man in love. So I must ask you, are you the one who put it there?"

Her hand flew to her chest as her cheeks blushed. Jackson could tell she didn't know whether to take his granddad seriously or not.

"I don't want to speak for Charlotte, Gramps, but I can answer that question easy enough. Yes."

Her gaze flashed to his and he didn't waver. If there was ever a time for her to know how he felt, it was now. Any man willing to get called out by his grandfather for being in love deserved an answer to his proposal. But he sensed she still wasn't ready, and he didn't want to force the point, so he let the moment pass.

"There you are!" Kiefer said. "I finally tracked you down."

Jackson greeted his cousin and made the proper introductions between the bride and groom and Charlotte. He almost spewed his champagne when out of the blue Ashley asked if another wedding was planned for the near future. Was she a mind reader?

Charlotte smiled graciously and blushed again, but still didn't venture to answer. He couldn't let that make him feel daunted. If there was ever a time to go out on a limb for the woman he loved, it was now.

As things were winding down, and he'd said his final good-bye to Kiefer and Ashley and, of course, his parents and grandfather, he escorted Charlotte back to the car. He'd left his mother with some flabbergasting—to use her word—instructions, but she'd agreed to carry them out to the T, had even cried a little about it.

He also banked on Charlotte needing another good night's rest so he could finish planning.

Making his job easy, Charlotte was nearly asleep on her feet by the time they got back to the hotel. "Looks like you're ready to turn in."

"Sorry I'm such a drag!"

"No, you're not. You're carrying my baby. It zaps the energy out of a person."

"So you understand?"

"Believe me, I do. Plus Drew and Evan are going to meet me in the bar for a quick drink. I've almost got Drew convinced to come visit before summer is over."

"That's wonderful."

"Since I met you luck has been on my side and my life has taken a turn for better. You know that, right?" He hugged and kissed her long and hard, hoping his message had sunk in, then said good night. Before his sons arrived he needed to talk to the hotel staff to help him make those special arrangements for Sunday evening.

He'd asked Charlotte to marry him, she'd yet to say yes, but he still intended to tie the knot right in his own backyard. Hopefully before tomorrow was over, she'd come round.

He'd often heard that a wedding in Savannah was destined to last as long as the city's ancient oaks. That sounded about right to him. Good thing he'd shopped for her ring online at the best jeweler's in his hometown, in case she still needed proof about how he felt. He had it in his jacket pocket. Jarod had dropped it off last night, along with some expedited official paperwork.

Walking down the hotel hall toward the elevator, Jackson couldn't help but think he was wearing down Charlotte's resistance, so he grinned.

Charlotte had a great night's sleep filled with dreams of celebrations and dancing and happy faces. It made her miss her family, what was left of it. Her brother, Don, had made a career in the service and was rarely in California. Her sister, Cynthia, her husband and their three adorable kids, her nephews and niece, her baby's cousins. She missed them all.

It occurred to her it was time to phone both of them and break the news. She promised herself she'd do it as soon as she was back in LA. Maybe by then she'd have made up her mind what to do about Jackson and his proposal. She could imagine their jaws dropping when she announced, *I'm pregnant.*

Jackson was already up and whistling away in the bathroom while she was still yawning and trying to open her eyes. Where Jackson got all his energy Charlotte didn't have a clue. Usually dealing with estranged families drained a person, but he seemed focused and happy, and she hoped she had something to do with his good state of mind.

He popped his head around the corner from the bathroom. "I got tickets for us to tour the Mercer house this morning. I pointed it out to you yesterday when we were at Monterey Square, the place with the huge statue of General Pulaski?"

She knew exactly which square he meant, it had been her favorite, and she considered it the prettiest of the ones he'd taken her to. "Yes. The *Midnight in the Garden of Good and Evil* house?"

"Yes, that one, the Jim Williams story."

"Neat. I'd love to peek inside." Last night, when he'd said "So let's get married" she had been on the verge of saying yes. Every second they'd been together she'd felt her love for him growing stronger and stronger. Did it really matter that he wanted to marry her *because* she was pregnant?

"You feel like walking today? We can take the water taxi across the river and walk from there."

"After all the eating I've been doing, that sounds like a great plan." Fortunately, she'd worn comfortable shoes for the plane ride. When she'd finished with her morning routine Jackson was dressed and waiting for her.

"I'll make sure you're back in time for a nap this afternoon, too."

"Since our plane doesn't leave until midnight, that's probably a good idea. I'll have plenty of time to pack tonight before we leave."

"But I've made some special plans for dining tonight. Maybe you can pack this afternoon after that nap. I want you to be rested to enjoy our evening."

"Sounds romantic." And he'd probably want his answer then, too.

He took her hand. "If all goes as planned it will be," he said, guiding her out of the hotel room. "Oh, one more thing—you know how you said it was too bad you'd only get to wear that knockout dress once?"

"Yes?"

"Wear it again tonight, okay?"

What did Jackson have planned? "Sure, if that's what you want." She didn't know why but chills rose the fine hair on her arms over his request.

Once downstairs they went out the waterside exit, passing the pool on the left and the pretty grassy area on the right. "Oh, it looks like they're setting up for a small wedding today," she said on the way to the water taxi.

"Well, they are famous for their wedding packages here."

"Looks charming." Only a handful of round tables were set up with white tablecloths, making a half circle around the small gazebo at the center. Someone had already draped cream-colored organza fabric at the entrance, and another employee was in the process of hanging crystal prisms on varying lengths of string, catching the light and casting rainbows everywhere. Maybe she should take notes and add them to all the mental notes she'd taken last night at Kiefer and Ashley's wedding.

Jackson was right, Savannah was a truly romantic city, and her old dream of having it all kept sneaking back into her heart.

A man of his word, Jackson made sure Charlotte was back at the hotel by mid-afternoon to pack and rest up before their special dinner plans. Later, as promised to make the man she loved happy, she put on the dress from yesterday's wedding, feeling just as elegant today.

She thought back to the day she'd bought it, the first time she'd noticed something different had been going on with her body, and the one purpose she'd had in mind while she'd searched for the perfect dress—to make herself a woman Jackson couldn't live without. Had she been successful? Maybe over dinner tonight she'd give him her answer.

Jackson had also put on the dressy suit he'd worn to the wedding yesterday, looking handsome as always, and very Southern. She'd noticed his speech had changed a little since coming back to his home state, sounding a little slower and warmer, and she really loved the Georgia accent.

She studied him. His brown wavy hair had got curlier in Savannah, just like hers had, and the light tan he'd picked up over the past two days made his bright blue eyes stand out even more. She wondered if their baby would get his classic nose or her own nondescript one. Or his shocking blue eyes. For no reason he smiled at her like he had a big secret, and the grooves on both sides of his cheeks highlighted that grin. Damn, he was sexy, and she suddenly had the need to tell him exactly what she was thinking.

"You are *so* good-looking."

He grinned. "And you, my lady, are a goddess." His eyes seemed to sparkle when he said the last word.

Well, that did it. They didn't have to leave the room, as far as she was concerned, because she'd been acutely aware that since they'd arrived in Georgia they hadn't made love. She might be pregnant and a little more tired than usual, but all he had to do was look into her eyes with those killer blues and touch her just so and, well, right about now she'd pretty much sign up for anything he had in mind. If he happened to whisper he loved her, she'd definitely give him her answer.

"So you want to get together?" she offered playfully and hopefully.

He took her into his arms and kissed her thoroughly, the kind of kiss that would require a reapplication of lipstick once they were done, and she started thinking they were definitely on the same page. But then he stopped kissing her. "Call me old-fashioned, but I'd kind of like to wait until after you decide if you want to marry me or not."

Was he blackmailing her by withholding sex? "Seriously?"

"A man's got to stand his ground for honor's sake." He winked.

Again, there was that secret worry that his proposal had been more about honor and not enough about love.

A minute later, with one last fluff of her hair and that reapplication of peach-colored lipstick, they left the hotel room just as the horn of another container ship blared its arrival and floated by their window.

"I'm gonna miss it here," she said.

"We'll make a point to come visit often, then."

She tossed him a look and got chills. He obviously wasn't backing down on his offer to marry her, making all these future plans and all. Maybe the guy really did love her for herself and not just because she was pregnant.

When they caught the elevator and ended up at the main floor, instead of heading for the five-star hotel restaurant, as she'd expected, he escorted her outside. She immediately remembered the small private setup on the golf-course-green grass near the gazebo and watched for it.

"Oh, look, isn't that just beautiful?" she said, wondering what the occasion was. Obviously it was a small and private affair.

"It sure is." He put his hand at the small of her back and guided her toward it.

She resisted him. "We can't crash someone else's party."

"Of course we can. Do you see anyone around? Let's just go and have a look."

Only because she was dying to see everything up close, especially now, since small clear glass vases of bright summer-colored gerberas had been placed at each perfectly set table, she agreed. "But isn't this taking nosy to a new level, at the expense of someone else's private affair?"

"I don't see it that way." Once they got close enough for her to see the fine hotel china and silverware, Jackson cleared his throat and raised his hand. "Can we get some help over here, please?" he said to a nearby waiter.

Her heart palpitated and her face flushed. "What are you doing?"

"Hold on, don't freak out."

The silver-haired server, wearing a white waistcoat, immediately snapped to attention. "Yes, Dr. Hilstead. Are we ready?"

"Just give me two minutes first, please."

Charlotte's heart went still as Jackson dropped to one knee and took her hand. With the other hand, he fished inside his jacket for the pocket and something small.

"I love you. I've been trying to prove it all weekend, and I hope you've caught on. Because I mean it. I'm a better man because of you, and I want to spend the rest of my life with you. I love you with all my heart, and I want us to be a family. Charlotte, since I met you I've discovered I'm full of love. There's room for my sons, and our sons or daughters, but most especially for you. Right at the center. Forever. Do you believe me yet?"

Her face crumpled. How had she not known his proposal had been sincere from the very start? He was a man of his word, but also a man of the heart. If he said he loved her, he meant it. "Yes. I believe you."

"Then will you marry me?"

"Yes."

Jackson's expression of joy promised to plant itself in her heart for life. "Thank God." He stood and kissed her, then flashed a beautiful ring as he gave some high sign. She could have sworn she heard muted applause.

"We'll hold the record for the world's shortest engagement." He slid the ring on her finger and she took a moment to admire the pure solitaire diamond's beauty.

With Jackson's affirmation and a snap of the head waiter's fingers, soft classical string music began to play the Pachelbel concerto, and a group of people came out from what seemed nowhere.

Now her heart thundered in her ears. She recognized Jackson's parents and grandfather—how could she ever forget him?—and both of Jackson's sons, plus a few other people she remembered to be relatives of his, one being his aunt Maggie. Nearly dizzy with wonder, she couldn't speak, even though her mouth was open.

A husky man around Jackson's age came toward them and Jackson introduced him to her. "This is my old college roommate, Jarod. Or Judge Campbell these days. He's a county judge, and he's managed to pull a few strings for us, and since we were here for a wedding, I thought why not make it two? Jarod's going to perform the ceremony. Are you ready?"

Her chest clamped down so hard she didn't think she could draw her next breath. Of course she wanted to marry Jackson, but right this moment? Right here? It was all his family and friends, and she didn't have anyone to represent her. She didn't want to spend one second ruining this moment with sadness, but the emptiness flicked her hard.

"He's going to marry us now?"

Jackson gave the most confident nod she'd ever seen. "Remember our saying? Life is all about what's happening right now. So what do you say? Let's get married."

"But I don't have anyone here, Jackson."

"We can get married again in California and you can invite the whole hospital if you want, but I can't wait another second to be your husband." His swoon-worthy words sank in and they seemed to be accompanied by the scent of magnolias. She was sure she'd never forget this singular moment when the man she loved asked her to be his wife. In front of a crowd!

"Actually," he said, "you do have someone here for you, and he's the perfect person to walk you down the aisle. All we have left to do is say *I do*. So if you'll excuse me, I'll just go stand up there..." he pointed to the decorated gazebo "...and wait for you." He smiled so reassuringly she couldn't think of a single reason to refuse tonight as the night to take her vows.

Doing as instructed, Charlotte turned to see Dr. Gordon standing at the back of the lawn, a sweet smile on his face, wearing a white summer tuxedo jacket and black slacks, and holding a small bouquet, which was apparently meant for her to carry. The head of the waitstaff walked her to him, and Jim Gordon proudly held out his elbow for her to clamp her arm onto. And, boy, did she need something to hold on to right now because Jackson had just knocked her for a loop! It seemed a lifetime of stored-up feelings had been unleashed as she took her place beside her mentor, and she'd never felt more alive in her life.

Her chin quivered and her eyes welled, and Jim gave her a fatherly, encouraging look. "Don't worry, I'll get you there, dear. It's time for your happily-ever-after. Now, on the count of three, follow me."

With that, she took his advice and dived into the moment, the what-was-happening-right-now part, and quickly remembered the special bridal walk from all the movies she'd watched growing up. *Step, together, step, together.* She thought about her mother and knew this would have made her ecstatic. And on wobbly legs, in front of a new family she couldn't wait to get to know better, she made her way to the gazebo, with the help of her mentor and stand-in father. There, the handsomest groom in the world, and the most perfect *imperfect* man she could never have dared to dream of, waited for her to say *I do.*

EPILOGUE

CHARLOTTE LOOKED UP at Jackson, holding her hand while she lay on the examination table. He smiled reassuringly and squeezed her hand.

"So at twenty weeks we do the official ultrasound. Are you ready?" the magenta-haired sonography tech said.

Charlotte studied the young woman's brow piercing while she considered the question. Was she ready? Now that she was married and she and Jackson were a team, any potential outcome of what they might find out about their baby seemed far less scary. "Yes," she said.

Jackson grabbed her hand again as the tech squeezed cold gel onto her stomach and began moving the transducer around her growing abdomen. Soon a pie-shaped section appeared on the screen and shortly after that a profile shot of their baby's head appeared. They gasped together in wonder. Charlotte's other hand flew to her mouth. Her baby looked perfectly formed with a cute upturned nose and a really big-looking head. Was there a thumb in the mouth?

"I'll snap that picture for you, if you'd like. Or maybe you'd rather wait in case we can identify the sex."

Charlotte's gaze jumped to Jackson's and he nodded, indicating, like they'd previously discussed, it was up to her. "I'd like *that* picture, please."

"Done." As the technician moved on, she described every part of the fetus's anatomy that came into view. "Depending on whether or not you want to know the sex, you may want to look away during this next portion." She held steady at the point she'd left off, waiting for Charlotte's reply.

Charlotte smiled contentedly, knowing without a doubt since she'd married Jackson that no matter what the sex of their baby, their love for each other and their future child would see them through any and all the challenges in life. Whether it involved DNA or not.

Right here and now she saw for herself that her baby was perfect in every way, growing as it should be. Jackson had been okay either way about knowing or not, so he kept quiet, just gazing benignly at Charlotte as she finally made up her mind.

He bent and kissed her forehead as she closed her eyes. Did she want to know the sex today? Would knowing add or detract from the wonder of her pregnancy? Since passing through the first trimester, she'd loved being pregnant. Feeling her body change and knowing something she and Jackson had created together grew inside her had put her in an incredibly happy place.

If there was ever a time to think of Dr. Gordon's recipe for living it was now. *Life wasn't about what might happen, it was about right here and now.* She had proof of a perfectly forming baby on the computer screen. Sonography didn't lie. Then she thought of her mother, because since the wedding she'd been doing that a lot. Her mom had once told her all about the day she'd been born. Back in the day they chose two names for every pregnancy. One for a boy and one for a girl. People gave generic gifts at showers, and the parents had the joy of discovering the baby's sex at birth. She'd loved hearing the story about the day she'd been born and how happy her mother had been that she'd had a girl.

Because she'd started to show, the women at work all seemed to want to share their own birthing stories, and one lab technician's stuck out in her mind. The ultrasound had indicated the baby was a girl, and they had only got girls' baby clothes and items at her shower. The problem was, she'd wound up delivering a boy! Her mother-in-law had had to return all the baby items and buy new ones, adding stress to the shock. They'd been expecting a girl and now had to adjust to having a boy. The ultrasound wasn't always one hundred percent accurate.

Charlotte turned to Jackson, his brows lifting as he waited for her decision.

"Let's do it the old-fashioned way and wait to find out when I deliver."

He laughed and clapped. "That's a great idea."

"Then look away," the technician said as she continued the test.

"You're peeking!" Charlotte teased Jackson, both of them giddy with excitement for their future as they stared at each other for the next few moments rather than watch the monitor.

"I'm not, I swear. You know I'll be happy with whatever we have…" he bent and kissed her, and she remembered why she hadn't doubted for one second how much he loved her since his amazing proposal in Savannah "…because whether it's a she or a he, our kid will make us a family."

Charlotte had lost the heart of her family way too early when her mother had died. Things had never been the same and when she searched her heart she realized that for years and years she'd longed for a family of her own.

Until she'd met Jackson, she'd never dared to dream it could actually happen. "I like the sound of that."

"Our family?"

"Yes, *our* family."

* * * * *

Look out for the other great story in
the SUMMER BRIDES *duet*

WHITE WEDDING FOR A SOUTHERN BELLE
by Susan Carlisle

And if you enjoyed this story, check out these
other great reads from Lynne Marshall

A MOTHER FOR HIS ADOPTED SON
HOT-SHOT DOC, SECRET DAD
FATHER FOR HER NEWBORN BABY
200 HARLEY STREET: AMERICAN SURGEON
IN LONDON

All available now!

MILLS & BOON®

MEDICAL ROMANCE™

THE ULTIMATE IN ROMANTIC MEDICAL DRAMA

*16/03

MILLS & BOON®

Mills & Boon have been at the heart of romance since 1908... and while the fashions may have changed, one thing remains the same: from pulse-pounding passion to the gentlest caress, we're always known how to bring romance alive.

Now, we're delighted to present you with these irresistible illustrations, inspired by the vintage glamour of our covers. So indulge your wildest dreams and unleash your imagination as we present the most iconic Mills & Boon moments of the last century.

Visit **www.millsandboon.co.uk/ArtofRomance** to order yours!

MILLS & BOON®

Why not subscribe?
Never miss a title and save money too!

Here is what's available to you if you join the exclusive **Mills & Boon® Book Club** today:

* *Titles up to a month ahead of the shops*
* *Amazing discounts*
* *Free P&P*
* *Earn Bonus Book points that can be redeemed against other titles and gifts*
* *Choose from monthly or pre-paid plans*

Still want more?
Well, if you join today we'll even give you
50% OFF your first parcel!

So visit **www.millsandboon.co.uk/subscriptions**
or call **Customer Relations on 0844 844 1351***
to be a part of this exclusive Book Club!

This call will cost you 7 pence per minute plus your phone company's price per minute access charge.

Lynne Graham has sold 35 million books!

To settle a debt, she'll have to become his mistress...

Nikolai Drakos is determined to have his revenge against the man who destroyed his sister. So stealing his enemy's intended fiancé seems like the perfect solution! Until Nikolai discovers that woman is Ella Davies...

Visit **www.millsandboon.co.uk/lynnegraham** to order yours!

MILLS & BOON®